B.LUSTIG

AUTHOR'S NOTE

I give you a big box of pain, angst, frustration and hurt, combined with a shot of happy flutters, a dose of fun and a pinch of humor, all wrapped in a pretty purple bow.

Have fun unwrapping!

Sidenote:

I created B. Lustig to publish books that give you a heavy dose of angst, big mouthed heroes and women that like to challenge them. I like to write the messy stories because I believe true love can overcome anything.

However, if you are looking for the mess that comes with blood, guns and crime lords stealing your heart? Yeah, I hate to break it to you, but you've got the wrong book. You need a Billie book that gives you alpha males and sassy females ruling the underworld guns blazin' and spilling blood.

This ain't it. Check out the back for all my Billie books!

'Roadtrips aren't measured
by mile marks, but by moments'

EVEN IF THOSE ARE SPENT WITH A ARROGANT
ASSHOLE PISSING YOU OFF MOST OF THE TIME

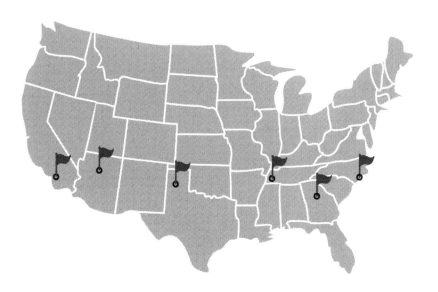

CALIFORNIA

- I'M DEFINITELY NOT A CALIFORNIA GIRL-

The strobe light blurs my vision, and I blink a few times to adjust my eyes. My body vibrates with the loud music as I look at our spot at the bar to find my uncle Johnny.

I remember walking into this club for the first time.

It seems like yesterday.

An eighteen-year-old with a know-it-all attitude and a smart mouth, trying to cover up the nerves that somersaulted through my stomach. Mad at the world, cursing her uncle and determined to make him regret he ever dragged her to Los Angeles.

She was a piece of work.

I liked her.

Unfortunately for me, the rest of the world hated her.

"Destined for the gutter," Johnny once said. *"Destined to fail."*

I knew he was bluffing, that he was just pushing the right buttons to put my ass in gear. And he was right, because all that young, inexperienced girl heard was a challenge.

I was going to prove everyone wrong.

I was going to show exactly what I'm capable of.

And I did.

Working for the LA Knights was both a pain and a joy, but I was good at my job.

I still am, but lately it feels like it's time to move on.

A hand reaches up at the far end of the bar, and a smile forms on my face when I meet my uncle's gaze. His back is leaning against the bar top, with Robert Davis, my future ex-boss, right beside him. Together, they look like the epitome of success, with their expensive suits and ivy league haircuts. Both men hold a clear resemblance, easily passing as brothers if you don't know who they are. I know my uncle sees the man as his friend, regularly seeking him out for advice, especially since my grandfather died a few years ago.

Adjusting my glitter top, I make my way over to the bar, my hips swaying with every step I take in my black heels. I'm a bit shaky, shown by the nervous flutter that has been running through my muscles since I got into the cab to come here, but I have no clue why.

Maybe it's because it's my last night.

Maybe it's because for some weird reason this feels like the end of an era. But then again, it could also just be the sushi. Who knows, really?

"Gentlemen." A smile slides in place as I give both of them a nod in greeting, eyeing the empty shot glasses in front of them. "Is this the example you want to be setting for your staff, Mr. Davis?" I joke, winking.

An amused frown creases his forehead. "We won the Stanley Cup; we're allowed to celebrate. Besides, I own this club, but you're right," he agrees, then a fake scowl washes over his face. "Johnny, behave yourself."

Johnny eyes me with a glare.

"Thanks for throwing me under the bus, kid," he mutters with a ghost of a smile.

"No problem. So, where's mine?" I ask, moving my head back and forth between the two men. They both give me a surprised look, the clear question between the two making me chuckle.

"You drink?" Mr. Davis asks. He doesn't wait for my response as he raises his hand up in the air, holding three fingers up to the bartender, excitement written on his elder face. "For the last five years, you wouldn't even touch a glass of wine in my presence. On your last night, you're asking for *shots*?"

I shrug. "Sorry, sir. I take my job seriously. Besides, we both know hockey players come with drama. I had to be sharp twenty-four-seven."

"Not gonna argue there." He grabs the freshly poured shots from the bar and hands me one as Johnny gives me a proud look that makes me emotional, though I have no clue why. Ignoring the lump forming in the back of my throat, I raise the shot in the air with an innocent look. "Cheers."

"Cheers." They respond in unison, before we all throw our heads back when the glasses touch our lips.

Ugh. Tequila.

I hate Tequila.

The liquid burns through my body and my stomach starts to roar in response while both men do their best to keep a straight face. My eyes go moist, albeit for a completely different reason this time.

A shiver runs over my back, and I eagerly grab a lemon wedge from the dish on the bar to replace the bad taste.

"You did a damn good job, though, sweetheart." Mr. Davis continues when he is able to relax his face again. "I'm sorry to see you leave. Are you sure I can't make you another offer? Maybe throw a new car in the mix?" He winks with a knowing look, referring to my early birthday present from Johnny.

When I started working for the LA Knights, I was aware that I'd be driving a company car. But the big surprise was the black SUV that was waiting for me on day one. Johnny pretended he was stupid, but he must've pulled a few strings to butter me up when he handed me the keys to my dream car. He never admitted it through the years, but I know it was a peace offering after basically kidnapping me, and I was more than keen to accept it. When I handed in my resignation, I was sad to see it go. But last week, Johnny had a big smirk on his face when he handed me the registration papers with my name on it. *"Happy birthday,"* he said before I threw my arms around his neck.

And the uncle of the year award goes to...

"How about you buy me another shot and I'll think about it?" I flirt, bumping my shoulder against Mr. Davis.

"Oh, God. She's really not on the job anymore." Johnny shakes his head as Mr. Davis drums his fingers on the bar top in excitement.

"You heard the girl," he calls out to the bartender. "Three more!"

The corner of my mouth rises in an evil grin, and I exchange a look with Johnny, silently asking for his approval. My tolerance for alcohol used to piss him off when I was still a teenager, as I used it to my advantage all too often, though it still got me in a ton of trouble. But now, a proud glint is visible in his eyes.

Robert hands me another shot and gives the other to Johnny. "Now, sweetheart, I like to see this wild side of yours, but don't fall off your expensive shoes. Okay?"

I softly chuckle, bringing the glass to my lips, and I again feel the tequila surging through my body. My stomach is hurling in defense, telling me it's not on the same page as my head, but I'm not the one to back out of a challenge.

"Don't you worry about me, sir. I'm stronger than I look." I slam the glass on the bar, then put another lemon wedge in my mouth. The sour taste shuts my eyes instantly, and I let out a small shriek to pump myself up as the hair on the back of my neck stands at attention. They follow my example, and Robert shudders when the liquid flows through his body, a pinched look on his face.

"You're not working for me anymore; you can call me Bob," he orders, his expression still tense from the shot. "You want another one?"

He looks from Johnny to me, and we both nod in agreement, even though I'd rather have something else. Tequila is definitely not my poison.

"I have to warn you, Bob. You do realize she's related to me?" A warning flashes in my uncle's eyes, combined with an amused smirk that matches mine. "My niece can do this all day without so much as waggling an inch in her high heels."

My eyes automatically roll before I look around us to see if anyone heard him calling me *niece* out of habit.

Now that I'm leaving, it's not a big deal anymore, but it's still not something I like to tell everyone. Being the niece of the General Manager of the LA Knights and getting free passes is one thing. Being the niece and getting a very high paying, most sought-after job without any credentials?

Yeah, not something I'm comfortable sharing.

Before you know it, I'll be eaten by all the media sharks this city is crowded with. It has already been enough of a hit to my ego that it was the sole reason I got the job, having barely finished high school before Johnny took me to LA with him. But like I said, I like challenges.

So, I overcompensated.

I worked my ass off, didn't ask for any favors, and made sure no one ever questioned me. Considering Robert Davis just asked me to stay, I think I have succeeded with flying colors.

"You're shitting me." Robert's wide-eyed gaze moves from me to Johnny in total disbelief.

"I will deny it if you ever tell someone, but yeah. She can drink like a sailor." Johnny shrugs, then brings the shot to his lips. "Frustrates the hell out of my sister. Gave us quite the worry when she was a teenager."

Slightly annoyed, I glare at him, making it clear I have no desire to give my boss an opening to learn more about my troubled teenage years. Luckily for me, Robert doesn't ask any more about it.

Rebel Rae, they used to call me.

It started out as a joke from Johnny when I was fifteen and convinced the entire class to skip the last period to go to the riverbank instead. Cheeky stuff like that still pulled a silent chuckle from most of my family after I faced the consequences. But by the time I hit eighteen, alcohol and drugs were part of daily life, and the only one still laughing was me.

In the last five years, I tucked that version of me away, as far as possible, making sure she'd never show her face. In the beginning, it was hard, but after Jimmy's accident, I knew I had to get my shit together. I knew I needed to change before I'd lose everything.

Mimicking him, I take the last shot in my hands and raise it up in the air.

"Cheers." I beam, repeating the move once more.

The sharp taste hits the back of my throat, and goose-bumps trickle onto my arms.

"Okay, next time you are in LA, we are going out. We'll have some fun, and you can show me exactly how much you can handle." He wiggles his eyebrows at me with a playful smile, the professional distance now completely gone.

Johnny punches his arm. "That's my niece, you perv."

Mr. Davis throws his hands up in the air, placating. "I was talking about dancing or something." He turns his head to me, and I notice how the tequila changed the features on his face. "I mean no offense. You're beautiful, honey, but you're a little too young. Besides, wife number four is already in the making." His dark brown eyes look at us with a boyish gleam while his attention is grabbed by something behind me.

"In fact, there she is right now. Johnny, Ms. Stafford, this was fun, but if you will excuse me?" He taps Johnny on the shoulder, giving me a quick nod, then walks over to a gorgeous exotic woman with long black hair.

I watch how he gives her a longing hug, and she returns it with a shy smile, like a woman in love, her cheeks turning a soft pink.

"Why is it that he is already working on his fourth wife, and you didn't even make it to number one?" I mock, turning back to Johnny.

"Because he's rich enough to afford four divorces," he snorts, then orders two rums, neat.

"Well, you could at least afford two."

"I could, but then what would you inherit when I die?" he counters, grabbing his tumbler while handing me the other.

"Good point. Don't marry. *Ever.*"

Johnny was only seventeen when I was born, and I'm like the baby sister he never had. And with him being only forty years old now, he is the big brother I always wanted. After working together for the last five years, we've become even closer. In fact, I think he's the only person who knows me underneath my thick skin and sunshine smile that gets me through the day.

A brief smile creases his face until it changes into a slight scowl as he looks at something over my head. My gut tells me to stay put, but my curiosity makes me ignore that feeling, so I turn around. Cursing myself, I let out a grunt when I see Sean behind me with that lopsided grin of his that used to melt my panties off.

He's looking hot as always in his white t-shirt that's perfectly hugging his hard chest.

He is fit, tall, and with his thick brown hair and piercing blue eyes, he looks like a fucking Disney prince. But even though I can still acknowledge he's handsome as fuck, I have too much pride to give him the satisfaction of letting him know that.

Annoyed, I twist my body back to Johnny.

"Goddammit," I hiss, grinding my teeth. I didn't exactly expect to be able to avoid him the entire night, but I had high hopes. *Foolish Rae.*

Johnny exhales loudly, annoyed as well, then reaches out his hand to Sean with a fabricated smile while I finish my drink in one go, knowing I'm gonna need it.

"Kent, having a good time?" he asks, feigning sincerity.

I feel Sean's arm wrapping around my neck, his nutty signature cologne enveloping me while I suppress the urge to shrug him off. It used to turn me on like crazy. Now it just makes me want to gag.

"I am, thanks." He takes Johnny's hand, a satisfied tone in

his voice, and I don't have to look up to see the big smirk he has on his face. "Can I talk to Rae for a second?"

Johnny silently asks me for confirmation, and I bite my lip in indignation, giving him a short nod.

Johnny hates him. He's not allowed to say it out loud because it will be front-page news if tabloids find out the Knights' General Manager hates his star player. But I know he does. He never liked him because of his super star attitude, but Sean's behavior toward me only made that worse. You don't go cheating on the General Manager's niece and not expect to become number one on his shitlist.

"You have three minutes, Sean. Three." Not being able to stand his touch any longer, I jerk his arm off and place my back against the bar. Johnny nods to Sean, slamming his shoulder in that way men do, then he quietly walks away.

"What do you want?" The irritation runs through my veins, while I try to keep a composed stance, along with a hard smile on my face to keep up appearances. The asshole isn't worth my time and certainly not worth my energy. I already wasted enough nights waiting for him, and the only reason I'm giving him a chance to speak is because I want to avoid making a scene. And like the superstar jackass that he is, he will definitely make a scene if I won't even talk to him.

He dips his chin to look at me, then bites his lower lip in a smoldering attempt.

"Are you still mad, babe?" he coaxes, making a cute face. The backs of his fingers softly stroke the skin on my upper arm at a calculated pace while he waits for my answer.

I can't believe I once fell for his bullshit.

"Not mad, just not interested. I'm over it."

Really, I'm fuming.

"So, you are really leaving?" He tilts his head a little, opening his mouth before he closes it again. His light blue eyes sparkle with disbelief, as if it's impossible for anyone to leave him. Maybe it would've been if I hadn't found him with his mouth on some other girl's face, but I did, and now we're here.

"Yes, I'm leaving tomorrow."

He moves closer, tucking the braid hanging over my shoulder before gently pushing back a strand of my blonde hair behind my ear. I can feel his breath fanning my cheek and his hand caressing my skin. It used to make me weak in the knees, sparking the lust he fueled with his touches. Now all I feel is disgust because I can't even guess how many girls he touched before he would come home to me.

"Come on. S*tay*. We can still make this work, baby. You can move in with me. I'm really sorry, babe. You know I only want you."

I snort. "Not true. There is a whole list of skanks you want."

"I'm sorry. *Really.*"

I shake my head, slapping his hand away with a warning glare. "I'm sure you are, but like I said, I'm not interested anymore." I meet his pleading gaze with a phony smile. "Let it go, Sean. Go have a drink with your friends. I'm done. We're done. The longer we're seen together, the sooner TMZ will be announcing we're a *thing* again."

He wraps a hand around the back of my neck and pulls me even closer, making it hard for me to stay calm and collective. The aggravation is building up in my stomach, and I close my eyes to make sure I don't do anything stupid, even though my hand itches to smack his face. I've done my fair share of stupid shit in my life, and I believe everyone deserves a second chance, but I don't give second chances to cheaters. Cheating isn't being stupid; cheating is being disrespectful.

And that doesn't fly with me.

"But we *are* a thing, babe," he whispers, trying to be seductive.

He leans in, brushing my cheek with his lips. I wait for the tingling to start, combined with the weightlessness his kisses used to give me every time our bodies connected, but all that's left now is disappointment. An explosive emotion if you combine it with the agitation that has already settled in my chest.

"We *were* a thing, Sean. Past tense," I retort, slowly but firmly pushing him a few steps back. "But that wasn't enough for you." I do my best to keep a straight face, not willing to give him the pleasure of watching me lose control. But really, it feels as if I'm a ticking time bomb and he's holding the remote to detonate. "You know, it's insulting that you actually think I would still want to be with someone who cheated on me for months. And not with one girl, no, a fucking bunch of them. I'm better than *that*, and I'm sorry that you just found out now, but you are too late, Sean. Congratulations on winning the Cup."

I move past him to walk away, refusing to look at him for another second. The jackass might have a whole harem waiting for him, but I sure as fuck won't be part of it any longer. I'm sure there is some other girl who will be willing to keep him occupied at night. But he's a persistent motherfucker, always has been. It's the reason we started dating in the first place. My aggravation hits a peak when I feel him snatch my wrist, tugging me back. Instantly, my eyes shut while my heart starts to race at a frightening pace, as I can feel my muscles tense. I try to ignore the jittery feeling in my belly, but it's only heightened when he opens his mouth once more.

"Rae, baby, stop fighting it, we both know—" His words are lost in the echo of my hand slapping his cheek, a sound that rings in my ear like the bells of Santa on Christmas morning. My palm burns when it connects with his skin, but it's a good burn. *A glorious one.* One I've been dying to feel since I first found out about his side chicks. I still had to work with him and keep everything professional. I've been the star of self-control for the last few years. It was a skill I needed to learn to be able to do my job in the right way, working with cocky athletes, and that only grew more and more with experience. But since my ass is getting the hell out of Dodge within the next twelve hours, I don't have to behave accordingly anymore.

And frankly, I don't want to either.

Maybe, if I didn't have a few shots five minutes ago, I would've restrained myself. But I did, and I'm done listening to his bullshit.

I will never accept infidelity.

From anyone.

His eyes close for a second, a growl rumbling in this throat before he snaps them open again. They are now filled with anger and confusion. His eyebrows draw close together, and for a second, I think he might return the favor.

"Let. Go," I order, my tone quiet but menacing. My heart is slamming against my ribcage, as if it's trying to find a way out of my body, fueled by adrenaline.

My eyes focus on his hand still wrapped around my wrist as I look up and see him clenching his jaw, like he's about to lose his calm. I smirk in question, silently daring him. He might be pissed, but I'm furious.

I can see his Adam's apple bob as he swallows, clearly debating what to do as he keeps peering down at me with a frustrated look. His eyes quickly glance at the people around us, then he mutters something I can't really hear before he finally releases me. A pleading yet angry look stares back at me as he runs a hand through his brown hair, but the memory of his lips on another girl refuses to give me the ability to have a normal conversation with him.

"We're done, Sean." I end the conversation once more, then stride away from him, walking toward the restroom to calm my nerves.

Those three Tequila shots should have made my nerves totally numb but the adrenaline rushing through my veins erased any effect it had three minutes ago.

For months, I believed him when he said there was extra practice, never realizing extra practice was him doing exercises with whatever pussy he could get. It wasn't until I went to the rink, looking for him, that I realized there was no fucking practice. I felt so stupid when I found him fucking an intern in the locker room.

I take big steps with my chin held high, making sure to not show my emotions. But I'm burning up inside, feeling like my organs are being liquified. That felt exhilarating, but also triggered a wave of shame I don't really want to let out right now. I can't believe Sean Kent fooled me, even though I've always known he was a cheater.

Did I really think I was anything special?

Maybe I did.

Maybe I hoped for it after he told me he loved me.

I walk past the VIP deck until I reach the hall that leads to the bathrooms, when a rough hand claps my wrist once more.

"What the—" I mutter while my anger rises to an ultimate high. Twisting around, a growl escapes my throat, not hesitating to slap Sean one more time.

Instead, I freeze, my heart dropping to the floor when I look into a set of unexpected blue-grey eyes. They give me this intense stare, as if he can look right through me, and I suck in a deep breath while my heart starts to race. His brown hair sits messily on his head, in big contrast with his blue button-up shirt that hugs his athletic physique in a breathtaking way.

Jared James Jensen.

Best defender of the LA knights, hot as fuck, and another royal pain in my fucking ass. He is the epitome of your all-American athlete; handsome, arrogant, violent, trash-talking, cheating asshole. Add his politician dad in the mix and he's untouchable. *A privileged ass.*

I glance back and forth between him and the scowling girl who now has her hand pressed flat against his chest, standing between his legs while his hand is still tightly wrapped around my wrist. The scorching feeling of his fingers against my skin makes my cheeks feel flushed for a different reason than the anger Sean just ignited, and I swallow hard, trying to pull myself together.

Shit.

2

JENSEN

I narrow my eyes at her, seeing the clear shock on her face when our gazes lock.

"Hey, are you okay?" The tone of my voice sounds concerned, and her brows move up in confusion, as if I caught her off guard. She throws a curious glance at the brunette still pressed against my body before her brows furrow together, her confused look now completely replaced by one of the famous glares I normally get when we talk.

Or bicker. Whatever.

The judgment is dripping from her face, forming an amused smile in the corner of my mouth as I stare into her brown eyes. They sparkle in the dim lights of the hallway, with specks of gold glistering at me like fireworks. Within a split second, they flash with anger, resulting in a deep exhale from my chest.

Right. There she is.

"I'm fine, Jensen," she snarls. "Although, since my resignation doesn't officially start until tomorrow, I feel obligated to mention *that* is not the wisest thing to do." She points at the girl with disdain, then yanks her wrist from my grip to continue her way to the bathroom, leaving as fast as she appeared and storming off like a damn tornado.

"You should go." I ignore the brunette's shrieking of *"what the fuck"* when I push her to the side without a second thought, before I rapidly trail behind Rae stomping farther down the hall. A jolt of electricity hits me right in the chest when I circle my arm around her waist to halt her, placing myself in front of her. Her chin moves up to look at me, all hot and fuming. For a brief moment, I just blink, taking in her haunted face as my heart jumps out of my chest, the reaction confusing the fuck out of me.

Dismissing the feeling, I let her go, cocking my head as she stares at me in question for stopping her once again.

"You're upset," I announce, roaming over the freckles of her nose and her now blushing cheeks. Her light blonde hair is braided, hanging loosely over her shoulder, and I resist the urge to reach up and feel the silky strands between my fingers. Her eyes darken in suspicion as she straightens her shoulders, putting her poised stance back in place. No doubt preparing for our usual bickering.

She's hot. Always a treat to look at, with a snarky mouth that both pisses me off and amuses me. I love to ruffle her feathers and push her limits. We'd be a good match if there wasn't one problem; Rae Stafford and I don't get along.

Ever.

"Don't worry about it, Jensen. Just make sure you don't end up on TMZ with your tongue in a brunette tomorrow," she sighs dramatically.

Showing my irritation with an arrogant smirk, I take a step closer to grab her hip with one hand, bringing the other up to cup her cheek. Confliction shadows her face when I bring mine closer, and her lips part in anticipation, even though her eyes keep glaring at me.

I frustrate her. I can see it every time she's yelling at me for flirting with a girl that isn't my girlfriend, or when she shoves another press statement in my hands to fix whatever thing I fucked up. She always stays professional, never dropping her perfect act, but I can see the annoyance in her almond-shaped eyes. They're beautiful as fuck when she's mad at me.

"Why?" I ask with a breathy tone, our noses almost touching. "Should I go for a blonde instead?"

I softly hear her gasp for air, and when I look in her eyes once more, she bites her lip, staring at me through her thick lashes.

"You'd like that, wouldn't you?" Seduction is seeping through her voice as a challenging smile ghosts her soft pink lips, putting my dick on high alert. This time it's *my* eyes that widen in confusion, not sure if I heard her correctly, but I'm all here for it. My grip on her hip becomes more demanding, as I press the tips of my fingers into the fabric of her black jeans, with a clear vision in my mind. A flirty counter is sitting on my tongue, eager to push this a little farther, when she suddenly rolls her eyes at me, and I know the moment is gone.

"You know what?" She throws her hands in the air. "I don't care anymore. Do whatever you want. Fuck whoever you want. I hope you at least have the decency to tell Emily she will never be enough, but then again, none of you ever do," she spits, referring to my girlfriend, then quickly darts past me toward the fire exit with big strides.

Fuck.

"Rae!" I call out, rubbing a hand over my face.

I want to go after her, ask her if she's alright again, but instead, I watch her perfect ass stomp away with swaying hips while I clench my jaw in regret. The look on her face as she stormed past me told me she was already upset about something. I should've just let her go, but when she's in front of me, I just can't help myself. I feel the need to push her buttons, trying to make her lose control of her perfect act. It annoys the shit out of me that she's always composed and poised. I want to push out the side she doesn't show anyone. A side that's wild and thrilling, that says *trouble* in the best sense of the word. A side that matches the spark in her champagne brown eyes.

I crave to see that side of her.

She never snaps, though. God knows I've tried hard enough to find ways to piss her off. Making comments to the press. Flirting with a few girls too many. For the last five years, she has been up my ass about every girl I talk to, accusing me of all sorts of shit. I didn't even deny it, just because I liked to see her worked up, to get her eyes shooting daggers at me. I get under her skin, and I like it. Having this asshole curiosity inside of me that's wondering just how thick her skin really is. Like a piece of glass that I just want to crack. But other than the returning scowl, she's been able to keep a straight face every single time.

Calm, steady, professional.

After Rae has disappeared through the door, I turn my head and see the brunette who originally had my attention. Glaring at me.

Obviously.

"Sorry about that." I smirk, sauntering back toward her like nothing happened.

She huffs in response, flipping her hair like a diva as she

storms off with a thundercloud above her head. I shrug, laughing, because I can't really blame her, but I also can't be bothered to chase her.

Deciding I need another drink, I walk to the bar to order another bourbon, when someone takes the barstool next to me.

"You're late, *mate*." I glare at my best friend over the loud music, throwing my phone in front of me on the bar top.

He's wearing a black dress shirt, and his brown hair is combed back, making him look slick instead of like the nice guy that he is. You would swear he was a Wallstreet banker or something instead of a publishing book nerd.

"What the fuck are you wearing, Bodi? This is a party, not a wedding," I taunt, bringing my drink to my lips.

"Don't mock my sophisticated look, *mate*. I don't need to put on a tight shirt to get some attention," he counters with his thick Australian accent.

Raising a hand in the air, he grabs the attention of the bartender to order a drink, then glances at my dark blue shirt that's hugging my torso with an unimpressed look.

A ghost of a smile forms on my lips. "That's because you've got nothing to show off." Taking another sip, I turn around and lean against the bar.

Even though we have been best friends since we were twelve, we couldn't be more opposite. He is a handsome librarian. I am a rough hockey player.

He wants to make the world a better place. I just want the world to leave me the fuck alone.

"In the end, I want a woman who wants me for my brain instead of my ripped body that will most likely disappear around age fifty," he points out, stirring his Jack and Coke.

I snort before a fake cough comes from my throat. "*Pussy.*"

"Yeah, yeah, whatever. Did you see the show?" He changes the subject.

"What show?"

"PR girl slapped Kent." A wide smile spreads across his face, his drink hanging mid-air as he waits for my reaction.

"Rae? Rae Stafford? She slapped him?" I frown, incredulously. "What? When?"

Dots are starting to connect in my brain, and suddenly, I realize why she was all worked up.

"Yup." He looks over the rim of his glass with a knowing look in his eyes.

"Like across the face?"

"Bitch-slapped."

I blow out a whistle in awe, a weird feeling of satisfaction forming in my chest, combined with a sense of pride.

"No shit. Why?" The question leaves my lips, followed by a heavy sigh, regretting pissing her off some more after that happened.

"Something about him wanting to get back together and her telling him to fuck off." He shrugs. "She stormed off after that."

I nod, tipping my head back in appreciation.

Good for her.

When word got out that she broke up with Sean, I figured it was only a matter of time before he got his ass kicked by her, because it was a given more skeletons were about to pop out of the closet. When nothing happened over the last few weeks, I was starting to believe she didn't have it in her. But I guess I was wrong. I said enough to her to deserve a solid bitch-slap, though I never got one. But Sean did. I'm not sure if I should be disappointed about that, but I am a little. I always wondered what would happen if you pushed that girl over the edge, and even though I'm not keen on getting slapped by a girl, I'd like to be the one who makes her lose control.

To burst her perfect bubble.

"What the fuck are you smiling about?" Bodi looks at me with raised eyebrows.

"I'm just surprised." I shrug. "Normally, nothing can make her fall out of line."

"You mean, nothing *you* have ever tried made her fall out of line."

I snicker. "Yeah, that too."

"Your mother called me."

I choke on my bourbon, my gut tightening, when I realize what Bodi just said.

"My mother?" I almost sprain my neck while I move my head to look at him.

This can't be good.

He nods, agreeing, then moves his glass to his lips with a big smirk, though I'm not sure what's funny about my mother calling. She only calls if she's pissed, or she needs something. Usually, both.

"What the fuck? Why?" I don't have a very warm bond with my mother. She mostly annoys the shit out of me because she wants to control every single thing in my life. Not because she is the caring, loving kind; you know, the kind of mother that waits for you when you get out of school with cookies and milk. Or even the kind that sits in the front row of the school play. No, being the perfect politician's wife, Kathleen Jensen, nothing matters more than her status. She won't even let her baby boy stain that. She actually said that to my face more than once. And she still couldn't understand why she had an eight-year-old with uncontrollable anger issues.

Go figure.

"Because you won't pick up the goddamn phone," he scolds as his brows knit together.

"There is a very good reason for that," I start, then pause for a brief moment. "I'm avoiding her." I know I can't ignore my mother forever, but I've been doing a great job of it for the last two weeks.

"Yeah, well, so was I. But somehow, she was coming through my phone anyway."

"Fuck, rather you than me," I mutter, turning my gaze back to my glass.

"You are such a good friend—*asshole.*"

"Hey, you are my best friend. I would kill for you." I offer him a dramatic look as he glares at me, unimpressed. "I'd die for you. But when it comes to Kathleen Jensen? It's every man for himself. Just ask my brother. I learned these tactics from him."

"Great, next time I'll stay home when your parents throw another elite party or some shit."

I snap my head toward his, gaping. He replies with a satis-fied grin, successfully cornering me. There is only one thing worse than having to attend my parents' official functions and that's attending them without my best friend talking shit about everyone who passes by.

"You're right, I am an asshole. Please don't leave me." I pout.

"Whatever." He rolls his eyes. "You didn't tell me your old man is running for governor."

I sigh with a dismissive shrug. "Why do you think I'm avoiding my mother?"

When my mother told me my dad was planning to run for governor, I knew a whole list of demands was about to be fired upon me. They allowed me to become an NHL-player, but they'd never allow me to stray further than that. I can be the rebel out of their three children, but only if it doesn't jeopardize my father's political career. In interviews, they are asked about my career and answer the questions with a proud voice. But really, they mostly care about where I live, how I live, and who I'm dating, to make sure their perfect picture stays intact.

Ordering another Bourbon to numb my senses, I search his face. "What did she want, anyway?"

"To ask when you will propose to Emily," Bodi calmly answers like he's asking me to take the trash out.

I feel the hairs stand up on the back of my neck, a feeling of panic gripping my heart and a lump forming in the back of my throat as I watch the face of my girlfriend flash before my eyes. She's hot. She's sweet. *Sometimes.* My mom loves her. She fits the perfect picture. But proposing right now? That freaks me the fuck out. I'm not even sure I want to get married. Marriage reminds me of my parents. If that is called a marriage? Happily ever after? Till death do us part?

Fuck no, I'll pass.

"Not anytime soon," I mumble, grabbing the fresh drink from the bar. I take a sip, welcoming the feeling of the liquid burning through my chest. The searing sensation doing a good job of pushing the panic to the back of my head.

"She called to ask you *that*?" I ask when he stays quiet.

Knowing it's my mother, there must be more. Kathleen Jensen always wants something. When she gets you to agree on one thing, you better prepare for whatever else she still has up her sleeves.

"*That,* and if you could hurry the fuck up because she wants to book the venue for the engagement party."

"Engagement party?" I blurt out louder than I intended.

My eyes alarmingly flash around to make sure nobody heard me. The last thing I need is for TMZ to announce my engagement tomorrow. An engagement that won't happen in the first place.

"When you will be coming home," Bodi continues, unaffected, "and what you would think of a September wedding."

"It's July?!" I screech, my panic attack coming back at full force.

I look at Bodi with widened eyes, my heart now jumping out of my chest for a whole different reason than before. The smirk on his face tells me he's enjoying this way too much.

"The woman is insane."

"She is *your* mother." He chuckles.

"An engagement party? A September wedding?" I move my head closer to Bodi's, making sure no one overhears. "She doesn't even bother to ask if I want to marry. Fucking crazy woman. She is out of her mind."

I slightly shake my head. My mother has always been controlling, telling me no, *forcing* me to fall in line, but this is taking it to another level. You can tell me to be somewhere, to wear a suit and act accordingly. But telling me to get married? And when? That one is new. It's also not going to happen.

I stay quiet for a while, feeling the panic being replaced by irritation boiling up inside of me. It pisses me off. *A lot.* I'm so sick of my parents bossing everyone around. Bossing *me* around. They may have married to enhance my father's career, knowing appearance is everything in politics, but that doesn't mean it's what *I* want.

I glance at Bodi when I feel his worried gaze on me. I know he doesn't like my mother, this being the main reason. He butts heads with her all the time, pissing her off every time he gets the chance. But he supports me, stands by me, like the selfless friend that he is, even though he always questions why I do what she says most of the time.

"What the fuck did you tell her?"

His face lights up and a smug grin stretches among his cheeks, telling me I'll probably enjoy whatever comes out of his mouth next.

"I told her you'd probably burn the house down to avoid ever coming home if she would dare to ask those questions again."

A smile splits my face. "My hero."

Then he adds with a straight face, "I also told her the Botox must have damaged her brain if she thought your wedding was going to be a high society event. Then she started yelling and swearing all kinds of things. It was quite entertaining."

Snorting to keep my drink in, I start to laugh, my eyes locked with his in admiration.

"She really went all in after I told her your wedding would probably be in Las Vegas. Or some southern barn. If there would be a wedding at all. I think I mentioned something about how you'd rather have a baby out of wedlock than ever get married."

He keeps a stoic face. "She yelled something about Emily never going for that and then, after I asked her who was talking about Emily, I couldn't make out any more words, so I hung up." He downs the rest of his drink like a pro and turns his body toward the bar with a satisfied smile on his face, as I try to catch my breath, unable to stop laughing.

"You're welcome."

"You are going in my will, you've earned it," I joke when I'm able to breathe again.

"Thanks, buddy, but I think your new *wife* won't go for that." He winks, but I hear the serious tone in his voice. We can joke about this, but the truth is, the world has expectations. My mother has expectations. My father has expectations. But so does my girlfriend.

"I'm never going to marry."

Bodi pulls a face. "Then you might as well break up with Emily, because she will never go for that either," he states matter-of-factly. "Did you talk to her about it? About marriage?"

"She brought it up a few times." I pause. "I kinda brushed the subject away."

Bodi keeps his eyes fixated on me, silently asking me for more than that.

"I like Emily. My parents love her. She's the perfect fit for my family."

"But is she the perfect fit for you?"

Looking up at the ceiling, I let out a grunt, annoyed he always asks the questions I don't want to answer. "How the fuck would I know, Bodi?"

We stare at each other, my jaw ticking, when my phone vibrates on the bar in front of me.

A message appears on the screen, telling me Emily is sending me an image.

"Speaking of the devil," I mumble, expecting some kind of half-naked pictures of herself from the photoshoot she was doing this afternoon, but instead, I cock my head when I look at the screen. I raise my eyebrow, not immediately knowing what I'm looking at until I recognize Rae's pretty blonde braid on her shoulder. My hand is on her cheek, and we are standing so close, it looks like I'm an inch away from kissing her.

I look around, stunned, wondering who the fuck could have taken this picture while Bodi gives me a quizzical look.

"What is it?"

"It's Emily," I explain, when my phone pings again.

EMILY: **I always knew you were fucking that PR trailer trash. Don't come home. WE ARE DONE. Asshole.**

HOME. The word alone makes a sarcastic grin shower my face, since it's *my* penthouse she's referring to. But when I realize how this night is going to end, my annoyance level goes from zero to the moon.

"What in the hell?" I close my eyes and pinch the bridge of my nose, handing over my phone to Bodi.

I'm a flirt. I flirt. *A lot.*

Emily knows this. I've been caught a little too close with some girl a whole number of times. She always stays. I have my suspicion she deep down doesn't care as long as she can be with a Jensen. It wouldn't even surprise me if she'd run off with my brother, if he would give her the chance. I know this will be over in about three hours. She will fight me, slap me, forgive me, kiss me, fuck me, and all will be well in the world. We have done the circle about twenty times. But just thinking about it instantly triggers a headache, because I simply can't be bothered to deal with it.

I just know it is expected.

"Fuck me. Is that Rae and you?" Bodi squeaks, wide-eyed.

"Yup."

He looks closer at the picture, zooming in on the screen with his fingers, then brings his attention back to me, impressed, when he realizes this was fifteen minutes ago.

"You dirty bastard. Did you kiss her?" He chuckles, eyes beaming.

"You think Kent would be the only one who got slapped tonight if I did?" I huff. "Of course not, you moron. She probably would have chopped off my nuts before she left."

He lowers his head a little to lock his eyes with mine, holding up my phone in front of my face. "Yeah, right, she looks like she is really pissed."

I bite my lip, looking at the picture, imagining how I would have kissed her. Instantly, I feel my dick twitch in my jeans, my heart jumping with excitement. Pushing the strange feeling away, I snatch the phone out of his hand and put it back in my pocket.

"Guess I have to ignore my mother dearest a little longer."

"Just forget about them. Forget about your mother. Forget about Emily. Let's go away for a few days. Take a break? Get us settled on a nice beach, with cocktails and some *new* ass to tap? You won the Stanley Cup, and as of right now, you're a free man. Let's take advantage of that for a few days and deal with this bullshit after we have some fun," Bodi suggests, keeping a close eye on me.

That sounds damn tempting. To leave it all hanging and

just enjoy ourselves in a foreign country. Somewhere hot. Getting wasted before noon, with cheap sunglasses perched on my head. But my father's run for governor lingers in the back of my mind. As much as I want to tell my family to fuck off, I don't want to make it harder on my siblings if I bail on my responsibilities.

"That is the best idea ever, but it will only postpone the shitstorm I'm going to get. Might as well get it over with."

When Bodi doesn't reply, I look at him, cursing the judgy look he's giving me.

"He's running for governor, Bodi," I explain.

Bodi wheezes, disappointed, but doesn't push any further. "So now what?"

"Now, I'll do what I always do." I pour the last of my drink down my throat and slam the glass on the bar, ready to call it a night. "I grovel."

"You need me to keep your pretty face in one piece?" he calls out against my back when I walk away.

I glance over my shoulder with an incredulous look, as my feet never stop.

"Stupid question, McKay. Let's go."

"Great," he sputters before I hear his footsteps follow my track.

3

Rae

The next morning, Penelope is waiting for me in my office with a smile creasing her face, clearly excited to take over my job. Considering she was picked out of fifty-four applicants, I can't blame her.

"Good morning!" She holds a Knights cup in front of my face, the liquid inside still steaming, and I gratefully take it from her hands as a scent of cinnamon greets me.

"Tea?"

"Ginger, with a bit of pumpkin spice. Just how you like it."

Rounding my desk, I take a seat, starting the final hours of my employment, before looking at the girl in front of me. Her brown hair is perfectly styled, her dark blue pantsuit is impeccable, and her nails seem fresh from the salon. She definitely looks a lot more prepared than I did when I sauntered into this building for the first time with my white Converse sneakers still covered in dirt.

"Are you ready to sign your life away?" My gaze locks with hers over the rim of my cup as I softly sip the hot tea.

I'm joking, but part of it is true. Working as a PR

Specialist barely gives you room to have a life. Christmas, your birthday, 4th of July, it doesn't matter; you have to be able to jump up and fix anything media related within the hour. It's thrilling, and exactly the kind of distraction I needed, but it's also a huge responsibility. Trying to bend the truth just enough to turn it in your favor, but not so much that it cracks and ruins the player's reputation. Or the team's.

"I'm ready!" She claps like a seal on crack, making me shoot her a dull look.

Well, at least she is still motivated.

FOR THE NEXT FEW HOURS, I hand everything over to her. I tell her who to watch out for, offer her tips to keep each member of the team in line as much as she can, and give her the files I made for all of them.

They may be rough and tough on the ice, but they are damn drama queens when it comes to their personal lives. Either they are screwing around when they shouldn't be, pissing off their wives, or getting into bar fights. And yes, I'm being completely biased and judgmental because of my lying and cheating ex-boyfriend. Really, they aren't all as vile as Sean Kent, but nonetheless, I kind of feel the need to prepare her as well as possible.

When we are finally done, she wishes me luck, then gets up to give me a minute, walking out the door. My eyes move to the side, looking over the Los Angeles International Airport with a heavy but content feeling inside of me. When I look outside now, it's hard imagining I had the shutters closed for the first few weeks of my employment. I get up, sauntering toward the window to watch the planes one last time.

It took me six months until I was able to watch the planes. Six months before I could do my job without being distracted, holding my breath in horror every time I heard a plane fly over the building. I kept waiting for the loud sounds of a crash to confirm my fear. But after a while, the fear passed, and I started to watch them every now and then. Facing my fear without getting on an aircraft myself.

With my arms wrapped around my body, I follow the plane that's about to land on the strip, my face instantly tensing at the sight of it, a habit I can't seem to shake. I swallow hard, pressing my lips together until the landing gear touches the ground and the plane slows to a safe speed.

A relieved breath leaves my lips at the same time I hear the door open behind me, and I glance over my shoulder.

"Hey, kid, you ready?" Johnny closes the door behind him as he enters. Wearing dark jeans and a polo, he's apparently introducing casual Monday. I quirk up one brow in suspicion.

"What are you up to?" I twist my body to face him, resting my back against the window.

"What are you talking about?" A coy smile forms when he takes the seat in front of the desk and loosens his tie. He carelessly places his right leg over the left and leans back like he's ready for the weekend, even though it's only noon on the first day of the week.

"In the five years I've worked here, you've never been dressed in jeans." My eyes rake up and down his body before they darken to a glare. "You better not be planning to fucking hop on my road trip."

"Five days in a car?" he scoffs. "As much as I love you,

I'm not ever spending five days in a car. I didn't become a millionaire to enjoy less comfort."

"Then, what?"

"Nothing," he blurts, too quickly for me to believe him, his neck flashing a slight red.

"Oh my God. Do you have a date?"

"No," he huffs. Again, the look on his face lacks credibility, like a toddler being caught red-handed with his little paws in the cookie jar. I hold his gaze, pursing my lips as I wait for a better answer than that.

"Maybe," he replies, drawing a long breath. "It's just a lunch date."

"With who?" I titter in excitement. Johnny never has serious relationships, and even though part of me believes he'll be the forever bachelor of the NHL, I wish him a partner in life. A love that matches the one my Nana had with my grandfather.

"I already said too much."

"Johnny!" I screech, adamant. "It's me! Share!"

He steadfastly shakes his head. "I'll tell you on Friday if it's worth talking about."

I hold still, narrowing my gaze, before I crack a grin and roll my eyes. "Fine," I mutter.

If someone would have told me five years ago that this was going to be my life, I would've laughed my ass off. My LA job was always drama and stress, but I liked the responsibility that came with it. Always ready to make sure everyone and everything involved with the LA Knights was always exposed and represented in the right way. Pulling it off every single time was both addictive and thrilling, like balancing on a skyscraper, never knowing when you'd crash, and part of me will miss the job.

"It would still make me feel better if you would take Frank with you," Johnny says.

"Give the man a break." I give him my sweetest smile, casually grabbing my cup of tea from the desk. "I'll be fine." Brushing his words away, I watch his blue eyes darken to a seriousness he rarely gives me.

His troubled gaze locks with mine as he purses his lips like he's got something to say, the look bringing a slight worry to my chest.

"What?" I finally blurt.

"My sister was right."

My eyebrows raise in curiosity. "What do you mean?"

He leans back, taking a deep breath before crossing his arms in front of his chest. It's one of those looks that screams *'Caution: preach ahead.'*

"When I first took you to LA," he starts, "she told me you would never really ground here. *'That girl is more southern than she realizes herself,'* she said." He pauses, cocking his head. "I guess she was right. Since you've decided to go back home, you look more relaxed than I've ever seen you. And I've known you your entire life." A sad chuckle comes from his mouth before he looks at his feet, lost in thought.

"Maybe I was wrong for bringing you here," he adds.

"Johnny." I sigh, closing my eyes for a short moment. "You saved me. If you hadn't brought me here—" I shake my head, pushing away the tears that are pricking in the corner of my eyes. "I would probably be dead in the gutter right now," I say with a thankful gaze.

The corner of his mouth slightly rises, amused. "No chance, kid. You are too smart to end up in the gutter. You're not Jimmy."

"I wasn't far off," I counter.

"You were never going to end like him."

"Maybe." I shrug with my lips pressed to a thin line. "But I wouldn't know how lucky I was if you hadn't brought me to LA. I wouldn't appreciate home if I didn't have anything to compare it to."

Johnny always gave me more credit than I think I deserve, but I *know* he's the one that saved me. I hated him for it and was determined to make a run for it as soon as we arrived in LA. But he pushed me. He threatened to force me to face my biggest fear if I didn't get my shit together, backing me up against the wall. Little did I know, it was the biggest gift he could've given me.

His eyes land back on mine, this time with a proud look that has me shooting him a coy smile.

"When did you get so wise?"

"When you dragged me here, gave me an all-consuming job, and forced me to grow up." I stick my tongue out at him, done with the heavy talk.

"Fuck, I *did*, didn't I?" His laugh echoes through the room, then he looks at his watch. "You better get going. I don't want you driving in the dark."

I hum in agreement before I get up and put the last of my stuff in my brown leather weekender. Then I move toward Johnny with a heavy feeling in my feet.

He grabs my face in his hands with a stern gaze.

"Now remember, you call me every morning and—"

"And every night when I'm in my hotel room. I know," I interrupt, finishing his sentence. It's the same thing he says every single time I make this trip. Twice a year. "Let's not make this any harder than it already is."

He lets go of my face to grab me in a tight hug, and I wrap my arms around his body, breathing him in.

"Shut up, smartass." His tone is soft, a slight crack seeping through it. "I'm gonna miss you."

Even though I can feel the tears waiting until they can run down my cheeks, combined with a lump forming in the back of my throat, I do my best to keep it together. "You know you are going to see me this Friday, right?" I scoff, not knowing how to respond to Johnny being all sentimental.

"Don't ruin the moment." He moves back to look me in the eye. "I'm going to say this one last time and never again after that. I'm going to miss having you around all the time, kid. Call me whenever you need me, okay?" His lips connect with my forehead, and I close my eyes to take in the moment. I'm grateful for him, knowing he will always have my back. He might not be my dad, but he's definitely the next best thing.

"Thank you for everything, Johnny."

"Don't worry about it, kid. I'd do anything for you."

"True. I'm in your will, right?" I joke.

He laughs, giving me a slight push toward the door. "Get out of here, *Rebel*. Before I put you back to work."

"Fine," I mutter with a smile, then I walk away and throw my weekender on my back with one hand. He walks me to the door at a fast pace, knowing I don't want to make a big deal out of it.

I'm not good at goodbyes. They always bring me back to the finality of it, and I'll do everything to avoid that feeling at all costs. I've already been through it too many times.

"Don't forget to call!" he calls out when I walk through the revolving door.

"I won't!" I yell back.

When I get outside, the sun warms my face, and I put my sunglasses on as I cross the parking lot, heading toward my car. Halfway along the lot, I turn around to look back one last time, taking in the big brick building that got so much of my time and energy for the last five years. I feel sad and relieved at the same time. Not knowing what to do next is both scary and exciting. But not knowing what I need is even scarier.

And I don't know what I need.

I don't even know what I want.

It took me a long time to get to the point of admitting that, always putting up a front of confidence. But the truth is, I don't know. I like to believe I once knew, before… But really, I have never known. All I know is that I want and need something that I will never have again. To settle the void in my heart.

I inhale deeply, framing this image in my head before I turn around to get going with a somewhat peaceful feeling, ready to take on the next phase of my life. It will be frustrating, and it will probably be hard. But I'm ready as much as I can be.

The satisfied feeling gets slammed out of my chest when I roughly bump into something in front of me. Or should I say *someone*. Dropping my bag in shock, a shriek erupts from my lips as I lose my balance while I expect to fall on my ass. I feel my heart jump when two firm hands grab my upper arms to keep me on my feet, making me look up to apologize as I stare into a pair of familiar blue eyes.

Blue like the shallows of the ocean, the sun making them glint in a way that steals my breath.

Startled, I take him in, captivated by the feeling of his arms while a hint of his fresh and fruity cologne hypnotizes me.

"Dear Lord, Jensen, you almost gave me a heart attack," I

snap, feeling busted as fuck. Even though he pisses me off, he also makes my stomach make weird flips every time he peers down at me.

"Bad conscience?" He grins as he lets go of my arms, then reaches down and picks up my bag.

"Something like that," I murmur, tucking it over from him. His eyes lock with mine, his gaze waiting, for what I don't know, but regardless, my heart starts to pound against my ribcage. I quickly take a step back, knowing I need the distance to keep my head clear when it comes to Jensen. I've learned to stand my ground against him over the years, to raise my chin and call him out on his bullshit, but that doesn't mean that it was an easy task. The intense look in his eyes combined with his handsome face makes me weak in the knees, while his arrogant mouth fuels my anger more than anyone else on the team. Well, that was before Sean cheated on me. Now, Jensen is a close second, being a walking mind-fuck if you'd believe how ridiculously my body responds every time our paths cross.

The fact that he pushed me a little more this weekend, in a way that had me looking up at the ceiling for a long time while lying in bed, hasn't made it any easier.

"Well, anyway," I say, putting my ever-professional smile on my face one final time. "I have to go. Good luck with everything." I move to the side to walk past him, when he grabs my arm again with force.

"Wait, we have to talk." The abrupt action makes me drop my bag again, this time pissing me off for real.

"Can you bring her bag to the car?" Jensen picks it up, handing it out to someone behind me, and I turn around with a confused frown.

"Oh. Hey, Bodi." I look at his best friend giving me a small wave, then he takes the bag from Jensen's hand. My head moves between both of them, not sure what's going on, until Jensen holds up his hand in question.

I cock my eyebrow at him with a quizzical look. "What?"

"Keys," he demands.

My first reaction is to make a smartass comment about how I don't respond well to people commanding me, or how I'm not one of his sidekicks, but when I look at Bodi's pleading brown eyes, my interest is piqued. Bodi is definitely the better man out of the two, from what I've learned over the years, and I doubt he'd make a silent appeal if it wasn't worth my while. I still shoot up my eyebrows in defiance, but my curiosity wins. Instead of throwing a fit, I drop my keys in Jensen's hand with a glare tugging on my lips. A fatherly sigh escapes Bodi's throat, then he grabs the keys from Jensen's hand.

"Be nice," Bodi scowls at Jensen, who rolls his eyes in return, ignoring him by putting his focus back on me, that same penetrating stare slipping into place.

I watch Bodi walk toward my black SUV, a few yards away, then he opens the trunk to throw the bag in like he owns the damn thing. An amused smile crosses his face when he feels my eyes on him before he sits his ass on the tailgate and pulls out his phone, getting comfortable until we are done with whatever Jensen needs my help with.

Not really keen on doing any more damage control for one of the Knights' notorious players, I move my gaze back to Jensen, crossing my arms in front of my body, with a slight glare. "If this is about the brunette from Saturday, you have to take it to Penelope. I'm not on the job anymore," I say, popping my hip.

"Actually," he drawls, taking out his phone, "it's about a blonde."

"Really?" I grunt, annoyed, as he starts tapping on the screen, until he holds a picture in front of my face. "You had to go for another—" My breath hitches when the photo reaches my retinas. "*Fuck me.*"

JENSEN

"Really? You had to go for another—*fuck me*." She stops mid-sentence when the recognition hits. Her eyes are full of ferocity as they move back up to meet mine, sparked with a new level of fire I haven't seen before. I might become the second person she slaps in forty-eight hours.

"What the actual fuck, Jensen?"

Holding my phone in the air, she takes a step forward with a furious glare, a blonde strand of her hair falling in front of her flawless face. The hairs on the back of my neck stand up when her honey-scented shampoo enters my nose, making it hard for me to concentrate.

Bad timing, Jensen.

"Who took this picture?" she growls, fumbling with her necklace.

"I don't know," I admit, running a hand through my hair. "Emily sent it to me Saturday night when I was still at the club. Someone sent it to her, but she won't tell me who." I lightly shake my head. I was up until two in the morning fighting about it, then continued my denial on Sunday. Emily was livid, telling me how she always knew I was screwing around with "PR girl."

God knows how she ever got that idea.

She didn't give in this time, though. Sunday afternoon, she just kept packing, and after she walked out with her bags, I worked on finishing the bottle of scotch for the next two hours before I went into another short coma, exhausted from my own pleas. Trying to sleep this mess away, I woke up this morning, expecting my girlfriend to be sitting in the kitchen with a scowl on her face. Like she always does. We fight, she's pissed, sometimes she throws shit at my head, we kiss, we make up, and all is good in the world and all that shit. But instead, I found Bodi sipping his morning coffee at the bar with a bored look in his eyes. It's when I realized it's only a matter of time before my mother will be hanging on the phone, nagging me with her judgment and instructions to fix shit with Emily.

Yay.

"God, if you could just control yourself for *once*." Her brown eyes are spitting fire, and I can't help but notice how beautiful they are, while at the same time, her accusations piss me off.

"How is this my fault?" I yelp back at her, my rage going through the roof in a split second. My blood starts to boil in my veins like it always does when she pushes my buttons. She likes to point her perfect finger at me every damn chance she gets. Going head-to-head with me to put me in my place. Normally, I enjoy it more than I should, loving how she never backs down while I always try to push her farther over the edge. Desperate to watch her lose it, even though I know I'm in the wrong.

But this time, it's different. This time, *she* is in the

goddamn picture too. Okay, so maybe I'm the one who started it, but that's not the damn point. Is it?

"If you wouldn't feel the need to flirt every goddamn second of your fucking life, it wouldn't look like you are kissing *me* instead of your supermodel girlfriend, *asshole*."

"I didn't take the fucking picture!" I snap, wanting to pull my hair out of my head.

"Who did?"

"I don't know!"

"I didn't give someone the chance to take this picture in the first place!" Her sharp voice feels like a knife going through my head, numbing half of my brain. I let out a frustrated grunt, pinching the bridge of my nose. I've been testing the boundaries of my relationship for years now, never really crossing the line, but trying to push them aside to keep my girlfriend somewhat interested. Every single time she was pissed, we'd both put in more effort and were solid for a few more weeks. But the one time I step too close to Rae, Emily doesn't believe me.

It's fucking ridiculous.

Everyone knows we can't stand each other.

Glancing at Rae, who is still glaring at me like a fucking warrior, I roll my eyes. I've been fighting with a woman for the last thirty-six hours. My head just can't handle another one right now. Especially not with Rae Stafford. This girl is too feisty for my current energy level. My shoulders drop with a sigh.

"I'm sorry, okay?"

She gives me a skeptical look, her eyes wary, calling my bullshit like she always does.

But I mean it this time, even though she still pisses me off. Chances are, she will get a shitstorm of media attention toward her as soon as this picture gets into the wrong hands, and I didn't mean for that to happen. Because experience says it will happen, eventually. Rae is used to handling stuff like this, but we all know it's totally different when you are the subject of the attention. She always did her best to keep her face out of the tabloids when she was dating Sean Kent, but the times she ended up there anyway killed her inside. I could see it every time she walked into the locker room with a haunted hint in her eyes.

We stare at each other for a few seconds, neither of us backing down while the tension grows thicker. Time seems to freeze, my heart starting to race, and I ball my hands to fists until I notice her gaze soften a little. An unexpected pang hits my chest, seeing the torn and frustrated look on her face, and I rub my hands down my cheeks as my jaw clenches.

"Great, my last day in LA and I end up on TMZ," she softly grunts. "Well, thanks for the heads-up."

Abruptly ending our conversation, she walks past me with a big sigh, way too quickly for my liking.

A little stunned, I turn my head to enjoy the view of her swaying hips prancing away from me before I realize that isn't why I'm here.

"Hold up, I need your help." I catch up with her, and we walk toward her car while Bodi closes the trunk and drops his back against the rear of the Mercedes SUV, his arms folded in front of his chest.

"I told you, talk to Penelope," she replies, never slowing down.

"Stop." I circle her waist to halt her, the same way I did last night, and another spark goes through my body. I clear my throat, pretending like that didn't happen, when she looks up at me through her fluttering lashes. "I need you to release a statement. Emily is pissed. And my family will be too as soon as they see this picture all over the internet."

I notice her eyes narrow in confusion before she looks at me with a straight face.

"Isn't she always when this shit happens? I'm sure she will turn around; she always does." She casually waves her hand in the air, dismissing the conversation.

"This time it's different. She packed her bags. She says she's done."

"Oh, for fuck's sake, you've done this more times than I can count, and *now* she decides she is done?"

"And I quote: 'I've always known you were into that PR girl. You see here four times a week,'" I clarify, my hand still on her belly to keep her in place.

She places her fists at her sides, looking at me like she will bite my head off if I dare to flinch. Tempting, but I still stand frozen.

"That is fucking ridiculous. We bicker all the goddamn time. Why the fuck would she think that?" she scolds.

"I don't know. To be honest, I don't really care, but my dad is running for governor. I have to fix it before I taint his perfect reputation." I shrug, honestly.

She holds my gaze, her face turning grim, before pricking her finger against my chest. "What the *fuck* have you been telling her?"

Again with the accusations.

"Why the fuck would I tell her anything?" I lift my eyebrows.

Why the fuck would I pretend for her to be interested in me? Everyone knows she is clearly not, and I have enough pussy to entertain my ego without getting rejected by Little Miss Perfect over here.

Her brown eyes turn dark, eying me with more suspicion. But then a frown deepens on her forehead, making it a pain to stay pissed at her. She frustrates me, but fuck, she's so cute when she's pissed. Especially when she goes all Nancy Drew on me.

"Fine, give me your phone. I will give her a call," she finally offers in a breathy tone, holding up her hand.

I rub my neck, averting my face. "Yeah, about that…"

"What?!" she barks, her impatience palpable.

I look back at her and give her my sweetest smile, hoping for once in my life it will work in my favor.

Who the fuck am I kidding?

Most women drop to my feet whenever I give them a small smile and some sweet talk, but with Rae, it hasn't worked once so far—I'm not expecting it to stick now.

"She changed her number."

"Fucking hell, Jensen."

"And her best friend called me a *cocksucking piece of shit* when I asked for her new number," I add while I'm at it. Might as well throw it all out there.

"Are you?"

"Am I what?"

"Cocksucking?" She daringly tilts her head, crossing her arms. Good to know she still has some humor.

I grimace at her *funny* comment, then take a step forward to crowd her space. "You want me to show you how I prefer pussy over cock every single time?"

She blinks, looking up at me through hooded eyes, clearly regretting opening her smart-ass mouth.

"Okay. That's enough, Jensen." She pushes me back with her hand pressed against my abs. She ignores my question, but my dick certainly can't, with her hand so close to his presence. My jaw ticks, disregarding the twitching of my dick while she lets out a deep wheeze, completely unaware of the torture she's bringing upon me.

"The girl must really be serious this time. Good for her." She sounds more stunned than angry. "So what the fuck do you want me to do?"

"I need you to release a statement and tell Emily that there is nothing between you and me. *Face-to-face.*"

Biting her lips, she stares at me, and I can see the wheels turning in her head, thinking about the situation. Standing in front of her, looking at her perfectly plump lips, makes me itchy to move into old habits and make a flirty comment, but I keep my mouth shut. For a second, I wonder why I've never kissed the girl, just to find out how those luscious lips would feel on mine.

"Fine." She snaps my focus back to her eyes as she glances at the watch on her wrist. "I need to hit the road in an hour; that way I'll still be in my hotel before dark. I'll send an email to TMZ and then I'll talk to Emily for ten minutes, but after that, you are on your own. Where is she?"

Here is the tricky part where I need to give it my all.

Blinking, I give her my smoldering look, figuring it can't hurt to give it another shot or at least do my best to not get slapped by this pretty blonde.

"Yeah, about that too," I tell her, carefully. "She's in New York."

Hopeful, I wait for her response, anxiously staring at her blank expression, even though we all know she will lose her shit soon enough. After a few seconds, Rae widens her eyes and drops her jaw incredulously, and I swear I can see the steam come out of her ears like it does in one of those cartoons.

"Jared James Jensen," she rumbles, her tone ominous and sexy at the same time, as if she's speaking to my dick directly. No one calls me by my full name other than my parents, and I rarely respond to my first two names. At times, I kinda forget my name is actually Jared James. But hearing them roll off her lips in such a dominant way?

I want more.

"You better be talking about some nice hipster café uptown or something. You know, where they serve all those different kinds of herbal teas and vegan pies, Jensen, because there is no way in hell am I going to New York right now. Are you crazy?" Her face is hard and tense, her voice full of frustration, already knowing I'm not talking about whatever fucking café that is.

"Specific, really. Do you go there often?" I can't help a laugh breaking from my chest, but when she gives me a death stare, the curling of my mouth goes back to a firm line.

"Come on, Rae, please." I fold my hands together, begging. "The jet is already waiting. We can go right now and have you back here by midnight. You can drive home tomorrow."

Something I can't detect flashes in her eyes, and I see her muscles go rigid for a brief moment.

"I don't fly," she deadpans.

I scrunch my nose, not following. "What do you mean, you don't fly?"

"I don't fly." She shrugs, a serious look on her face.

"Don't bullshit me. Come on, Rae. We can go right now and have this sorted before dinner."

"I have to be in Jacksonville by Friday. I'm leaving today."

"I'll fly you to Jacksonville." I push further.

"I don't fly, *Jensen*," she repeats, seething this time, with her glare returning in its full glory. There is a familiarity to it that I enjoy, but there is something else that is situating in my bones the longer I look at her.

"What the fuck? Why?" I blurt. "Are you afraid of flying?"

"No!" she snaps, as her expression turns darker with rage.

"Then, what?!"

"It's none of your goddamn business!"

My skull feels like a nutshell she's trying to crack, which is probably the result of my excessive drinking for the last two days. Or the previous female yelling my brain had to endure. Either way, it's making it a pain to think straight and stay calm when I just want to toss her over my shoulder and kidnap her to get this over with. I have a feeling she won't appreciate that, though.

"Fucking hell, come on, Rae."

Can't she for once be on my side?

"No, Jensen. I don't owe you shit, and I'm going home. *Today.*" She scowls, her voice firm and without any room for discussion. Her sparkling brown eyes stare at me for a moment before she sighs, her face softening a little. "But I have no plans for the next few weeks, so if you need me to come to New York, then Sunday will be your first option."

"Sunday is too late. My mother will be on my back within the hour, demanding me to fix this." The words leave my lips before I think, and I hear Bodi mutter *"idiot"* behind me, making me realize I'm fucking this up. *Blame my hangover.*

She blinks, pursing her lips, her eyes shooting daggers once again. "You have two options, Jensen. It's either *'thank you, Rae, for giving me some of your time. You are the best,'*" she mocks before her voice turns in a roar I didn't know she could produce, "or you can figure it out your goddamn self!"

Her anger hits me in waves before she storms off to Bodi without waiting for my response.

"Fine, Sunday," I yell back to her.

"Fine! See you Sunday, *asshole*." She stops in front of Bodi and holds up her hand while he rubs the back of his neck, an apologetic smile breaking through his lips.

"Sorry about that." He nudges his head toward me, completely disregarding me as if I can't hear him. *Asshole.*

"Whatever. I'm used to it by now." Bodi drops the keys in her hand, and she walks to the driver's seat, never giving me a second glance. I groan, pissed, as Bodi saunters over to me with a gleeful smile on his face, my feet moving to meet him halfway.

"Well, that was entertaining."

Ignoring him, I think about how the rest of the day will play out, knowing the paps will be eating this up like cake. With my father running for governor, it will be in every daily paper by tomorrow, and I'll be expected to fix it. The only option I have is hiding out at home, hoping it will pass in a few days. But the thought of going home freaks me the fuck out, so with a brain only half functioning, I seek out another option. In the split of a second, I decide I need to get the hell out of this city. I'm not staying in LA. I'm leaving, and I know exactly where to go.

Picking up my pace, I trot past my best friend. The second he sees the determined look on my face, he rolls his eyes, joggling his head.

"Whatever you're up to, *don't.*"

"Get in," I roar at him, making my way to the passenger seat of her car.

"Really, Jay, are we really going to do this?"

"Yes."

"We don't even have our stuff with us." He lets his shoulders hang, looking up at the sky.

"You got your laptop. I got a credit card. What more do we need?" I counter.

"She's going to hate you."

I groan, pricking my finger into his chest like a growling bear. "I'm not staying in LA. And if I want to avoid my family for a few more days, what better excuse than to be driving across the country?"

"Jay, seriously." Bodi rolls his eyes, making a futile effort to convince me otherwise.

"Do you have anything better to do?"

"That's not the point," he mutters in response.

"You said we needed a break. Here it is," I hiss, opening the door.

I put on my seat belt and press on the start engine button, when the passenger door pops open. Automatically, I let out a shriek, thinking I'm being carjacked or something, until I notice those same blue eyes catch mine, accompanied by a cocky smirk.

Confused, and frankly, a little shocked, I watch Jensen get in, then I glance to the backseat when I hear another door opening and notice Bodi doing the same.

"Err, what the fuck are you doing? Your car is right there." I point my finger at the black Camaro on the other side of the parking lot. I can't forget what he's driving because he almost hit me with the damn thing a few months ago. Apparently, the man drives like he skates.

Without mercy.

"We are going with you." The words leave his body with ease, like I've missed some agreement in our last conversation. I'm pretty sure we said Sunday, though.

He pulls his black hoodie over his head of messy hair, then places his aviator sunglasses on his nose, looking like the infuriating bad boy that he is. I watch him put on his seatbelt and get comfortable, leaning back as he crosses his arms in front of his body. Tucking a lock of hair behind my ear, I ignore how he makes my skin pebble with goosebumps when he pins me with a daring look. I close my eyes, inhaling deeply before I exhale and plaster a kind, yet forced, smile on my face.

"What do you mean, *you are coming with me?*" I grunt.

"We are coming with you to North Carolina, and on Sunday, we can drive to New York together."

My eyes bulge as I just blink, stunned, because this has to be a joke. Some kind of sick prank that is another lousy attempt to piss me off.

Slowly, I turn my head to Bodi, who just shrugs as if it's the most normal thing in the entire world. He isn't fazed by Jensen's latest idea. A stupid one, if you ask me.

"No," I point out, "the two of you are getting the fuck out of my car, and I will meet you in New York on Sunday." A jittery feeling bubbles in my stomach as I'm wondering why I'm still hoping this is a joke, because I know it ain't. The determined look on his annoyingly handsome face says it all. Jensen doesn't joke, nor does he listen. I honestly think it's not in his DNA to listen to anything other than his own wills and wants. I've had so many discussions with the boy, always with the same outcome. He always does whatever the fuck he wants. Consequences be damned. I guess that's what you become when you are a spoiled little boy coming from an elite family.

No is not in their vocabulary.

Lazily, he keeps his attention on me, and I can feel his piercing eyes burning through my skin, even though his sunglasses block me from looking into them.

"Look, it'll take about one more hour before both our faces are on TMZ, so about two more hours before the first paparazzi bitches are hanging around my house. I'm not dealing with that shit."

"And how is that *my* problem, exactly?"

He leans his head against the window, ignoring me, and I can see the movement of his eyes shutting behind his glasses, clearly getting ready to take a nap in my passenger seat.

"You literally can go *anywhere* else," I cry with my hands in the air, wrinkling my nose. "You have a jet waiting for you!"

"I haven't been on a road trip in a while. Now just let me sleep for a few hours. I've had a rough couple of nights."

Pinching my lips together with a shake of my head, I desperately look over my shoulder for some backup. Bodi's playing with his phone but brings up his eyes when I call out his name.

He offers me a coy smile, looking nothing like the douchebag beside me, with his green flannel shirt, his chocolate brown hair, and his kind eyes. I give him a hopeful look, trying to spur him into action to drag his best friend out of my car. But instead, he shrugs.

"I've learned to just roll with it," he explains, then moves his focus back to his phone.

He's no fucking help at all.

I close my eyes, taking a few deep breaths. "I just can't get rid of you, can I?"

"Like he said." Jensen points his thumb to the backseat without looking up. "Just roll with it."

I drop my head on the steering wheel in defeat, my skin connecting with the cold leather.

He has no boundaries. Like at all.

"Fuck me," I mumble, opening my eyes again, my skull still in the same position.

"I would love to, but I'm not in the mood right now." I

jerk back up, slapping his arm in response, making him duck a little into the door with a chuckle, before my head connects with the wheel once more.

How am I still dealing with this shit? And how am I now doomed to Jared James Jensen as my road trip buddy?

"Hey, just look at it this way..." I gently twist my head to see a lopsided grin forming on his handsome face, his eyes peering at me from under the safety of his glasses. "You won't be alone, and we can take turns driving. I'm guessing your folks will be very grateful that there are two strong men who can protect you for the next three days."

I straighten my back, our eyes staying locked as I think over his words. His sunglasses hang on the tip of his nose, his gaze now fully focused on mine, making my heart beat a little faster. If he didn't annoy the shit out of me, I'd admit he looks cute with his bad boy look. Who am I kidding? He's sexy as fuck. Too bad he's also a douchebag and a pain in my ass.

My ego doesn't want to agree with anything he says, but he has a point. I love road trips, but I've done this trip many times before. Even though I like some alone time, after day three, I'm mostly bored. Letting them tag along means I at least have someone to talk to. And by someone, I mean Bodi.

"Five," I correct him.

"What?"

"It's five days."

"Fuck me," he grunts, pinching the bridge of his nose.

"I would love to, but I'm not in the mood right now," I sass, throwing his words back in his face.

He smiles like a damn Cheshire cat, and I swear I can see a little approval in his eyes. "Cute."

He holds my gaze, staring at me with an intensity that

grows by the second. A tension that's different from the frustration we are used to fills the space between us, so I avert my gaze to snap out of it, convincing myself I'm imagining things. If he smiles like that the entire trip, I'm in serious trouble. His smile is contagious. I want to stay mad at him, but unwillingly, the corner of my mouth curls up.

"Don't make me regret this," I try to scold. Obviously, I fail miserably.

"Never." He winks, beaming, making me roll my eyes.

"Dear Lord, give me the strength to not kill this boy in the next week," I mumble while I drop my head back to the wheel, gently bumping it a few times, even though I know any prayer will be futile.

He's totally going to make me regret this.

TWO HOURS of awkward silence later, we have just passed Barstow, and Jensen seems to be sleeping like a log. It isn't until he starts snoring softly that I turn around to Bodi, wondering if he really is asleep or if he's just faking it.

"This isn't for real, right? No way anyone can sleep this deep in a car." I glance to the backseat. Bodi's still on his phone and I'm seriously curious as to what he has been doing for the last two hours.

"Nope," he says, popping his *P*. "It is."

"Really?" I wave my hand in front of Jensen's face, trying to detect any awareness. His face doesn't change an inch, so I test it one more time by tapping his nose like a child, expecting him to snap at me but giggling inside. When nothing happens, I slightly shake my head in disbelief.

I hear the sound of Bodi's iPhone locking, followed by the

unbuckling of his seatbelt, moving himself to the middle seat before popping his head into the front of the car beside mine.

"It's because he drank a lot and slept a little. Pour some alcohol in the bastard and he's knocked the fuck out. The only reason he was up this morning is because I woke him."

He smells clean with a hint of coco wax that is keeping his small brown crest of waves perfectly styled. He is truly handsome, with his perfect mix of a desirable body and kind eyes, looking completely different from his rugged best friend. Not my type, but add his Aussie accent in the mix, and I can only assume he does well with the ladies.

I move my eyes back to the road while I try to suppress a yawn.

"You didn't sleep much either?" he asks.

"It's hard to sleep when your dipshit ex-boyfriend keeps calling you the entire night."

"Yeah, thanks for the show, by the way. The fucker deserved it." He sniggers, reaching in front of me to grab the bag of gummy bears that lay in the cupholder before popping one in his mouth.

"That wasn't supposed to happen. None of it was supposed to happen," I clarify, though a proud grin seeps through.

The fucker deserved it, let's be honest.

"But?"

I take a deep breath, trying to tone down the annoyance I feel every time I talk about Sean before I speak, but I already know I'll fail. I want to let it be done, but I can't help but still want to kick his ass.

"But the son of a bitch just won't stop."

"Yeah, he doesn't like to be told *no*, does he?"

"That's an understatement, but then again—none of

these arrogant jocks ever do," I mutter, wondering if I should tell Bodi more. He stays silent, only hearing chewing gummy bears, waiting for me to tell him more.

"I think that is the problem. I didn't think we would marry, have kids, and live happily ever after. I wasn't planning a future with him. So, when I found out he was cheating on me, I was hurt and embarrassed, but mostly relieved. We should have fought about it, then he should have moved on to the next groupy he could find. *That* was supposed to happen."

I point my finger in the air, trying to make a point.

"But?" he repeats.

"But," I continue, drawing out the word, "now he's trying to mess with my head, telling me how he never felt more for a girl than he does for me. How he wants to have a future with me. How sorry he is. Blah blah blah."

"Do you believe him?"

"Fuck no." I glance dubiously at him before moving my eyes in front of me. I know the only reason Sean is still interested is because I'm not. He likes the chase, which became clear after the long list of girls he screwed around with.

"Do you *want* to believe him?" The tone in his voice is sincere, creating a sense of trust inside of me that makes me relax into my seat.

"Hell no. My ego just can't stand how he keeps talking to me like I'm this naïve little girl that he can sweet talk back into his bed," I grunt.

"And here I thought only men had ego issues." He laughs while reaching into the bag of gummy bears again to find the flavor he wants.

"Oh no, sometimes I wonder if I should buy my ego a house. It's pretty big." I shrug shamelessly. "But not as big as those athlete's motherfuckers." I point my thumb at Jensen beside me. "They need skyscrapers to fit their ego in."

He lets out a laugh. "Yeah, or a shopping mall."

We both laugh, and I like how comfortable I feel around him.

"How did you guys meet?" I ask curiously, catching his eyes in the rearview mirror.

He looks up and locks his eyes with mine with a ghost of a smile.

"Boarding School. We were twelve when we went to the Shepard's Boys Facility in Vermont."

"Really? You went to boarding school?" I cock my eyebrow at him. I figured Jensen went to boarding school, coming from a politician family and all, but I never would have guessed Bodi went to boarding school as well.

"Oh yeah. A very rich father and an alcoholic mother is the sum for a kid shipped off to boarding school." He shrugs.

"They don't have boarding schools in Australia?"

"My uncle lives on the East Coast. With my mother going in and out of rehab, my father was never sure if I could go home during the holidays. Staying with my uncle was the better option."

For a second, I see pain in his eyes.

"I'm sorry."

"Oh, don't be!" He dismisses my look with a genuine spark in his eyes. "My parents tried; they just didn't know how to raise a kid in their situation. They thought they did what was best for me. In a way, I guess they did. I met Jay, and we vowed we would do better than they did."

"Did you?" I hold my hand up for a gummy bear, my eyes on the road as he drops a few in my hand.

"Definitely. Jay's goal was to become an NHL player by twenty-five. Mine was to have a publishing company."

"Well, he succeeded," I say, glancing at the sleeping guy beside me. The muscles in his face are relaxed and calm, his normal smug look completely gone. My hand wants to reach out and brush his cheek, and my heart jerks, surprised by the sudden affection I'm feeling.

"What about you?"

A proud look washes his face. "Ever heard of Kayman Publishing International? Or KPI?"

"No shit!" I blurt in awe. "KPI is yours?"

KPI has brought on five best sellers in the last year, making it the number one publisher in the business right now. Not that I make it my business to know shit about publishing companies, but my cousin Kayla wants to be a publicist, and she mentioned KPI a few times.

He nods, taking another gummy bear.

"Whoa, I'm impressed," I admit, holding up my hand again. We both stare at the road ahead of us, unfazed by the sudden silence that occurs.

"You know… he's not that bad," he whispers, changing the subject, cocking his head at Jensen to make sure he doesn't wake up. I turn around to look at Bodi in question, then roll my eyes at him.

"I'm serious."

"I'm not saying he is a bad person. In general," I hiss, turning my eyes back to the road to avoid his eyes laced with a hint of judgment.

"Goldilocks, listen to me." I laugh at his newfound nickname for me as he proceeds, "He is *not* like them. He puts on a grand act. In fact, sometimes I wonder why he wouldn't pursue a career in acting, but that's all it is. *An act.*"

"Bodi, he can be a good friend or son or whatever. But in the end, they are all the same. They think it's normal to cheat on their wives and hump around with whoever they want. It's fine, it's just not something that *I* support. And after Sean, that became even more clear."

"No, he doesn't." I see him shivering his head in the corner of my eyes when he adds, "He never cheated on Emily. Not *once*. He is not like Sean."

"You realize I've been writing about twenty statements to cover his tracks?" I sigh, unconvinced, but also a bit puzzled why he even brings it up.

"Stating what? How he didn't cheat on Emily? That he didn't sleep with any of those girls? I know what you wrote. I'm just telling you it's also the truth. I know you don't trust him, but trust me; he is not like Sean. He has never cheated on Emily." He looks into the rearview mirror, keeping his gaze focused on mine with an intensity that demands for me to listen. I don't peg Bodi for a liar, nor a person who would be a wingman when his best friend goes on a cheating spree. If that's even a thing.

"Then why pretend he did?"

"Like I said, it's an act. He is not as bad as you think he is. Trust me, give him a chance. He might surprise you." He blurts the words out at high speed, as if he doesn't want me to reply, then points at the upcoming gas station, dismissing the conversation. "Can you pull over? You need coffee, and I need food."

"Yeah, sure," I reply, a little dazed, as his words keep lingering in the back of my head, wondering if I've been judging Jensen too harshly this whole time.

FLAGSTAFF

ARIZONA

- YOU DO KNOW IT'S HAUNTED, RIGHT?-

6.

JENSEN

When I wake up, I stretch out my arms to get the stiffness out of my back, glancing around the now empty car as I let out a big yawn. My cheek feels dead, and I rub my stumbled jaw as I look in the sideview mirror to check the damage. Wrinkles of my hoodie are embedded in my cheek, but at least my head feels a little less heavy than before.

I look around the gas station, trying to find a familiar face. When I can't find one, I shrug my shoulders and decide to get some air while I wait for them to get back.

The hot air hits me when I exit the car, sucking in a deep breath as I close the door, then lean against it. With my sunglasses protecting my eyes from the bright sunlight, I pull my phone from the back pocket of my jeans.

Three missed calls, five text messages, and two voicemails.

Damn, that's a lot of action.

I pinch my lips together with a groan before I unlock my phone, assuming the worst.

One missed call: mother—nope. *Ignore.*

One missed call: Kay—not right now. *Ignore.*

One missed call: Unknown number. *Ignore.*

I dial the number for my voicemails and listen while I try to rub the stiffness out of my neck.

"*You have three new messages*" rings through my ear before a loud beep makes me shut my eyes for a brief second, the high tone tensing the muscles in my neck.

"*Jared James Jensen.*" My mother's voice makes goose-bumps shower my body. "*Why do I see your face on the internet with some trashy blonde? Again? No wonder Emily is upset. Call me when you get this—*"

I guess we went live. No surprise there. Even though I knew leaving the city was futile, I still hoped shit would hit the fan tomorrow, or tonight at its earliest. At least at a point when LA is nothing but a small dot in the rearview mirror. Not when we are… where are we anyway?

I move my head, twisting and turning until I read a sign. Topock Arizona Marina.

Great, we're in boondocks, Arizona. Well, at least my chances of being recognized around here are slim if this is a one-horse town like it seems to be.

Without feeling the need to listen to the rest of it, I press the *delete* button before putting it back to my ear to listen to the next one.

"*Jensen, little bro, buddy.*" I hear the smile on my brother's face when I recognize his voice.

"*Thank you for making mom lose it again. As always, it was very entertaining. Rumor is, the girl in the picture is Rae Stafford. Kudos, Jensen. She is hawt!*" He calls out the last word, and I laugh at his theatrics. "*I sure hope you are serious about this PR girl, because I've watched the girl put you in your place a few times, and I would love to watch that every Christmas for the rest of our lives. Besides Emily, she's hot and all, but fuck me—she is goddamn boring.*"

"*Is it true? Is he breaking up with Emily?!*" I hear my little sister bellow through the phone, resulting in a small grunt from Finn.

"Shut up, Della. Anyway, call me when you get this, because I want to hear the full story."

I chuckle while deleting the message, envisioning how my mother probably stormed into his home office, demanding that he tell her what the fuck I'm doing. I can just hear her rant about how I'm throwing my life away and that it's time for me to grow up.

Whatever the fuck that means in her books.

I guess putting a ring on Emily's finger and knocking her up with a few babies. The thought alone suffocates me, resulting in a shiver running down my spine while I listen to the last message.

"Hi, Jared, this is Lisa Thompson from US Time! Magazine. We would like to ask you to comment on your relationship with Rae Stafford. I'm willing to give you an exclusive—" Hell fucking no.

Aggravated, I delete the message before it ends, letting her words run through my mind. My eyes shut, the sun burning on my skin.

Relationship with Rae Stafford.

There is none. We're nothing; we're not even friends. Still, I hate how reporters now know her name, igniting a primal urge to protect her from the vultures of the media. Wondering how viral we're going, I google my name, secretly hoping it's not front-page news already. Call it wishful thinking because the knot in my gut tells me I'm not that lucky. The picture of Rae and I is the first that pops up, giving me an answer instantly. It's out. It's everywhere. The world knows.

Great.

I'm used to it. Being the son of a politician makes you a

well-wanted subject for any story they can come up with. It's been like this my entire life. I've been pretty secluded in boarding school, but as soon as I went to college, the shit-storm began, and it never really stopped. As I recall, now, eleven years later, I have knocked up about ten girls, and have been engaged at least a handful of times, but the best one has to be the story that I'm moving to Europe to lift Emily's modeling career to another level, leaving me a devoted stay at home dad for our future children. I laughed my ass off reading that. Like I would ever move to fucking anywhere for any girl. Or be a stay-at-home dad—*fuck no*. That sounds like torture on a daily basis.

"Good morning, *sleepy*!" A joyful voice snaps me out of my thoughts, and I look up at the gorgeous blonde that is the source of my massive hangover. A glare forms on my face as her appearance shines brightly at me, like the sun bursting through a dark cloud.

Okay, maybe she's not, but I'd rather blame her than take responsibility.

Sue me, I never said I was a good guy.

"What are you so chipper about?" I snarl, having no patience for her perky attitude right now.

She rolls her eyes, then glances at Bodi behind her.

"I think we took the wrong dwarf. This seems to be *grumpy*, but I'm pretty sure I ordered *sleepy*." She cocks her head, a daring smile ghosting her lips.

Bodi chokes on his Coke, and I shoot him a menacing death stare, narrowing my eyes, then moving my attention back to blondie.

"Funny."

"I know, I'm hilarious," she says dryly, then holds up two bottles of Coke. "Coke or Cherry Coke?"

"Got any Jack to go with that, baby?" I step a little closer, like I did this weekend, crowding her with my body, never shaking the need to push her buttons. It's like a never-ending story, but since Bodi pointed out I'm basically single, it's a bigger challenge to not cross the line I've been balancing on with Rae. To see just how far I can go with her.

Her eyes grow to slits as her eyebrows pull together. "If it's Jack you want, I can just slice you open and you can suck it out of your blood. I'm sure there is still plenty in there. Let me put these in the car, and I'll go fetch a knife."

"Dark." I nod in approval, my voice throaty. "I like it."

She moves herself away from me with both Cokes in her hand, and I quickly snake an arm around her waist. I pull her back, placing her side against my chest. My face is only inches away from hers, and I'm totally in her personal space. My nostrils flare when I smell her honey scent again, and I resist the temptation to bury my nose in her hair while sparks jolt through my body. I hold still for a second to find my words as she tenses in my arms. Like a deer caught in head-lights, her eyes are wide, waiting for my next move, as if she's wondering if I'd go in for the kill or the kiss.

Unwillingly, my attention moves to her now parted lips, looking desirable as always.

Find your balls, Jensen.

"Cherry Coke, I'm in the mood for something sweet." I softly pull the bottle out of her hands before I let go and give her a gentle push to make her walk to the driver's seat, even though my hand is itching to pull her back against my body. She shoots me a pissed glance as she struts away, and I keep my eyes trained on her, waiting for one of her snarky comments. When it doesn't follow, I turn my head to my best friend with a slight grin. Bodi is softly shaking his head.

"*What?*" I mouth at him.

"You're an asshole." He smirks, peeking his head above the open door, his brown hair flopping in front of his forehead.

"Nothing new there," I murmur, then reach over the black metal of the hood, right before she gets to the door. "Give me the keys. I'm done sleeping. I'm driving."

She stops, cocking her head in a way that is both slightly terrifying and captivating while a fuming glare forms on her pretty face. She blinks, then leans her arms on the other side of the hood, mirroring me.

"I'm sorry, I don't speak *dog*. Can you repeat that in English?" Her eyes are on fire, and it turns me on more than it should.

I let out a deep, sarcastic sigh. "Oh, so that is why you don't respond to any of my commands. And here I thought you were just a puppy that needs some more training," I reply, sweetly.

If I thought her eyes looked livid five seconds ago, I was wrong. She clenches her jaw, and I'm sure the big SUV between us is the only reason I'm not jumped yet. I've seen a look like this on her many times over the last few years, and it seems like it gets sexier every single fucking time. But this is a whole other level of rage I seem to have triggered. It's the level where I want to shut her up with my mouth covering hers. Putting out her fire by making her explode in my hands first. Anything to feel her flames against my body.

"Puppy, bitch, call me whatever you want, but I will more than likely bite your balls off before I listen to any of your commands, *asshole*."

"Does that mean you want your lips on my balls?" I wink.

"ARGH!" she cries out, closing her eyes for a brief

moment to take a deep breath. "Fuck you. Get in the damn car," she *commands* as she leads by example.

"Oh, come on, that one was a little funny," I say while I do the same. I quickly lock eyes with Bodi, who is avoiding my gaze with another reprimanding shake of his head.

He definitely used to be more fun.

"Besides, why can't I drive?"

Ignoring me, she puts her sunglasses on her nose, then starts the engine and moves the car back on the road. I can feel her anger flooding my way, and I tilt my head to look at her.

"Come on, baby, you can't ignore me for the rest of the week."

Accepting her nonverbal challenge, I throw her a smoldering look while she glances at me every few seconds. Her frustration seems to simmer down slowly, the features on her face growing less stern every time she meets my gaze.

"Baby," I repeat.

She growls, keeping her focus straight ahead as I watch her grip the wheel a bit tighter.

"Baby, I'm sorry. You know I'm just messing with you. It's what we do, right?" I move my hand back and forth between the two of us. "We piss each other off. I'm an asshole and you love to tell me I am. I would freak you out if I was going all good guy on you," I joke, trying a different approach. Part of me means it. We've been bickering and nagging each other for so long, I don't even know how to not get on her nerves. I push her buttons and she pushes right back.

She starts to shake her head, a smile now haunting her lips, encouraging me to keep going.

"Baby, talk to me," I plead, fluttering my lashes like a damn Ken doll.

"Stop calling me *baby*. I'm not your goddamn baby," she grunts.

I smile, finally getting a reaction from her. I'd rather have her bitching at me than ignoring me. It seems out of character, considering we have been bitching at each other for the last five years.

"Oh, good, you're talking again. Tell me, why can't I drive?"

"Are you kidding me?" she sneers, adamant, her brown eyes wide and bright. "Have you seen yourself drive? I want to get this thing to North Carolina. *In one piece.*"

"I'm an excellent driver," I huff, slightly offended by her remark. I've never crashed a car. I won't deny I've had a few close calls, but I've never actually crashed.

"Jensen, you drive like you are on *Grand Theft Auto.* You can do that with your Camaro, but you are not touching my car."

"Whatever." I roll my eyes. "How can you afford this car anyway? Isn't it a company car? I mean no offense."

I know being the PR rep of the LA Knights must mean good pay, but I'm guessing not enough to be able to buy such an expensive car as this.

"Offense taken, jackass," she says, outraged, before she adds, "And yes, it *was* a company car."

I wait in anticipation while I watch her tone it down a little. "But if you must know, it was a gift."

"A gift? You got an eighty-thousand-dollar car as a gift?" I can't hide the disbelief in my tone since gifts like that are only given by family members or rich sugar daddies. My stomach turns as something clicks in my head, and I stretch my neck up high, blinking in confusion as a wave of jealousy is thrown over my body in bucketloads.

"Oh my God, Rae. Were you fucking Davis?" I screech as bile forms in my throat, disgusted just thinking about it.

"What?! No! What the fuck? Gross, you moron!" she cries, giving me an incredulous look before putting her focus back on the road.

I push out a sharp breath, feeling somewhat relieved at her words, before I relax back into my seat. I stare at her, still wide-eyed and waiting for her explanation. It might not be my business, but the racing of my heart disagrees, wanting to get all the details to change the vile image in my head.

"I got it from Johnny."

"What now?" I snap, my eyes bulging out of my head this time. "You were fucking Johnny? Right, like that's so much better! The guy is like fifteen years older than you!" My voice is deep and angry, roaring at her with a possessiveness that surprises me.

She slaps my arm, matching my foul mood. "No, you disgusting son of a bitch. Johnny is my uncle," she chides. "And he's *seventeen* years older."

Uncle?

Before I can process what she's saying, she connects her hand with my body again, this time with her fist against my shoulder.

"Ouch!"

"Besides, how dare you suggest I'm a fucking gold digger. I'm not like your little *indiscretions* or your super-model girlfriend. Talk to me like that again and I will be aiming for your eyes. With my *fists*." The look on her face tells me she means business as she holds her finger up in the air, reprimanding me like I'm a little schoolboy while a strand of her blonde hair flips wildly in front of her eyes. I ball my hand into a fist to resist the urge to push it behind her ear, suppressing the smirk that is dying to stretch my face.

Fuck, she's sexy.

When I raise my hands in surrender, she turns her focus back to the road. With her hands back on the wheel, I inhale deeply, thinking about what she just said.

"Johnny Pearce is your uncle?" I rub my arm, feeling the sting of her fist connecting with it, a little in awe because of the strength she hit me with.

Damn, the girl throws a good punch. Like she's a fucking warrior princess.

"Yes, Johnny Pearce is my uncle," she repeats, her voice filled with annoyance.

"How come I never knew this?"

"Oh, I don't know," she mocks, "*maybe* because every conversation we've had for the last five years was revolved around your little *skanks*. Forgive me if I don't feel the need to tell you about my family tree when I'm doing my best to keep your reputation at a high level. Oh, or maybe it's because it's none of your goddamn business." The corner of her mouth lifts in a sarcastic smile before it's replaced by a scowl. "It's no one's business."

"So, it's a secret?"

"Not a secret. Just something I don't share unless I have to." Her voice grows soft, the fire now missing as she speaks. "It's hard to be taken seriously when your uncle is the big boss of the team. I couldn't have that."

"Does Kent know?" Bodi asks from the back.

She sighs at the mention of his name, her expression tensing within a second. As much as I always thought I annoyed the shit out of her, it is nothing compared to the frustration that washes over her face just by Bodi mentioning his name. I tilt my head to see her face a little better, because there is something else I see there that I'm not liking one bit.

Hurt.

Sean Kent really hurt her, making me hate him even more.

Being teammates, you can't get along with everyone in the team. Kent and I serve a common cause. A goal. Bringing the team to victory and winning the Stanley Cup every single fucking season. On the ice? That is exactly what we are made to do, and we work like a well-oiled machine. But as soon as the skates come off, the guy irritates the shit out of me. I've come close to punching him in the face more than once. The noticeable hurt in Rae's eyes brings that feeling rushing through me.

"Yeah, he knows." I can hear the disappointment in her voice. "He was jealous of Johnny and I being so close, so eventually I had to tell him. Ironic, huh? He got jealous of his boss, even though he was the one fucking around like a stray dog."

"I'm sorry," I offer, and I mean it. I'm an asshole, dancing the line of flirting on a daily basis, but I don't condone cheating.

"It's fine. Should've known better. *Never date a hockey player*, right?" she jokes, causing a pain that stabs right into my chest at her words.

"Right."

7.

JENSEN

I t's after six when we drive into Flagstaff, Arizona. The leftover liquor in my body has definitely lost its effect, so I'm dying to put some more in over a nice fat juicy burger or something. Anything to ignore the buzzing of my phone that has been going off with unstoppable notifications for the last two hours.

I try to stretch out as much as I can in the car, feeling the soreness of my muscles. My body is aching for some movement, and frankly?

So am I.

Letting out a feral yawn, Rae takes a turn to the right on route 40, and I see a familiar sign on the top of the building in front of us. The orange neon letters on top of the Brickstone building have been shown on TV more than once, and anyone who has ever heard of Flagstaff knows exactly what the most famous and infamous hotel is called.

"We are not—you're not staying at the Monte Vista, right?" I ask cautiously, keeping my eyes on the hotel that is featured in almost every paranormal series there has been in the US. I once saw this documentary where people heard knocks on their doors, calling for room service when literally no one was even in the hallway.

I'm not a scaredy cat, but it freaked me the fuck out.

"Yeah, I stayed here the last time. It's close to the road and at a good rate. I mean, it's not the Four Seasons, but it's better than a motel."

"You have *got* to be kidding me?"

"Why would I be kidding about a hotel?" She shoots me a glare, pulling up to the parking lot and parking her car next to the Monte Vista Lounge.

Clearly, she isn't aware of the infamous ghost stories of the Monte Vista Hotel, or this girl really has balls of steel. Probably both.

"Have you ever heard about the stories? This place is haunted," I explain with wide eyes, giving her a nervous laugh. I know she is tough, tougher than any other girl I know, but you can't tell me she wouldn't be at least a little freaked out if she knew about this.

The engine is killed, and she turns her body to face me directly, her hands resting on her lap.

She looks at me with a stoic face before glancing to Bodi for an explanation.

"I'm Australian. I don't know shit." He raises his hands, palms facing our way.

I grind my teeth. It pisses me off that she wants his confirmation before even taking me seriously.

"You don't believe me? I'm dead serious. There are dozens of stories about guests who heard freaky shit and ghost chasers that detected some weird shit too."

"Ghost chasers? Like ghostbusters?"

"Yeah."

Her eyes are back on me, her face not showing an ounce

of understanding. I keep her gaze, waiting for her to say something. To show me she isn't some warrior princess unaffected by paranormal activity that is making me feel like a goddamn sissy boy.

"Jared James Jensen, you are not seriously telling me you are afraid of ghosts?" She cocks an eyebrow, her lips in an amused grin, and I clench my jaw at her comment. Her fingers are casually playing with the gemstone of her necklace.

I guess she isn't.

Fuck me, is she really playing me like that? Putting me on the spot like that? I'm not scared of ghosts, but I would sleep much better in a hotel that isn't known for their paranormal activity. Besides, I wouldn't want her to be screaming in front of my door in the middle of the night.

I mean, I'm really just thinking about her right now.

"Don't worry, my plan is to drink enough to make me pass out so I'll be able to ignore a fucking bomb attack, but I wouldn't want to mess with your good night's rest. After all, you are the one driving." I keep my face straight, although I'm doing my best to suppress a grin. My ego is too big to tell her straight up that I would rather go to another hotel, but my ego is definitely *not* too proud to manipulate her into getting on the same page with me.

She furrows her brows, probably discussing with herself if she should take the bait or not. Leaving her hanging to think over my words, I slide my phone in my pocket and reach out to open the door of the car.

"But you are right, it's probably nothing. Besides, you have already slept here, right?" I don't wait for her reaction and get out of the car, then open the trunk. While I reach for her bag, acting like a gentleman, she gets out and joins me, casually dropping her hip to the tailgate, her arms crossed in front of her body. Her face is relaxed, but her eyes flash me the seed of uncertainty I just planted in her head.

Mission accomplished.

"Exactly what kind of stories did you hear?" she asks cautiously.

I ignore the snickering of Bodi, who is still in the car, pretending to be working on his phone, when really, I know the son of a bitch is listening to our entire conversation.

"There are a lot." I shrug. I push a few boxes to the side, then drop my ass on the tailgate to sit next to her, holding her suspicious gaze.

"A lot? Like *what?*" I watch how she nervously swallows, then push my smug grin to the back, knowing I have her exactly where I want her. When I'm done telling her all the spooky details, we will be booked in the Marriott around the corner.

I'm a spoiled boy; I want a good bed, a clean room, and the option to dip into the indoor pool would totally make my night—and I want it minus the poltergeists of Arizona.

"Let's see," I say, mirroring her body language. "There is the story about two people who were murdered there and tossed onto the street below. There is the Phantom Bellboy."

"The Phantom Bellboy?"

"Oh yeah, rumor is, he knocks on everyone's doors in the middle of the night, calling out for room service." The blood seems to leave her face momentarily, and it's getting harder to keep a straight face.

"And there is this lady that was known to always be sitting in front of the window in her room. She sat in this old rocking chair the entire evening. Then when she died, multiple people on the staff claimed to have seen the rocking chair start rocking," I pause, "by itself."

The horrified look on her face tells me I hit the jackpot, but as quickly as the fear came, it's gone. I hold her gaze, pinning her with my eyes until the sound of a plane makes her look up. Her face grows stern, and I cock my head, watching how her eyes stay fixated on the sky.

"You okay?" I ask, curious.

She blinks, snapping her attention back to me.

"You are just trying to scare me, Jensen. Nice try, though." She takes her brown leather weekender out of my hands. "Come on, Bodi, move your ass out of my car."

Stunned, I stay in place, wondering what the fuck just happened.

Is she kidding me?

"I'm not trying to scare you." I try again, shoving Bodi's laptop bag into his arms as he exits the car, then pushing the button to close the trunk before trailing behind the blonde pain in the ass prancing away from me. "It's just common knowledge about Monte Vista."

"I'm sure we'll be fine."

Cursing, I follow her as we walk into the most haunted hotel in Arizona. Or is it the fucking country? I'm not sure, I just know it's a stupid plan.

"Good evening!" she quips to the man behind the big mahogany desk. There is an oversized rug on the floor that looks like it's my grandmother's, and the walls look like they could use a fresh lick of paint. Glancing around the foyer, a shiver runs up my spine, as if the dead are already greeting me with their presence.

Great.

The receptionist greets her with a big smile, his brows

quivering as if he likes what he sees, and I glare as he quickly glances lower than her face. Moving my body close to Rae's, I rest one elbow on the desk, giving the asshole a daring smile.

She's mine.

Well, not mine, but she's with me. I mean... I think.

"Hey." I purse my lips, my eyes narrowing, silently telling him to back off. Aware of my subtle threat, he swallows hard, then changes his stance.

I feel Rae's head slowly turn as she looks up at me, barely a foot of space between us. She frowns, then her eyes darken when I shoot her a sweet smile. We stare at each other for a moment before she returns her focus to the receptionist.

"I have a reservation."

The receptionist starts to tap his computer. "Under what name, miss?"

"Stafford."

"Ah, yes. A standard queen, right?" He glances at Bodi and I, a clear question in his curious eyes.

"Yes. And I was wondering if you have a double queen for these guys? Preferably on the same floor?"

"The room next to yours is a double queen, and it's free."

"Perfect!" She beams, giving me a pleasant smile that does something to my heart before we hand out our IDs and he grabs the keys off the key rack.

"Can I ask you something..." She leans a bit closer to read the receptionist's name tag. "*Carlos.* Will I be able to sleep tonight? We've heard some rumors about this hotel," she whispers, secretly, shooting me a mocking wink as I irritably roll my lips inward. He follows her gaze back at me, then moves his face closer to hers with a playful grin that I want to wipe off his cheeks.

"Don't worry. They are just rumors. Nothing ever

happens here. But if you or your *friends* are scared, there is always someone at the front desk to help you."

"We are *not* scared. Thank you very much." I jerk the keys out of his hands, then gently push Rae away from the desk before picking up her bag from the floor. "Goodbye, *Carlos*."

A chuckle escapes her lips as I continue pushing her forward, with Bodi trailing behind us. "Don't be rude, Jensen."

I sigh when a flutter goes through my stomach at the sound of her joy ringing in my ears, making me close my eyes while pressing my lips together.

"I'm not rude. I'm just hungry." My hand is still on the small of her back as I walk us toward the stairs. I'm starving for a burger and craving a certain blonde.

"Yeah, that must be it," Bodi huffs, laughing, shooting me a look that screams *bullshit.*

Grinding my teeth together, I narrow my eyes at him while we make our way up the stairs.

"Shut up, asshole."

"You're in trouble," he mouths with a smug grin.

Yeah, tell me about it.

"What do you want?" Jensen asks, still standing, as Bodi and I slide down into one of the booths. We just had dinner at the steakhouse around the corner and I think it was the first conversation Jensen and I had without stabbing each other's eyes out. The three of us mostly chatted about safe subjects, like who will win the Superbowl and if pineapple should go on pizza. Though Bodi looked like he wanted to bury us alive when Jensen and I agreed that pineapple works great on pizza. It was a nice change.

"Long Island Iced Tea, hold on. Let me grab some money." I reach into the front pocket of my pants while Jensen lets out a loud grunt. When I look up, he rolls his eyes at me before stomping off toward the bar to place our order.

"What? What did I do?" I give Bodi a confused look. He's settling into the booth with his hands draped over the back of the bench, an amused smile creeping.

"He's not going to let you pay." His eyes say *duh*, sparkling with amusement. "Remember, ego the size of a skyscraper?"

"Right." I twist my body a little toward him, glancing over at his appearance. He changed his flannel shirt for a grey dress shirt, and his sleeves are rolled up. His brown waves sit perfectly styled on his head, and with his bright smile, he's a billboard for stability to any potential women lurking around.

"How are two best friends so different?" I ask as my eyes roam back to Jensen leaning against the bar to wait his turn. His white t-shirt and dark hair make him stand out in every way, claiming every ounce of attention in the room. His bulky physique and permanent scowl make him intimidating as fuck.

"We're more alike than you know."

"How so?" I keep my eyes trained on Jensen, the hard muscles in his back making me ache to feel them underneath the tips of my fingers. He has been pissing me off from the first day we met, but I've never denied that he's handsome as hell. It's something I could look past whenever his snarky mouth started growling at me, but the constant blushing of my cheeks when his eyes rake over my body, or the flutter in my lower belly when he smirks make it hard to deny the attraction I seem to have for this infuriating man. He knows how to push my buttons, and he seems to enjoy every second of it. Like I'm one of those stuffed animals that says *press here* and a sound comes out. I want to bite his head off every single time he annoys me, and I'm ready to stomp off, but something keeps me drawn to him. Making me wonder if there are more buttons he can push.

"I'm just more polite," Bodi continues. "But he and I? We're built out of the same wood. He just doesn't flaunt it unless you deserve it. He doesn't trust easily. Blame his upbringing."

"Hmm," I hum, still fixated on the man that pisses me off as much as he turns me on. Biting my lip, I let Bodi's words settle in my mind, when suddenly, Jensen turns around with a tray filled with drinks, and our eyes lock. The tension quickly forms as he saunters back to us, and I avert my gaze, shooting Bodi a smile to hide my discomfort.

The corner of his mouth curls a bit, looking right through my actions, but he doesn't address it.

"I told you, he's not that bad," he says instead as he gives me a penetrating look, right before Jensen sets the tray on the table in front of us.

"Long Island for you. Beer for you. Beer for me. And a shitload of shots for all of us."

I look at the shots in front of me with wide eyes. "Don't you think you had enough for the weekend?" I put the straw of my cocktail in my mouth, taking a sip before our eyes lock again.

His eyes are focused on my straw with parted lips, a hunger in his eyes making me blush like a damn peach, and I quickly put my drink back on the table. I exhale softly with nostrils flaring, trying to fake annoyance, when really, there is a fire forming between my legs. I can't deny the effect he has on me, even if my feelings keep tossing me around like a damn ping-pong. One minute, I'm drawn to him, dying to feel his lips on mine, while the next, I want to punch the smug smirk off his face.

"What is it?" I ask, after I clear my throat to pretend I'm unaffected. His ocean blue eyes hold me hostage with a glint of lust, and I can feel my organs burning me from the inside. He shoves himself into the booth on my other side, getting a little closer than necessary, like the provocative ass that he is. His fresh scent enters my nose, and without thought, I suck in a deep breath to bottle it in my mind.

"That's a surprise." He winks before he sighs loudly, pulling out his phone, only to shove it back in his pants with a scowl. When I notice him declining a call with a grunt, a frown covers my face.

"Everything okay?"

He waves his hand in the air. "Don't worry about it."

"You want one?" He holds a shot up, and I gratefully take it.

"Yes, please." Anything to rein in whatever he is unleashing inside of me.

He hands one to Bodi, then grabs another one from the table. He puts the glass to his lips and throws his head back without waiting for us.

A feral roar erupts from his chest, as he slams the glass back onto the table.

"Always the gentleman," Bodi sneers at his friend, then mimics the move by pouring a shot down his throat while I do the same.

"Maybe you should stick to your cocktail, baby. I wouldn't want to have to carry you out of here." He smirks.

The look on his face tells me he's full of shit.

The look on mine tells him he's underestimating me. Like many did before him. I wiggle my ass on the bench, straightening my back with confidence.

I press my tongue against my teeth with a grin splitting my face. "I hear a challenge, *hockey boy*."

"Maybe." He moves his face closer to mine with a seductive smile haunting his lips. "Are you up for it, *princess*?" The nickname slightly offends me, being anything *but* a princess. I can be a royal pain in his ass, though, if he keeps it up. Grabbing another shot from the table, I slowly bring it to my lips in reply, my eyes staying locked with his the entire time. The tension turns palpable, making my nipples hard as rocks, and for a split second, I hope his focus doesn't move down to my chest with my desire on full display. I hear a soft moan, and he licks his lips when I swallow the contents down, my tongue going numb from the burn of the vodka. With a straight face, I softly put the glass back on the table, defiance filling my eyes, then take a sip of my Long Island to wash the smooth yet bitter taste away.

Game on, hockey boy.

He keeps staring at me with an amused smirk, his arm placed behind my neck, resting on top of the booth. Finally, his eyes darken, and an evil grin flashes on his handsome face, exchanging a look with Bodi.

"Alright! Miss Poised is ready to party!" He drums his fingers on the table in excitement before gesturing his hand toward Bodi, telling him to grab another shot as he grabs two himself.

"Ready?" He winks, holding up the next shot in front of me. Our fingers touch briefly, sending a tingly feeling right to my stomach, and I press my legs together again as I take the shot from his hands.

"You don't know what you're signing up for, *hockey boy*."

"Maybe," he replies, his voice low and gruff, "but I can't wait to find out."

AN HOUR LATER, I'm tipsy and feeling more relaxed than I've felt in a long time. I stopped counting shots a while ago, figuring Jensen was going to pass out pretty quickly, but the fucker has a better tolerance than I thought he'd have. I'd expected him to relax a bit more with each shot, but so far, the alcohol has only raised the tension between us and made his flirting appear more frequently, taking every chance he gets to touch me.

"I gotta ask, Rae." Bodi stares at me with fuzzy eyes when I place my now fourth empty cocktail glass back on the table. "Where the fuck did you learn to drink like that?"

"Yeah, not a talent I expected you to have," Jensen pitches in as he brings another shot to his lips. When the contents disappear, his face turns sour, eyes shut like he's sucking on a lemon before he fixates them back at me. His brown hair seems to get messier every time he runs a hand through it, but it doesn't make him less attractive. In fact, the amount of alcohol now surging through my body makes it a challenge to keep my distance. To not run my fingers over the skin of his arm or place my hand on his leg.

"What? You didn't think *Miss Poised* could handle her liquor?" I playfully scowl at Jensen, bumping my knee against his.

"Oh, you don't like that nickname?" I can feel him twirling a strand of my hair through his finger, the careless affection igniting a need to move closer to him.

I look at him intentionally. "It just shows how badly you know me."

He purses his lips, straightening his shoulders as he inhales through his nose, nostrils flaring with irritation. His tongue darts out, and he moves his face a little closer. "I guess that goes both ways," he counters, a little offended. Our gazes lock, both filled with a defiance that reminds me of all our bickering moments in the past. I'm hating and enjoying that we're back to this part of our relationship, where I can see the desire in his light blue eyes.

Determined to stand my ground, I let the alcohol give me

the courage I need to hold his piercing gaze while I can feel the skin on my neck go flush.

"Yeah, okay, guys." My attention shifts when Bodi gets up from the table, yet Jensen's head stays in place, his attention burning through me. "I'm gonna head out. I'll see you both in the morning."

I give him a smile and a short wave while he waits for his friend to acknowledge him. When he doesn't, he rolls his eyes and winks at me. "Good luck."

I watch him walk away, the hairs on my arms rising as I feel Jensen's fixated gaze still pointed at me. But I put on my big girl pants and suck in a breath, then turn my head with an innocent look.

"What is it, Jensen?" I muse.

"Give me a layer."

"A layer?" I parrot, a bit puzzled and not sure what that means.

"Yeah, give me a layer." He moves closer, then suddenly lets his head hang as he mutters some curse words. Shooting me an apologetic gaze, he pulls his phone out of his pocket for the tenth time.

He glares at the device, and I watch amused as he finally turns it off, throwing it on the table. "Fuck the hell off!" He lets out a grunt, then puts his attention back on me with a smile, as if nothing happened.

"Give me a layer," he repeats.

"Are we talking about clothes? Because hell no." The screech that comes from my mouth covers up how I really wouldn't mind taking off his clothes.

"Fucking hell, Rae." He blinks. "Let's not go there. No, I'm talking about *you!*"

"I don't follow."

He takes another strand of my blonde hair between his fingers, gently tugging.

"For the last five years, I knew there was more to you than the pretty blonde in a pencil skirt," he explains, his lips now only a few inches from my face. The warmth of his breath makes it almost impossible to concentrate as I'm being consumed by his demanding energy. My brain has a hard time processing his words, but the few brain cells I have left seem to take on the job of keeping up my indifference.

"You know what a pencil skirt is?" I joke, trying to break the tension.

"I know there is more than the uptight piece of work that you are," he goes on, undisturbed. "I've been dying to peel every single layer off you until the real Rae Stafford finally shows her true colors."

"Who says this isn't exactly who I am?"

"Nah-ah. I can see it. There is a spark in your eyes that you've tucked away, deep. But I'm gonna find it, Rae. I'm gonna find the real you. You can't hide behind professionality anymore."

I bite my lip, feeling exposed. "Is that a threat?"

The features on his face ease a bit before he whirs, "I'm too smart to threaten a girl who throws punches like you do. Besides, you can just show me who she is."

I let out a loud laugh, and when he does the same, I can feel the tension simmer down a little bit. We grow quiet, and I give him a grateful smile, loving how he hasn't tried to piss me off in the last hour.

"My turn." I beam.

"Your turn? I didn't know we were taking turns," he bellows, incredulous.

"We are, *hockey boy*. Why are you turning your phone off?"

His eyebrows move to his hairline before rubbing his face. "Does it matter?" he grunts.

"I'm curious." I shrug. "Who are you avoiding? Emily?"

"Emily. *Right.*" His gaze turns glossy, as his thoughts seem to drag him under. The man turns into a lone teenager in front of my eyes, the worried look on his face making my heart hurt and confusing me at the same time.

"Come on. Tell me," I press, snapping him out of his own mind.

He locks his eyes with mine; they're laced with something I can't decipher. Hurt? Pain? Disappointment? Discouragement?

"My mother. Who wants to talk about Emily. Or, actually, scold me about it."

"Why?"

I know we can't all worship our mothers like I do, but avoiding them seems a bit harsh. Even for Jensen. From what I've seen, his family is pretty united. His parents support his profession, even though I'm sure it's not the best job for a politician's son, and I know they attend a few games every now and then.

"I promised her I'd stay with Emily until my dad was elected. You know, keep up the happy family picture."

"You don't love her anymore?"

"I don't think I've ever loved her. Not that I know what love is. My mom set us up all those years ago. She was the perfect girl on my arm, but we don't really have chemistry, let alone something called love. Whatever the fuck that might be."

I narrow my eyes, my heart weeping for him.

"I don't know love either," I confess, hoping it will open

him up more, my eyes focused on the table. "Other than the love from my parents. But I guess that's a given."

"Not really, because my mom's a raging bitch." A cynical chuckle comes from his lips.

Rapidly, I swat my hand against his chest. "Jensen, you can't say that."

"Why? Is Hell going to be unleashed on earth if I do? Are you going to call the newspaper?" The last sentence cuts me like a sharp knife, fast and hurtful.

Disappointed, I frown. "I'd never do that."

"I know. I don't know why I said that."

With one quick move, he circles his arm around my back, pulling me flush against his body, our lips almost touching. My heart starts to race like a madman on crack, having no clue what his next move will be, but too curious to make a kick. Instead, I stay still, enjoying his arms holding me close.

"Do you want to know what you do to me?"

I suck in a sharp breath, completely frozen in his hands, feeling paralyzed for a brief moment as I try to gather my words, not fully understanding what he's implying.

"N-no. Yes. I don't know."

His blue eyes darken, turning a deeper blue shade that reminds me of the sky at night, completely sucking me in. My heart pounds while I wait in anticipation as I watch the specks in his eyes dance like stars. He's always been intimidating, throwing in a bunch of words he knows will bother me, hoping to push me over the edge. I can handle Jensen. I can handle the rugged, no nonsense hockey player. I did that every day for the past five years with a whole roster of those assholes. Sure, Jensen has always been the hardest to handle, but every single one of those players kept me sharp, and after a while, I knew exactly how to play their behaviors in my favor. I knew how to benefit from being on the receiving side of their tantrums. But this is completely new territory. This unmistaken tension throws me off guard, giving me no idea how to respond. When my eyes dart to his mouth, I want to press my lips against his, desperate to taste him as I automatically part my lips.

"Rae," he reverberates against my lips, and for a moment, I'm expecting him to close the distance.

"Yeah?" I crack, waiting.

I close my eyes, thinking he's about to kiss me yet feeling unsure about it, when finally, he leans his forehead against mine. The heat of his head feels comfortable, as if I can *feel* a connection forming between us.

"I think we should call it a night." His breath warms my lips while disappointment makes my shoulders slump.

"Right. Yeah. You're right."

He pulls away, letting go of my body, and I push down the ball that has been forming in my throat. I instantly feel beaten by the lack of his touch.

He inhales loudly, moving his chest up and his shoulders square as he gives me a troubled look before a genuine smile slips into place.

"Come on. Time for bed."

F rantically, my hand slams against the door as I curse myself.

Me and my damn big mouth.

I freaked out when the dipshit threw his ghost stories at my face, but I figured I'd be fine.

I was.

But after whatever he pulled tonight, I kept staring at the ceiling, feeling something happening between my legs while my mind kept going back to his piercing gaze trained on my body. In other words, he fucked with my head, making it extremely difficult to fall asleep because his eyes were haunting me to stay awake. Add my annoying ex-boyfriend who keeps calling me, and it was impossible.

And that was all cool and fine, until it wasn't, when I heard a noise echoing through the entire room, making my horny mood become replaced by a horrified one. I just lay there, eyes pressed shut, hoping I'd fall asleep anyway, but after ten minutes, I was done.

This shithead is going to fix it.

I don't know how.

But he is.

"Jensen, open the door."

When nothing happens, I knock again, hitting the red wooden door harder because of his lack of a reaction.

"Goddammit, Jensen. Open. The. Goddamn. Door," I practically growl against the wood.

I don't care how long I have to stand here. *It's his fault.*

Shit, I hope he's not passed out like he vowed he would be. I quickly start to count in my head the number of drinks he had. Definitely two scotch at dinner. A shit ton of shots at the bar. And a few beers in between.

I feel my heart drop to the floor, and I let out a shriek when he abruptly opens the door.

"What's wrong?" His eyes are wide, a grimace sitting on his lips, and his face is washed with worry.

Okay, so maybe I shouldn't have sounded so panicked.

My eyes roam over his toned chest that is missing a shirt, and his jeans are replaced by the sweat shorts he quickly purchased down the street. The fabric is hanging loosely on his hips, and I can't resist looking down. Swallowing, my eyes notice the happy trail that is disappearing into his pants, and I lick my lips without thinking. When my focus moves back up, he's looking at me with an amused grin, my mind doing a backflip in embarrassment.

Shit.

I push him back with force to ignore his smirk, storming into the room.

One of the beds is directly next to the door, and the room is small, not giving me a lot of space to pace angrily, so instead, I spin on my heels to face him.

"You!" I shove my finger toward his chest. "It's all your fault!".

"Will you hush?" he hisses. "Bodi is asleep!"

He looks at me confused, blinking, then runs a hand through his messy brown hair. Jensen's out of bed look might be my favorite so far. He shouldn't be doing that. In fact, it should be forbidden for a man as sexy as him to do that without a shirt. With that ghost of a smile on his face.

He shuts the door, pressing his back against it, then crosses his arms in front of his chest. He seems tired yet amused, doing all sorts of things to the nerves between my legs, now filled with desire. *Again.*

"Okay, little hellcat, what the fuck are you talking about?" he rasps, the gruff sound of it humming through my core.

"You messed with my head!" I stalk toward him with an angry whisper and press a pissed finger into his chest. "*You* got all these ghost stories in my head. *You* freaked me out. I was fine not knowing shit. I slept here three times before today, but no, *you* felt the need to fill my head with stupid stories about phantom bell boys and freaking dead women! *You* fucked it up for me. Thanks to *you*, I can't sleep." I stick my finger back into his chest with every *'you'* I say.

I don't know why I'm as pissed at him as I am, and I'm not sure I'm really pissed either. More like annoyed, and maybe a little scared.

Oh, who am I kidding? I'm terrified.

And I sure as hell am not going to sleep in that room all by my fucking self. If he's such a big shot, he can go sleep there, and I'll sleep here with Bodi, taking his bed.

"Rae Stafford, you are not seriously scared of a few ghosts, are you?" He cocks his head and puts on a mocking voice, totally throwing my own words in my face. I want to strangle him, but getting any closer to him would be playing with fire considering my panties are totally damp just by looking at him. I can play it tough and just punch his face; it would be a dream come true, but that doesn't give me a place to sleep. No sleep means not being able to drive.

That means this dipshit will totally be claiming my car. My ego can't have that, so I decide to go with the truth, totally pulling the *damsel in distress* card.

"Fuck you, Jensen. I'm scared as hell." I pout, putting every ounce of cuteness I have into the battle. "With every crack I hear, my heart is pounding in my chest, thinking that fucking bell boy is going to knock on my door or that old lady is going to make that rocking chair in my room move. I have a fucking rocking chair! What if someone really died there?" I freak out a little more from just talking about it, and goosebumps trickle down my arms, picturing that rocking chair in my head.

I look up at him. His face softens, and he looks at me with care. It's a look I haven't seen before, and a tingly feeling goes through my belly. It makes me want to reach out for him. It makes me want to wrap my arms around him, embracing the comfort of his body that is matching his face right now. Like he feels my need for affection, he places his hand on the back of my neck, locking our gazes.

The warmth of his hand on my body both calms my heart and makes it pound harder at the same time.

"Hey, calm down. You'll be fine," he soothes.

"No, I won't. Not being by myself in that freaking ugly ass motherfucking room. With those weird baroque black sheets and those ugly ass pieces of furniture. Seriously, I don't know why you would want to haunt that place because it's nothing anyone would want to stay in. Have you seen my room? It really is fucking ugly. I'm not going back there. You go sleep there," I ramble.

He snickers. "Yeah, this room is ugly enough for me. No need to switch it up now."

He glances around the room over my head with a serious look as he slowly starts massaging the nape of my neck. It feels electrifying, and I tilt my head a little, leaning into his touch.

"I'm not going back," I whisper, trying to hide the rasp in my voice.

"Well, I'm not going to send you back, but I don't have many options for you."

I turn around, making him take back his hand, and look at the two queens next to each other. I can feel the warmth of his chest radiating against my back while he stands directly behind me, and it's taking everything inside of me to not lean back against his body.

The room is just as ugly as mine with Bordeaux flowery sheets and a dirty-looking carpet on the floor. Bodi is sleeping in the bed next to the bathroom. I cock my head at his sleeping position with a frown. He's all over the place, looking like he was spit out by a hurricane.

"Damn, he always sleep like that?"

"Yup, sometimes he even wakes up backwards."

I cock my eyebrow at him in disbelief.

"I'm not joking." A sweet smile forms on his lips before his eyes darken again. "I'm also not going to give up my bed," he announces with that annoying hint of amusement visible in his eyes. "But you're welcome to join me."

That bastard.

"You've been waiting for this, haven't you?" I glare, my fear suddenly completely gone.

"No, no," he says, chuckling, "don't turn this around. I've

been waiting to go to the Marriott down the street, but you basically told me to suck it up. *I did.*"

"You've not once mentioned the Marriott down the street! There is a Marriot down the street?"

"Only because you were all like *'you're not afraid of ghosts now, are you Jensen?'*" He puts on a whining voice.

"Argh!"

"What's wrong, Rae?"

"I hate you."

"You can hate me while I protect you from the old lady haunting you with her rocking chair. Come on, get in. We need to get up early."

He gets in the bed, holding the sheets up as he waits for me. I stand statue-still, conflicted about what to do. My ego doesn't want to give in, refusing to admit he played me, but I also really, *really* don't want to go back to my room. Just thinking about it makes me shiver, while getting in bed with him makes me shiver for a whole different reason.

I narrow my eyes at his smug grin, my arms crossed in front of my body like a mad toddler. "Don't you dare pull anything, Jensen."

"I'm gonna sleep on my side, with my back to you. I swear I'll behave. Scout's honor." He puts three fingers in the air.

"You were a boy scout?" I cock an eyebrow, calling *bullshit.*

"Until they kicked me out, yeah."

I chuckle, moving my feet to the edge of the bed before I slowly get in. The warmth of his body comforts me in a soothing way, and I instantly relax.

"Why did they kick you out?"

"Because I kept harassing Mrs. Robins to make sure I got kicked out."

"Really?"

He turns his head to face me, a relaxed, lopsided grin on his face. "I didn't want to be a boy scout. My dad forced my brother and me. I wanted to play hockey. I had to be creative. He didn't talk to me for a month after they kicked me out."

"A month?" I hiss, incredulous.

"Hmm," he muses.

"Then what?"

"He realized I wasn't going to be the perfect boy they wanted me to be if he wouldn't give me something he could hold against me. I've been playing hockey ever since. You know the rest."

We stay quiet, looking around the room before he kills the bedside light, letting out a deep sigh. A sadness seems to creep over his body, radiating against me.

"Why did your dad force you to be a boy scout?" I ask after a while, my voice reverberating through the room.

He stays silent, as if he's thinking carefully about his next words, while I turn on my side to look at him. I can make out his silhouette in the dark, while his blue eyes shine bright as they reflect the moonlight coming through the window.

"There are a lot of things my brother and I have to do." The tone of his voice is flat, clearly etched with something that lays heavy on his heart.

"Oh."

His body rapidly turns on his side, our faces now only a few inches apart.

"I'm sorry," I offer, not knowing what it is I am sorry about, but realizing his life might be more gloom than he shows to the world.

"Don't be."

Our eyes lock, connecting in the shimmering light pouring through the darkness of the room, a feeling of comfort washing over me at the same time my heart starts to beat louder.

"Rae?" he finally hums, a gruffness laced in his voice.

"Yeah?"

"If you don't want me to touch you, you should turn around and go to sleep." The words are pushed out of his lips, as if he has a hard time voicing them, and for a minute, the boldness tucked inside of me seeps through, dying to tell him to go for it.

But instead, I nod. "Yeah, sure."

We both switch sides, our backs now only a few inches apart as we lay beside each other in the queen-sized bed.

"Goodnight, babe."

The corner of my mouth curls, loving the flirty tone in his voice.

"Goodnight, Jensen."

10.

JENSEN

I wake up from the warmth that's glued against my chest, cracking an eye open and squinting at my surroundings. My lips are being graced by a pile of hair as I turn my head to the side with my eyes still halfway closed.

Sucking in the scent of her hair, my body lingers in the blissful stage of awareness, but I'm still too sleepy to move a muscle.

It took her a while to fall asleep. I'd been listening to her breathing, anxious to hold her against me as I thought about how fucked up my world is right now. I'm on a road trip to hide from the paparazzi, bolt from my expectation, and definitely avoid my mother. I have a relationship I'm expected to fix, yet all I can think of is the blonde lying next to me. The one that stirs more feelings inside of me than anyone ever has, good or bad. When her breathing slowed, and I knew she fell asleep, I turned on my back, looking at the ceiling with a weird lump forming in my stomach.

I feel like a hurricane has stormed through my life the last few days, and now I'm looking at the debris, knowing I have to fix it all.

But I don't know if I want to fix it.

I don't know whether to fix the old house or just build a new one.

Slowly waking up, I enjoy my arm wrapped around her warm body and fully open my eyes. The morning is starting to kick in, the room now a little less dark than before. Rae's head rests on my chest with even breaths while her slender arm is draped over my stomach. Without thought, my hand reaches up, running my fingers through her silky blonde strands, enjoying the comfort it brings me.

My mind argues with me. Telling me I shouldn't get this comfortable. That I shouldn't feel this comfortable.

I have a girlfriend. Sorta. Technically, I don't, but the whole reason I'm staying the night in a hotel in Arizona is because I need Rae to help me get Emily back. I need her to get my mother off my back until I figure out what I'm gonna do with this whole *marriage* thing. Or what I'm gonna do with my parents trying to control my entire life. I'm not like my brother Finn. He falls in line effortlessly because that's who he is. He's a well-known and respected lawyer, attends all the right events, hangs out with the best connections, supports more charities than I can remember, all while being the perfect all-American son without him even trying. And my sister… well, she's a senior, so other than showing her face at events, she's still off the hook.

But me?

Fuck, man. I just wanna skate and chill. When I think about marriage, I think about watching a movie on the couch, going skiing on Christmas, heading out for a Sunday drive without a destination. Not showing our faces on every red carpet and posing for Instagram pictures every five minutes.

That's not me.

The truth, though? I'm not sure what is *me*.

All I know is what is expected of me.

And holding a woman in my arms like Rae Stafford is definitely not expected of me.

I MUST HAVE DOZED OFF, because when I open my eyes again, morning has fully arrived, lighting the room with a heavy dose of natural daylight. My head is resting against Rae's, and I brush my lips over her hair, giving myself a minute to wake up. I clear my throat before I exhale loudly while a sense of peace settles in my chest. A smile creases my face, and I turn to the right, glancing around the room. My eyes grow big when I meet the smug grin of Bodi, sitting fully dressed on the edge of his bed.

"Christ, what the fuck, Bodi?" I hiss as my heart starts to race.

It's not like I was hiding Rae in my bed, but having him stare at us for God knows how long, like a creep, it gets me fired up. Or maybe it's the bucket of reprimanding that I know is going to be thrown in my face any minute now. Pretty sure it's both.

"Good morning, *sunshine*," he sings, then leans on his knees with his eyes still trained on me. "What's this, mate?" He circles his finger in the air with his thick Australian accent.

I rub my hand over my face while pushing out a breath. "She got scared. I offered to share my bed."

"Oh, wauw." He dramatically grips his heart. "Such a gentleman. The cuddling? Was that required too?"

"Shut up."

"No, you shut up, *mate.*" He now glares.

There it is. One bucketload, coming right up.

"What are you doing?"

I hold his gaze, keeping my mouth shut.

"I'm serious!" he continues. "This is the one and only time I'm pointing this out, because I honestly don't care what you do. But we are here to fix things with Emily, right? Keep your parents happy?"

"Right."

"That isn't Emily!" he whisper-shouts.

"I know, okay?!" I huff, rolling my eyes.

"Do you? Because you're playing with fire, Jensen. And as much as I'm dying to watch you play with fire, or better yet, burn the whole house down, I need to make sure you know what you're doing before your mother starts stalking me again. And I love you, but truth be told, I'd rather be a life target for the army looking like Pikachu than have another discussion with your mother."

"I'm dying to see that." I blink.

"Shut up."

His green eyes peer down at me, filled with—I don't even know what? It's not judgment. It's not disapproval. It's a look of interest, as if he's trying to make me aware of something, waiting for the coin to drop. "What are you doing?"

"I don't know," I admit, scratching my head.

I have no goddamn clue. My mind tells me I crossed a line last night. A bigger one than ever before. Yeah, I talk to other girls. I stand a little too close, and I twitter in their ears. But spending the night cuddling is a whole other level. I know that. It makes it harder and harder to pretend and keep up appearances with Emily, and it's wrong.

But then why does it feel so damn good?

"Yeah, well, you have five more days to figure it out. That is, *if* the paparazzi won't find out you're driving across the country with a girl that isn't your girlfriend. I got your back." He folds his hands together. "I really do. But you have to figure it out. Five days, Jensen. Do you hear me?"

I let his words run through my now dazed head, knowing he's right. I can't keep avoiding my life forever. At some point, I need to make decisions instead of bluffing out of anything that is supposed to be part of my future.

"Do you hear me?" Bodi repeats.

"Yeah. Yeah, I hear you."

"I'm gonna get us some coffee and save her the embarrassment of waking up hugging you like a damn koala with an audience. I've brought her bag to our room." He points at the weekender now sitting on the floor. "I'm gonna see if I can buy us some clothes. I'll be back in thirty minutes, yeah?"

He gets up, then gives me a mocking salute before he disappears through the door. The door closes with a heavy thud and Rae startles before she slowly stirs awake, now twisting and turning in my grip.

Her golden-brown eyes look up at me in confusion, then take in the room, before she quickly sits up, her cheeks turning pink. "Oh, shit. I'm so sorry!" She pulls the sheets to her chin, even though she's dressed, and a chuckle comes from my throat when I look at her flush of embarrassment. She looks adorable.

And I need to grow a pair.

"Hey." I place my hand on the small of her back. "It's okay."

"No. No, it's not. You shouldn't be cuddling with other girls! Your mom will hate me if she finds out. *And* Emily." She shoots me a look full of doubt.

I smile. "True. But there were ghosts, Rae. I couldn't leave you unprotected, could I? Besides, my mom hates pretty much everyone."

She snaps her head, meeting my gaze, before slapping my chest. "Shut up, *asshole*," she scolds, though I can see a smile trying to creep in.

"Look, don't worry about it. Just let me pick the hotel tonight, okay?"

Her lips purse, looking at me like they need to be kissed, and I move my attention back to her eyes to distract myself from the desire that's lurking inside my body like the Big Bad Wolf, dying for a taste of Little Red Riding Hood.

"Yeah. Okay, that's fine," she complies, then gets out of the bed, making the sheets send a cold breeze over me. "Where is Bodi?"

"Getting coffee. It's almost time to hit the road. He brought your stuff."

I point to the bag, and a grateful smile slides into place on her face. "That's so sweet of him!" She grabs the bag from the floor, beaming. Her hair is messy, and her face free from makeup, like a blank canvas. My dick appreciates her modest curves being hugged by her dark blue pajama shorts, and I flex my hands hard to get rid of nerves that run through them.

"I'm gonna go and take a shower, okay? I won't be long."

I nod my head, absently. "Yeah, of course."

I watch her prance toward the bathroom, shamelessly checking her out.

Fucking hell, if this is how the rest of the week is going to be, I'm in serious trouble. She's hot as fuck, and her perky little attitude only makes it more fun to get under her skin. But as much as I try to get under hers, I'm pretty sure it doesn't compare to how badly she's getting under mine without even trying. It makes me realize Bodi is right. I have a lot of shit to figure out. And I'm not sure if having Rae Stafford around me for the rest of the week is going to help me find peace—or if she will unleash the fury that might be waiting for me at the end of the road. She might become the death of me.

But looking at her right now, it makes me believe I'd die a happy man.

"Jensen?" She twists her body around, meeting me with her fiery brown eyes, and I swear my heart stops for a split second when our gazes lock.

"Hmm?" I muse, licking my lips.

"Thank you," she says, shyly, "for last night. I owe you one." My mind instantly goes into the gutter, wanting to take her up on that with her naked body pressed to mine. I tilt my head, narrowing my eyes at the thought of having her at my mercy. "You know I'm gonna collect that, baby."

"Shut up." She rolls her eyes, the corner of her mouth raised in half a smile as she opens the door to the bathroom.

"Rae?"

She halts, the doorknob in her hands. "Yeah?"

"You're welcome."

With a straight face, she stares at me until her eyes soften and she gives me a radiant smile. It's one I haven't seen before, making a pang go through my chest as she goes into the bathroom, and I let out a frustrated grunt.

Yeah, I'm in some serious shit.

few hours later, I'm sitting behind the wheel again, my eyes focused on the long road ahead of me. Bodi is working on his laptop in the backseat while Jensen has been silently staring out of the window for the last couple of hours. There is an awkward silence between us, and I have no clue if it's because of how we woke up together or if something else is on his mind.

When I woke up in Jensen's arms, I felt mortified. Comfortable as fuck. But also mortified.

I've been reprimanding him for the last five years, scolding him for hanging around with those homewreckers, and now, I'm the one who's the homewrecker. I know it's not completely true since he told me it's more an arrangement than a relationship, but it still feels wrong.

But part of me can't seem to forget how I felt when I woke up listening to his heartbeat, his arms wrapped around my body, feeling the warmth of his skin against my cheek. Every time I push the thought away, the feeling away, it gets bounced back inside my body within seconds.

Safe.

He made me feel safe in a way I haven't felt since the

crash. My mind keeps telling me it's nothing, just a coincidence, but my heart keeps corrupting my head with silly thoughts… like wanting to touch him.

Kiss him.

Run my fingers through his short hair.

"Are you close to your family?" Jensen's voice snaps me out of my daydream as if he could hear my thoughts, and I glance at him, a bit puzzled.

"Back home? Your family? Are you all close?" There is a serious wonder in his eyes that has me thinking he's looking for something in my words.

I shrug, not sure how to reply. "I mean, I haven't seen them much in the last five years. Only twice a year. But I know they are there when I need them."

"That's good," he replies softly. "Any siblings?"

"A little sister. She's ten."

"Ten? She's a caboose baby?"

"Something like that," I mumble.

"What about Johnny? Are you close to him?"

Hesitant to disclose my relationship with Johnny, I press my lips together in wariness. If he's asking because he's my uncle, there is no harm, but I have to remind myself this is also his General Manager he's asking about. Even though this might be a personal interest, I have to keep it professional.

I narrow my eyes at him, snapping my focus between him and the road. "Why do you ask?"

Before he can open his mouth, the ringing of my phone echoes through the Bluetooth of the car.

Speaking of the devil.

Johnny.

"Shit," I mutter, gripping the wheel a bit tighter as I contemplate what to do. He doesn't like me driving all the way to the East Coast by myself, but I'm not sure how is going to react when I tell him Bodi and Jensen are tagging along. When I called him last night, I thought he'd already seen the picture on TMZ, but when he didn't mention it, I decided to postpone the inevitable. I know his schedule, and it's packed with meetings today, so I figured I wouldn't have to deal with him before tonight.

I figured wrong.

"Are you gonna take that?" Jensen questions. A deep sigh escapes my throat, knowing this conversation will be a pain, while ignoring Jensen.

I stop the car on the side of the road, parking it in the grass.

"What are you doing?" Jensen asks anxiously as I grab my phone out of the center console.

"I need to take this."

"Rae! We are on the interstate! Are you crazy?! You can't get out!"

"Yeah, Goldilocks, I don't think this is a good idea," Bodi chimes in.

I neglect their worry, exiting the car before I check the road for any traffic. It's not very busy, and I make sure I have enough time to make it to the grass on the left side of the car. "I'll be right back."

Jensen's eyes are shooting daggers at me as he yells shit that's muffled by the door I slam shut.

He can wait.

He's not going anywhere.

"Hey," I answer the phone while I walk away from the car.

"Can you explain to me why your face is mentioned as Jensen's new girlfriend?" Johnny's voice is calm as always, but

I can hear the frustration seeping through. "You wanna tell me something, Rae?"

"It's a misunderstanding." I run a hand through my hair. My ears register the sound of a car door opening, and I watch as Jensen exits my car with a furious glare on his handsome face.

Dammit.

"A misunderstanding? Rae, this picture looks like it's a bit more than a misunderstanding."

"You know how Jensen is. He flirts. He was getting on my nerves again at the party. Someone snapped that picture. There is nothing going on between us, I swear." I hold my hand up to Jensen, silently telling him to keep his distance, but like the caveman that he is, he just storms at me like a raging bull.

"Get in the damn car, Rae!"

"No!" I mouth with a scowl.

"You're getting in the car right now!"

"I'm talking to Johnny!"

"Yeah, and I'm not going to tell him you were run over by a truck on the interstate! Get in the damn car, Rae!"

"There are no trucks!"

"Who is that? You're on the interstate, Rae?" Johnny grunts in my ear.

Abruptly, the hairs on my body stand up and the sound of a roaring plane engine has me glancing to the sky with a jerk before my focus moves back to the scowling man approaching.

"Get. In." He grinds his teeth, stalking the last steps toward me until he's huffing in front of me, peering down with his nostrils flaring while the sounds of cars flashing by drown out his heavy breathing.

"Shut up, Jensen," I hiss, covering the phone with my hand. "I'll be right there!"

"You are with him right now?!" Johnny screeches with a shitload of suspicion.

"Thanks," I mouth to Jensen before I let my head hang, wheezing. "Yeah. He and Bodi are coming to Jacksonville with me."

"He and Bodi?! What the hell is going on, Rae? Are you dating Jared Jensen now?"

"I'm not, Johnny. I would've told you. Emily broke up with him because of the picture. He asked me to come see her in New York and convince her there is nothing going on between us."

"Y'all have phones, don't ya?" Johnny's southern accent comes through in its full glory, telling me he's pissed.

"She changed her number. She doesn't want to see him."

Johnny stays quiet for a moment as if he's gathering his thoughts while my eyes stare at Jensen's chest, unable to lift them to his eyes, because I can still feel his raging energy coming at me.

"Doesn't explain why they are there with you," Johnny finally responds.

"I don't fly," I state matter-of-factly.

"I *know* that," he replies, the tone of his voice impatient.

"I don't know, okay? They jumped in the car when I left. Said they needed a break. I figured you'd be happy that I'm not driving by myself anymore." I'm totally bluffing, trying to turn the conversation around, and I'm pretty sure he knows it. He stays quiet, but I can hear his heavy breathing through the phone, the sound of cars rushing by muffling the sound of my heart rate that starts to race. Finally, he speaks.

"This conversation isn't over yet. Put Jensen on the phone," he orders.

"You wanna talk to Jensen?"

"Yeah," he says with a tone that says *duh*. "Put him on the phone and get back into the car. I don't wanna tell my sister you got hit by a car."

"Okay," I drawl out the words, rolling my eyes, then press the phone against Jensen's chest. "He wants to talk to you."

He places his hand over mine, our fingers touching. As soon as the phone is within his grasp, I move past him, a whim of his fresh scent heightening my senses as my feet move back to the car. I can feel his eyes burning through my back, his gaze waiting until I'm safely inside the vehicle before he finally puts the phone to his ear. Then when I open the door and start to climb in, I hear him say, "Mr. Pearce? Hi."

AMARILLO

TEXAS

- COME ON, JUST DANCE WITH ME, HOCKEY BOY-

12.

JENSEN

I wait for him to say anything, with the phone pressed against my ear, my chest still tight from the freak moment that sassy blonde just gave me. Who gets out of the car on the fucking interstate?

"Look Jensen, I don't know what you're doing—"

"Nothing, sir," I interrupt before his authority-filled voice does the same with me.

"I wasn't finished." The force in his voice shuts me up, and I clench my jaw. "Don't bullshit me with some kind of fairytale about your girlfriend and you, or how you need my niece to fix whatever mess you made of your life. I know you've always had a thing for her. I'm not stupid, and I also don't care. But if I find out you're using her in any kind of way, I'm going to make life in the NHL real hard for you. Do you understand?"

"Yes, sir."

"Good. Since you decided to hijack her trip back home, I'm holding you responsible for her wellbeing. You have her home by three on Friday. In one piece and happy. Got it?"

"Yes, sir."

The satisfaction is crawling into his voice while I wait until he's finished. "Who's driving?"

"Rae is, sir. She won't let us drive."

"Put her back on the phone."

"Yes, sir." I hate the way he's talking to me, and if he was anyone else, I'd tell him to go fuck himself. He can be my boss, but no one bosses me around like that unless you share my last name. But I know that picture will get Rae a lot of questions when she arrives back home, and I don't want to make it any worse by picking a fight with her uncle. Even if the dick is only eleven years older than I am. I walk back to the car, pulling the driver's side open. Rae turns to me, a frown pulling on her forehead. Without saying a word, I hand her the phone, and she swiftly grabs it from my fingers. Her fingers graze mine, and our gazes lock when a spark flies through our hands.

I have got to stop doing that.

"Yeah?" she asks, a little reluctant while her bright eyes never leave mine, making my heart rate speed up a little. "What?! No!" Her tone is stubborn, and I do my best to hide the amused grin that's lurking in the corner of my mouth.

I love it when she's feisty and fired up.

"That's ridiculous. I'm fine, Johnny!" She lets out a deep grunt, rolling her eyes, then exhaling loudly.

"I hate you right now," she huffs, directing her scowl toward me. I have no clue if she's talking to me or to Johnny, but something tells me it's the smartest thing to shut up while I stand in the open door as the tension wraps around us like a thick curtain. Our gazes stay sealed with the sound of cars rushing by, reminding me we are on the side of the damn interstate, yet I'm unable to break our connection.

"You've put it in my name." Pause. "Fuck you, Johnny." Pause. "Whatever." Pause. "Fine." Pause. "Shut up."

Amused at her reaction, I watch as she hangs up, then slides her body out of the car until she hits the ground right in front of me. Our bodies are almost touching. I dip my chin, holding back the smile that wants to slip in place as I peer down into her pretty gold eyes. Bright specks are dancing around her irises, like fireflies in the night. The sweet scent that invades my nose has me sighing in contentment while I try my hardest to keep my focus on her glare.

"Apparently, you're driving. *Asshole.*"

I chuckle. "We're back to name calling?"

"We are if you're turning my uncle against me to get your way." She roughly pushes me to the side, stalking around the car to hop into the passenger seat.

"I didn't," I tell her, still standing in the open door when she gets back in. She buckles up with a grimace plastered on her face, then crosses her arms in front of her chest like a damn toddler, looking defiant as fuck.

"Just get in the fucking car, Jensen."

Damn, her spunk is cute.

"Rae, babe, I swear." My tongue darts out, licking my lower lip, trying to keep the smile off my face as I climb behind the wheel. "Come on. Rae?"

"Just drive, Jensen!"

A grunt escapes my lips, and I throw my hands in the air, then glance at Bodi in the backseat. He shrugs, shaking his head.

"Fine," I mutter.

Starting the car, I hold her phone out to her as I drive the car back onto the interstate. Without a word, she yanks it out of my grip, then throws it on the floor, snapping her head toward the window.

Her small fit stirs me alive, and I silently laugh. I shouldn't think she is cute right now, but fucking hell, she is. The way her nose wrinkles when she's mad. The slight pout on her perfect, plump lips. The hostility comes at me in waves, turning me on even more. It's tempting to throw out a flirty comment, yet I push away the desire. Giving her a minute to calm down.

Eventually, the mood in the car changes back to slightly awkward as we all stay quiet, listening to the sound of Bodi's fingers connecting to his laptop, some country song on the radio softly echoing through the car.

"Well, that answers my question," I state when we're well on our way twenty minutes later. I can feel her holding back, doing her best to keep shutting me out, but it doesn't take long before she can't resist responding.

"What question?"

"If you're close to Johnny."

She narrows her eyes at me, grumpy as fuck.

"What makes you think that?"

"You talked to him for a minute, and he somehow managed to get you right there," I point at her. "While I took the wheel. What did he tell you?"

"Nothing."

"I hardly believe that."

"Just drop it."

"Come on, babe. We have a very long road ahead of us. You're gonna ignore me the entire way?"

Her head snaps my way. "You're gonna keep talking my ear off if I do?"

"You bet your ass I am."

"I hate you." Her eyes narrow, and her nose scrunches like before, resulting in a warm fuzzy feeling forming inside of me as I look into her adorable face.

"I hardly doubt that. Nobody can hate me," I pipe up with a smirk.

"Your mother," Bodi chimes in from the backseat. "Leo from tenth grade. The mailman you keep calling names. I bet Emily hates you right now. Really, the list is endless."

I glare over my shoulder, meeting his smug smile with those gleaming eyes.

Asshole.

"Okay, we get it." Turning back, I glance at Rae staring at me with her mouth open in shock. "What?"

"Your mother hates you?"

"Not sure if she hates me——"

"She hates him," Bodi interrupts while his fingers never stop typing.

"*Thank you for your input,* Australian dickhead," I seethe, then answer Rae's question. "We don't really get along."

Though that might be the understatement of the year. Kathleen Jensen always adored her oldest boy, the good-looking boy that knew how to behave and when. I think she might love my seventeen-year-old sister Della, motivated by the fact that she can treat her as her own personal clone. But I was the boy that came home with dirt on his clothes, split lips, and messy hair. I was the one who always messed up her plans, even when I didn't mean to, and she never tried to hide her resentment.

"How come?" Genuine curiosity is written on her face, along with a pinch of pity that annoys me. I don't want pity from anyone.

"Because I'm not my brother? Because I don't do everything she wants? Because I annoy her?" I shrug. "Who knows, really?"

"You annoy everyone. That's not enough reason to hate someone."

"Gee, *thanks.* Are both of you done insulting me?"

"Never."

I roll my eyes, then hold her gaze for a few seconds. "So, you *don't* hate me anymore?"

"Don't change the subject." She scowls, though I can see amusement etched on her lips.

"Tell you what," I start, "how about I tell you about my mother and you tell me about Johnny?"

A heavy grunt rumbles from her throat as she rolls her eyes, then slouches down in her seat like a child.

"Fine."

"You go first."

"What? Why?!" she cries, giving me a wary look.

"Because I asked first."

She stays quiet for a moment, staring onto the road as if she's contemplating how much she wants to share. Giving me that same feeling I've always felt looking at her; there is more to her than she shows.

"Johnny is the brother I never had. He knows me best," she starts, shrugging her shoulders while staring at the road with a vacant look.

"Have you always been close?"

"In a way, yes. He was only seventeen when I was born, and he was the youngest of three, so to him, I was his baby sister. When he got into UNC, he called me every other day and came home every chance he got to take me to the zoo or the park. Then he graduated, moved to LA, and I saw him less frequently, but he always made sure we stayed in touch.

After—" She swallows her words. "In my teenage years, I was a bit of a troublemaker—"

"A troublemaker?" My ears quirk up, suddenly on high alert. If she's admitting there is a rebel inside of her, I'm dying to get it out of her. Poke the bear a little.

"Pretty much," she agrees. "I drove my family nuts. Still do sometimes, I guess."

"How?"

"Different subject, *hockey boy*." She dismisses the question. "At some point when... well, Johnny threw me into his car, and he drove us to LA, forcing me to work for the Knights. I hated him for it, but I also respected his motives. I ignored him for a few weeks, but eventually, we grew closer again." I can hear her voice hitch when she sucks up her words, telling me there is something she doesn't want to share. But I can't help trying one more time.

"Are you gonna show me this side of you?" I wiggle my brows up and down.

She swats my arm in return. "Shut up. Your turn."

"You know I'm gonna get back to this point eventually, don't you?" Having her admit something I've been seeing for ages triggers excitement inside of me. If she thinks her small disclosure of her rebel side will be enough for me, she's wrong. Now I want more. Now I want to peel back the layers until I've found her.

Until I've found the real Rae.

"Oh, what a surprise!" Sarcasm hits my way, her brown eyes still glaring at me in defiance, though she doesn't seem as annoyed with me anymore. "Not today, though, smartass. Now, stop dodging and answer the question!"

"What was the question again?" I tease.

"Jensen." Her lips growl my name, making me blink at

her in fake shock, an *O* forming on my lips as a flutter runs through me. Her demanding expression grows my dick tight against my jeans, giving me a hard time keeping my face from tightening.

"Why do you think your mother hates you?" Her voice sounds soft like honey, and my relaxed mood is replaced by irritation, making me rub my face in frustration. My parents are never something I want to talk about, but the authenticity she gives me makes it hard to keep up my dick-ish stance.

"Right," I mumble, not sure where to start. "Well, growing up in the public eye might make it seem like we have it all, but really, we are just a bunch of string puppets. We are supposed to behave a certain way."

"Like how?"

"Say the right thing. Act the right way. Show we are a happy family, I guess?"

My family memories mostly contain events where we need to be on our best behavior, acting like model kids while my parents were chatting with important people who could help my father's career as a politician. I hated it. My life felt boring and stale for as long as I remembered, and I took every chance I could to roam off, play outside, climb trees, or just get away from it all. Hockey saved me from dying of boredom.

"But you weren't? A happy family, I mean?"

I shrug. "Not sure what a happy family is, but I hated it all. My mother was always busy organizing the next fundraiser, always too busy for us, and she hated it when I didn't do what she expected me to. I was mostly raised by nannies."

"I'm sorry, Jensen."

"I guess I don't know any better."

The number of times I wished I had a normal family. A family that spends their Christmases around their decorated tree, baking cookies on Christmas morning. A dad that watched your games, or a mom who cradled you to sleep after a bad dream. But the truth is, I don't even know if that exists.

For all I know… it's just a fantasy.

WE MAKE it to Amerillo right before dinner, and after a quick stop at a food truck, we book a room at the nearest hotel, then freshen up. Bodi and I are waiting for Rae to join us for drinks, and I can't help my eyes searching the door every five seconds. In just twenty-four hours being in her company, we've grown into a routine that feels natural. A balancing mix between a push and pull of our characters clashing that keeps me on my toes and has the image of Rae roaming through my head when she's not around.

Finally, my waiting is rewarded, and my glass stills mid-air when a gorgeous blonde enters the hotel bar. Her silky hair is hanging in a thick braid over her shoulder, her brown eyes beaming through the room when our gazes lock.

"Fucking hell," I mutter.

I lick my lips when she sways her petite hips covered in black jeans, making a few male heads spin as she glides through the room.

She's with me, fuckers.

"You okay, mate?" Bodi shoves his elbow into my ribs, trying to snap me out of my fixation. "She's getting in your head, isn't she?"

"I'm not sure if she's getting in or everything else is

getting out," I admit, honestly. The whole reason I went back to the stadium was to find Rae. To make sure she could help me fix whatever bullshit I had going on with Emily, knowing my family would be nagging me about it. But the more time I spend with Rae, the less I think about fixing what is supposed to be fixed.

"I'm pretty sure it's both."

I watch Bodi bring his glass to his lips in the corner of my eye, a smug tone in his voice. "Christ, mate. Stop staring."

"I can't."

She walks the final yards while my heart pounds against my ribcage until she stops in front of our table. Her vibrant smile lighting the room.

"Hey, boys."

When I stay gawking at her pretty face, her eyes widen in embarrassment, and she examines her black crop top. "Oh, God. Do I have a stain somewhere?"

"No!" Bodi blurts. "You look great. Just different from what we're used to."

She drops her attention to her jeans and red boots, then takes a seat beside us with an amused grin.

"Is it the boots?"

"It's everything." Our eyes meet, and she bites her lip, keeping her attention focused on me for a brief moment. "You look good."

"Thank you." Her cheeks turn a light pink. "Right," she says, changing the subject. "What are we drinking?" Her fists drum on the table.

13.

I ignore the accelerating of my breathing, keeping a straight face as I snap my attention between both of them.

"Truth or dare?" My brows quirk up.

Bodi shrugs, then holds his tumbler up in the air. "Sure. Why not."

I reply with a smile before my focus turns back to Jensen. His handsome face is still fixated on me, his dark hair now perfectly styled. I can see the hunger etching through his eyes, pinning me down with a growing desire. I give him a daring look, moving a bit closer with my head resting in my hand as I pop my elbow up on the table.

Damn, he's hot when he's staring at me like that.

"What? You scared, Jensen?"

I've never been a shy girl. I'm the friend you push forward when the cops ask you what the hell you're doing on a deserted airstrip. The one who asks for clarification when the entire class can't keep up with that intimidating science teacher. I'm bold, and I can be blunt about what I want; my rebel phase is the proof of that. In the last five years, I created a persona that was sophisticated, composed, and serious, that helped me act like the professional I had to be. She made sure no one saw the real Rae. But Jensen seems to bring the wild side alive again, rising from the ashes like a phoenix.

He leans in, his lips now close to my face. I can smell his aftershave, a toxic scent of fresh and spicy notes, mixed with the whiskey on his breath that makes my head spin a little. Since the first time we met, this man has done something to me. He knows how to tick me off and get me all riled up. But since he jumped in my car, there has been a different meaning to that phrase.

"Now that I know there's a rebel tucked inside of you… I need to meet her," he growls, demanding. The low, vibrating tone shivers along my spine as I keep a straight face. I needed yesterday to adjust to the chemistry we have, getting used to his smart-ass comments and heavy flirtations, but today, I've grown into our back-and-forth. I'm even starting to enjoy it, taking advantage of the fact that my answers don't have to be perfect anymore, now that I'm no longer on the job.

"Ha! She's on a holiday for the foreseeable future. Besides, I doubt anyone would've taken me seriously on the job wearing jeans and some boots," I explain jokingly.

"Oh, I definitely would've." It's a statement that leaves no room for questioning, flushing my cheeks. Not sure how to respond, I stay quiet while the room seems to close in on us. As I look into his shiny blue eyes, the world around us seems to fade; the only thing left is an invisible chord that keeps us connected. A chord that right now seems to feel like a lifeline, as if our hearts are beating at the same pace.

Bodi breaks the magic, clearing his throat, and I jump a little with embarrassment. I can't deny the attraction I feel toward Jensen, but it seems like Rebel Rae wants to crawl her way out every time Jensen gives me one of his smoldering looks.

"Fuck," I blurt awkwardly, offering Bodi an apologetic smile, then changing the subject. "Something light. Schnapps or something. That will set the mood."

"What mood is that? Because I'm already in one." Jensen throws his head back in frustration, pouring the contents of his glass down his throat, though the thirst remains in his eyes. Bodi rapidly kicks him under the table, and I can hear a grunt coming from Jensen's throat, turning a smile on my face.

"Shut up," Bodi orders, glaring at his best friend before he smirks at me.

"Fine. I'll shut up. You want schnapps? What kind?" Jensen asks. He tries to hide his frustration, but the deep frown on his forehead tells me he has a hard time with it.

"Peach!" Clapping like a seal, I bounce in excitement and get up to get a tray of shots, using it to take a moment to pull myself together. I knew this was going to be a challenge the second he dropped his ass in my car, but now that I've experienced the warmth of his body against mine, I can't stop thinking about what it would be like to feel that warmth between my legs. To feel his lips all over me.

When I get to the bar, I ask the bartender for a double rum, throwing it down my throat in one go for some liquid courage while I feel my phone vibrate in the back pocket of my jeans. Already knowing it's Sean, I pull out my phone with grinding teeth, decline the call, and then return to the boys with a tray filled with shots.

I've got my hands full. No need to waste time on my ex-douchebag.

"Okay, you first!" I point at Bodi. "Truth or dare."

He huffs, stirring his Jack and Coke. "Dare."

Jensen chuckles beside me, and I look at him rubbing his hands together with an evil smirk. "I was already hoping you'd say that."

He gets up, walking to the bar, and we watch him with confusion, before Bodi mutters, "*Oh shit,*" under his breath.

"What's going on?"

Bodi just shakes his head, rubbing his hands over his face. When Jensen gets back, he holds another shot in his hand, placing it in front of Bodi.

"*Dare*, mate."

Bodi keeps a straight face, though his brown eyes are shooting daggers at his friend. "I hate you." His lips purse, before he presses his tongue against his teeth.

"What's that?" I ask.

"It's on you if I chuck up my dinner, you know that, right?" Bodi replies, as they both ignore me.

"Ah, come on, pussy. It's been ages. I think you can handle it," Jensen pushes, his features getting more animated by the second.

Bodi holds his stare for a brief moment before he shakes his head, picking up the shot.

"Asshole," he hisses, then throws his head back as he pours the liquid down his throat, his hair flopping with the jerk of his neck.

"What is it?" I smack Jensen's arm, having no idea why he's snickering like he just made Bodi eat shit and sold it like chocolate.

Before he replies, Bodi's eyes shut in agony while he lets out an excruciating groan, slugging the shot glass back on the table. He quickly places his hand in front of his mouth, gagging, as Jensen starts to laugh uncontrollably. A whim of anise wrinkles my nose.

My eyes widen as Bodi tries to fight his need to puke up his guts, and I screech, both entertained and shocked. "What the hell did you give him, Jensen?"

"Sambuca. The fucker once lost a bet," he heaves, still laughing, "resulting in doing ten Sambuca shots in a minute. He's had a trauma ever since."

Bodi's face is now completely pale, inhaling and exhaling slowly, trying to get rid of his nausea while I watch Jensen having the time of his life.

"You're an asshole." I laugh, turning his attention to me.

"I know."

My head quivers as I hold a peach schnapps in front of Bodi's face. Drops of sweat are forming on his forehead, and his grimace is telling me he definitely needs some cheering up.

Poor guy.

"Drink up. It will get the taste out of your mouth."

Eagerly, he grabs the shot out of my hands, downing the thing as if his life depends on it. When he places the glass back on the table, a shiver runs through his body, and he lets out a loud shriek that makes me wince.

"Dear Lord," I mumble with a heavy southern tongue, gripping my heart. I feel Jensen's eyes calmly move my way.

"Where the hell did that come from?" he asks in a gruff tone. The stumped look in his eyes makes it undetectable to tell if he's turned on or appalled. My brows move to my hairline, not sure what he's talking about.

"Your accent. You've been hiding that for five years?"

"Maybe?"

He leans closer, burying his nose in the loose strands falling around my face, just above my ear. Right away, the hairs on my neck stand up as his breath fans over the sensitive crook of my neck.

"It's sexy."

My eyes stay focused on Bodi, pushing back the tension building in my core.

"Okay, I'm back." A smile slides into place on Bodi's face before he points his finger at his friend with a determined look. "Payback is going to be a bitch, Jay."

"I can handle it." Jensen shrugs, grabbing my neck with his rough palm. "You're up."

"Nah-ah. You first." My chin raises with defiance as I enjoy the scorching feeling of his hand on my body.

"Fine," he grunts, letting go of me.

"Truth or dare," I beam, resting my elbows on the table.

"Please say dare. Please say dare. Please say dare," Bodi chants in a whisper.

"Truth."

"AH! Pussy!" Bodi gives Jensen a shove while I enjoy the familiarity between the two men. They clearly know each other through and through, but they also have a great level of respect for each other that's noticeable within their banter. It reminds me of how Kayla and I are together. How we can bitch at each other all day, much to my grandmother's dismay, but to us, it shows how much we love each other. It's our love language. The more I bitch at you, the more I love you.

"Okay," I start, cocking my head as I lock my eyes with Jensen waiting for me in anticipation, "did you ever cheat?"

I don't know where my brazenness comes from. I don't

even know why I think this is a good time to give in to my curiosity, but for some reason, I do. I blame Rebel Rae.

His handsome face grows stern, and for a minute, I regret my question, cursing Rebel Rae back in her crate. He holds my gaze for a moment until the corner of his mouth curls, amusement washing his face. When I'm convinced he's not mad, I softly push out a breath.

"Why are you asking, Rae?" He mockingly tilts his head. "You of all people should know the answer to that question?"

Insecure, I share a look with Bodi, who's smiling like he's loving the entertainment I provided. Too cocky to chicken out, my eyes find Jensen's, knowing I'm playing into his hands by pushing this through.

"I don't," I admit.

"Well, well. What are you saying, Miss Stafford?" He narrows his eyes. "That you might have been wrong about me?"

"I'm asking you a question." I roll my eyes at his dramatics, holding back my grin.

He rests his elbows on the table, slowly leaning in, and I can feel my heartbeat speed up once more. A tingly feeling runs through my hands, and I play with my nails to keep them busy, when really, I want to rake them through his hair.

"For the last five years, you've been scolding me for *cheating*. I believe you've told me *'I should keep my dick in my pants'* more than once." He leans back, his arms crossed in front of his body, with an arrogant smirk. "But one night in my bed and you're starting to doubt yourself? You're starting to wonder if I'm really a cheating asshole, or you're just a judgmental little pain in the ass?"

"I never said I doubted myself," I huff, adamant, even though I know he cornered me successfully.

Remind me to put Curious Rae back in her crate next to Rebel Rae.

"You wouldn't be asking me that question if you didn't, baby." He grabs the arms rest of my chair, pulling me closer. "Admit it. Admit it, and I will answer your question."

"Not how this works, Jensen. It's your turn. You answer."

His eyes move back and forth, roaming my face, and I swallow hard when they lower to my lips, his tongue darting out to lick his own. I can feel the blood rush through my head, as I wonder how his lips would feel on mine while I squeeze my thighs together.

"*NO.*" The word rumbles out of his body, as if he wants to make sure I understand the meaning of it, yet he doesn't explain anything else. "Now say it."

"Say what?!" I screech, our faces still too close.

"That you were wrong about me."

"Why? You're still an asshole." I can hear Bodi tittering beside us, and my eyes quickly dart to him enjoying the show.

"Not denying that. Say it, Rae. Admit it. You *like* me. And don't roll your eyes at me like I'm wrong, because you know I'm right."

"*Like* is a big word," I sputter.

"You. Like. Me."

"Fine!" I throw my hands up in the air, leaning back in my chair to create some distance while grabbing a shot from the table. "You're alright."

"Ha! I knew it. Now repeat after me, 'I'm a judgmental pain in the ass.' But say it like you mean it. Really pull the words from your toes." He balls his fist, raising it in the air to enhance his assertion. I blink at him, while I put the glass to my lips until the sweet taste of peach welcomes my tongue.

"Never gonna happen, *hockey boy*," I reply while smashing the glass back on the table.

"Fine. My turn. Truth or dare, Rae?" Jensen's blue eyes gleam with pleasure as I wonder what is going on in that head of his. Normally, I'd rather choose dare, not feeling the need to disclose anything with anyone. Answers always result in more questions, and before you know it, they know your life story. Mine is definitely not worth sharing if we want this to stay a happy night. But after what he pulled to Bodi, I have a feeling giving Jensen a dare will probably be a bad choice for me.

"Truth."

Jensen holds my gaze intensely, his eyes acting like lasers as if he can read my mind before his lips start to move. "Were you in love with Kent?"

My heart falls when the words reach my ears, joined by a pounding drum in my head. A tightness forms in my chest while I'm rushed back to that first moment Sean told me he loved me. We hadn't been dating for long, but it didn't matter because it made sense. He took me on a date to the beach, just us, with a bottle of wine and some crackers. Simple, just how I like it. We'd been talking for an hour, cuddling, and just enjoying each other's company, when those eight letters left his lips. The moment was right. The setting was right. *He* was right.

But I couldn't say it back.

I froze. I freaked out. And when I finally calmed down, I told him I wasn't capable of loving anyone. Not after what I'd been through. Not when I know love can leave you as quick as it arrives. I asked him for time. Told him that one day I'd be able to say it back.

"Rae?" Bodi's voice snaps me out of my daydream, and I glance at him before my eyes move back to Jensen, now looking at me with hawk eyes, worry written over his face as if he's not sure he wants the answer to this question.

"No," I finally admit. "No, I was never in love with him."

Relief showers his face, confusing me before I take another shot to calm my heart down, then put on a smile to lighten the mood.

"Who's next?"

JENSEN

Many rounds of this stupid game later, I've learned two things about Rae Stafford.

She doesn't like to answer personal questions, and she can drink like a sailor.

Unless it's gin.

After the three of us devoured the two dozen shots of pink schnapps, I ordered the same amount of apple gin shots, and I'm not regretting it. With every shot she takes, her eyes glow even more, she becomes chattier, and to my amusement, more flirtatious.

"No!" she cries, laughing. "The two of you seriously got arrested for *streaking*?" Her hand drops to my knee, like it has been doing for the last ten minutes, and the heat of her palm burns through my jeans. "How come I never read about this in the paper?" she jokes.

"Because his daddy has a big army of lawyers that wiped out all evidence," Bodi explains, with a grateful look. "I don't like his mum and dad, but I have to admit, I was glad they took care of that."

"Must be convenient to have a dad with connections."

She winks, squeezing my knee before she licks her lips. The same lips that seem to have a deep connection to my dick.

"Not as much as it may seem." Sure, I'm glad there is no evidence of my drunk streaking adventure, but ninety-nine percent of the time, having a parent in politics just means you have to think about every move you make. Being the black sheep of the Jensen family allowed me a few missteps along the way, but my parents made sure it was never more than that. Not because I didn't try, but because they threatened to make life really hard for me, and God knows they can.

She examines my face, any restraints completely gone until her eyebrows raise in recognition, looking around the room. "I love this song!" She jumps up, grabbing my hand. "Come on, *hockey boy.*"

"What? Where are we going?"

"Dance with me!"

Bodi chokes on his drink while I blink at her, wondering if she's joking.

"Err, no." I glance at the dance floor filled with line dancing people.

"Come on, *hockey boy.* We're in Texas! I got my boots on." She raises a boot from the floor. "We *have* to dance! Don't tell me you don't have a few moves?" Cute as she is, she wiggles her hips.

"I really, really don't." I laugh sheepishly while my eyes take in her radiant smile. She scrunches her nose in disbelief, creating a fuzzy feeling inside me that wants to reach out my arms and cuddle her on my lap. To kiss her hair at her silliness and hold her like she's mine.

"Oh, come on. Just follow me." Pulling harder than expected, she jerks me off my chair and onto my feet, dragging me onto the dance floor. I look over my shoulder, a bit shocked at her sudden strength, locking eyes with Bodi, who's waving at me with a gleaming look, enjoying this all a little too much.

Australian bastard.

"Rae, babe," I plead. "I really can't dance. I play hockey, for crying out loud."

"Exactly. If you can move your feet on the ice, you can move them on the dance floor. I'll show you."

She leads me to the floor and places us in a line, surrounded by people who clearly know what they are doing. I awkwardly look around me, feeling like a fish on dry land before my focus is back on Rae.

"Okay, pay attention." She starts to move her feet while glancing at me. "Step, step, step. Kick, step, slide." She repeats the move while I soak her in, enjoying every move she makes with her slender body.

"Jensen! Pay attention."

"Right. I'm not doing this," I announce, rubbing my neck. Placing a hand on my side, I eye her with a bored look, hoping she'll let it pass. No such luck.

"Come on, handsome. Humor me."

"Handsome?" I feel the corner of my mouth tucking at her new nickname for me.

"That's the part you listen to?" Her eyes roll, then she brings her focus back to her feet. "Look, it's easy." She shows the step one more time, and I just look at her, moving her legs and hips with ease. Following the rhythm with the rest of the people. She keeps going, undisturbed, before her eyes find mine again.

"Jensen!" She scowls. "Come on! Don't be such a bore."

"Nope, not doing it." As if the universe is working with me, the music changes to a ballad, and my brows quirk up. "I will do *this*, though." Grabbing her hand, I gently tug her into my arms, pulling her body flush with mine. I rest my cheek against her temple, then fold my arms around the small of her back. I feel her sigh, and I'm not sure if it's in defeat or contentment. But she slowly drops her weight against my chest and our bodies merge.

She makes me want to cross the line I've never crossed, enticing me with her Bambi eyes and with everything she does. Her blunt words are like a cold shower on a hot summer's day, completely freaking me out, but feeling so good once you're used to it. My mind is telling me to run before either of us gets hurt, but my heavy heart keeps me locked in place like an anchor.

We stay quiet for a while, swaying our bodies together to the music like we've never done anything else. Her body seems to fit with mine perfectly, like my missing jigsaw puzzle piece, while her hands rest on my biceps as if she's claiming me unintentionally. When Bodi finds my gaze, I can see his chest move with a heavy exhale, pursing his lips, before his eyebrows raise with a thumbs up.

I roll my eyes at him, not willing to let him ruin this moment. He shrugs, a smug look plastered on his lips, then drops his thumb over his shoulder, telling me he's leaving. He takes another shot from the table, then mockingly forms a heart with his hands, bringing a smile to my lips, and I flip him off.

Jerk.

"Jensen." Rae's sweet voice reverberates against my chest, growing the arousal inside of me, as I watch Bodi walk away.

"Yeah?"

"I was a *judgmental little pain in the ass.*"

Fazed by her confession, I pull my body back a little,

wanting to look her in her eyes. She's staring at me with big tipsy eyes, biting her lip innocently.

Fuck, she shouldn't do that.

"You what now?" Amazement is audible in my voice, and she rolls her eyes.

"I'm not gonna say it again," she says, then wraps her arms around my back, ending the conversation when she pulls me against her body once more.

A chuckle escapes my lips when I do the same, cupping the back of her head with my hand. My lips brush against her blonde hair, enjoying its softness.

"I heard you, baby."

I hear a hum coming from her chest, vibrating against my ribcage. Instead of speeding up, my heart rate slows, beating in union with Rae's as I rest my chin on her head.

"This is nice," she muses. "I think I could stay like this forever."

I'm not sure if it's the alcohol that's making her say things she normally wouldn't, but either way, I can't help smiling. I can't help feeling the same. Wanting to bottle this moment forever. The smartest thing is to leave. To end this before there is no way back. Before something happens that we'll both regret. But I can't. I want to see where this goes. I want to do everything I shouldn't, for once doing whatever the fuck I want. For real this time.

"Me too, babe."

15

I 've never been in love. The only form of love I've known is what my parents gave me, like a warm safety blanket, cradling me throughout the world. When that disappeared overnight, I never wanted anything else. Convinced that my heart couldn't find and lose that again without completely shattering in my hands, I settled for the love of my family, knowing I can never handle more. But feeling my body ride the melody of the music with Jensen's arms wrapped around me, it reminds me of that safe feeling. My ear rests against his chest as his ribcage slowly but steadily moves up and down with each breath. I can feel his heart beating against my temple, the sound soothing me into a sleepy state.

"This is nice. I could stay like this forever."

I feel his lips on my hair, a soft moan going through my body. "Me too, babe."

The sense of his lips on my head opens a can of feelings I've never felt before. A toxic combination between an exciting rush and a completely Zen and mellow state. Like a drug, taking me into a different state of being. The ultimate high.

He grabs me a little tighter, breathing me in as if he's trying to suck up the moment like I am before his grip loosens.

"We should probably call it a night, babe."

The tone in his voice seems torn, like he doesn't really want to end this moment, but nonetheless, his words hit me like a cold shower. They knock me off my pink cloud as disappointment hits my body. But today, the rebel inside of me has seen life after five years, and she isn't ready to get back in her cage.

"Why?" My voice is soft but clear when I look up into his hypnotizing eyes. The reflection of the light strobe dances around the blackness of his pupils, peering down at me with a troubled gaze.

His roughened hand reaches up, stroking my cheek with the backs of his fingers. He keeps his eyes locked with mine with a brooding look that burns right through me. A tendril of panic seizes my chest, fearing what is going through his mind. But my chin stays in the air, fueled by my level of alcohol, because I don't see why we can't give in to this undeniable chemistry we have.

We are no longer working together, he made it perfectly clear his relationship, or lack thereof, is fake as fuck, and frankly, my intoxicated mind just wants to fucking kiss him. When heat rises to my cheeks, I'm feeling like it's impossible to hold his gaze, but finally, his withdrawn look softens. He places two fingers under my chin, forcing me to look up at him as his light blue eyes pin me down with urgency. The desire quickly becomes palpable, and when his attention lowers to my lips, I hold my breath, waiting for his lips to cover mine. His hand cups my cheek as he leans in, and I can feel his whiskey breath over my face as he brushes my nose with his. Our lips are only an inch away, and patiently yet eagerly, I wait for him to close the distance. To finally feel his soft lips against mine, feeding the hunger that's become excruciating over the last hour.

"I really want to kiss you." His thumb softly strokes my lower lip in a scorching way, and I hopefully stay quiet. "But I don't want TMZ to write anything else about us."

That feeling of safety I just experienced vanishes into thin air, like someone literally knocks it out of my chest. I know he's right, and I should be pleased he's being thoughtful about this. That he's trying to keep our heads out of the tabloids. But it still feels like rejection. I suck in a deep breath before I let go of his body.

"Yeah." I stiffly push a strand of my hair behind my ear, looking at the hardwood floor, then grab my necklace to keep my hands busy. "Yeah, you're right. We should call it a night."

Abruptly, he takes a step back, leaving me standing there. Something changes in his stance when he squares his shoulders, his cocky grin back in place, reminding me of the Jensen I've known for the last few years.

"With my luck, it won't take long before someone snaps a picture of me. Of *us*," he explains, rubbing his neck. "We'll create a shitstorm if we are seen together again."

My body tenses as he emphasizes "us" while his eyes wander around the bar with caution. Letting my head hang for just a second, I close my eyes as I rub my forehead to hide from the humiliation that surges through my body. Three minutes ago, I felt safe, allowing myself to give in to the lust Jensen sparks inside me. And now, I'm standing here in front of him as he talks about me like I'm his dirty secret.

"Right." I nod, plastering a composed smile on my face,

as I brush his words away. "Of course. You're right. *Definitely* don't want that."

I want to smack the presumptuous look off his face, calling him out on the fact that once again he's putting us in the position to create a shitstorm anyway. But feeling embarrassed enough as it is, I decide it's not worth my energy.

Taking a step back, I give him a clumsy wave, now feeling conscious of everything I do. "Okay, well. Goodnight."

Quickly, I turn around, determined to disappear as fast as possible, walking like my feet are on fire, but I'm putting on a brave face. I want him to call me back. To kiss me senseless, erasing the world around us.

But I know I shouldn't.

There are so many reasons why I shouldn't get involved with Jared James Jensen, even if it's just for a night. He's bad news. If I'd allow myself to get feelings for anyone again, it definitely shouldn't be Jensen. It should be someone loving, caring, loyal, smart. Someone who makes me laugh, and who gives me a fluttering feeling in my stomach.

Yeah, that definitely isn't Jensen.

16.

JENSEN

The next morning, I feel as shitty as when I went to bed last night. I watched her stomp out of the bar like someone lit a fire up her perky ass, with heavy shoulders, regretting my words the second they were spoken out loud. I enjoyed the carefree posture she'd been giving us all evening, and I saw it dissolve in a split second because I decided playing *safe* was the right thing, for once. Even though I think it was the smartest thing to do for both of us, my mind kept thinking about her disappointed face and how much I wanted to kiss her. I know she said she agreed, but I could detect the hurt in Rae's eyes, and it's been haunting me the entire night.

God, I'm such a moron.

For hours, I was looking up at the ceiling, wondering what my life would look like if I didn't have the pressure of my family resting on my shoulders. They think I'm the rebel child, always wanting more than the privileges my family provides. A selfish piece of shit. One of the things thrown at my face many times. I guess when I grew up, I decided to act the part, doing whatever the fuck I wanted. When I moved to LA to skate for the Knights, it was like I felt somewhat free

153

for the first time. Yeah, I still attended most of my parents' events, and yeah, I started dating Emily when my mother arranged it, but other than that? I did whatever the hell I wanted, whenever I wanted, no matter the collateral. I guess it compensates for all the times my parents still find a way to make me play my part in our happy family.

"You look tired, mate," Bodi points out, as we step into the elevator. "Late night?"

I take a deep breath, pushing the button to the ground floor.

"Nah, just stuff on my mind."

"Stuff. Cryptic," he replies skeptically, with a smug tone in his voice.

Placing my sunglasses over my eyes to hide the fatigue, I ignore my best friend, knowing he's gonna bring it up sooner or later anyway. Bodi isn't the one to keep his mouth shut about anything. In fact, he's the one who keeps telling me to take the damn plunge and tell my parents to go fuck themselves. Trust me, I want to. But I can't abandon my siblings, and I can't risk my father taking away the one thing I live for. They've got connections anywhere, even in the NHL, and playing hockey is the only thing I love to do. I have never told anyone how my father threatened to kill my career, keeping it tucked away as deep as possible. But really, it's been hanging over my head like a thundercloud ever since. I'm sure Bodi will tell me to do whatever I want and tell my parents to go fuck themselves. That I'm a grown ass man. And he's right, I am. But he has no clue how difficult my family can make my life if I completely go rogue. Many men have crumbled under my father's influences and I kinda like my life as it is. Well, at least when it comes to my hockey career.

When the elevator doors open, my heart stops as my eyes

land on the pretty girl that kept me up last night. She's wearing jeans and a hoodie, swaying around on her sneakers to a country song in the foyer with a foam cup in her hands. Her blonde hair shines bright from the morning sun coming through the windows, like her personal spotlight.

She looks stunning.

"Oh, let me guess. It's Goldilocks that's been keeping you awake, is it?" Bodi snickers as we walk toward our third traveler.

"Shut up," I snap, right before Rae's brown eyes lock with mine. They glitter like gold, her smile reserved as if she's back to professional Rae, and I clench my jaw in response. I've been enjoying a relaxed, happy Rae, and I'm not ready to see her go just yet. If anything, I want more of her. A lot more.

"Good morning, Goldilocks." Bodi holds up his hands, shooting her a friendly smile when he notices her discomfort. Before she can reply, his phone rings, and he mutters something to excuse himself.

"Good morning," I say, taking a step closer to her when Bodi walks away. I want to fold my arms around her and take in the sweet scent of her shampoo. But instead, I shoot her a coy smile.

"Morning." She looks at me in anticipation, holding her cup in front of her lips as if she's hiding from me, though I can see a ghost of a smile lingering under the surface and a feeling of relief twists inside me.

"You okay?" she asks, taking a sip.

A whim of cinnamon and honey enters my nose, a scent that is the exact sum of how I look at her. The perfect mix between spice and sweet, filled with sass.

"Yeah. Are you?"

"I'm good."

"What are you drinking?" I ask, curious.

"Ginger tea with pumpkin spice."

Quirking up my eyebrows, my lips curl. "Tea with pumpkin spice?"

"Do you want a taste?" She doesn't mean to flirt with me, but the question has me glancing at her lips nonetheless, desperately to know if they taste like cinnamon too. "They don't sell it everywhere. I had to go and ask the chef if he had pumpkin spice."

"Bet he didn't mind giving into your request." I smirk.

She shrugs with a straight face. "He wanted a kiss in return."

"A kiss?" My jaw ticks. My eyes blink, *I think.*

"Oh yeah. He wanted a real one, you know? Tongue, hands in hair. The whole charade. I mean, I thought it was a little much for a bit of pumpkin spice, but I really like my tea with pumpkin, and he was kinda hot. Old, but hot."

"Hot?" I parrot, my eyes narrowing.

"Yeah, like George Clooney hot? Anyway, I just went for it. We only live once, right? So I went like—" Her lips part, her eyes hooded as her tongue darts out, accompanied with a soft moan. "And then, he went like—" Her head twists, completely going for it as she kisses the air.

Pressing my tongue against my cheek, I watch her public display of affection for the sky as she reenacts her morning activities.

"Rae?"

"Yeah?"

"Are you fucking with me?"

She presses a hand to her mouth to stifle her giggles. When her hand falls back down, a smile from ear-to-ear sits on her face, her eyes mischievous.

"Yeah, but the look on your face was fucking worth it. Were you jealous, *hockey boy?*"

Yes.

If I could turn green, I'd probably be the damn Grinch right now.

"No," I lie, as she keeps looking at me with that sassy look that tells me I'm full of shit. Holding her gaze, I gently pull the cup out of her hand. A shiver runs through me when our fingers connect, and I straighten my shoulders, keeping up an unaffected stance as I bring the cup to my lips.

My senses hit a peak when the spice lands on my tongue, followed by the sweet taste of honey. "Not bad."

"Not bad?" she huffs, incredulous, pulling a face. "There is no other way to drink tea."

Defiance laces her face as I watch her, amused. My pulse quickens as I look into her eyes, examining the freckles sprinkled on her nose. Her face looks fresh, clean from make-up, and it hits me once more how beautiful she is. Since the first time she introduced herself to me, I was captivated by her beauty, always desperate to get a glimpse of her. I've always seen her in work clothes, with make-up on her face, and her hair perfectly styled. She has always been gorgeous. But having her standing in front of me with the morning sunlight making her glow, I realize that was an understatement. Rae in her pure form is mesmerizing.

An enigma I want to crack.

My train of thought is broken when she frowns, waiting for me to say anything.

"Look, Rae. I'm sorry about last night, okay?" I blurt.

Her cute face turns serious before she mockingly rolls her eyes.

"Don't be such a drama queen, Jensen. We're cool."

"We are?" I ask, slightly confused.

I walked out of the elevator, hoping she wouldn't be uncomfortable around me. That we could keep going as we have been for the past two days, keeping the bickering to a minimum. Though I enjoy the banter we throw at each other, I like her better when she's smiling rather than scowling. But seeing her unaffected about what happened last night leaves me more disappointed than I expected.

"We are, *hockey boy.*" She pats my chest, then turns around. "Come on, Memphis is waiting for us, and I'm desperately in need of some good fried chicken."

I stare at her, speechless, as backs away from me with a smug smile. My breathing speeds up, and I'm wondering if I should be stupid and kiss her just to throw her off or be happy that nothing changed. Rolling my lips, I take a step forward, having every intention of being stupid and kissing her numb. But then, before I can act on it, I feel my phone buzzing in my pocket at the same time Bodi walks back inside.

"Change of plans," he tells us, tugging his phone back into his jeans. "I need to be in Atlanta today."

"Today? Why?" Rae asks.

"There is an author I want to sign, and he's only in the states until tomorrow. That was his assistant. He wants to meet with me today. Can you drop me off at the airport? I will meet up with you tomorrow when you get to Atlanta."

We both nod, and he pulls the key fob out of Rae's hand.

"I'll go and get the car."

I keep my eyes trained on Rae, excitement building in my body like a little schoolboy when I realize I'll have her to myself for the next twenty-four hours until my phone buzzes once more.

Pulling it out of my back pocket, I then dip my chin to look at my messages.

UNKNOWN NUMBER: It's Em. I miss you. Can we talk? Call me.

UNKNOWN NUMBER: I'm sorry. I was a bit drastic. I love you.

SHIT.

"Are you coming?" Rae's voice snaps me out of my trance, and I look up to her cheery grin, waiting for me at the entrance of the hotel.

Without any hesitation, I delete the message, not giving a fuck. I know it's postponing the inevitable, but I'm not giving a shit. In a few days, Rae will walk out of my life, leaving me with nothing more than a faint memory, and I want to make the best out of it. I want to make memories that will have me smiling when I'm eighty and sitting on my damn porch. Everything else can wait.

"Y-yeah. I'm coming," I respond, tugging my phone back into my jeans.

WE DROPPED Bodi at the airport, and a few hours later, we're well on our way to Memphis, and Rae hums along with the radio with her feet on the dash.

Emily keeps calling me, and after the third time, I put my phone on complete silence. I should be pleased that getting her back won't be a lot of work and that my mom will be happy to hear that her perfect picture isn't in jeopardy. But my mind keeps trying to envision my future. Asking myself what life will look like in five, ten, or even twenty years from now. What fate has in store for me. But every time I try to think ahead, think about my future, Emily is not part of it.

But to be honest, when I look at my future, I don't see anything other than all the things that aren't revolving around me.

I see my father becoming governor.

I see my mother planning event after event.

I see Finn becoming a part of the Supreme Court.

I see Della going to Yale, like she always wanted.

But when I look at myself? What does the future hold for me?

I'm blank.

Empty.

"Are you close to your siblings?" Rae suddenly asks, turning her head.

A little thrown off, I glance at her. "Why are you asking?"

"I don't know. I guess because you don't really get along with your folks. Makes me wonder if you and your siblings get along. Or if you are… well,—"

"Alone." I finish her sentence.

"Yeah."

I push out a breath. "We are. We're really close. They are the only reason I've been able to keep up with all that political bullshit. That… and hockey."

"Did they have a hard time growing up in the public eye? Like you?"

I shake my head. "Finn always wanted to be a lawyer. For him, doing what was expected came naturally. He liked going to events, listening to the grownups' conversations. Learning the way people acted. I just wanted to play. Climb trees, build huts. One time, I took all the sheets from the house and turned his room into one big fort. Finn was studying for some kind of test, and he just warned me, unfazed about the fact that I was turning his room into my personal playfield. When my mother walked in, she freaked. Finn, being the big brother that he is, took the blame, but my mother didn't buy it for a second. She knew Finn wouldn't do shit like that."

"But you would." Rae chuckles.

"I would."

I have never been the model child, even though I tried my hardest. I did my best to do whatever my parents wanted me to do. Shake hands, dress up in a tie and suit, but the truth is, my attention was always drawn to the wrong things. Having a chat with the smoking server at an Easter brunch. Getting stains on my clothes because I followed a dog into the bushes. I wanted to explore. To go on adventures. But living with my parents was predictable and has sucked the life out of me since the day I could walk.

"What about your sister?" Rae shows me a sparkling smile, leaving me speechless for a second as I stare at her, thankful she can't see my hunger-filled eyes through my sunglasses.

"She's the princess," I say, turning my focus back to the road. "My mother treats Della like her little clone, and I think for the most part Della liked being the favorite of the family. But now that she's older, the cracks are starting to show. She is more of a rebel than my mother knows."

"How old is he?"

"Seventeen."

Rae whistles. "Sounds like the perfect age to piss your mother off."

"Right. She does it more often lately." I laugh, thinking about my sister with pride. She's always been the baby of the family, and I love her more than anything. But over the last year, she's been reaching out to me a lot, frustrated about our mother, and I've been enjoying every minute of it.

"I bet you support her rebellion, don't you?" She leans against the door, her elbow propped up on the window with her hand supporting her head as she glances at me with amusement. A silly smile tugs on my cheeks, looking at the blonde girl next to me.

"Absolutely not. I fucking cheer her on. Giving her all the inside scoop on how to piss her off even more."

A loud laugh sounds through the car, showering me with goosebumps from head to toe. The ringing of her laughter makes my heart jump for more.

"You're an asshole, Jensen."

"I know, babe."

For a brief moment, we stay quiet, as I linger in the comfortable mood she's getting me in with a grin splitting my face. It's weird how some things work. Last week, I couldn't stand the girl, thinking she was the most rigid one there was. Hot as hell, but rigid as fuck. And now, she's sitting next to me as we drive cross-country like we've known each other our entire lives.

"Tell me something I don't know about you." She bites her lip with a mischievous glint in her eyes that turns me the fuck on, my brows quirking up.

"Like what?"

"I don't know? Something I can't google."

I drop my head back, breaking out in laughter. "You're looking at me like you want to know all my dirty secrets?"

"Oh my God, if you're talking about your sex life, then no," she screeches. "Just tell me something no one knows."

I think hard, asking myself what I'm willing to share with her.

"I'm not going to be playing for the Knights next season."

I glance over to watch her reaction, and like I expected, her jaw drops, giving me a dubious look. She pushes her sunglasses lower on her nose, showing me her sparkling eyes.

"You look like a dork, doing that," I say, even though she looks fucking adorable.

"You're leaving the Knights? You just won the Stanley Cup."

"I know."

"Where are you going?"

I rub the back of my neck, letting out a grunt. "I don't know yet."

No one knows. Not even Bodi. I decided before we won the finals that I needed a change. That no matter what happened, I was going to do something different next season. I hoped we'd win, making it the perfect ending of my time in LA. But regardless, it was time to change it up. To take on a new challenge. Lately, life has grown stale, and I'm desperate for something new. Something exciting.

"You don't know yet?"

"Nope." I pop my *P* with a level of nonchalance that feels good. I'm looking forward to a new city. Maybe that's why I'm not really making a lot of effort to fix things with Emily just yet.

"Are you a free agent?"

"Yeah."

"Any preferences?"

"Any club that isn't on the East Coast."

Her brows pull together in question. "What's wrong with the East Coast?"

"Nothing." I pause. "Everything. It's closer to my parents."

"That bad, huh?"

I shrug, giving her a *it-is-what-it-is* look. "Right now, it's a five-hour flight. I can hide behind practices and games, telling my mom I can't make it half of the time. If I'm residing on the East Coast, that will be an hour, two tops. She will be on my back more than ever."

She hums in understanding before I change the subject.

"What about you? Tell me something I don't know about you?"

"Well, since my childhood isn't public record, there is a lot you don't know about me, Jensen." She tilts her head as she looks at me.

"You told me you had a wild side, the other day. How wild?" I ask, wiggling my eyebrows. "Are we talking about skipping class and skinny dipping? Or drugs and getting arrested."

Her eyes widen, averting her gaze as I notice her cheeks getting flushed.

"All of the above?" I ask while I drive the car to the gas station we're approaching. A hint of amazement is detectable in my voice. And she lets out a grunt when I park the car next to the gasoline pump.

"Share, Rae," I growl. I want to hear all the dirty details that will make her fall from her pedestal in my head. Right in the mud where I want her to be. Dirty with that sassy mouth of hers.

But she presses her lips to a smile stripe, shaking her head with her eyes closed.

My head moves to her side before I start to tickle her to get a response.

"No!" She breaks out in a hysterical laughter, trying to push my hands off her body.

"Tell me, Stafford!"

"NO! Jensen! Stop." Her words come out broken, barely able to speak between her continuous screeches. My body hangs over the center console, getting closer to hers with every jerk of her limbs trying to hold me off. She lowers into the seat, almost lying down while hands keep tickling her sides, pricking my fingers into her skin as my nose gets closer to her hair. The sweet scent of her shampoo greets me, and I halt, startled when I look into her hooded eyes as she stills underneath me. I hear my heart pounding in my head as my lips part. My breaths grow shallow while a heat builds in my groin.

"Tell me, before I'm forced to use my teeth."

She gasps, and our connection deepens as she gives me a longing look.

"You're supposed to say something that will make me talk," she says, her voice gruff, going straight to my already aching dick. "Not make it tempting to keep my mouth shut."

Her delicate hands move up to my arms, slowly drawing circles with her thumbs in a scorching way. Like magnets drawn together, I lean in, unable to break our connection and determined to finally find out what she tastes like. To find out how her plump lips feel against mine. She closes her eyes when our noses touch, my lips only an inch away.

"Yo!" A knock startles us, and I throw my head up while feeling my heart slamming against my chest.

"What?!" I bark, glaring at the gas jockey who is peeking through the window with amusement.

"You need me to fill her up?"

Rae awkwardly moves her body back up, and I let my head hang, pressing my forehead against her shoulder as I push out a breath. She rakes her fingers through my hair, the sensation making it even harder to straighten my body when the guy knocks on the window again.

"Yes!" I whine, rolling my eyes at him. "Fill it up!"

Getting back into my seat, I rub my hands over my face with a groan, then look at a still smiling Rae.

"You get an A+ for effort." She smirks, then opens her door.

"I'm going to get it out of you, baby!" I call to her when she gets out, slamming the door before sticking her tongue out at me.

I laugh.

Cheeky little brat.

JENSEN

I'm staying in the car while Rae is inside to grab us some snacks when I pull my phone out of my pocket. I sigh when I notice the dozen calls from Emily before I see the missed call from my agent. Curious, I call him back, holding my phone close to my ear in anticipation. I nervously tap my finger against the wheel, eager to hear the interest from other teams now that we won the Stanley Cup yesterday.

My jaw ticks in excitement, knowing there has to be some serious interest from different teams. The dial tone sounds harsh until Kay answers the phone.

"You've been ignoring me, Jensen," he speaks, a bit grim. "Heard you've been busy."

"If it makes you feel better, I've been ignoring everyone. What do you got for me?" I ask, running a hand through my hair. I have no desire to waste time with small talk and certainly not to discuss whatever might be going on with Rae.

"There are offers from the Bruins, the Penguins, and the Devils." The words come out of his lips as if he's telling me the items on a McDonald's menu, and my ears heat up at the sound of it.

He's shitting me. He has to be.

"I think I heard you wrong, Kay. Because I could've sworn you just said *the Devils*. As in the Jersey Devils?"

He keeps quiet, and I feel a sharp pain of agony going through my chest. With impeccable timing, Rae gets back into the car with a smile splitting her face as she holds up a bag of gummy bears and some barbecue chips. I send a small smile her way, then pinch the bridge of my nose.

"Come on, Kay," I drag out the words, feeling fucked. "What was the one thing I've always said?"

"No Metropolitan Division."

My frustration echoes through the car. "That's three teams from the Metropolitan Division!"

There is no chance in Hell I'm going to move back to the East Coast. You might as well ball and chain me right now and put a fucking gag in my mouth while you're at it.

"What do you want me to say, Jensen? These are the teams that are interested right now. You just won the Stanley Cup. You're wanted back home."

"I sure as fuck am not going back home," I counter, adamantly.

"Just think about it for a few days. They are all offering a shit ton of money."

He keeps quiet for a moment while I tighten my grip around my phone, the anger now feeling like a firecracker up my ass, ready to take off.

"I don't care! I'm the best defender in the league right now, Kay. You find me a team in a different Division, or I'm going to find myself a different agent!"

I hear him sigh through the phone, but I shake my head, even though he can't see me refusing to budge.

"Come on, you're being an asshole, Jensen."

Slamming my fist on the wheel, the fire bursts inside of me. "Watch me be an asshole if you don't find me a different team!" I roar, then I hang up the phone, letting the device fall in my lap. No fucking way am I going to play in the Metropolitan Division, no matter how much they'll offer me. I'll be signing my life away, and that's not going to happen.

Not now.

Not *ever*.

"Bad news?" I spin my head to Rae, who's cautiously eying me.

"That was my agent. All East Coast teams."

She nods her head, then places her hand on my arm, trying to comfort me.

"That sucks, but it's only been four days. There will probably be more."

Her gentle touch seems to calm me down, and I feel my frustration getting pushed to the back of my head. When she squeezes my bicep, I feel a tug in the corner of my mouth.

"Yeah, you're probably right."

"Well, and if that's not the case... you can always just go into witness protection."

"I'm pretty sure that's only for when you testify against a criminal."

"You have money," she huffs, flipping her hair. "You can make it happen."

I start the car, laughing. "Shut up, dork."

"Just saying." Her shoulders shrug, before propping her legs on the dash and opening the bag of gummy bears in her lap.

"I don't buy it, you know?" She eyes me with suspicion as she brazenly purses her lips before popping a gummy in her mouth.

"Buy what?" I ask, curious.

Pointing at me, she moves her hand up and down. "This. You."

"What about me?" Amused, my eyes widen.

"Your whole *asshole* attitude. I think it's one big act. A way to keep everyone at bay. But deep down, you're a good guy."

I snort.

"You are!" she bellows. "I can see it when you talk about your sister. You love her. Your brother too. They mean the world to you."

"Of course, they do. They are my siblings."

"Na-ah. You can hide it from me. But I see it. I see you, Jared James Jensen."

It's not even a question. It's a statement. One that makes my heart expand, even though I'm trying to keep it as small as possible, making sure no one can step on it. But somehow, she hits her target with just three words. *I see you.*

"I'm a piece of shit."

"You're not." She pauses, and I glance over at her. "You just act like one."

I smile at her, soaking in the kindness in her eyes, making sure I keep the look she's giving me forever imprinted in my head. She might be wrong, but that doesn't mean I can't cherish this moment forever.

The ringing of her phone echoes through the car, and she startles at the loud sound of it. "For Pete's sake," she murmurs with a southern drawl that has me laughing, shaking my head as I look at the dashboard to see who it is.

June.

"Who is that?"

"My aunt. Hi," Rae says when she presses a button to

answer the call. Her voice is soft and she kinda shrinks, sinking deeper into her seat.

"Rae, honey, Johnny tells me you're bringing these two boys home. Is this true?"

"Uhm, yeah."

"And you're dating one of them? What's his name?"

Her cheeks grow flushed, panic lacing her eyes.

"Err, I'm sorry. I can't hear you." She makes a cracking sound, and I watch her, entertained. "We're driving into a tunnel. I'll see you Friday. Love you!"

Before June can say anything else, she leans in again, hanging up the phone by pressing the button on the wheel as I stare at her with amusement.

"Keep your eyes on the road, *hockey boy*." She glares, rolling her eyes.

"Nothing. Very original, the whole tunnel thing. I bet that wasn't suspicious at all."

"See, this is one of those moments where you *act* like an asshole, but you don't *have* to."

"There is no fun in that." I wink, and I swear I can see her breath hitch.

"Just drive."

MEMPHIS

TENNESSEE

- I THINK ICE CREAM IS AS IMPORTANT AS FRIED CHICKEN -

The warm juice lands on my tongue, and I close my eyes, letting out a desperate moan. Sucking in the flavor, I feel like I'm in heaven, loving the most gorgeous piece of meat I've ever had in my mouth as I eagerly swallow, hungry for more.

"What?" I frown, looking at Jensen staring at me like I told him I hate puppies, completely shocked.

I don't, for the record.

Ferociously, I tear my teeth into the piece of chicken in my hand, letting out another moan when the crunchy skin takes residence between my teeth.

"I have never seen a woman eat chicken like that." Jensen holds his chicken mid-air, his sunglasses still covering his handsome face, yet I can see his eyebrows peeking above the metal of the frames.

"Like what?" I ask, brazen, as I take another bite.

"Like you're a dinosaur, ripping apart a baby rabbit."

"That's disgusting." I shake my head.

"Says the woman going all feral on some fried chicken."

"What? I *really* like fried chicken."

"Yeah, no shit."

With our fried chicken in hand, we walk down Beale Street, enjoying the last rays of sunshine of the day. The bright pink of the sky, combined with the sound of a trumpet on the street, gives me a content feeling.

"So, why did you quit?" I turn to Jensen with a frown, not sure how to answer that.

The truth is, I don't even know. I liked my job. I liked organizing everything, and to a degree, I even liked cleaning up whatever shit landed on TMZ. It was great pay, way more than any average twenty-three-year-old earns, and I lived in a nice apartment in one of the better neighborhoods of the city. Life was good. I was happy. Then one day, about a year ago, I woke up realizing it wasn't enough, and I haven't been able to shake the feeling since. My co-workers like to believe it was because of Sean and his dick-ish behavior, and I'm sure most of the team thinks it too. But really, I felt like that way before I found Sean with some other girl in the locker room, plowing her down like he was digging a hole to China.

"I don't know," I admit, popping the last bite of my chicken into my mouth.

"You don't know?" Jensen asks as he holds still, surprised. I turn around while he watches me carefully, as if he was expecting a different answer.

"Oh God." I playfully roll my eyes. "Let me guess, you think I'm heartbroken, and now I'm running home to cry and lick my wounds?"

"Something like that, yeah."

"Not a chance. I've been wanting to quit for a while now," I start, continuing our walk. The scents of different kinds of foods tickle my nose as I roam over the crowded street, while my ears take notice of the southern drawl of the people around us. I never considered myself a southern girl until I moved to LA. Suddenly, I appreciated my boots, my southern habits, and the southern hospitality that was embedded into my soul. I hid my accent, trying to blend in, but still I felt like a fish out of water most of the time. "When Johnny took me to LA five years ago, I hated him. I wanted to stay, even though I hated everything at home. I wasn't a happy teenager."

"Well, that's hard to imagine," I hear Jensen mumble behind me.

A little offended, I spin on the spot, pointing my finger into his chest. "Just as hard as a politician's son complaining about how bad he's *supposedly* been treated."

His jaw ticks, his gorgeous eyes blazing, though they have the color of the ocean. He pins me down, shooting a shock of —well, something, through my body, but I keep my chin up in defiance nevertheless.

Finally, his eyes soften, the fire simmering down. "Sorry."

My brows shoot to the sky while I do my best to not break out in a smile, my jaw almost dropping to the floor. "What now?"

I tilt my head, narrowing my eyes with a smug look.

He shows his teeth, a fake smile splitting his face as he glares at me in a threatening way. "Don't push it or I'll make you regret it."

It sounds more like a promise than a threat, and instantly, my heart starts to pound a little faster.

"Anyway," I continue, taking a step back to create some distance between us. "When I arrived in LA, I got the structure that I needed. A routine that kept me out of trouble and occupied. It took me a while, but I think at some point I was happy." Staring at the ground, I continue, "But after a couple of years, I couldn't shake the feeling that something was missing. I did a great job fitting into the glitz and glam of the city, but really, I was…" I pause, my thoughts trailing off.

"Lost," Jensen finishes.

"Yeah." I bring my head up, looking into his sunglasses-covered eyes, feeling that same weird feeling he's been giving me for the last two days.

Understanding.

Safety.

He gets on my nerves most of the time, pissing me off with almost everything he says, but at the moments that matter, it feels like he gets me. Like he knows me. It freaks me out and comforts me at the same time, like I'm safely cradled in his arms, standing on the edge of a cliff. He's able to make me fly or crash unapologetically.

"Watch out!" Jensen's eyes widen as he calls out to me, and I twist my head to look behind me. I yelp, startled, as a football flies through the air, coming directly at me. Naturally, I step aside without a second thought and follow its movement as it slams into Jensen's chest, his chicken flying out of his hands.

"What the—" The look on his handsome face grows stern, and his hands are up now holding a piece of air instead of the chicken that was there two seconds ago. His white shirt is covered in grease and barbecue sauce, and the look on his face makes me believe he's about to yell at someone. I press my lips together, trying to suppress the chuckle that is dying to come out.

"You couldn't catch it?" He scowls from under his sunglasses.

"I don't catch."

"You don't catch?"

I snort, folding my hands in front of my mouth when I

look at him glaring back at me. He seems broader than usual, looking damn sexy with his fuming stance. He looks like he's ready to rip someone's head off. It will probably be me if I don't stop laughing, but I just can't help myself.

"I don't catch," I repeat, shaking my head.

"Who doesn't catch?" Jensen frowns. "Nobody! If you see a ball, you catch it. You place your hands up in the air, and you at least *try* to catch," he adds, unsatisfied.

"I don't," I say, shrugging my shoulders with my smile still in place. Special thanks to Jimmy Kavinsky, who threw a volleyball into my face in eighth grade. After that, I was done. I vowed then and there I wasn't even gonna try anymore. I don't catch.

"Come on, grumpy." I grab the napkin I'd pushed into my back pocket earlier and take a step forward as my hand reaches up to wipe the barbecue sauce off his cheeks. "We'll buy you a new shirt. You can keep it as a memory when our trip is over and you've forgotten all about me," I joke.

He stays quiet, placing his hands over my hips to tug me a little closer, and I can feel my breath hitch. He takes off his sunglasses, and his eyes dart to my parted lips. My mouth turns dry while I keep my head up, a strand of his dark hair flopping in front of his head. When he opens his mouth, his voice is soft and deep, rumbling through my entire body.

"You're hard to forget, babe."

JENSEN

W ho the fuck doesn't catch?

She literally stepped back like someone threw a fireball at her with the calmness of a fucking jedi. Other than the screech that left her lips, she looked like she was cool as a frog while she followed the path of the football with her eyes as it hit me right in the chest. Remind me to never throw anything at her that can break.

We buy a black home-of-the-blues shirt that doesn't look as lame as all the other touristy shit, then roam the streets like we've been doing all evening. We talk about the team. We talk about my growing up in the public eye on a bench watching the sunset. We laugh about the drunks sauntering on the side-walk, and I joke about her love for fried chicken until I figure out the other thing she has an obsession with.

"Your favorites are fried chicken and ice cream, and you manage to look like that?" My eyes rake up and down her body with an appreciative smile.

"Like what, exactly?" she cries "What's wrong with my body?"

"Abso-fucking-lutely nothing, baby," I say, her cheeks turning a soft pink.

I pay for our ice cream, and we both take a seat on the sidewalk, watching the people pass by.

"You know. I didn't take you for a dark chocolate kinda girl."

She takes a lick of her cone, her tongue darting out in a sensual way as she quietly eyes me. "What did you take me for?"

"Something fruity. Fresh. Lemon, maybe. Raspberry. Or orange."

Satisfaction is shown on her face, a small faint smile tugging on her plump lips. "Actually, there is this ice cream parlor in Jacksonville that sells Orange Chocolate ice cream. That's my favorite."

"Why doesn't that surprise me?"

She gives me a coy smile, then my phone rings, and I take it out of my jeans to see who it is.

Mom.

Rae glances at the screen, giving me an encouraging look. "Just answer it. You know she won't stop until you do anyway."

I know she's right. My mother has been calling me ten times a day ever since she saw that picture of Rae and I, and with my luck, she'll up that to twenty if I'm not giving her something to keep her quiet for a few days. Or at least until I'm in New York.

Not looking forward to this, I sigh, then press the green button before moving the phone to my ear.

"Hello, mother," I say while my eyes keep looking at Rae eating her ice cream, following every move of her lips. Her tongue dashes out with every graze, making me grow uncomfortably in my jeans. She really should stop doing that.

Not the best moment to talk to your mother, I can tell you that.

"Jared James Jensen." My mother's piercing voice cuts through my brain like a damn knife, making me roll my eyes. "How dare you ignore me for three days! Who do you think you are? You have a reputation to uphold. We can't have you roaming off with some gold-digging whore with elections right around the corner!"

"She's not a gold-digging whore, *mother*," I snarl, looking into Rae's bright eyes still beaming at me.

"*Moi?*" she mouths, jokingly gripping her heart. Her light-hearted stance has me only annoyed by my mother instead of fuming, and I'm silently thanking her for it.

"Not to mention, Emily. That poor girl. *Humiliated!*" she keeps going, not even listening to what I'm saying. "Where are you, Jared?"

"Memphis."

"Memphis?!" she parrots, repulsion distinct in her voice before she continues to rant through the phone. "What are you doing in Tennessee? I demand you take a plane right now and get your ungrateful ass in New York to fix whatever you ruined with Emily!"

"Or what, *mother*?" I don't know where my sudden rebellion toward my mother comes from, but something has me acting differently. Or should I say, *someone*. When I look into Rae's glistering gold eyes, I don't care about whatever my mother is ordering me to do. I don't care about whatever threat she's holding above my head or what I agreed upon. All I know is this moment, with this girl in front of me.

I want her.

I want her with every fiber of my being, and I don't think I can hold back any longer.

"Excuse me?" my mother replies, after a shock of silence.

"Or what, mom?" I look up at the sky. "I'm twenty-nine. You can't exactly tell me what to do."

"You've always been a pain in the ass and your father and I let you, but we made an agreement! You're staying together with Emily until your father is elected. I don't care if you love her or not, although she's the best thing that ever happened to you. Then again, you could never see what's good for you. Enough with the bullshit, Jared. You're coming home! Now!"

"No." The word leaves my mouth quicker than I expect, but I feel it everywhere in my bones. It's as if the sky breaks open, the sun shining through after a rainy day. I'm done bowing down and doing shit I don't want to for the greater good.

"No?!" my mother screeches through the phone.

"No," I repeat with force this time, catching Rae's bright brown eyes. Without waiting for a reply, I hang up the phone while I throw my ice cream on the floor. My eyes never leave Rae's as I look into her beautiful face. A burning desire to strip her naked forms inside of me, running a shiver up and down my spine. Like I'm jumping a cliff, ready to dive into the water.

My hand reaches out to cup her cheek while the other pushes her blonde hair behind her ear before I hold her face in my hands.

"What are you doing?" Her eyes are sparkling with excitement, yet her voice is etched with surprise.

"Fuck it."

"What?"

"Fuck it," I say a little louder this time, then cover her lips with mine. She freezes for a moment when our lips connect, and I press her against my face like I'm drowning and she's my breath of air as I'm swimming toward the surface. Her lips taste like honey mixed with cinnamon and chocolate, a flavor combination now forever reminding me of her. Hesitantly, she parts her lips, and I take it as my cue to delve in, completely claiming her like she's mine. A moan vibrates against the back of my throat as I place a hand to the small of her back, tugging her closer against my chest. Her hands grasp onto my shoulders with the same hunger I'm experiencing, and for a minute, I forget we're in the middle of the street. Every stroke makes me want more, thinking about how I could kiss her forever, right at this moment. I grunt when she digs her nails into my skin, turned on by the desire that seems to ripple through the both of us.

"We should stop, before I tear off your clothes in the middle of the street," I heave, even though I crash my mouth against hers once more.

"We should." She bites my lip, and my breath falters before I press my forehead against hers, our noses touching. "But I really don't want to," she confesses.

"I know." I pull her up, then take her hand in mine before I drag her behind me down the street.

"Where are we going?"

I glance over my shoulder, shooting her a wink.

"Somewhere I can have you for myself."

He slams me against the wall as the hotel elevator moves up, pressing me into the surface while I feel his cock rolling against my hips.

"Fuck, I've been wanting to do this for a long time now." His hand reaches into the front of my jeans, rubbing over the fabric of my panties.

"A long time?" I huff, barely registering what he's saying.

"Oh yeah. Every single time you called me a lying cheat, I wanted to make you shut up with my lips covering your wet pussy."

My eyes widen at the bluntness of his words, gasping as the image plays out in my head. He notices while he keeps placing scorching kisses on my neck.

"You want me to lick you, baby?" He undoes the button of my jeans, giving him better access before his finger runs through my folds and my legs buckle underneath me. "You want me to bend you over so I can eat you out like you're my dessert?"

I can't push anything out other than a moan, the sensation of his lips on my neck almost becoming too much.

"I got you, babe." He holds me up with one arm while

the other keeps stroking through my wetness. "You're so wet for me."

When the elevator doors open with a ding, I snap out of my bliss, my cheeks now turning a bright red, fueled by a combination of embarrassment and lust. I push him off me as I try to redo the button of my jeans in a hurry. A sigh of relief escapes my lips when no one enters, but before I can properly pull my jeans back over my ass, Jensen squats down, pressing his shoulder against my stomach as he lifts me in the air. "Don't bother."

I let out a shriek while he takes big strides out of the elevator and through the hallway until he stops in front of our room. We took a room with two queen sizes, sticking to the bullshit story we were going to sleep separated, but we both knew it was inevitable we'd end up in bed together. Or at least, I sure as fuck hoped we would. His fingers reach for the keycard in the back of my jeans, roughly throwing it open, then he closes it with his foot. I screech in excitement when he throws me on the bed, and I wait in anticipation as he crawls over my body until his entire form is flush with mine.

"I want you so bad, Rae," he rustles against my lips.

"Then take me."

The warmth of his hand moves underneath my shirt, pushing the fabric up until he has full access to my breasts. Eagerly, I drag my shirt over my head, then arch my back to undo my bra, ready to feel his skin against mine.

"God, you're sexy." His hand cups my breast while he sucks on my nipple, and I moan in pleasure. He rolls his fingers over my sensitive pebble as he migrates his lips farther down, and my legs automatically fall open.

"You want me, don't you?" he breathes against my skin, his blue eyes glancing up at me with a hint of insecurity.

I nod, biting my lip, desperate to feel him kiss me between my legs.

"Say it."

I grunt with hooded eyes, as he slowly drags my jeans and panties down before throwing them on the floor. He brings his head back between my legs, his breath hovering above my aching pussy.

Dragging his finger through my core, I throw my head back as he sucks in a deep breath. "God, you smell addictive. Say it, Rae." Without waiting for my reply, he presses a soft, sweet, and scorching kiss on my opening, that makes me shudder before he does it again. "Say it, and let me taste you, baby."

"I want you!" I sigh, loud and frustrated, opening my legs a little wider.

"Good girl," he whispers against my lips before I can feel his tongue digging into my walls, then I feel him move up to circle it around my clit.

"Oh, God," I moan, gasping for air.

"God can't make you feel *this*." He softly pulls my clit with his tongue, and I arch my back, bringing my hips closer to his mouth. "Or *this*." His lips take in my inner lips, playing with them in his mouth as I feel his nose graze my delicate nub.

I don't know what the fuck he's doing, never having experienced anything like this in my life, but all I know is I don't want him to stop. A fog forms in my head as he keeps working my pussy like I'm the sweetest thing he's ever eaten, flying me straight to cloud nine. My hands delve into his soft hair, pushing him even more between my hips.

"Oh, please, Jensen."

"You like that, baby?" A finger plunges inside of me.

"Oh, yes. Don't stop," I huff, desperate for more. "Please don't stop."

His tongue keeps licking me unapologetically, like he hasn't had dinner in weeks, while I lay there completely surrendered, at his mercy. I want him to drag it out for as long as possible, utterly enjoying this complete bliss. His hands push under my ass, and he brings my hips up, then starts to drag his tongue everywhere over my pussy in a scorching way, never touching my clit. Softly teasing me, by placing gentle and affectionate kisses everywhere but where I want him to.

It's excruciating.

It's delicious.

"You taste so damn good," he grunts, as he keeps going, never missing a beat, while one finger starts to tease even lower. Surprised by the pressing feeling against my ass, my mouth falls open in surprise as I gasp for air, loving the intensity it's bringing me while he keeps working my body to make me reach my peak.

I can feel my orgasm lingering under the surface, dying to break free.

"Please, Jensen," I cry at the same time his tongue flicks my clit at a fast pace, setting off that explosion that was forming inside of me. My legs shake, and a desperate grunt comes from my lips. I literally see stars as my eyes shut before I open them again, bringing my head up to look at him. His lips are shining with my wetness, and I lick my lips at the sight.

I crook a finger, motioning him to come back up. A lopsided grin splits his face as he drags his body over mine. He hoovers above me, and I lick the seam of his lips.

"Hockey is not the only thing you're good at," I flirt, running my hands through his hair.

He quickly gets up, plucking a condom out of his back pocket before taking off his pants and boxers. "Oh, there is a lot more I'm good at, baby."

With his teeth, he tears a condom wrapper to roll the rubber over his long, thick shaft eagerly bopping against his stomach.

He jumps on me, and I laugh as we bounce on the bed, until I feel the tip of his cock sliding through my folds. Shutting my mouth, I look at him, enjoying the intensity in his eyes. I've always had them in anger, irritation, pinning me down as we were arguing about whatever we argue about. It used to drive me nuts, but now all I can think about is how I want him to stretch me wide, slamming into my body like he owns it with that exact same intimidating gaze. As if he can read my mind, he softly pushes his length inside of me, his eyes closed as if he's savoring the sensation.

"Fuck, you're tight," he huffs, then presses a domineering kiss against my lips.

Giving me time to adjust, he gently starts to thrust, burying his face in my neck.

"You feel even better than I imagined," he hums against my sweaty skin. My teeth sink into his shoulder as I take this moment. Our damp skin connected, the panting of his pleasure tickling my ear while my arms are wrapped around his ripped torso, as he rides me like it's just him and me left in the entire world.

Our world.

His grunts grow more intense with every push he makes. My body tightens around him, my heels digging into his toned ass as I clench my thighs, wanting to feel him deeper inside of me. I can barely think straight, the feeling of his cock filling me up taking over every thought without effort. I've thought about this moment too many times I dare to admit since he crowded my space in that hallway last weekend. For the first time, there wasn't just annoyance in his eyes when they hauntingly glanced down at me. No, I could see the arousal, the desire, the hunger etching through the handsome features on his face. It's the last thing I see before I fall asleep, and it's the first thing on my mind. Him hijacking my road trip made that even worse, but I can't say I'm not happy he did.

I'm ecstatic.

"You feel so good, Jensen." I scrape my teeth over his earlobe, and he throws his head back, just enough for me to watch how his eyes roll up in what looks like a state of euphoria.

"I can't hold it," he grates out, before his lips find mine again.

His movement becomes desperate, plowing into me like a maniac while I enjoy every second of it. Finally, I can feel him tense against me, a feral look flashing in his eyes when he releases inside of me. With a few final pumps, he doesn't stop until he unloads every drop, then his body flops against mine, his breath fanning my neck. I run my fingers over his spine, enjoying the warmth and weight of his body on top of mine. Like a blanket of comfort after a rough day.

After we've caught our breath, he rolls off of me and onto his back, an arm over his eyes, showing off his chiseled chest.

"Damn, woman. I think you broke me."

"Oh, really?" I snicker. "Where is your big mouth now, *hockey boy*?"

"Probably somewhere lost between your legs." He smirks.

"Really, because I don't feel anything." Jokingly, I lift my head, looking between my legs.

Abruptly, he reaches out, pulling me so that I'm now on his chest, looking down at him with a seductive grin.

"That's because I made you come so hard, your pussy will be numb for the next hour."

"Hour?" I screech. "Don't underestimate the stamina of my pussy, you arrogant fuck. But that's okay, if your sweet little dick needs to regroup for an hour, I'll wait. I am kinda hungry, anyway." I avert my gaze, taunting, looking for the room service menu.

He blinks.

"Don't ever make another sentence with my dick and sweet. Gives me chills." He shudders underneath me, and I let out a giggle. "The only thing my dick needs is your lips wrapped around it to make you shut up for two seconds, you little witch."

He tickles my side, and I cry in laughter, squirming on top of him.

"Stop!" I yell, laughing. "Stop!"

He holds still, his playful stance clear in his eyes. I like this Jensen. The lighthearted one. The one that jokes with me, even though I frustrate the hell out of him. The one that isn't mad at the world.

"I can't wrap my lips around your dick if you keep me occupied," I say, like a smartass, fluttering my lashes.

His jaw ticks, and his playful gaze is quickly replaced by desire until he opens his mouth with a husky tone. "Get to work, then, baby."

I FEEL CONFUSED, like a cat thinking she's a dog while I lie next to Jensen in bed later that night, looking up to the ceiling. I can't sleep, because my mind keeps wandering off to Jensen's lips on mine and how I want more. How I felt when we melted together as one. Every time his lips now find mine, it's pressing, demanding, yet delicate and affectionate at the same time. Like he calculates every move with a determination to get me completely undone and into a useless puddle in his hands. I've been wanting to kiss him ever since he dropped his infuriating ass into my car, but nothing prepared me for the actual experience. It was scorching, in the best fucking way, and I can't seem to think about anything else. It makes me believe I'm fucked.

After the third round, the fatigue hit us both, and I turned on my side, my back facing Jensen, reminiscing about our night before my mind completely took over in a fucking girly way. All of a sudden, I'm freaking out, wondering if this is a onetime thing, but mostly if I want it to be. It's the middle of the night, and my head is now filled with a list of pros and cons. Coming to the conclusion that we will never work anyway and trying to wrap my mind around the most likely fact that this will indeed be a onetime thing. Or at least until we arrive in North Carolina.

He rolls over, pressing his chest against my back while tugging his arm under my body to pull me tighter. His deep exhale tickles my ear, telling me he's awake.

"Don't think so much. You'll crack your skull," he murmurs against my neck.

"I'm not," I lie through a whisper.

"You are. *Stop*. Forget about tomorrow. Forget about what comes next. Let's just enjoy this moment. Just be with me."

I'm about to argue with him, telling him all the lies I

came up with to convince him this is nothing more than a night of fun when I feel his lips on the back of my neck. It's lingering long enough to create an uncontrollable flutter in my stomach that makes me realize I'm in trouble. Jensen isn't supposed to make my stomach backflip like a gymnast. He isn't supposed to spoon me like sleeping with me is the most natural thing in the world. And he sure as fuck isn't supposed to give me affectionate kisses that have nothing to do with sex.

But mostly—it shouldn't make me smile like a Cheshire cat. A very content, purring in pleasure, Cheshire cat.

Yeah, I'm utterly and completely fucked.

ATLANTA

GEORGIA

-LAST NIGHT WAS INCREDIBLE -

21.

JENSEN

I wake up the next morning feeling light as a feather, with a calmness inside me that wasn't there before. Rae's naked body is plastered against my chest, the swell of her ass pressing against my morning wood, and I let out a small grunt.

I graze my nose against her neck, breathing her in. She smells sweet like honey, with a hint of sweat etching through.

"Good morning," I murmur, pressing my mouth against her skin.

She hums something, keeping her eyes closed, and my hand wanders over her stomach, stroking the soft skin, having every intention of waking her up with my tongue between her thighs. Softly, I start kissing her neck. She slowly begins to stir awake, when my phone starts to buzz on the nightstand.

I groan in annoyance and reach out to grab it.

"What?" I rumble.

"What is this? The animal shelter? Sorry, I couldn't hear you over all the barking. I think I have the wrong number because I'm looking for my brother. Not a damn beagle," my sister's sassy voice says.

"A beagle? You know damn well I'd be a fucking pitbull if I were a dog."

"One," she starts, "you are a dog—most of the time. Two, you might bark like a bulldog, but you'd be a cute little chihuahua with a tutu. More bark than bite."

"If I'm a chihuahua, you're one of those damn pugs. You know, with the flat faces?"

"I hate you. I'm uninviting you to my birthday."

"That's not for another two months."

"I know."

"Good morning, Della," I drawl, glancing at Rae, who's looking at me with a lazy glaze in her gorgeous brown eyes. Her blonde hair is spread out over the pillow while her naked body is covered with the white sheets, the first rays of sunshine lighting up her bright eyes.

She looks like a goddess.

"Good morning, big brother. How have you been? You almost gave our mother a heart attack last night."

"You mean it didn't work?" I joke.

"Nope. She's still alive and kicking. I was silently applauding you, though."

My lips curl. "Thanks, sis. I'm just going to avoid her until I get in New York and fix whatever needs to be fixed."

"Which is what? Your loveless relationship? You don't really want to get back together with Emily, right? I don't like her."

"I thought you got along with her just fine? You go shopping with her."

"Because mom makes me," she screeches incredulously, "but she's boring. She only talks about how many followers she has or how much money everyone has."

I sigh, pinching the bridge of my nose, just thinking of

Emily. When we started dating, she was fun. She was hot. She was also busy most of the time, so even though we were dating, I still did whatever the fuck I wanted. It wasn't until we became official, and she started hanging out with my mother, that I realized I was in deep shit.

Suddenly, she was invited to family events, spending Christmas with us on the East coast, and before I knew it, she silently moved herself into my condo. It wasn't until Bodi made me realize I never really had a decent conversation with her that wasn't about fashion, who fucked who, or whatever new designer bag she wanted next, that I knew it wasn't going to work out. I'm a simple guy, but I still look for a bit more than that in a relationship.

"I know. It's just—"

"It's just you agreed to stay together until dad is elected?" Della interrupts.

"You know about that?"

"I'm seventeen, Jensen. Not eight. Besides, I'm the only one still living at home. You think they could hide something like that from me?"

"Right." To me, my little sister is just that. My little sister, but last year, she showed me how much she grew up. Even though I've always been close with her, I love how she and I seem to grow even closer lately. Sharing our daily life but mostly confiding in each other about our family frustrations.

"Just let it go, Jensen," she says, after a few silent moments while Rae brushes her fingers along my arm in a way that I'm sure is meant to be comforting but is actually arousing.

"What do you mean?" I ask, my gaze locked with Rae's, making it that much harder to hear Della. A lopsided grin haunts her face. A taunting and sexy look, seductive, combined with the sparkle in her eyes.

"Don't take her back. Just leave it. Leave *her*. Fuck dad. If he isn't going to be elected as governor because you broke up with your girlfriend, he shouldn't be elected anyway. Because clearly, it's not about him, then. Is it?"

I whistle. "Don't let mom hear you. She might ground you, Della."

"Whatever. I just think it's bullshit."

"Our reputation reflects—"

"On him. I know. I've heard it just as much as you did growing up. I'm not running for governor, though, and neither are you. It's bullshit, and you know it. Listen to your little sister and just do whatever you want. Dump the superficial bimbo."

"Okay, who are you and where did you hide my little, dumb sister? She's about yay high, with a smart mouth, and looks like a clone of Kathleen Jensen?"

"You're the one fake dating some girl you don't even like to please mother, and *I'm* the dumb one?"

"Ouch, burn, sis." I chuckle.

Rae's hand moves lower, her fingers now running through my happy trail, and I do my best to stay focused as she gives me a playful grin.

"Stop," I mouth, still listening to my sister telling me to do whatever I want.

"What?" she whispers back, innocently.

"—but you know how she gets," Della tells me, even though I'm hardly listening. "How is that girl, though? Tell me more about her?"

"Hmm?" I hum, distracted by the little vixen beside me.

"That girl! Rae Stafford? Have you seen her after that? I think I've seen her at one of your games. Are you dating her?"

I silently gasp for air when Rae wraps her hand around my cock and starts stroking it up and down.

"Err... No!" I reply, louder than intended. "Yes. Euh, I'm still seeing her every now and then. Actually, Della, I gotta go. We'll talk in New York, okay?"

"What? Why?"

"Bye, sis!" I blurt, hanging up the phone and throwing it beside me on the carpet floor. I lick my lips when I turn my face toward the little minx that's fucking with my head.

"What are you doing?" I growl, as I pull her closer.

"Just telling you a good morning." Her gold eyes peer up at me in amusement, and for a brief moment, it feels like something goes through my heart. The image of Rae waking up in my bed on a regular day flashes through my mind as quickly as it's gone, and I frown in confusion.

"What is it?" she asks, noticing the change on my face. Quickly, a smile forms on my lips while my thumb moves up and down her jaw. I don't know what this girl is doing to me, but I do know it's something I haven't felt before. Like every time I look into her eyes, I'm craving for more. Desperate to feel her next to me. To hear her piss me off with her snarky comments, or make me laugh when she rolls her eyes at me.

"Nothing. Good morning, baby."

"Good morning." She beams.

22

If anyone told me last week that I'd be driving across the country with Jared James Jensen and I'd enjoy myself, I'd tell them they must have bumped their head with a rock. Because there is no way Jensen and I would be able to be in the same room for longer than five minutes without killing each other, let alone share a car for eight hours a day.

But here we are.

I'm staring out of the window, humming along to the radio with my feet on the dash, secretly stealing glances at Jensen. He's wearing a light grey t-shirt that's bringing out every line of his muscles, with some light washed jeans he bought in Memphis yesterday. His sunglasses sit on his nose, giving him that bad boy look that makes him breathtaking.

He looks amazing.

Last night was incredible.

This morning was wonderful.

Part of me thought it would be awkward with Bodi leaving, no longer working as the middleman whenever Jensen and I would have a go at each other. But in reality, that awkward feeling was quickly replaced by comfort the second Bodi got out of the car.

"That was your sister, right? On the phone this morning?" I turn my head. He's leaning into the door, his head resting on his hand while he holds the wheel with the other.

I'm not sure if he's holding back, but he hasn't been driving like a madman like I expected him to do. Instead, he's driving as comfortably as I feel. Cruising over the highway without a care in the world.

"You mean when you were distracting me."

"You didn't complain." I shrug.

"I don't think I can ever complain when you put your hands on me." A smirk lifts his lips, and I can feel his eyes burning through my body from under his sunglasses.

"Keep your eyes on the road, *hockey boy*." I chuckle, averting my gaze to tame the butterflies in my stomach.

"She told me to do whatever I want," he tells me, after a while. "With Emily."

I let his words sink in, having no clue what he wants. Seeing him lighthearted like he's been the last couple of days has really showed me that Jensen mostly does what is expected, and rarely does what *he* wants.

Part of me wishes he wants me, because I'm quickly getting addicted to the feeling he's been giving me. But also, my pros and cons list pops into my head again, shoving the ridiculous thought of me and him to the back of my mind.

"What is it you want, Jared James Jensen?" My voice is composed with a teasing tone as I look at him.

He holds my gaze, and it intensifies within a second, leaving me unprepared for the answer coming from his mouth.

"Right now?" he huffs. "*You.*"

I swallow hard, shocked by his bluntness. My eyes bulge out of my head, and at this point, I'm glad I'm wearing sunglasses that are functioning as a shield. My heart starts to race. He keeps moving his head back and forth between me, and the road, searching my face while goosebumps trickle my body.

"Like," he starts when I'm lost for words, "I don't know what the fuck we are doing. Or what's gonna happen next week, or even when we get to Jacksonville, but right now, I want you." He rubs the back of his neck. "Right now, I want to enjoy whatever the fuck we have going on whenever you're not pissing me the fuck off."

I snort, returning to my defiant self, trying to lighten the mood. "You mean when you piss me off."

"Shut up, little witch." He smiles. "You drive me nuts most of the time, but the last three days I've felt better than I have in a while, and I don't want to think about what comes next other than the road still ahead of us."

His hand reaches out to my neck and gives it a small squeeze.

"Let's just have fun. Okay?"

I nod in agreement. "Okay."

It's a simple agreement. A simple confirmation, but I can't help a heavy feeling settling in my bones. Something tells me I'm making a commitment I can't uphold, but he's right. Who the fuck knows whatever the hell we're doing. I sure as fuck don't know, and until we both go our separate ways, I don't even want to think about it. If anything, it seems like the perfect closure of my LA life.

Not to mention the fact that he made my body explode like fireworks on the 4th of July, and I never pass on a good fireworks show.

Suddenly, he tugs my neck, leaning over to press a bruising kiss on my lips while keeping one hand on the wheel.

Before he lets go, he softly bites my lip, then straightens his back, just in time to avoid driving into the car in front of us. He yanks the wheel to the side, followed by a loud honk of the car beside us while I get jerked against the door.

"Shit!" he mutters at the same time I say, "Ouch."

"Fuck, are you okay?" he asks, frantically, when he gets the car back on the right side of the road. The back of his hand strokes my cheek, looking for any distress on my face.

"Are you trying to kill me, hockey boy?" I do my best to keep a straight face, but I can feel a smile dying as it tries to push through.

When he notices how fake my glare is, he rolls his eyes. "There are easier ways to kill you, Stafford."

"What?!" I yelp, gaping. "You wouldn't get away with it."

He chuckles, bringing his hands back to the wheel.

"Pfft, I'm the son of Asher Jensen. I'm pretty sure I would."

"Oh, so *now* you wanna pull the *my-daddy-is-a-politician* card?" I quirk up an eyebrow.

"Are you kidding me? That's the *only* time I'm gonna pull that one."

"To get away with murder?" I deadpan, folding my arms in front of my body. I press my lips together while inside, I'm smiling like that damn Cheshire cat again. I love how our bickering changed to bantering. I love how our aggravation turned to flirting. And most of all, I love how it all feels normal.

"Hell yeah, what else would I need it for?"

"You're the worst."

"I know." He smirks.

23

"Did you know he was the youngest Nobel prize winner at the time?" Jensen asks as we stand in front of Martin Luther King Jr.'s birth home. The house looks like an ordinary southern home, with yellow paint and brown shutters. But the knowledge that he lived here, someone that had such an impact on our modern-day society, still makes the hairs in the back of my head stand up, even though it's a warm summer day.

"Really? How do you know that?"

"I paid attention in history class."

I turn my head, the disbelief dripping off my face. It's hard picturing the bad boy of the NHL as a model student. Actually, it's impossible.

"What?" He chuckles.

"Nothing," I tell him. "Just didn't take you for a history nerd."

He wraps his arms around my waist, spinning me so that I'm facing him, then dips his chin.

"I said I paid attention. Not that I was a history nerd." He takes my sunglasses off my face, placing them on top of my hair, while his other arm keeps me tight against his chest.

"What are you doing?"

"I want to look in your eyes when you are being a pain in my ass."

"Isn't that always?"

"Actually, yeah." He brings his hands to cup my cheeks, giving me a sweet affectionate kiss that has me moaning against his lips. "Come on, let's grab some food. Bodi will join us later."

He takes my hand in his, leading us out of the park.

"So, what are you in the mood for?" I ask as we walk down Edgewood Avenue.

He pulls me closer before wrapping an arm around my neck. "That depends. Are you on the menu?"

"Just for dessert." I seductively bite my lip.

"Hmm, I can wait for dessert." He kisses my hair, bringing that flutter back. "I think."

We walk in unison, glancing around the streets of Atlanta. The diversity is noticeable on every corner of the street, giving it a vibrant and alive atmosphere.

I like discovering new places, roaming new cities and learning about new cultures. Part of me is disappointed that I'll probably never be able to travel to the other side of the world, but when I walk in a city like this, it makes me realize there is so much more to see in my own country.

"Sushi!" Jensen suddenly shouts, pointing at a sign that says Nagasaki Sushi. "Do you like sushi?"

I pull a face. "Do they have fried chicken?"

"Err, I don't know. But they have fried shrimp?"

"Close enough."

We walk in, choosing a booth in the back of the restaurant with dim lighting. He orders a few sushi rolls, along with some fried stuff for me, and two glasses of wine. Settling into his side, we wait for our food to arrive, while we make up stories about the people around us. I laugh at the ridiculous narratives we come up with, my mood getting giddier by the minute.

"I bet he's a big-time lawyer. A well-known name in the city." Jensen nudges his head toward the man in a suit toward the front of the restaurant, before lowering his voice to a whisper. "But secretly, he's an accountant for the gangs of Atlanta."

"What! No way! He's clearly a civil rights advocate, trying to help the homeless."

He pulls a face. "You're crazy. Just look at his face! It screams trouble."

"*Your* face screams trouble." I shrug.

His gaze darkens, that playful glint showing in his eyes as he licks his lips. The look that makes me turn into a puddle every time.

"You want me to show you how much trouble I am?" My mouth turns dry, and the butterflies go on high alert again when he leans in. His breath warms my face, and I part my lips in anticipation before he kisses me. The kiss has me swooning deep inside. Filled with affection and domination, it's set in a perfect balance. A kiss that makes my brain stop functioning, and I couldn't care less. His tongue moves along the seam of my lips, automatically parting them with a moan, right before the food is placed on the table. Jensen lets out a grunt, giving me another peck as if he has a hard time letting go.

"Good evening." The waiter beams when we both give him a coy smile, mine with flushed cheeks. He places the food on the table, then lets us be before we dig in. For a minute, we are silent, enjoying our food, though he tugs me closer to him, rubbing my back in a sweet way. It feels as if we've been doing this for months instead of days. As if we are two people who know each other through and through. With my previous boyfriends, there was always a level of awkwardness, of embarrassment. But with Jensen, I don't feel insecure telling him how I feel, or feel the need to make things prettier than they are. He has already seen me growling and grunting more times than most men have anyway. No, with Jensen, everything feels real instead of make-believe.

My phone is laying on the table, face-up, and something lights up the screen. His eyes glance toward the device, noticing a message coming through.

Sean.

"Is he still trying to get you back?" he asks, still chewing.

"Apparently," I grunt, taking a bite of my fried shrimp, enjoying the soy sauce on my tongue.

"He calls you a lot?" I can hear the aggravation in his voice, and it warms my heart, enjoying his possessive behavior more than I should.

"Every day," I say, honestly. "Every night too."

"Every night?!" he asks, a slight shock on his face. He throws his chopsticks on the table, then wipes the corner of his mouth with his napkin. Leaning into the booth, he rests his arms on the back.

"He called you last night?"

"Hmm, every night. I put my phone on silent."

"Do you ever pick up?" The look on his face seems interested. But the ticking of his jaw tells me he's having a hard time keeping a straight face. I'm not sure what has aggravated him, but for some reason, it changes my lighthearted mood too.

"Why would I? I know exactly what he'll say."

"Yeah, what's that?"

"I love you, Rae. Take me back, Rae. I'm sorry, Rae. You know you're the one, Rae. I will never get better than you, Rae. A lot of pleading, basically."

I haven't picked up Sean's calls since we left LA, mostly because the man in front of me has kept me occupied every single minute. But also because it doesn't matter. I'm moving back home. I'm not going to get into a long-distance relationship with the guy who cheated on me. How stupid is that? I'd be basically giving him a wager to cheat whenever I'm not around.

"Do you want him back?" His deep voice cuts through me, now completely pissing me off. I can hear the judgement in his voice, combined with a disappointment that shoots right through my heart.

"Do you think I'd be fucking with you if I wanted him back?" I sneer, offended. Quickly, I slide away from him, crossing my arms. Maybe I'm overreacting, but I don't care. The suggestion pisses me off. I know I don't owe him shit; he and I are nothing but a few blurred lines that will be straightened the second we drive into Jacksonville. But I am insulted that he would think I'd use him like some kind of rebound before running back to Sean Kent. He might not know me very well, but I'm pretty sure he knows me a little better than *that.* Especially when I'm the one who's been scolding him for five years about the photos on TMZ with any girl who wasn't his girlfriend.

I'm not like that shit.

I don't do that shit.

And I'm disappointed he'd even feel the urge to ask. I assumed he thought more of me.

He shakes his head, pulling me back against his body in

one swift move. "Oh, no you don't. Don't you dare fight me because I asked you a fucking valid question." He fists my hair, so he can tug my head back to look into my eyes. I can feel his warmth enveloping me, covering me in a blanket that instantly simmers my irritation down, but not completely. "I know you're not some bimbo begging for his attention. But you also didn't out him in the tabloids. You haven't outed him with the team. I know what he did. You know what he did. Yet you haven't said a word to anyone. It's not hard for me to wonder if that's because when this is all over, you want to give it another shot. Give *him* another shot."

"You know what he did?" I frown.

"Come on, baby." His thumb rests in the corner of my mouth. "He's my teammate. It's no secret he fucks around every chance he gets."

The embarrassment washes over me, and I turn my head out of his grasp. I tried to keep it a secret, at least for the outside world. He's one of the star players of the LA Knights. I was already getting hate for dating him, let alone if I started calling one of their favorite players a cheater. I told Johnny because he's my uncle, but other than that, I kept my mouth shut. Told everyone the spark died down between us and we grew apart. But really, he killed the spark by sleeping around every chance he got.

"Hey," Jensen says, grabbing my chin to force me to look at him again. "It's not your fault. We all know he's a player."

"You all know? The entire team knows, and no one cared to tell me? *You* didn't care to tell me?"

He grinds his teeth. "It's not like we were exactly on speaking terms, were we? You bite my head off every chance you get."

"And this proves exactly why," I growl, pushing him off me and climbing out of the booth.

"Rae."

"Fuck you, Jensen."

Ignoring him, I stomp off.

"Rae, goddammit." I hear him mutter behind me.

I don't know why I'm suddenly so mad at him again. Why suddenly he seems to piss me off like he has for the last five years. Maybe it's the humiliation of finding out he knows I was being cheated on yet didn't care to tell me. Maybe it's because I now have a hard time trusting men that have women lining up because of their celebrity status. Maybe I'm just confused about the last few days, knowing they will hurt me in the end. *He* will hurt me in the end. Or maybe I just need someone to throw my frustration out on. But it could also be his offending words, implying I'd sleep with him before I run back to my ex. Either way, I'm pissed.

The warmth of the summer night hits me in the face when I walk out the door and start to follow the pavement back to our hotel. The smokey smell of meat being grilled enters my nose, and my stomach starts to roar in protest when I walk by a BBQ food truck.

Ugh, I should've never listened to that dick.

"Rae, I swear to God, stop, or I will——" I hear him groan behind me. I keep walking, like an angry child, not in the mood for whatever pretty words he has for me, until I feel his arms circle my waist from behind, his mouth now flush with my ear.

"What's happening, baby?" The rumble of his voice drums all the way to my core. "What made you all fire blazin' at me?"

"Let me go!" He tightens his grip on me.

"Not a chance in Hell. Kent might be the kind of guy that will let you storm off in a fight, but I sure as fuck am not. You should've known that by now. I love to fight with you. What I don't *love*"—he twists me around in his arms, then crowds my space until my back is pressed against a brick building. His blue eyes look haunting, turning me on instead of scaring me away—"is you running out on me. This isn't going to work if you don't talk to me. Talk. *Now*."

"I don't wanna talk to you, *asshole*." I narrow my eyes, trying to ignore his addictive, fruity, musky scent as I look up at him. Like berries freshly picked after rainfall, quenching my thirst.

"We're back to *asshole*?"

"If the shoe fits…" I trail off, turning my head to piss him off even more.

"What did I just do, Rae?" he shouts, incredulously. "Tell me, because I don't get it. What the fuck did I do wrong?"

Closing my eyes, I push the emotion away, not willing to give him the satisfaction of my tears. Frustration washes over me as I swallow hard. My mind is telling me he's an asshole, but also telling me to not be so damn defensive. To stop acting like a raging teenager. But for some reason, my emotions seem to be all over the place, dribbling around like a damn basketball. My mind has never been so clear and so confused at the same time. I don't like the question he asked because I want him to think better of me, but also because the question made me aware of Jensen's reputation, making me wonder if I'm simply the next flirt before he goes back to his girlfriend.

I don't want to be that person.

I *refuse* to be that person.

His hands move to the front of my neck, cupping it before

he brushes his nose against mine in a domineering yet affectionate way. "Talk, Rae."

"I'm not a cheater." I finally tremble out the words.

Confusion etches through his features. "I never said you were, baby."

"You basically implied it by asking me if I want him back. Why would I be with you if I did?"

His eyes widen as if the realization hits, then he cups my cheek.

"I hurt you."

I nod, trying to swallow the tears away. His thumb starts to brush my skin, and I lean into his touch. He drops his forehead against mine, then closes his eyes as he lets out a deep wheeze.

"I'm sorry, Rae. I didn't mean to hurt you."

"I know," I hush against his lips. My hands move up, holding his handsome face between my palms. My fingertips run through his rough five o'clock shadow, and without thought, I press my lips against his.

The act feels good. So good.

Like his lips are made for mine. Like his body is forever melted to be draped over me, fitting like a glove. Before this week, I couldn't imagine taking anything from LA but a distant memory, let alone staying in touch with anyone. Now when I look into the future, all I see is him.

Jared James Jensen.

He's clawing his way through my dead bolted heart, and the scary part is that he's succeeding. Holding a crowbar up in the air, he's almost through the door. I can feel it. And it's scaring the shit out of me.

As if he can feel my fear seeping from my body into his, he slowly pulls back, tugging me closer against his chest.

"What are you so afraid of, baby?"

That you'll leave like everybody does? That you'll find out I'm damaged goods?

That I'm falling for you…

"Stop," he commands gently in my ear. His lips land below my ear, pressing a sizzling kiss on the sensitive spot. Feeling the warmth of his lips against my skin makes my thighs clench together as I close my eyes and fist his shirt in desire.

Fucking hell, I'm terrified of being with this man.

But fucking hell, I want him in any way possible.

He grips my chin, tilting my head so he can look at my face. "Open your eyes."

I do as he says, parting my lips and looking into his eyes. They remind me of the blue of the ocean, and for a second, I wish I could drown in them forever. Swim in the safety of his gaze, knowing he will hold my hand and have my back.

"I want *you.* Don't think about anything else. We will figure it out, okay?"

I hold still, searching his eyes for any deceit or betrayal, to look for any lies, but I can't find any. They radiate only truth.

"Okay," I finally say with a cracking voice, knowing I don't have a choice.

Neither of us seems to know where we are going. But it doesn't matter. I can't let go anyway.

24.

JENSEN

I can see the conflict in her gorgeous eyes. I can see the words sitting on the tip of her tongue. Silently asking for the clarity we both crave, because there is no hiding our feelings anymore. Within twenty-four hours, my heart set its eyes on her, and there is no way back. I can feel it running through my veins, and I can't give her comforting words right now. The ones where I tell her I want more than just this road trip. I want more than just this week. The ones where I tell her that I want to get to know her more and see where this goes. But my parents' expectations are lingering in my head, and I don't want to drag her into the madness of the Jensen political family. Not yet, anyway. I need to do this carefully, before they start to throw threats that will affect Rae's family. Not to mention me being traded. Who knows where I'll be playing next year.

"I want *you*. Don't think about anything else right now. We will figure it out, okay?"

"Okay." Her voice cracks, stinging my heart. Maybe I'm wrong for keeping her hopes up, dangling false promises in front of her face when I have no clue if I can keep them. But that's all I got right now.

So, I just kiss her. Desperate, scorching, and filled with urgency and unspoken wishes. Hoping she can feel what I'm feeling, praying it will spark her confidence in whatever this might be. The kiss consumes me, taking my breath away, and I cup the front of her neck, breathing into her mouth.

"You drive me crazy, Rae."

"You're already crazy." She smiles, bringing us back to the light mood we were in before dinner. I feel the corner of my mouth rise.

"Maybe."

Her hands roam over my back, and I close my eyes, enjoying her touch, completely transfixed by every stroke. When my eyes lower, I reach up, rolling the gemstone of her necklace through my fingers.

"Who gave you this?" I realize how jealous I sound when I hear my own words, too late to change my tone of voice. Smooth, Jensen.

A ghost of a smile meets her beautiful features. "Jealous?"

"Maybe."

"My mother." My brows raise, and I scold myself inside for my possessiveness, ignoring the vibration in my pocket.

"Is it a gemstone?"

She nods. "My family owns a jewelry business. They work with gemstones."

I cock my head, my eyes roaming the freckles on her nose. I didn't expect that answer, and I feel a bit embarrassed for assuming it was from Sean. Like she was still hung up on the guy, even though she told me she isn't.

"Your phone is buzzing, Jensen," she muses, looking at me with hooded eyes.

I clear my throat, blinking. "Right."

Reluctantly, I pull it out of the back of my pocket, taking a step back but keeping my hand on her waist.

Bodi.

"Hey, mate," I say, keeping my eyes focused on Rae. She's biting her lip, her back still pressed against the wall. Her blonde hair is now messy, the direct result of my fingers running through it in a demanding way.

"Where are you two at? I'm at the hotel. Let's have a few drinks before we call it a night," Bodi tells me.

"We're downtown. We'll meet you there in twenty minutes."

"Alright, see you then." I hang up the phone, then tug her against my chest again.

"That was Bodi. He's at the hotel. He wants us to have drinks."

"Okay, let's go."

I look at her, searching for any leftover distress showing on her face.

"Are we good?" I ask, not completely satisfied.

Just like us players, this girl can put on a serious game face, and I don't want her to feel like shit with a fake smile.

"We're good, babe."

My eyes widen, and my dick twitches.

"You called me *babe.*"

"So?"

"You never call me *babe.* Just Jensen."

She rolls her eyes. "Well, okay, then, *Jensen.* Let's go."

She grabs my hand and starts to tuck me behind her down the street.

"No, don't stop. I like it." I drape my arm over the back of her neck, pulling her into my side as we start walking back to the hotel. "Turns me on," I whisper against her neck, resulting in a chuckle that warms me inside. I can listen to her laugh all day.

"You'd fuck me out here in the street if I'd give you the chance, wouldn't you?"

I let out a torturous moan, glancing up to the sky, something intense flaring inside of me.

"If I say yes, will you let me?" I joke halfheartedly. I'm not going to fuck her in the middle of the street, but I sure as fuck won't say no if she pulls me into some dark alley right now. I've been dying to get her pressed against the wall the entire day. To bury myself inside of her once more and completely get lost in her delicious body. To still my hunger by eating her out, drinking up her juices like a glass of sweet tea on a hot summer day.

"No," she says firmly, as expected. "Not in the middle of the street."

I can hear the suggestion in her voice, and I frown, wondering if I'm hearing her correctly.

"Wait, is there anywhere else you'd be game?" I ask curiously as we walk on together.

"Depends on how public we're talking." She smirks, tilting her head to look at me.

I clench my teeth together. "Rae Stafford, my sweet princess, have you ever had sex in public?"

Her fingers thread through mine while the other holds onto my waist.

"Haven't you?"

"Err, I have. But I didn't expect you to be such a dirty girl."

"Pfft, please. You can call me a princess, but that doesn't mean I am one. I'm not a saint, Jensen."

Remembering her supposed rebel phase, I run my tongue over my lip.

"Okay, tell me. Where is the craziest place you've ever had sex?" My mouth turns dry when I think about all the places I'd love to have her for myself, suddenly aware of all the available possibilities. The jet, the beach, the locker room after a winning game, the movies, the bathroom stall in some trashy bar. The list is endless, really.

She grunts. "Are we really going to do this?"

"Fuck yeah, we are."

"Fine," she huffs, then points her finger at my face. "Don't get jealous, though."

Lifting my free hand in the air, I press a kiss to her hair. "I won't."

"Craziest, huh?"

I nod, waiting in anticipation as we hold still to continue along the crossing.

"I think the janitor's closet, senior year."

"That's not that crazy!" I blurt, thinking back about the many times I took Macy Anderson to the janitor's closet when I was a freshman in college.

"While he was on the other side. In his office."

"Wait, what?"

"Oh yeah," she continues, "our janitor, Mr. Cohen, had his own office. Or, actually, it was more like an office space. There was a desk in it, and a file cabinet, but not much more could fit in. Not sure why he needed an office anyway, but he did. One day, Kyle Sanders and I sneaked in right before lunch and started making out. It couldn't have been more than ten seconds before we heard Mr. Cohen come in. Kyle peaked through the hole, and apparently, Mr. Cohen was taking out his lunch, getting comfortable. We held quiet for five minutes, but after that, I was done waiting."

She reveals the words without any shame.

"You had sex in the janitor's closet with someone on the other side of the door?" I laugh.

"Yup."

"Damn, I wish we went to high school together."

"What about you, *hockey boy*? What is your wildest memory?"

"I once fingerfucked a girl in the queue for Space Mountain at Disney World."

"You didn't!" Her head slowly moves up, her bright eyes shocked.

"I did."

"Jared James Jensen," she reprimands, bringing that desirable feeling back to my already growing cock. "What about all the kids waiting in line with you?"

I shrug, laughing. "She was wearing a big vest that covered everything up. Besides, she was glued against my chest, so to everyone else, it looked like we were happily in love, hugging our way through life."

"Were you?"

"Was I what?"

"In love."

"No," I say, short and quick, before I process the question properly. Love to me has always been something unattainable, only existing in fairytales and movies. I 'liked' girls; they turned me on. And for the most part, I liked spending time with them. But I never have felt that dying desire to be with someone.

Not until now, that is.

"I don't think I've ever been in love," I confess.

"Me neither." Her disclosure makes me happy, pushing away the hint of jealousy that was waiting to start growling with possessiveness.

"Tell me something, though," I whisper, my lips flush with her ear when I see the hotel come into sight while Bodi is waiting in front of the entrance. I notice her brows quirk up in anticipation, as she bites her lip when she feels my breath fanning her skin. "Name the one place you'd want to have sex at least once in your life. What's on the bucket list?" My tone is husky, turned on by the thought of being part of her deepest desires.

Her chin twists, looking at me with a flirtatious gaze, then she eyes Bodi on the streets. When she realizes he hasn't seen us yet, she stops in the middle of the sidewalk, fisting my shirt in a demanding way that quickly has my heart racing. Our chests are now joined as one, and she's staring at me with a dangerous glow to her irises, as if she's daring me to fulfill whatever is going to roll off her tongue any second now.

"On the hood of a car." She pauses, and my lips part in lust, envisioning her request in my mind. "I want to be licked into oblivion while the cold metal is pressed against my ass, my pussy hot like fire as I look up at the stars on a summer night.

I swallow hard, blinking. My dick is getting painfully large inside my jeans, and the thought of Rae, spread out on the hood of my black Camaro, makes my world spin like a madman.

"What the fuck, Rae," I huff, flustered, lost for any other words. I rub my palm over my face, clenching my jaw to prevent myself from throwing her over my shoulder, taking her to my room, and fucking her until she's passed out.

She snickers, like the little witch that she is, her cheeks now flushed with desire, and her eyes naughty as fuck.

"You asked." She shrugs, then gives me a sweet peck on the lips, turns, and walks away, right in time for Bodi to notice us.

"Hey, Bodi!" She beams at him, leaving me completely stunned on the sidewalk, like she just told me what her favorite meal is.

I know what my favorite meal is from now on.

Fuck me.

25

M y heart races. My panties are growing wet, yet I plaster a big smile on my face before I wrap my arms around Bodi, taking in his clean scent.

Stupid me. You don't go telling the man you want to rip your clothes what you're yearning for the most, if there is no chance of him complying with your request right away. I can feel my pulse beating like a drum in my neck, and a lustful ache growing in my core. The thought of my legs, spread wide, on top of the hood of a car, makes it a challenge to keep my brain cells doing a proper job.

"Hey, Goldilocks," Bodi says, his voice soft. "You okay?"

"Hmm." I nod.

He smiles, looking at me through his friendly eyes.

"Why are you blushing?" His hands are on my shoulders, and my mind can't catch up quick enough to come up with a logical response.

"Hands off, McKay," Jensen growls behind me, then his arms slide around my waist as his chest connects with my back.

The difference between both men is huge. They are like day and night. Yin and yang. Jensen is rough, blunt, and intimidating, with his no nonsense stance and his big mouth. Bodi is composed, kind. The nerd in high school, who turned out to be a hot scientist. Or publisher, in his case. But I do get it now. I do understand why Bodi told me they are more alike than meets the eye.

Both of their hearts are pure.

Jensen acts like the careless hockey-er most of the time, but I see it. The kindness that's tucked deep into his body. I can see it in his eyes every time he looks at me, mixed with the craving he can't seem to lose.

Nor can I.

Bodi moves his head back and forth between the two of us, then rests his gaze on me, a grin splitting his face.

"I guess the fucker won you over, huh?"

I lean my weight against Jensen, settling into the warmth that radiates from his hard chest.

"Won me *over* is a bit exaggerated. But he's not as bad as he seems," I joke, faking indifference.

"Shut up, little witch." Jensen softly bites my ear, and I pull back, a chuckle rolling off my lips.

"Right," Bodi drawls, clearly not buying my lame attempt of a brush off now that he's seeing Jensen's lips on my body. "Come on, let's have drinks."

We follow Bodi inside, settling for three seats at the bar while Jensen never lets go of my body. Bodi orders three Old Fashions, then excuses himself. "I'm going to the bathroom. I'll be right back."

I watch him walk away from us, until he's completely out of sight, then quickly turn back around to Jensen with a scowl on my face.

"What are you doing?" I hiss, slapping his thigh.

"What?" he yelps, his hand still running over my thigh.

"You're all over me."

"You say it like it's a bad thing?"

"What about Bodi?"

"What can I say, baby? I'm hooked, and I get really shitty when I don't get my next fix." His lips land on my neck, and I giggle, pushing him off.

"Stop, Jensen!"

"Baby, he's not stupid. Besides, he's my best friend. He wants me to be happy. And you make me *really* happy." He pulls my stool closer to him, placing me between his legs. His hands roam over my body, shamelessly stroking the skin underneath my shirt. I let out a tortuous moan, his palm glowing on my skin.

"I can't get it out of my head now," he drawls. His lips scrape my cheek, my flesh prickling at his touch, and I automatically close my eyes.

"What's that?" I crack, my mouth turning dry.

"How I want to spread you out over the hood of my car. Running my tongue between your folds, treating you like a cake tasting."

My eyes shoot open, the mental image clear again, and I turn my head to grab his chin. Our eyes lock, filled with arousal.

"Fuck," I breathe, horny as fuck.

"I know." He grins with an evil look.

He moves his mouth over mine, devouring its softness, his kiss slow and thoughtful. Our tongues dance together, sending shivers of desire through my body. His moan vibrates to the back of my throat, making my heart race like a drumroll. The kisses of this man are scorching, making me addicted to his taste and his touch. Every move seems pre-thought, slowly building me up to that point where I'm like jelly in his hands, ready to drop my panties in the middle of the bar. Feeling a man's hands on my body has never felt as good as Jensen's rough palms on my skin.

"Hey, guys." We quickly break loose when Bodi's voice reaches our ears, and my cheeks immediately turn a bright red as I try to wipe my mouth subtly with the back of my hand.

Ignoring my embarrassment, he takes his seat next to me with a pompous look on his face.

"What did I miss?" he asks, casually moving a hand through his hair.

"Jensen told his mother *no*," I blurt, a lousy attempt to change the subject, which will have zero effect, I'm sure. Jensen frowns at me, and I shrug my shoulders. It was the first thing that popped into my head that could deflect the fact that we were sucking face in the middle of a bar.

Bodi turns his head toward Jensen, beaming with pride, though I can see a hint of suspicion.

"Did you?"

"Technically, I hung up when she started ranting. I haven't answered her calls since."

"No way."

"Fuck it." Jensen shrugs, repeating the words he told me after he hung up the phone with his mother two nights ago. An amused smile forms on Bodi's lips, glancing at me as if he knows I'm part of Jensen's motivation.

"Fuck it?" Bodi echoes.

JENSEN

M an, that feels good.

"Fuck it."

The more times I say it, the better it feels. As if every time I speak the words out loud, the universe is shifting a little in my favor, even though nobody knows how that will turn out.

"And then you kissed Rae," he asks rhetorically. I breathe out, knowing there is no use denying it anyway. Bodi knows me better than anyone. He will look right through whatever bullshit I'll try to feed him, and to be honest, I don't want to lie about it.

I don't want to deny the fact that this girl is making me feel alive for the first time in my life. I get that it's still early, and it's stupid it to be completely open about it, but if there is one person I don't want to hide shit from; it's Bodi.

"And then I kissed Rae." I glance at Rae, staring at the ground with her lips in a firm stripe.

"Good choice, J." He nods playfully, and I respond with a long sigh, not loving the fact that Rae seems to feel more uncomfortable by the second. I turn and tilt my head, glaring at his amused grin. We stare at each other, as if I'm hoping my death glare will have him sinking to the floor. One can hope.

"You're fucked," he mouths, silently, making me shake my head.

I know.

Trust me, I know.

"Right." Rae glides from her stool, a flicker of embarrassment still visible in her eyes. "I'm going to call it a night."

"You're leaving?" I quickly grab her wrist. I don't want her to leave. I guess this is awkward for her, but I want to be able to hold her in front of my best friend. Kiss her when she's being a smartass and pull her hair when she's pissing me off.

"Yeah, I'm tired. I'm going to let you two hang out, and I'll see you in the morning." I search her face for any sign of fatigue but can't find shit.

"You don't have to go, baby."

She smiles, awkwardly. "It's okay. I'm tired. I'll see you in the morning."

Her body turns, ready to walk away, but I place my knee in front of her stomach, pulling her between my legs once more. "Rae?"

"Hmm?" She twists her head, her gaze dripping with desire as she swallows.

"Fuck it." I smirk right before I crash my mouth against hers. My hands slip into her hair, holding her head still so I can have my way with her, pushing my tongue in with a passion that's running through me from head to toe. Her sweet honey taste has me acting like a druggie on a relapse; I want to keep kissing her forever. Claim her taste as mine from this day forward.

When I pull back, I press my forehead against hers, my

palms still in her soft and silky hair. "Fuck it, baby," I whisper against her rosy lips, hoping she can hear the words that are not coming from my mouth.

Fuck it, I don't care who's watching.

Fuck it, I don't care what everyone thinks.

Fuck it, I don't care what everyone wants.

Fuck it, because I want you, and I'm not letting you go. Not now. Not ever.

She pushes out an amused breath, softly nodding.

"Fuck it," she repeats, then presses another sweet peck on my lips before I let go of her. I slowly let her walk out of my grasp.

"Goodnight, boys."

"Night, Goldilocks." Bodi's grin is splitting his face in two, and I roll my eyes, then sigh, bringing my glass to my lips.

"Whatever you're going to say, save it," I grunt.

"Oh, no. We are going to talk about this, mate." His know-it-all smirk, combined with his annoying Australian accent, is a little irritating, but it doesn't come out of nowhere. If you don't want to talk about shit, Bodi is not the one you hang out with. He will kindly ask you to talk to him, and if you don't? He'll nag you until you do.

"I don't want to talk about it." I make a futile attempt.

"I don't care," he announces, turning his body to face me, his elbow resting on the bar with his glass in his hand. His brown hair bounces as he tilts his head. "Tell me, how long did it take until you were smooching with Rae after you dropped me off at the airport?"

"Smooching? People still use that word?"

"I just did."

I glare at him, my lips pressed into a thin line.

"Come on, tell me! An hour? Two? Five minutes?"

"Shut up, Outback Jack."

"Not until you tell me. Start talking, *hockey boy*," he mocks, using Rae's nickname for me to get under my nerves.

It's working.

"Memphis," I finally disclose.

"Huh!" He frowns. "That's longer than I'd expected."

I just chuckle, fear showering my body. I want Bodi to know. I want to tell him how I feel, but I'm also hesitant to voice it. If I say the words out loud, it becomes real. If it becomes real, I can no longer deny it. I can no longer deny the feelings I have for her. I'm too scared to voice it because I don't want to lie to anyone.

Not to Bodi.

Not to myself.

And certainly not to *her*.

But if this comes out, I don't know if I can protect her. To protect her from the hurt my family will inevitably cause her. I'm fighting the tightness in my chest that forms as I try to hold everything inside. Realizing I have feelings for her is hard enough as it is, and trying to hold it in makes it a torture, but I know I have to.

"J." Bodi's voice rings in my ear.

"What?" I drawl.

I know he means well, but I don't even know how much I can say without completely ruining this for myself. She looked up at me in fear on the street, earlier tonight, silently begging me to tell her how I feel; how we move on from this, and if we move on from this together. But the truth is, I don't know. All I know is I want her. But I'm not convinced that's enough.

"You don't have to be scared, you know," Bodi tells me, as if he can read my mind.

I take a sip from my glass, the orange peel in my drink

making my nostrils flare before I let my head hang. "I don't know, Bodi."

My voice cracks.

"Yeah, you do. Just because your mom doesn't want you to say what you want doesn't mean you have to listen. Just talk to me."

I rub my face. "I don't know what to do."

"She's getting into your head, isn't she?"

"I'm not sure if Rae is getting in, or Emily is finally getting out." When we started this trip, I had every intention of doing what was expected from me. To fix things with Emily, even though it was the last thing I wanted to do. They can call me a good-for-nothing-asshole, but I am loyal to my family. Even if they want to paint me as the bad guy.

"It's both, J."

I twist my head, looking at my best friend peering me down with his clear blue eyes. "You don't love Emily. You never have. Now I don't know if you love Rae, but I do know she's the only one that ever made you smile like a damn idiot for most of the time. It's starting to scare me," he jokes. "I know you are loyal to your parents. But why the fuck are you, mate? They don't do shit for you. I understood when we were still eighteen. But you're twenty-nine now. You don't need them. *They need you.* They want to keep up the appearance of being a loving family, but let's be honest, that's the biggest façade there is. Why are you pleasing them when they need *you?*"

I sigh. "They threatened to ruin my career."

Bodi pauses for a moment, letting my words sink in.

"How exactly?"

"My father knows everyone. If he doesn't want me to play. I won't play."

"That's bullshit, J!" Bodi spits, his jaw ticking as I see his face flare up. "Your dad is running for governor. Not fucking president."

"I'm pretty sure he has friends in the NHL as well."

"He probably does, but it doesn't mean he can control every team in the NHL. That's bullshit, and you know it. You're just taking it as an excuse because you are scared to death. Admit it." He shoves my shoulders, and I snap my head toward his with a glare. But I can't help the thought crossing my mind. Wondering if he's right.

"I mean it," he continues. "So your father has some influential people in his circle. And yeah, he might be able to get a foot between the door in some clubs. But, Jensen, you just won the Stanley Cup. Every single hockey team in the country is going to want you. Plus, there is hockey in Canada, Europe. You don't have to stay here. Besides, they could be bluffing. Ever consider that?"

I look at my best friend speaking the words that have crossed my mind for the last two days. Every time I look at Rae, I've been weighing out my options, thinking about how different my life could look, but also hearing one clear thought that stays in my head. Loud as fuck. Hearing Bodi say the same words that have been occupying my thoughts for the last few days feels like a ray of sunshine after a hurricane. The sky breaks open, showing all the possibilities that come after disaster. After a heartbreak. I want her to be a possibility. If she's not the one, I want to look back, knowing I tried. I don't want her to be the one that got away while I'm stuck in some lifeless marriage like my parents.

If anything, want to regret the decisions I made, not wonder what could've happened if I made different ones. Like I'm waking up after hibernation, I see it now. I'm not giving her up. I'm not giving *us* up. She makes me feel good. She makes me laugh. She makes me happy.

I'm not sure if that's love, but it's close enough for me to wanna say *fuck it.*

Fuck it all. Maybe that's a mistake, but I guess there is only one way to find out.

"Yeah, actually. I have."

Taking a sip of my drink, I can feel Bodi's eyes on me.

"Fuck me," he suddenly blurts. "You're going to do it, aren't you?"

I lick my lips, holding my glass in front of my face while I suppress the smile itching to curl the corner of my mouth.

"Do what?" I ask innocently, though I know what he's talking about. He's been dying for me to tell my parents to go fuck themselves for years, but I guess I never found a good reason.

Now I have.

"Motherfucker. That blonde little thing finally gave you that last push, huh?"

I shrug, downing the rest of my drink. "I don't want to give her up."

Bodi triumphantly slams his fist onto the bar. "I knew she would make you crack."

"Make me crack? What the fuck are you talking about?" I laugh.

"Oh, come on, you're falling in love with Rae. A blind man can see that."

I let his words sink in, waiting for that terrified twang to pop up. The one that has been jumping out like a damn surprise party every single time a girl would tell me they love me. I could never say it back, and I'd barely manage to reply with ditto, because there has always been this feeling inside of me that didn't believe in love. But hearing *Rae* and *love* in the same sentence gives me nothing but a content feeling. Like a cup of hot cocoa, warming my body after a cold day.

"Maybe you're right," I concede. "Maybe I have feelings for her."

My head starts to feel light, blinded by the realization that shines through my always clouded head. The fog seems to disappear, and I can feel the weight being lifted off my shoulders.

"You do, mate." Bodi slaps my back. "So, what's the plan?"

"To get her back home by three tomorrow, before Johnny Pearce wants my head on a platter," I quip. "I'm postponing the difficult talk until this weekend. I just want to enjoy the next couple of days, you know?"

Bodi nods, then takes a sip from his drink.

"How was your meeting?" I ask, changing the subject.

"What meeting?"

"The one you flew out here for? Did you sign that author?"

Bodi lets out a full belly burst of laughter, and my eyes widen, wondering if he's lost his mind. "What?"

"There was no meeting, dumbass."

I look at him, confused, not fully understanding what he's saying until it's like a lightbulb appears in my head.

"Motherfucker."

"I believe the words are: *thank you*, motherfucker." He smirks, looking fucking smug.

"You're shitting me, right?"

"You needed time alone with her. She makes you happy."

The look in his eyes is the reason why he's my best friend.

He grants me the world, and he will cross any boundaries if he thinks it will make me happy.

"You faked a meeting and flew out two days early so I could have a few days alone with Rae?" I ask, stunned.

"Actually." He drags out the word, giving me a fake smile. "I also sent that photo of you two."

I just blink. Confused.

"To Emily," he clarifies.

"You did what?!" I bark the words, more in shock than in anger, because the truth is, I don't even care who sent that damn photo. I'm just glad someone did, but hearing my best friend is the bastard who put this all together makes no sense. Then again, it also makes complete sense.

"Look, I know you don't want to admit it, but there is something going on between the two of you. I see the way you look at her, and if I'm honest—I've always seen the way she looked at you. There is a chemistry between the two of you, and with me around, that was easy to ignore. You're switching teams, you're moving to who knows where, and you needed to realize Emily is not it. I'm sorry I tricked you." He gives me a remorseful face before it returns to that smug grin. "But you basically forced me with your ostrich behavior."

"And this fake meeting?"

He shrugs. "With me out of the picture... I knew it was only a matter of time before you two would take the plunge."

"You're an asshole." I glare, even though I'm not mad at him. If anything, I want to kiss the guy for figuring out what I've been trying to tuck away.

"It worked, didn't it?"

I tilt my head, nodding. "It sure as fuck did."

"Now that we agree on that, are you ready to face your mother?"

Normally, the thought of facing my mother would drain my energy and suck up whatever good mood I might be in. But this time, I just smile.

"Fuck it." My heart fills with pride, ready to face her head on. Bodi is right. I don't need them. It's not like I go to them for some motherly advice or to discuss my season with my father. They haven't contributed anything other than a roof over my head, food on the table, and a feeling of never being enough. I have money in the bank, so number one and two haven't been an issue since I first signed my NHL contract. But it's time to stop looking for ways to please my parents. I'll never be what they want me to be, and I'm done pretending.

"Shit." Bodi smiles. "For real this time? You're going through with it?"

Rae's bright smile flashes in front of my face, and I know there is only one answer.

"Yeah," I pause, nodding my head. "I am."

JACKSONVILLE

NORTH CAROLINA

- I TRIED TO RUN, BUT ULTIMATLY I BELONG
HERE. THIS IS MY HOME -

27

JENSEN

T he sun is warming my face through the windshield of the car, and I let out a deep, happy sigh. I've been driving across the country with this sassy blonde for a while now, like I'm a lost boy, consumed by wanderlust. But really, I feel completely at peace, sitting in this car with my girl next to me.

Yes, *my girl*.

The world might not agree with me, and hell, she might not even agree with me at this point. But she is *my* girl in every way possible.

Waking up this morning, feeling her next to me for the third time this week, it gave me the realization I already felt lurking under the surface. I don't just like this girl. My feelings for her go deeper than I have ever felt before. She pisses me off with her snarky tongue and her snappy comments, but really, I haven't felt this thrilled in forever, and I know she's the reason. I love seeing her face in the morning and kissing her goodnight.

I want this.

I want her.

The thought has my mother's face flashing in front of my

eyes in the worst way. She's going to give me hell. My parents can't have any change of plans now that my dad is getting more popular every day. They've threatened to make my life miserable multiple times, but they don't see the big picture. You see, my life is already miserable. It's already filled with things I don't give a shit about, or things I don't want to do, just because my father is governor of New Jersey. If they want to make life hard on me, and end my reputation with their power, my career, or whatever else they want to hang above my head, I say let them. I'd rather pack my bags and live in bumfuck nowhere, waking up with Rae in my arms every single day, then play their show pony for another day. I made enough money to live comfortably for the rest of my life.

I'm ready to fight.

And I want to fight for Rae.

"You know you have to be on your best behavior?" Rae's sweet voice snaps me out of my daydream, and I give her a questioning look. She tilts her head, narrowing her eyes.

"What are you talking about, woman?" I chuckle.

"Meeting my family."

"Aren't I always?" I now laugh.

"You're an asshole," she deadpans.

"He really is," Bodi chimes in.

"See, Bodi agrees."

I point my thumb to the back of the car. "You gonna listen to that fucker over there?"

Defiant, she nods her head. "Definitely."

"I've been nothing but nice to you! *Really nice.*" My gaze darkens, thinking about waking her up with my tongue between her legs, my eyes still heavy with sleep.

Good morning at its finest.

"To me, yeah. I'm not complaining." She grins as I watch

her with amusement. "But to everyone else, you're your dick-ish self and I kinda want them to like you. Just show them my version of Jensen."

"What version is that?"

"Sweet, funny, sexy," she taunts, licking her lips before her face straightens again. "No, scratch that, don't need Nana to think you're sexy."

"Scared I'll run off with your grandmother?" I give her a faux seductive look.

"Ew."

"Yeah, seriously, mate. EW." I hear Bodi pipe up from the back.

"Just give them you," she continues. "The real you."

I glance at her, looking at her bright golden eyes showered with kindness. My chest moves up and down as I feel my skin tingling. The world seems to stop, forgetting everything else around me but the girl that's worming herself deeper into my heart.

"Eyes on the road, hotshot," Bodi calls out, and I snap my attention back in front of me as I swallow hard to push the emotion away.

"Yeah?" I say as casually as possible. "Who's that?"

"A warm, fun, caring person." The words leave her lips quickly, like they were already on the tip of her tongue.

The heat seems to radiate through my chest, fueling my desire to never let this girl go. My muscles relax, and I roll my shoulders, then bring my chin up with a cocky grin.

"Intimidating?" I joke, partly.

"You can be, if you want to be.

"But not to you."

"No, not to me." She shakes her head.

"Why is that?"

She smirks. "I'm not easily intimidated."

"Clearly." I smile.

"Why is it you never give people the real you?"

"This is the—"

"Don't give me that bullshit," she interrupts harshly, though eyes still peer at me with an overwhelming kindness. "I've been with you for the last seventy-two hours, and I know that brooding NHL playing asshole is not who you are. I already told you that before, and I stick by it."

I sigh, shrugging. "Maybe."

A few moments pass, and I stay quiet, thinking about her question.

"You didn't answer my question, though," she points out, still waiting for an answer.

I guess it's just something I'm used to. People treat me differently than they treat my brother. And they don't treat me the same as they treat my sister either. In my younger years, I was the rebel, the difficult one. I wasn't bad at learning, but I wasn't very good at it either. I didn't want to play piano, I wanted to climb trees. As soon as I realized I could never please my parents, I stopped trying, to an extent. I turned from the difficult one, to the feared one. The one who went through life growling and kicking, always trying to push his own way through. It only worked half of the time, but at least they'd rather leave me home when going to certain events because they couldn't risk me roaming off. Or God forbid if I did something to damage their reputation. Fine with me. I'd rather stay home and watch TV anyway. It didn't take long for me to understand that showing that side of me wouldn't make me happier, but the expectations lowered, which helped a little.

"Because it takes off the pressure if people expect less of

you," I admit with a heavy heart, a slight shame sitting in the back of my mind.

"Baby. I'm sorry."

I don't like that this is the first time she calls me that because I hear the pity in her voice, and I don't want it. I'm not a good person, I know that. I can blame my parents for everything, but *I* was there. I know the things I did.

"Don't," I say, my tone low and reserved. "I'm not some sad little kid. It is what it is."

She glances at me, biting her lip in that cute way she does. "Okay."

I turn my head, offering her a comforting smile, not wanting to ruin the mood.

I don't mind her asking about my childhood, but it does feel weird, since no one ever did. Bodi did, so I told him the gist, but Rae manages to give me looks that make me want to tell her every detail of my life story. She makes me wanna share every step that led me to this. To her.

"But I'll be on my best behavior, baby." I grab my snap-back from my head, putting it on backwards so I can see her better. "I promise."

The corner of her mouth lifts, her eyes beaming. "Good."

28

A little sooner than expected, we arrive at my family home, and Jensen parks the car in the driveway. A warm, fuzzy feeling settles inside of me when I look at the white house with a big porch. It's one of those homes that looks even better with Christmas lights, and just thinking about decorating the tree with Lily this year makes me giddy like a child.

"Nice house." Jensen lowers his head, taking in the building that represents my entire childhood. Suddenly, I'm reminded of the fact that my entire family is waiting for me inside, and I start feeling a bit nervous to introduce him to everyone.

"Thanks," I mumble as I get out of the car with a stone in my stomach.

Here goes nothing.

Leaving our stuff in the car for now, I hear the boys follow behind me, and when we reach the porch steps, I quickly turn to face them.

Bodi and Jensen both nod their heads, albeit with mischievous smiles on their faces, but I'm deciding to trust them. Sucking in a deep breath, I slowly exhale before I swing the door open.

"Surprise!" We all jump at the unexpected noise directed at us, and I blink at the two-dozen people standing in the hallway.

"What the—" I hear Jensen huff under his breath as I bring my head up to the banner hanging on the ceiling that says: *Happy birthday, Rae!*

You have got to be kidding me.

"It's your *birthday*?" Jensen grates.

"Err. Yeah," I say, awkwardly. "Surprise?"

My entire family, plus neighbors, are standing in the hall with party hats on and birthday horns in their mouths. The house is decorated with blue and purple garlands.

"And what, you forgot?" His breath tickles my neck as he hisses against my skin.

Of course, I didn't forget. But I didn't think they were planning a surprise party. I thought we'd have dinner; Nana would make some fried chicken, and we'd have cheesecake from Lou's for dessert. It's not like twenty-four is a special birthday?

"I didn't wanna make a big deal out of it."

"Maybe you should've mentioned that to your family," he mumbles.

"Not now, Jensen," I sing-song with a tight smile still in place, taking a step forward.

His firm hand grabs my shirt, holding me back for another moment as he puts his mouth flush with my ear.

"I'm gonna get you back somehow, Stafford."

Stiffly, I let out a chuckle before Lily runs into my legs, wrapping her arms tightly around my thighs.

"Hey, pretty girl." I grab her by the arm, then lift her

onto my hip before burying my nose into her blonde hair. She smells like her vanilla scented Disney Princess shampoo, and I suck in the smell, reminding me that I'm really home.

"I missed you," she says.

"I missed you too."

"Who are you?" She brings her head up, her dark blue eyes beaming at Jensen.

"I'm Jensen." He gives her a small wave. "And this is Bodi."

Bodi does the same, and she waves back to them sweetly.

"Are these your boyfriends?"

The entire room laughs, and I can feel my cheeks blush when I glance at Jensen, not sure how to introduce him. Either of them.

"These are my friends." I go for. "This is Jensen, and that's Bodi. Boys, this is my little sister Lily."

"Those are weird names." Lily scrunches her nose, and I cover her mouth with my hand, offering the boys an apologetic smile.

"Lily," I reprimand, "I know, but we don't say that out loud."

Amusingly, both Jensen and Bodi cross their arms in front of their bodies with modest glares.

"Welcome, boys." My aunt comes to my side, taking Lily from me, then offers them her hand. "I'm June. Nice to meet you."

They both introduce themselves once more, like real gentlemen, and I can see my aunt give them both a look of approval.

"Johnny told me you were staying. Sorry, we didn't inform you about the party. Let me show you to your rooms, and you can take a minute to freshen up," she offers before she walks them upstairs, showing them the guest room. Jensen lingers, licking his lips when he brushes past me. His eyes move to my mouth, then quickly glance behind me at the people still waiting for me to greet them properly. He wants to kiss me; I can see it in his eyes. But instead, he just strokes my stomach, passing by before he trails behind Bodi, shooting me a wink as he walks up the stairs.

My heart flutters, and I let out a deep sigh, right in time, before the small crowd is hovering around me.

TWENTY MINUTES LATER, I have a glass of wine in my hand, a cupcake in my belly, and my cousin Kayla hanging on my lip as I tell her about the last week. And by hanging on my lip, I mean, she cornered me and is now interrogating me like the fucking FBI. But in her defense, I would've done the same if she brought a guy home for her birthday.

"Okay, so what about that Emily girl? Isn't he supposed to marry her or something?"

Anxiety hits me hard, just thinking about him marrying Emily, but the same question has been going through my own mind at least once a day.

"I don't know, Keeks." I take another sip of my wine, avoiding looking at her. "I don't even know when he might be leaving?"

"Is he still expecting you to go to New York with him?"

"I don't know!" I screech, looking up at the sky. I don't think he is, but who knows at this point. We haven't really talked about what happens next, both set on enjoying whatever time we have together. Technically, we are not together.

"Are you going to if he does?"

I slowly turn my head to her. Her curly brown hair is voluminous, with highlights shining in the sun, bringing out her bright blue eyes. The signature of the Lockheart family.

"Am I going to New York if he asks me to?" Fuck no. I'm not going to torture myself by convincing his ex that there is nothing going on between us. Besides, when I made that agreement, there wasn't anything going on between us. While right now I feel like a hypocrite even thinking about it, I don't want to make life harder on him either. I know he will have to go through a bunch of shit if he doesn't get back together with Emily.

"I don't know." I shake my head. "I really, really don't know, Kayla. I don't want to. But I also don't want to fuck up his life. Argh! How did my life get so complicated all of a sudden?" I growl. Bringing my glass to my lips, I down the whole thing out of frustration, then pull Kayla's glass out of her hand to continue with hers.

"Hey! That's mine!"

"You're nineteen. You're not allowed to drink anyway."

"June said I could," she mopes.

"Don't worry. I'll get us another one in a minute."

She mumbles something, but I ignore her, thinking about the man now walking through my childhood home. The truth is, I don't want him to go, but I feel like his leaving is inevitable. Our worlds don't match in any kind of way, and I can't expect him to shove his parents aside, even if they treat him like shit.

I'm terrified to bring it even up, because I don't think I can handle the rejection if he's planning to get back together with Emily after this weekend. Fake relationship or not.

"Speaking of the devil." I follow Kayla's gaze.

Bodi and Jensen step out of the kitchen and into the yard.

Jensen roams the yard, until his eyes lock with mine, shooting that same desire-filled look my way that I've become so familiar with. My heart jumps, and I hold his gaze with a faint smile, as we stare at each other like we're the only people around, until Johnny takes up his attention.

"Fuck, Rae. No chance that boy is thinking about his ex. He's smitten."

"He's not smitten." I blush, bringing my glass to my lips again.

"No, you're right. He's head over heels." Kayla boldly plucks her glass back, drinking the thing all in one go.

"Shut up, Keeks."

"You shut up. I almost had an orgasm watching him eat you with his eyes from a mile away. He wants you."

"You don't know shit," I counter.

"It's hard to deny when he is undressing you with his mind. Gah, he makes me swoon." She flutters her lashes, and I chuckle at her silly face.

"Yeah, you and me both, girl."

I look at Jensen again, making my heart race at just the sight of him, hypnotized by his fearless smile. I have no clue what's going on between us. All I know is that he makes me feel things I never thought possible, but I can't shake the sense that all good things come to an end. And I have a feeling our time is running out.

29

JENSEN

I look around the yard, seeking Rae's blonde hair. When I find her, my heart stops when our gazes collide, and it seems like the world stops too for just a brief second. I smile, clear desire dripping from my face, I'm sure. She does the same. My feelings for her seem to be growing bigger by the minute, and soon, I know I'll reach that point of no return. If I haven't already. Then I blink, and the moment is over, as I feel someone approaching me from the side.

"Jensen, nice to see you." Johnny offers me his hand with a genuine smile, and I grab it in greeting. Even though he's dressed the same, in dark jeans and a dress shirt, he looks different in the company of his family. More relaxed, maybe.

"Likewise, sir."

"How was the trip?"

"It was good," I reply genuinely, trying to hide the loop of memories involving his niece that's going through my head. "I've never been on a trip across the country, but it's been fun."

Johnny eyes me, and I swear I can briefly see a hint of wariness, and I don't like it. Now that I know how close he is to Rae, I want him on my side, and I have a feeling he's not going to be the easiest person to please. Not like her little sister, who I already wrapped around my finger by telling her how much I loved her collection of gemstones.

"It's a long trip, but it's a beautiful one," Johnny agrees. "Did my niece continue to give you a hard time?"

I think back to the first two days of our trip, and the glaring looks she gave me, but they are quickly replaced by her vibrant smile, fueling my good mood.

"At first, yes. But eventually, she loosened up."

"She's a good girl." His focus goes to Rae sitting on a bench in the back of the yard, with a girl that possesses her same vibrant smile, yet her hair is a chocolate brown. "She's been through a lot."

"I assumed so, sir." Though I'm not sure what he means.

"Did my sister give you and Bodi the guest room?" Johnny asks with a wary look.

"Yes, sir."

He nods, his eyes narrowing in a clear warning. "I suggest you stay there as soon as it's lights out."

I press my lips together, suppressing the laugh that wants to break out at his comment, acting like I'm twelve. Normally, I'd be pissed, but I don't think there is anything that can turn my gleeful mood.

My phone dings in my hand, and I quickly glance at it.

EMILY: I miss you. When will you be in New York?

I clear my throat, annoyed.

"Everything okay?" Johnny asks, eying my screen.

"Yeah. Everything is fine." I give him a tight smile, which he returns with a skeptical nod. He probably doesn't believe a word I'm saying. The mood becomes a bit awkward as we silently watch Rae, before I turn my attention back to Johnny. A sadness creeps into his features as he stares at his niece.

Suddenly, he looks older than the forty years he has been alive.

"She briefly told me she had a hard time as a teenager?" I ask, hoping he will tell me more.

"She did. We almost lost her." The words sound ominous, and a tight feeling enclasps my chest as I continue listening to him. "My sister couldn't handle her. Neither could my brother-in-law. I was the only one who got through to her, but I lived on the other side of the country. She hated me when I dragged her to LA, but I couldn't do anything else. This was the only way to let her keep her freedom and keep an eye on her."

My mind is running overtime, trying to understand what exactly he's saying. She told me she had a rebellious phase, but this sounds like there is more to it than just some teenager going to a few parties too many. My gut spurs me to keep asking questions, but for some reason, I feel like I should ask Rae first, so I keep my mouth shut.

"Glad you did, sir."

He twists his head to look at me, a coy smile now clearly visible. It could be nothing, but it feels like a small victory. "I like you, Jensen. You're a pain on the ice, but you're a good guy."

I expect him to tell me more, at least threaten me a bit like the big brother he seems to be for her, but unexpectedly, he stays quiet.

"That's it? You're not going to tell me you'll break my legs if I hurt her? That you will destroy my career if I break her heart?"

He snorts, amused. "From what I can tell in the tabloids, you have a few things to figure out first. Besides, the look in your eyes tells me you're fucked anyway." He slaps my shoulder, then squeezes it for a second. "Just be patient with her."

I smile slips in, knowing he's right.

I'm fucked, and I don't even care.

"I will, sir."

"Now, I apologize in advance, but my mother seems to be desperate for a word with you." He nudges his chin to my left. Rae's grandmother points at the chair next to her, silently inviting me to come sit. "Here, take this. You'll probably need it."

Johnny offers me his tumbler of whiskey, and I eagerly grab it, mumbling a thanks before I saunter toward the chair.

Evelyn Pearce has long grey hair that's perfectly styled, with green eyes that seem to follow me like a hawk. She looks like a classy, sophisticated lady, reminding me of my mother, but the fire in her eyes tells me she's completely different. Evelyn Pearce clearly isn't afraid to protect her own; you can see it in her entire stance. She's a lion.

"Nice to meet you, Jared James Jensen." She nods approvingly when I take the seat next to her.

"You too, Mrs. Pearce."

"Oh, please. Call me Evelyn. Or Nana. Whatever seems more fitting."

I chuckle when she winks at me. The woman is the epitome of a southern belle, and she must have been a gorgeous woman back in her day.

"I'm not sure I'm comfortable with that, ma'am."

"Suit yourself." The old woman pats my leg, and I smile at her, hoping to get on her good graces while bringing the glass to my lips.

"You're in love with my granddaughter." She states it with

a certainty that has me laughing and choking at the same time.

She is not wasting any time.

"Am I?"

"Oh, you don't fool me, boy. I can see it in your eyes when you look at her. How you stare at her just a little longer than necessary. Admit it. You're falling in love with her."

I sigh.

What is love, really? I don't know, but I do know I haven't felt like this before. Not with anyone. I don't even think I've ever witnessed it.

"I don't know, ma'am," I reply, honestly.

"Do you think about her before you go to sleep?"

"Yes," I say without hesitation.

"Do you think about her when you wake up?"

"Yes."

"Does your heart rate speed up when she enters the room?"

Automatically, my eyes find hers, feeling my chest expand. "Yes."

"That's love." The tone in her voice leaves no room for discussion, like she is an expert on the matter.

"That easy, huh?"

"Just because everyone treats it like it's rocket science, doesn't mean it is." She shrugs. "Have you told her?"

"No." I shake my head, adamant. Waking up this morning, I realized I felt more for her than I initially pretended to. Being with her feels natural, like I can be me instead of the person everyone expects me to be. But right now, my future is dictated by others, and Rae is not part of their plan. My parents might have given me this week, but I know there's a shitstorm coming as soon as I leave North Carolina. Something I'm not looking forward to. But it's also something I need to sort before I push this any farther. Just to make sure I don't let her walk into the lion den unprepared.

"Don't wait too long, boy." She pats my arm in an encouraging way, like grandmas do. "She already has a wall as big as a skyscraper built around her cracked heart, protecting it with her life. If anyone tramples it anymore, she'll put it in a vault and will never take it out again."

I tilt my head, replaying her words in my head, then grind my teeth together when I realize what she means. "Kent hurt her that much?"

"Who?" Her eyebrows move to her hairline, a strand of her grey hair falling in front of her face because of the sudden movement.

"Kent. Sean Kent? Her ex?"

Nana pushes the strand back behind her ear, then raises her eyebrows in amusement. "That stupid jock? No offense," she mutters, raising her hands in the air.

A chuckle leaves my lips as I throw the last of my whiskey down my throat.

"None taken."

"No," she huffs, indignant. "She didn't give a shit about that boy. She just kept him around for the *fun* stuff, if you get what I mean." She chatters the last sentence with her hand in front of her mouth, and I smile politely. But really, the thought of Sean and Rae together has me grinding my teeth. "I don't think she has ever been in love. Not really. Not like with you."

I snap my head to the old woman with wide eyes, shocked at the bluntness of her words. "You think she's in love with me, ma'am?"

Her eyes roll, as if I just asked the stupidest question.

"God, you children nowadays really like to beat around the bush, don't you? What do you kids call that? Playing hard to forget?"

"Playing hard to *get*, mother." June joins us with a beer in both hands. "Don't listen to my mother. When you get older, you don't really care about being polite anymore." She offers me a coy smile, then hands me one of the beers.

I place my empty glass on the floor next to me, then take the beer from her perfectly manicured hand. "Thanks."

"Mother, you are needed in the kitchen."

"What for?" Nana screeches, clearly not in a hurry to leave.

"Something with the cake. I think Johnny busted the side."

"I swear if that boy took a bite of that cake when I told him not to, he'll be getting a shitload of chores tomorrow."

"Mama, he's forty. Besides, he's leaving tomorrow, so he's not going to do chores."

"I don't care if he's eighty and senile; if he touches that cake, he's going to mow the damn lawn before he goes back to his fancy LA life."

I snicker as I listen to both women bickering, shaking my head at the love that's still detectable. When my parents are bickering, it's filled with venom, always a clear snarl to whoever is the recipient. Being around them is stressful, because you're constantly on edge, fearful of what you might be doing wrong this time. But these two women clearly respect one other deeply.

"Sorry about that," June says when Nana stomps off to the kitchen. "I hope she didn't scare you away? We're really a very friendly family. In general."

"No, ma'am. I'm a governor's son. I've been spending my

holidays with senators and other intimidating people since I was little. We've been drilled to talk to scary people. Though I'm sure your mother can be really intimidating, I'd rather talk to her than Judge Jefferson of the Supreme Court."

"Hmm, that makes sense," she muses, taking a pull from her beer.

We stay quiet, standing beside each other, and my eyes move through the yard. Bodi is chatting with Rae and her best friend, all three of them laughing about something he says. Her smile works as a beacon, lighting my world every time she laughs. Her energy draws my eyes toward her, even when she's not trying. It has always been like that, but I haven't really understood what that meant until the last few days. She's like my northern star in the dark of the night.

"She told me I'm in love with your daughter," I admit, bringing my beer to my lips. I'm not sure where my sudden honesty comes from, but I guess part of me is dying to know her opinion on the matter. The bitter liquid falls on my tongue, right when Rae finds me with her eyes and gives me a small wave. My heart jumps, and I give her a wink.

"I highly doubt that. I've heard you are a bad boy, but I doubt you will fall in love with a ten-year-old."

Confused, I turn my head. "I don't follow."

"Even though Rae is my daughter in every sense of the word, I'm not her mother."

My eyebrows quirk up.

"She's my niece. I'm her aunt. That's my husband. My sister was her mother." She points at Christopher, who's briefly been introduced to me, grilling burgers behind the barbeque. "We took her in after the crash."

My head starts to spin, and I'm not sure if I'm hearing her correctly.

"What crash?" I ask, a lump forming in the back of my throat.

She sighs, closing her eyes for a brief moment. "I already assumed she didn't tell you. When she was nine, they took a trip to the Bahamas. The plane had a malfunction. It crashed into the sea in front of the coast of Miami. My sister and my brother-in-law didn't survive, along with a hundred other passengers. Only ten people survived. Rae was one of them."

A tight feeling forms around my throat, and I just blink, shocked. It feels as if time slows down while a cold shiver makes the hairs on the back of my neck stand up.

How did I miss that?

"She doesn't fly," I breathe, suddenly realizing why.

June shakes her head. "When we arrived in Miami, the government arranged a flight for us back to North Carolina, along with the bodies of my sister and brother-in-law. But we couldn't get Rae onto that plane. She went ballistic. The only option was to drug her, but I refused. We rented a car to get back home. She has refused to fly ever since. I tried. Johnny tried. She doesn't fly."

"I didn't know." It's all I can say, trying to wrap my head around what I just found out.

"I know." June's voice is soft and friendly, but there is an urgency detectable. "I don't want this to be one of those cliché things, where you get schooled and questioned by every person in the family about the girl you fell in love with. Because, yeah, my mother isn't the only one who notices the longing looks across the yard. I think the whole party knows." She gives me a coy but loving smile. "And I'm pretty sure I know her well enough to know she feels the same. But she's been hurt and never fully recovered. Caring for someone scares her. She will push you away. But she's worth sticking around for."

My chin moves a bit up, my shoulders relaxing as I exhale deeply, believing every word she's saying.

"I know, ma'am. And I want to fight for her."

30

I'm catching up with my next-door neighbor Rita when I feel two big arms slide around my waist as a kiss is being pressed to the crook of my neck. Goosebumps trickle down my skin, accompanied by a heavy flutter in my stomach, my knees growing weak.

"Hey, baby," Jensen whispers in my ear, then tugs my back against his chest before he offers a wave to Rita. "Hi, I'm Jensen."

"Rita," she replies, fluttering her lashes like she's about to take off.

"Do you mind me stealing her away for a second?" He must be using all his charm because Rita's cheeks turn a rosy pink, and she nods her head with a flirtatious smile.

I mumble a *sorry* before he walks us backward, leading me to the gate on the right side of the yard that leads back to the driveway. When we are out of sight, he presses me against the sheltered part of the carport, his lips finding mine with passion. I moan against his mouth, fisting his shirt in my hand while my pussy is screaming to be touched.

God, this man turns me on so bad.

"I'm pissed at you," he breathes against my lips between kisses.

"You don't seem pissed," I muse, grinding my hips against his body. The bulge pressing against his zipper tells me he ain't as pissed off as he's telling me.

"I am."

"Hmm, why is that?" I'm only half listening, too occupied digging my nails into his back. He awakens every fiber in my body, effortlessly sucking me into his energy, dying to bury myself in his arms. As soon as he's within a two-yard radius, I can't break loose, even if I tried.

"It's your birthday." I can hear the disappointment in his voice, and my guilt makes me pause as I look up at him with regret in my eyes. I know it was a shitty thing to do, not telling him it was my birthday. I didn't want to tell him because I didn't want him to feel like he had to do anything about it. He was going to be pissed about that either way, but I thought it would just be a family dinner, like we always do. I figured I could tell him when I showed him the guest room, when we were alone. He'd probably growl at me, we'd have dinner with my family, and then I would make it up to him later. Never in a million years did I expect to walk into a surprise party with half the neighborhood present. For my twenty-first birthday? Sure. My twenty-fifth? I guess. But not for my fucking twenty-fourth.

"I'm sorry. I should've given you a heads-up. I didn't know they were making such a big deal out of it."

"Well, seems fair since it would kinda ruin the surprise." He smirks, running a finger along my jaw. "Why didn't you tell me?"

"Because—I don't know. This—" I move my finger back and forth between us. "I don't know what this is, and I didn't want to give you the feeling you needed to do anything for my birthday. Because you don't."

His gaze moves up and down my face, as if he's thinking about my words, then he presses a rough kiss to my lips that leaves me breathless.

"Give me tomorrow," he says, a certain urgency audible in his tone.

"What do you mean?"

"Give me tomorrow. Just you and me. You still owe me one."

"Okay," I agree. "What do you want to do?"

"Everything. Anything. Show me around. Show me where you grew up."

I bite my lip, shaking my head, not fully understanding. "What do you want me to show you?"

"The school you went to. Where you got your first kiss. Where you used to hang out. I want to see your world."

Goosebumps trickle over my body, a weird feeling of euphoria settling inside of me. I don't know what's happening, but a grin forms, and I eagerly nod my head.

"Okay, yeah. Sure."

"Yeah?" The back of his hand brushes my cheek, then he presses a soft kiss on my lips.

"Yes."

His thumb traces the seam of my lips before he drags my lower lip down. "You drive me crazy, Rae Stafford."

"Rae? Rae, where are you? It's time for cake." Nana's voice calls out through the yard, and I close my eyes while he presses his forehead against mine. Great timing, grandma.

"We should head back," I murmur.

"Hmm, I guess so."

His phone starts to vibrate in his back pocket, and I pull it out for him, pushing it against his chest with a smile. I'm tempted to see who it is, wondering if it's Emily, but I keep my eyes on his, pressing a chaste kiss on his lips when I reach up.

"Take that. It might be important."

"I doubt that."

"I'm going to blow out some candles." I break loose from him, my hand lingering on his stomach for as long as possible.

He looks at me like I'm the most amazing thing in the world, then nods. The man makes me swoon without even trying, feeling desperate for his touch.

"I'll meet you inside in a minute."

31

JENSEN

When I look at the screen, I'm happily surprised, so I pick up.

"Hunter Hansen, you still alive?"

A deep chuckle comes over the line, and I imagine his cocky grin.

"Are *you*? I've seen your name in the tabloids more than once last week, man. You've been busy."

"Oh, you know how that goes, man. You're seen with one girl, and you're a married man the next day."

"You must be heading for your divorce, then, because I've seen you with the same girl twice."

I drop my back against the concrete wall, a frown on my face.

"What do you mean?"

Hunter pauses, as if he's trying to break the news to me easily. "There is a new picture online of you and the blonde. You two are looking pretty cozy on the streets of Atlanta."

Letting out a growl, I rub my hand over my face.

"Shit," I mutter.

The first few days, I was careful, checking my surroundings, putting a Knights cap on my head to make sure no one recognized me. Anything to make sure the tabloids couldn't corner me by surprise. But after Memphis, I let my guard down, putting my main focus on Rae most of the time.

"Is it clear it's the same girl?"

"You mean Rae Stafford? Former specialist for the LA Knights?" Hunter asks bluntly, giving me a clear answer.

"Fuck."

"Yeah. I'm guessing your mother is not happy with you."

"Ha! Nothing new, right?"

"True. What are you doing in Atlanta, though? I thought you'd be celebrating your win in typical LA style?"

"Like you did with your last fight? You bailed the second you got the chance." I laugh, thinking back about his final fight last April. He got me front row tickets, and when he won, I went to congratulate him in the dressing room, but he was already gone.

"Are you still pissed about that, Jensen?"

"You brushed me off with a text," I whine jokingly. "I was a little hurt, yeah."

"I'm sorry, superstar. You know you have a place in my heart."

"Yeah, whatever. How is your woman doing?"

"Good! She's getting big. It's a boy, by the way." I can hear the pride in his voice, putting a smile on my face.

"No way! Another Hunter? I'm not sure the world can handle that."

"Tell me about it. Charls said the same when we found out."

I can't believe we went from clubbing together to Hunter having a wife and a kid on the way. I still remember when she walked into us at a club years ago, with a girl on each of our laps. I will never forget the hurt in her eyes, the pain that she physically felt when she saw him with another girl. But even under all the hurt, I could still see the love dripping from her face.

She loved him with everything she had.

He always told me they were best friends, but at that moment, it became clear that was bullshit. I never officially met Charlotte, but she gave me a glimpse of something I want one day. To find someone who still loves you after you hurt them. Because they simply can't stop.

"She's a good one, though. I've always known that," I offer.

"Yeah, man," he agrees, contentment in his voice. "She's the best. She asked me to ask you for dinner next time you were on the East Coast."

My brows quirk up at his invitation.

"I'm in North Carolina."

"Today?" Hunter sounds surprised, which seems logical since I normally avoid the East Coast as much as I can.

"Yeah, man, I'm in Jacksonville. Rae lives here."

The line stays quiet before I hear Hunter's amused voice ring in my ear. "Wait, you're at her house?"

"Yeah."

A whistle cuts through my head. "Must be serious, then."

"Shut up." I laugh.

"You're not even denying it?" he blurts, incredulous. "Oh, yeah, you are coming to dinner now. I want all the deets on this Rae girl."

I chuckle. "Alright, when?"

"Tonight. Charlotte is making fried chicken."

"Sounds perfect." I know Rae will love fried chicken on her birthday.

"I'll text you the address. And bring the girl."

Before I can reply, he hangs up the phone, and Bodi appears at the gate leading back to the backyard.

"Who was that?" he asks, putting his black and white flannel shirt back on. His hair sits messy on his head, and his lips look shiny, like they are covered in… lip gloss?

"What happened to you?" I frown.

"Nothing." He's good at the whole innocent look. Most of the time, you can't detect his lies because he keeps a straight face until the very end. But this time, he didn't hide the proof.

I bring my thumb to the corner of my mouth. "You sure? Because you got some lip gloss right about here."

"Shit," he murmurs, wiping his mouth with the back of his hand.

"Let me guess. Rae's cousin? The one with the brown hair?"

He clears his throat, then raises his chin with that same innocent look on his face. "She jumped me," he offers.

"Nice try, McKay." I grab his shoulder and squeeze, but he quickly slaps my arm away.

"Whatever. Was that Kay with a new offer?" he questions, smoothly changing the subject.

"No, it was Hunter. He wants me to come to dinner tonight."

"Oh, sounds like fun."

"And bring Rae," I add.

Bodi whistles, the corner of his mouth raising. "Bringing her to dinner parties. Pretty official, huh?"

"We are at her birthday with her entire family. I guess we're past the casual phase, anyway. Besides, it's fried chicken at Hunter's. That's hardly a dinner party."

"If the wife of the inviting party is cooking," he starts

with his best posh imitation, which is still crap, "and the wife of the attending party is asked to join—it's a dinner party."

"Whatever, asshole. You wanna come?"

"Nah, if you two are bailing, I think I'll go and have some more fun with her cousin."

"You do realize she's ten years younger than you are?" I cock an eyebrow, a smile breaking through.

"It's not like I'm going to marry the girl. We're just having fun. Besides, I'm not third-wheeling your dinner party."

We both walk back into the yard, looking over all the guests circling around the birthday cake.

"When are you going to tell her?" Bodi asks, nudging his chin toward Rae.

The question could mean anything, but I know what he's asking. I know because I've been looking for the right moment since yesterday, hoping I could corner her long enough tonight to tell her how I feel.

How I really feel.

But now that I'm surrounded by a few dozen of her closest friends and family members, that doesn't seem to be a good idea.

"Tomorrow," I say, firmly. "I'm taking her out tomorrow, and I'll tell her."

32.

I feel his eyes on me, and I twist my head to meet his gaze.

"Are you sure you didn't want to stay?" he asks.

"Pfft, are you kidding me? I didn't even want a party in the first place." When he asked me to follow him, I eagerly jumped up, more than ready to avoid another curious look my way. I don't think I can handle one more person asking what is going on between Jensen and me without acting like a bitch. The question bothers me because I don't have an answer. It reminds me of the uncertainty that I know is hidden somewhere. I can feel it in my bones, even though I try my hardest to ignore it.

"Your family isn't going to get pissed?"

I snort. "Have you ever seen me at a Knights party past midnight? I bail on every party, including my own. I think they're surprised I stayed for as long as I did."

Normally, I'd stay an hour, then Kayla and I would go hang out at the riverbank with friends. Even though she's four years younger than I am, she's always been one of my best friends. When she was fourteen, I'd drag her everywhere with me. Wherever I went, she followed. And as a fourteen-year-old being allowed to run around with the seniors? She was happy to do so. Considering she ditched me for Bodi within the hour, I was more than happy to oblige when Jensen asked me if I wanted to sneak out with him.

Like two teenagers, we tiptoed out of the kitchen before we ran to the front door, laughing and getting into my car as fast as we could. Most of my happy thoughts are before the crash, but ever since Jensen barged in, my heart seems to shine more every day. Like a slowly polished gemstone, showing more of its brightness bit by bit.

"Where are we going anyway?" I ask when he takes the interstate that goes to Raleigh.

A smirk forms on his face, then he reaches out to grab my hand. He twists his fingers through mine, placing our hands on his lap as his thumb starts to brush my thumb. There it is again, that infinite flutter. That feeling of bliss I'd like to keep forever.

"Are you hungry?" He kisses my hand, never letting go, and when I nod in agreement, I'm not just hungry for food. My skin pebbles in longing, desperate for him to kiss me everywhere. I'm hungry for him, and right now, I'm wondering if my appetite will ever be satisfied.

"Always." I smile.

"Get your head out of the gutter, woman," he grunts.

"Fine."

He lifts my hand, pressing a soft kiss against my fingers as we continue to ride in a comfortable silence.

"Braedon?" I question, thirty minutes later, when I read the sign on the side of the road. "What's in Braedon?" The vibration of the car is calming me.

"A friend of mine."

My eyes widen, and I swallow in surprise.

"We're going to a friend?" I know he just met my entire family, but for some reason, meeting his friend for dinner seems pretty official.

"He and his wife asked us to come over for dinner," Jensen explains.

"He and his wife? So, it's a dinner party?"

"You sound like Bodi. Saying how dinner with a couple is a dinner party."

"Bodi is right," I deadpan.

"Baby, it's just a friend and dinner, okay. Don't panic. It's casual, really."

When I stay quiet, I glance over at him. My lips are pressed together in a straight face, but really, I'm suppressing a beaming smile, trying to act casual. Deep inside, I'm excited he wants to bring me to meet one of his friends. Maybe it's not as official as meeting his family, but it certainly is something.

"You good?" His eyes hit me with worry. See, it's *something*.

"I'm good. I'm excited to meet them."

Relief washes over his face, combined with a sigh. "Okay. Good. That's good."

The look on his face makes me believe this is a big deal for him too. It makes me want to put on my big girl pants and ask him to stay. To be with me and figure out what's going on between us.

Five minutes later, he parks behind an old truck in front of a white house. Roses give the home a cozy feel, and as I look at the swinging bench on the porch, I can imagine that being someone's favorite place. We exit the car, and when Jensen is caught up with me on the grass, he grabs my hand, shooting me a sweet smile. My cheeks flush red as I push a strand of my blonde hair behind my ear. That weird feeling inside of me seems to intensify by the moment, and if he keeps giving me this Jensen, I think I'll just combust into flames before dinner is over. When walking up the porch steps, he places himself in front of me, cupping my cheek.

"It will be fun. Don't worry." I'm not sure if he's convincing me or himself, but I love how considerate he is being. He presses a kiss to my forehead, then leads us to the front door. Before either of us can ring the doorbell, a loud bark sounds on the other side of the door. Hearing some muffled commands, the bark dies down. I straighten my shirt with one hand, the other still intertwined with Jensen as we wait until the door opens and a tall, handsome guy smiles at us.

"Jensen! So glad you could make it!" I cock my head a little, staring at his familiar face. A black snapback sits backwards on his head, giving him a boyish look, yet his physique shows he's all man. My head cracks, wondering where I've seen him before, until my eyes bulge when I finally see it.

"You're Hunter Hansen," I blurt, more starstruck than I intended.

Smooth, Rae.

He brings his attention to me with a kind smile on his face as he offers me his hand. "And you're Rae Stafford. Nice to meet you." He winks.

I hold his hand for a second too long, and I can see a slight glare forming on Jensen's face, clearly not impressed with the gawking look I'm sending his friend.

"What?" I shrug. "It's not every day you meet a champion."

"I just won the Stanley Cup," Jensen deadpans, a little offended.

"Aah, don't be jealous." I wrap my arms around his waist,

looking up at him with fluttering lashes. "You're still my number one."

He grunts, narrowing his eyes, but still gives me a kiss, indicating he's satisfied for now. "You men have such big egos," I joke.

"Don't I know it." A gorgeous woman appears behind Hunter, beaming at me. Her dark blonde hair perfectly frames her face, and her sea-green eyes are laced with a sense of comfort, making me instantly like her. "I'm Charlotte."

I give her a short wave, glancing at her belly. "I'm Rae. Congratulations."

"Thank you!"

"How far along are you?" I ask, admiring her feminine curves.

"Twenty-one weeks." Charlotte proudly rubs her stomach.

Her belly is petite, covered by a denim dress shirt, but she has that pregnancy glow that people always gush about.

She looks beautiful.

"Nice to finally meet you, Jensen."

"Likewise, Charlotte." He gives her a slight nod.

"Well, come on in," she says. "I made fried chicken."

I freeze, feeling the corner of my mouth rise, splitting my face in half. Slowly, I twist my head toward Jensen looking at me with amusement.

"She made fried chicken."

"I know."

"You know?" I parrot, incredulous. We all walk into the house, and the smell of fried chicken enters my nose. I inhale deeply, my mouth watering just thinking about it while my stomach roars in excitement. "You didn't tell me we were having dinner at Hunter Hansen's house," I hiss, squeezing his side, as we walk into the big kitchen. "*And* you forgot to mention his wife is making fried chicken. We should've brought flowers or something. Wine, chocolate, anything! You get deduction points, *hockey boy*."

"I'm sorry, but *you* forgot to mention it's your birthday." I quickly glance between Hunter and Charlotte as we follow them into the kitchen, hoping they didn't hear him.

"*Today*." He emphasizes loudly, and I look for any hiding spots. When I can't find any, I give him a pained look, feeling like I want to crawl to China right now. A lazy grin forms on his lips, and he grabs my elbow, tucking me against his chest.

"I'm free of getting deductions today, you little witch." He folds his arms around my body, tickling my side before pressing a kiss to my hair.

"Hold up." Charlotte frowns from behind the white breakfast bar, the sound of boiling oil going through the room while we all look at her. "It's your birthday?"

I sheepishly give her a smile while Jensen still holds me tight in his arms. I'm glad he is, because really, I want to bury myself into his body, having no clue what they will think of me. Birthdays are not a big deal for me, but I know they are for everyone around me, always making me the odd man out whenever it's that time of the year again. After my parents died, I didn't feel the need to celebrate my birthday. The only reason I traveled back to North Carolina for it every single year was because Nana demanded it. And well, you don't say no to Nana.

"Yup. She forgot to mention it in the last seventy-two hours. I found out when we walked into her surprise party this afternoon."

Hunter and Charlotte exchange a look, a little perplexed. I wish I was a mind reader right now, because even though I normally don't care what people think of me, for some reason, I want to make a good impression on Jensen's friends.

And this doesn't make it seem like I'm doing a great job.

"Why didn't you tell him?" Hunter finally asks. I look for judgement with narrow eyes, but I can't find anything but curiosity.

"I didn't want to make a big deal out of it."

"I get you," Hunter approves. I glance between him and Charlotte, but I can't read her at all, so I anxiously wait for her to say something. She can't be a lot older than I am, but she holds herself with a confidence I admire, making me look up at her. Wanting to get on her good side. Although she doesn't look like she has a bad side anyway.

"Yeah," she finally begins, slightly shaking her head, "not gonna lie, I'd be pissed."

"I am," Jensen replies, indignant, though a smile haunts his face.

"This one tried that with his eighteenth birthday." Charlotte points her thumb toward Hunter before she turns her back to us to check on the chicken, while Hunter dives into the fridge.

"Yeah, she was not amused," Hunter titters, holding out a beer to Jensen. "Beer?" he asks when his hazel brown eyes land back on me.

I shake my head.

"Charls makes a good Dark 'n Stormy," he then offers.

"Oh. Yes, please!" I reply, then turn my focus back to Charlotte. "What did you do?"

She meets my eyes over her shoulder, a devilish grin forming on her pink cheeks. "Hit him over the head."

My eyes grow wide, pushing back a laugh when I imagine this tiny woman hitting the world's greatest fighter. Hunter shrugs, not even denying it, and I laugh even harder, kinda surprised. Thankfully, it makes the insecurity leave my body, and I relax in Jensen's arms still circling my waist, enjoying the warmth of his body against my cheek.

"You got beat up by your woman, Hansen?" Jensen mocks.

There is a level of comfort created around me that has me grinning from ear-to-ear. I want to ask Charlotte if I can help her with anything before my attention is grabbed by a soft whine coming from the screened-in porch door. Behind it stands a big brown dog with fluffy hair, looking like a big teddy bear. He's staring at me with gooey eyes, silently begging to come in.

Hunter sighs, then walks over to open the door for him.

"Oh, he's so cute!" I break loose from Jensen to go and hug the most adorable dog I've ever seen. He wiggles his tail in excitement, pressing his nose against my cheek when I lower myself to give him a good rub.

"He really isn't," Hunter mutters, taking a pull from his beer.

"Don't listen to him." Charlotte comes next to me, petting the dog with a loving look on her face. "This is Bruno. He came with my engagement ring."

My heart melts. "Oh my God. Really?"

Charlotte nods, her beaming eyes like a kid on Christmas morning. "I always wanted one. When he proposed, Bruno carried the ring."

"Who knew such a big bad fighter was really such a softy?" I mumble, only for Charlotte to hear.

"Ha!" she snorts, a face with triumph. "Trust me, in the end. They all are."

"I'm not," Jensen scoffs. "I don't do romance."

Charlotte huffs, amused. "I'll talk to you in a few months." Then she glances from me to him. "Or days." She gives me a suggestive wink, then walks to the fridge to make my cocktail.

"Come on, let's get outside," Hunter offers, and Jensen follows him to the porch while I stay back, taking a seat at the breakfast bar.

Charlotte makes us two cocktails, and I glance around the kitchen, until she turns around, tucking a loose strand of her dark blonde hair behind her ear.

"Hunter told me you and Jensen have been all over TMZ for the last week. That must suck." Holding two glasses in her hand, she takes the stool next to mine, placing one of them in front of me.

"Yeah." I blow out a breath, keeping my eyes trained on my glass while bringing it to my lips.

A little confused, I stare at her glass before looking back up to her.

"Mine is virgin." She cackles. I join her in laughter while the tension leaves my shoulders, the nervous feeling that was still lingering in my stomach now completely gone.

"You'd think that low of me?" She keeps tittering with a silly smile.

"I don't know?" I screech as we both shriek in joy, echoing through the entire kitchen. If there was any ice left between us, it's now completely broken. After a minute, we both manage to stifle our giggles and take a sip of our drinks.

"It's not always fun, right? Dating a celebrity," she says, stirring a finger through her drink.

My gaze finds hers in understanding. "How long have you and Hunter been together?"

She snickers, wrinkling her nose, then takes a big sip of her mocktail.

"Officially?"

I nod.

"Ten months." She raises her eyebrows with a knowing look, looking at me over the rim of her glass. I keep my eyes locked with her, waiting as she takes a sip and rolls her lips. "But we have a long history. We were best friends in high school."

"Really?"

"Oh, yeah. The not-spending-a-day-apart kind. When I look back at it, we've been in love since the first day we met, but we agreed on friends. After that, life happened, and the timing was never right."

"Then what happened?" I ask, hanging on her lip.

"It took him a while, but basically, he finally pulled his head out of his ass." She chortles. "He might be fearless in some ways, but he's always been terrified when it comes to admitting his feelings."

I avert my gaze, feeling her words leaving their mark on me. I know how Jensen makes me feel, and what I want. But I'm terrified to voice it, scared as hell that it might be the one thing that will make me lose what I have now. Even if that's not much anyway.

"Have you always been in love with him?" I ask, twisting my head.

"Yes." She pushes out a breath as if it still hurts to love him. "I tried to deny it, but it was useless. Whatever I did, he carved himself into my heart, and I couldn't get him out."

"How did you hold on?"

"I didn't," she admits. "At some point, I had to move on.

But like the asshole that he is, he strolled himself back into my life one day and refused to leave."

I shake my head with a laugh. "Those arrogant athletes."

"Right!" she bellows.

"Was it hard? Getting back together?"

"It was harder to stay away from him. I guess that's how you know in the end." A vacant look forms on her pretty face, and I watch her closely.

"What do you mean?"

"If you can't stay away. If you keep being drawn in like a magnet every time you are around that person. If your heart keeps holding on, even though it's already broken into a million pieces. To me? That's love." Her green eyes move back to mine. "It's shitty. But that's love."

My mind wanders off, thinking about my own heart. I've known it's been broken since I woke up without my parents. Knowing for sure it will never be mended again. Seeing how Charlotte looks at Hunter, even though she admits her heart has been broken into pieces, makes me wonder if I can do that. If I can give away my broken heart to some other hand. Hoping he will protect the pieces with his life.

I always thought I needed to hold what's left of it close to me until the day I die. But now, I'm not so sure. Now, I'm wondering if even though my heart is broken, if it's still capable of being loved.

JENSEN

After dinner, Hunter and I are out on the front porch, both with a hip pressed against the railing, and a beer in our hand. Deep pink and purple bands are painting the sky as they're slowly being pushed away by the coming of the night.

"Nice place you got here, man. Completely different from your LA shack," I say, glancing through the window.

"Thanks, man. It's Charlotte's family home. She has always lived here with her mom."

"You never wanted a new place?"

Hunter rubs his neck. "We thought about it. To start over together. Charls thought it would be weird for me, but to be honest, I've always felt more at home here than in my own home. It holds a sense of comfort, I guess. I don't know."

"No, I get you." There is a troubled look on his face, as if he has a hard time explaining it, but I understand what he means. I don't know everything about Hunter's childhood, but from what he told me, it wasn't fun. Charlotte saved him in many ways, acting like his lifeline.

"It's not just a house. It's a home."

"Yeah, basically." Hunter shrugs, letting out a content sigh.

We stay quiet for a while, staring at the sky.

"I hope that's in the cards for me. One day," I tell him, taking a pull from my beer.

"What is?"

"This." I open my arms. "A home. A family. *A wife.*"

"Well, rumor has it that your engagement is going to be announced soon." I look at my friend. His brown eyes hold a dare, and I can hear the words he's not saying out loud. I dare you to lie to me. I dare you to feed me your bullshit. A week ago, I would've. I would've told him Emily was a good girl, and we'd be a good match. But I don't think I have it in me to lie one more day.

"Yeah, not sure if Rae is ready for that yet." My mouth moves into a cocky grin, and his brows shoot up.

"So, you're really done with Emily?"

"Have been for a while now. She has hopes we will get back together every time we have another bullshit fight. She doesn't want to break up, but I'm not in love with the girl. Never have been. We were still together to make sure my father's election didn't get jeopardized, but I can't do it anymore. I can't give up Rae. I want her, man."

"Yeah, no shit, Jensen. You look like a lovestruck teenager."

"What?" I bellow, disbelieving. "I do not!"

Hunter holds his fist in the air, raising up a finger with every sentence that comes out. "You touch her every chance you get. You can't stop looking at her. You're smiling so much it's starting to scare the living shit out of me because I know you as a brooding son of a bitch."

"Like you?" I counter.

"Exactly like me! I was a fucking Grinch until Charlotte and I finally got together."

I eye him, taking another pull of my beer. "You sound like Bodi."

"Bodi is right."

I grunt, rolling my eyes. "If I'd get a grand every time someone says that."

"Well, Bodi is a bit brighter than you are, so don't blame yourself," Hunter taunts, and I hit his snapback of his head.

"Ay!" he chuckles, grabbing it from the floor to put it back on his head. "Just admit it, your head over heels for her. I know because I feel the same, man. I'd been trying to push it all away for years, feeding myself with bullshit, but when you know, you know," he pauses, "and I think you know."

I do know. Hunter is right. Bodi is right. Within days, I've fallen in love with this little pain in my ass that keeps me on my toes. She has me saying goofy shit, thinking ten times a day how cute she is, and *fuck me, where are your balls, Jensen?*

"Yeah," I finally admit, with a cracking voice. "I love her."

My chest expands as I finally say it out loud and suck in a deep breath.

"Told you." Hunter smirks, bringing the bottle to his lips. "You haven't told her yet, have you?"

I shake my head.

"Have you told your folks?"

The thought of my parents has me snorting in disdain. I've successfully ignored them for the last few days, even though I've been getting texts and calls from everyone in my family. It's only a matter of time before my mother will throw something in my face to make me do as she says. But I've been thinking about it for the last two days, lying awake with

Rae safely asleep in my arms. I've gone through every possible scenario, and none of them seems scarier than losing Rae. They can fuck up my reputation and trash my NHL career. They can disown me. They can make my life real hard, especially if my dad gets elected. But I don't care. The thought of a loveless marriage, to a girl I barely like, going to events that please my mother, saying the things my father wants me to say in the media, it all sounds like a nightmare. At first, I was okay, not knowing any better. I was fine with Hell, but Rae gave me a small taste of Heaven, and now I want it all.

"Not yet."

Hunter whistles. "Bet you're looking forward to that."

"Not really. They are threatening to end my career." When I say the words out loud, they sound ridiculous, but I've seen people with less end up with nothing just because they pissed my parents off. Blood doesn't mean shit to them.

"How the hell are they going to do that? You just won the Stanley Cup."

"They have people everywhere. I'm sure my dad can find someone in the NHL to get me benched just to mess with me."

I hold Hunter's gaze, who's blinking at me, then he shakes his head. "People are assholes."

"Don't I know it. I'm raised by them."

"You know I'm coaching in the USHL now?"

I frown. "I didn't. In Raleigh?" I ask, referring to the days he used to play hockey when he was a kid.

"Yeah. Peewees. Never expected to enjoy hanging out with twelve-year-olds, but it's fun." I've always known Hunter as fun and easy-going. He was a badass when he was in the fighting cage, but outside of it, he was the life of the party.

His bright personality has always been overshadowed by a pain that never left his face, though. If you didn't know him, you'd never see it, but I did. Hearing him talk about coaching the Peewees of Raleigh gives him a different stance, and for the first time, I can't detect the pain that's normally etched in his features.

"That's good, man. You got the girl. You got the family. You got the job. You got money in the bank. You got it all." Our gazes meet, and a pleased grin tucks on the corner of his mouth.

"I do, yeah."

I bring my beer to my lips, the bitter taste of hops landing on my tongue. "That's good. I'm happy for you."

"Thanks." The silence sits comfortably between us, before he twists his attention back to me. "I ran into Karl the other day."

I look up, my eyebrows knitted together, knowing who he's talking about. Karl Mitchels, head coach of the North Carolina Hurricanes.

"Karl?" I mock. "You're on a first name basis with the man?"

He chuckles. "I run into him once in a while. You know how it goes."

"Yeah, I guess."

"He told me he wants you on his team."

"He did?" I ask, cocking my head.

"Hmm," he muses, then points his beer at me. "But *your* agent shut him down before he could make an offer."

Yeah, that sounds about right. Kay has clear instructions.

"He has a *No-East-Coast* policy," I explain.

I know it sounds stupid for most people, but I really don't want to live on the East Coast. I'd rather take a team in

Canada or Russia before I start playing for a team this close to my parents.

"Why?" Hunter asks, confused.

I push out a breath, a grunt following with it. "Because I don't wanna live on the East Coast."

When he hears the words, his eyes widen, suddenly realizing why I'm against living here.

"Because of your family?"

"Yeah."

He lifts his snapback from his head, running a hand through his brown hair. I can see the cogs spin in his brain, and I press my lips together into a small stripe. There are unspoken words sitting on his tongue, and I prepare myself for a preaching I don't want to hear. I've heard it all before. I'm annoying myself, giving myself the limitations I did, but I don't know how to deal otherwise.

"Well," he starts, his voice small, "are you still set on that now that you have Rae?"

I frown. "What do you mean?"

"She lives *here*. In North Carolina. She made it pretty clear she's not going back to LA. You love her. You *just* said that."

I haven't even thought about that. I've been so wrapped up in finding enough balls to face my family to either accept her or go fuck themselves. I haven't thought about how Rae is not coming back to LA. In my head, we'd been waking up in my bed every single day, but not once had I taken into consideration that we will be miles apart after this weekend.

"You going to do long-distance with her?"

"No." I blurt, then clear my throat with frustration, rubbing my face. "I don't know?" Fuck, I don't want to do long-distance. I want to wake up next to her every day. I want

292

to cook her breakfast on Sundays and surprise her with fried chicken whenever the fuck I want.

"I didn't think about the how," I confess, a troubled look on my face. A heavy feeling now sits in my stomach, while a slight panic creeps up my spine.

Charlotte's voice sounds from the house, calling out to her husband, and he pushes away from the railing, giving me a reprimanding look that doesn't help.

"Well, you gotta figure it out. But something tells me she isn't going to settle for long-distance, not after what you told me Kent did to her."

"Tell me about it."

Her ex cheated on her from under her nose. I know she knows I'm not Kent, but I doubt she'll be happy with face-time dates and virtual kisses.

"The Hurricanes offer still stands and let me tell you something, it's a damn good offer. Better than any one I ever got. Besides, you were already planning on telling your folks to fuck off. Why stop now?" He smirks, walking backwards toward the door, like a fucking know-it-all, but I can't fully hide the smile that's trying to push through. I know he's right. Rae is the first step, but if I want her, I'll have to take control of my life in every way I can. No matter where I live.

"Just think about it," Hunter says before he walks through the door, leaving me alone with my thoughts.

Just think about it.

Right, I can do that.

34

I'm staring out of the window as we drive back home, a shitstorm of feelings sitting in my chest. It's like every time I tell myself to not make this thing between us any bigger than it is, Jensen will find a way to touch me, hug me, make my skin burn, and press a kiss on top of my head. My father was like that with my mother. Affectionate, sweet. He was the no-nonsense lumberjack kinda guy, with his flannel shirts and thick beard, but make no mistake, he was a pushover when it came to his wife. He loved her dearly. It was visible in every single touch. Every single look. It's the same look Hunter gives Charlotte when she does nothing more than walk across the room. His hazel brown eyes filled with amazement every time he looked at his wife.

Today, I've caught Jensen looking at me with that same admiration, and my heart can't help hoping I'm not imagining, while my sanity tells me to run fast. Run fast before it's too late. Before the last that's left of my heart shatters into a thousand irreparable pieces, leaving me broken forever. And then there's Charlotte's words, still lingering in my head like a song you can't get out.

"Can't I just sneak into your room tonight?" He gives me

a playful wink that has me gasping for air for more than one reason.

"No. If Nana finds out, she will drag you out of there in the middle of the night. Let's save ourselves from that kind of embarrassment," I say, feeling heat creep into my neck.

"Sounds like a challenge."

"Jared James Jensen," I scold, narrowing my eyes, though it's hard to keep glaring at him when he's giving me that lopsided grin.

His eyes darken, and he rolls his lips. "My name has never sounded as sexy as it does when it comes from your lips."

"Don't look at me like that."

"Like what?"

"Like you're about to swallow me whole."

He laughs. "Don't give me any ideas, then." The back of his hand brushes my blushing cheek before he turns his attention back to the road. A happy feeling crawls inside of me, still enjoying the perfect ending of this day. Having dinner with Hunter and Charlotte gave me a sense of peace I haven't felt before. Looking at their relationship, the small touches, and the loving banter, it felt natural. Relaxed. I want that. I crave that. That sense of comfort my parents gave each other, combined with the safety of a place to call home.

I glance at the man that seems to make me burn from the inside, staring at his sharp jaw. He has a vacant gaze in his eyes, focused on the road.

"Are you okay?" I cock my head.

When our eyes collide, a lazy grin forms, and my heart jumps.

"Yeah, I'm good." He grabs my hand, intertwining our fingers before placing them on his lap. For a second, I close my eyes, enjoying the warmth of his hand against mine as I pretend for just a minute this could be our forever. To pretend his father isn't New Jersey's next governor, and he doesn't have a reputation to take into consideration. To pretend we are just a boy and girl, enjoying every minute together.

"Do you ever wonder if you should change your path? If it's time for change?" he asks.

I twist my head, cautiously watching the troubled look that's darkening his face.

Is he talking about me? About us? Is this the part where he tells me that *it was fun, but I gotta go?*

Swallowing hard, I push the fear away that rapidly grows in my stomach as I feel my hand going damp in his.

"I do." I raise my chin, answering honestly. "That's why I moved back home."

There was nothing wrong with my LA life. It was fun; it was glamorous. It made me grow up. But in the end, it wasn't me. I knew this life was just a cop out until I was ready to face my demons back at home.

"LA is not me," I add, although I don't know why. I feel like I need to explain to him, to let him know I'm not going back to LA. Ever. And after that phone call with his agent, it became pretty clear he's not moving to the East Coast anytime soon.

"It's not me either." I can hear the sadness in his voice. His pained energy almost suffocates me. I want to wrap him in my arms and tell him everything will be fine, even though I don't even know what is hurting the most.

"Then why stay?"

He lets go of my hand, running a hand through his hair, and I hate the loss of connection. As if he's rejecting me.

"I don't know." When he glances over at me, I can see the confusion, the lost boy. It's only brief, gone within a second, but I saw it. He can hide a lot behind his cocky stance, ready to tell the world to go fuck themselves. But I see the craving for confirmation, for validation. The craving to be enough. I want to be the one who gives him that, but my own fear cripples me from saying anything.

So instead, I grab his hand once more, squeezing it, before I turn my focus back to the trees passing by, silently telling him I'm here.

I'm here, and I hope he doesn't let me go.

35

The next morning, I'm waiting for Jensen, resting my back against the car as I enjoy the warmth of the summer sun. My head pops up from my phone when I hear the front door open, and I stare at the sexy man walking down my porch steps. Hiding from behind the safety of my sunglasses, I gawk at him, keeping my face as straight as possible. His white t-shirt shows off his sun kissed skin, his jeans hang low on his hips, and his sunglasses cover his mesmerizing eyes. But it isn't until a smirk slides into place that my heart stops for a brief moment. Time seems to slow down as my cheeks soak up the burning heat of the sun, and I cross my arms, supposedly unimpressed. But really, I just try to hide my heart from jumping out of my chest.

He looks like a fucking GQ model.

"So, where are we going?" He nudges his head, closing the distance with big strides before placing both hands beside my head while I don't move from leaning against my car. A whiff of his fresh and clean cologne makes half my brain stop functioning as I look up at him. He leans in, brushing his lips on mine, and being greedy as fuck for him, I press my lips against his with much more vigor.

"Hmm, good morning to you too." A lopsided grin greets me.

"I don't know. This was your idea."

His lips find my neck, burying his nose in my hair, as he rests his hand on my shoulder.

"I'm starting to doubt that plan right now."

My eyes close, completely surrendered by his touch until the rest of my brain sparks back to life. "We are in my front yard."

"I know," he muses, undisturbed.

"Where I *live*."

"I know." He leaves a trail of kisses on my skin, each burning more than the one before.

"With my *entire* family." I emphasize the word. I'm pretty sure it will take Nana two minutes to realize I'm making out in the front yard and about three before she starts to yell to get a room, just to piss me off.

"I have a hard time keeping my hands off you," he huffs, grinding the bulge in his jeans against my stomach. "Especially when you're pressed against a car." He takes my hands in his, leaving me completely breathless as he covers my mouth in a demanding and dominating way. I knew telling him my dirty fantasy would make him horny as fuck, and I'm not complaining.

A grunt comes from my throat. "If you want to make my sex fantasy come true, I'm not going to stop you, but I'd really prefer it if we didn't do it in my family's front yard."

His teeth scrape the skin below my ear, a chuckle tickling the sensitive area. "Fine, let's go."

He pushes off me, giving me a wink, then rounds the car to get behind the wheel. A week ago, I'd never let him drive my precious car, but in the last few days, it's become such a familiarity to have him driving while I stare out of the window. I love the feeling of his hand on my thigh, knowing he's right there beside me as the trees pass by.

I show him my high school, my middle school, and even my pre-school. I tell him how I used to break my record every chance I got, by getting kicked out of class as fast as possible. I tell him how I spiked the punch at my sophomore winter formal. I show him the tree where I got my first kiss in junior high. I show him the park I used to play at as a kid, the community pool where I spent my entire summer when I was finally allowed to go by myself, and the cycling track where I used to hang out with all the boys. We buy chocolate orange ice cream at my favorite parlor, even though it's only eleven am, and we grab a burger at the local diner when it's almost lunchtime.

It's fun.

It's relaxing.

It's everything I never expected it to be with Jared James Jensen.

An infuriating, yet sexy, pain in my ass for the last five years.

But now it's all I want.

"Okay. I need one more." He wipes the corner of his mouth with his napkin, still chewing on the last bite of his burger. He's sitting across from me, looking hot as fuck with one arm propped up on the back of the booth.

"One more what?" I ask, smiling, before popping a fry in my mouth.

He rests his elbows on the cold surface, bringing his face closer to mine with that playful smirk gracing his cheeks. The one that weakens my knees and makes it impossible to resist anything he asks.

"Show me *your* place."

"What does that even mean?" I ask, rolling my eyes. With his dirty mind, it could literally be anything involving me naked. But when I see the sincerity in his piercing blue eyes, I understand he's asking for more than just a quick place to fuck.

He grabs my hand, my heart rate kicking up a notch. "Where did you go to celebrate? To cry after a long day? Where did you process everything life threw at you as a teenager? Where did you go when life got hard?"

I swallow roughly, my mouth turning dry.

"How do you know I have one?"

"Because in the last week, I've gotten to know you better than you know, Rae Stafford. And something tells me you're the girl that has a secret spot. Just for yourself."

I roll my lips, amused and touched by his comment, because he's not wrong.

But he doesn't realize what he's asking from me, because I've never shared that with anyone. It's my safe place, my comfort place, the place where I had my lowest of lows. But staring into his big blue eyes, I can't resist it. Can't resist *him*. Not when I see them flash with a kindness that's rare for Jensen.

I nod. "Okay."

His face splits, his eyes dancing with joy. "Yeah?"

I nod again, and he pays the bill with an excited smile spread across his face.

Ten minutes later, I direct him to a secluded place at the riverbank. It's a small spot, hidden between the trees. There is only room for one car, with barely any space to have as much as a picnic, making it less interesting for the young kids, and

I've always happily taken advantage of that whenever I needed to be alone.

He parks my SUV between the trees, and we both get out. The reflection of the sun shines on the water, as rays of sunshine push through the leaves of the trees. I suck in a breath of fresh air, then climb on the hood of my car like I've always done, taking in the calmness that surrounds me.

Jensen silently joins me, placing his body next to mine, our knees touching.

"It's not necessarily my happy place," I explain, his head twisting to look at me while he takes off his sunglasses. "But this is the place where I can order my thoughts. Where the world is quiet enough for me to process whatever life throws at me."

"Like when your parents died?"

My head snaps toward him, searching his eyes in confusion. "You know?"

He nods, grabbing my knee before he starts to massage my leg in a gentle and comforting way. "Is that why you freeze every time you see an airplane?"

I let out a confirming hum.

"Why didn't you tell me?" His deep blue eyes bore into me like he's searching for my soul, the tension almost making me stop breathing.

My eyes move back to the water. "I don't know?"

I hold still, sucking in a deep breath. "Because I'm sick of being an orphan? Because for once I didn't want that to overshadow everything I do."

I can see my words hitting him in the chest as he swallows with a pained expression. I know. It's raw. But it's honest. When my parents died, I hated the world, and for the longest time, I'd cry myself to sleep wishing I died on that plane too.

I love my family, and I will forever be grateful for everything they did for me. How they took me in and treated me as their own. But they are not them. They are not my parents, and it took me a long time to grasp that. But by that time, it was already too late. I was the rebel child, kicking and screaming through life, with whispers following me wherever I went.

Her parents died.

She is an orphan.

She is damaged.

She's broken.

I heard them all, and when you hear them on a daily basis, you start to live up to them. I was fourteen when I found out alcohol could make those whispers go away, not because they weren't there. But because I didn't care when I drank. I couldn't be bothered by anything, completely drowning in my fearless stance.

"Because people will expect less?" he asks, reminding me of his own words.

"Yeah." He told me how he acted like an asshole because it kept people's expectations low, making it that much easier. I acted like an out-of-control brat because people didn't have any expectations at all after my parents died.

"After the crash, people always treated me like porcelain. Always trying to say the right thing, to motivate me with kind words. But I could feel the pity. They had already put me in the *damaged* box because that was easier for them. More convenient. It's hard to be motivated when no one expects anything from you because of something that happens out of your control. To label you." I keep my eyes trained on the water, watching the ripples grow bigger and bigger every single time. Tears are pricking in the corners of my eyes, and I suck in a breath to push them away. "Johnny saved me by pushing me into a job he knew I wasn't ready for, and he expected the world from me." I pause. "Without telling me, he showed that he believed in me. That I was more than just that orphan kid from Red Wood Creek High School."

I can feel his fingers under my chin, and I close my eyes, not ready to see that same pity in his eyes, before he gently pulls my face toward him.

"Rae," he rumbles in a soft yet demanding tone. I hum in response, still keeping my eyes shut. A hint of his freshness penetrates my nose, combined with the whiff of the pine trees around us. It smells safe, like home.

"Open your eyes, baby." His breath fans my face, and I exhale softly, refusing to let my emotions out in front of him fully.

"Rae, open your eyes."

Finally, I let my shoulders hang, opening my eyes. When I look into his deep blue eyes, I see affection, something like love, I think, and even a bit of pride. His thumb brushes my jaw in slow, scorching strokes, soothing me.

"You've been pissing me off for five long years, but there is one thing I've known long before this week." He stops for a brief moment, a smile ghosting his handsome face. "You, Rae Stafford, can do anything you put your stubborn little mind to."

I chuckle, and when I close my eyes, tears find their way out. Bringing his thumb up, he wipes them off my rosy cheeks, then presses a kiss on my lips. But there is a difference in his touch, like something shifted, and we leveled up. His lips entwine with mine, and a satisfied moan vibrates against my throat, as his tongue starts to dance around mine in tentative strokes. Soft, slow, longing. A hand moves into my hair, holding my head as if he's scared I'll escape his touch. My heart races in my chest, at an exhilarating pace, yet it feels comforting, like coming home after a long run. A grunt comes from his lips when he breaks away, pressing his forehead against mine. His hands hold my head, compelling me to look him in the eye.

"There's also a lot of guilt," I confess, wanting to confide my darkest feelings to him. His brows knit together. "Before I moved to LA, my friend died. We'd been drinking all summer."

My tears seem to get free, and before I know it, my heart is flooded with emotions. "We all did it. We didn't care. Drinking made me feel less. And I didn't want to feel at all. It was wrong. I know it was." I stare at his chest, unable to look him in the eye. "We drove home completely fucked every single day. Nothing ever happened. We always got home safe." I pause. "Until one day, we didn't."

"What happened, baby?"

"Kelly, my best friend. She dropped me off at home. Then she crashed into a tree on her way home." The words leave my lips, and I'm now sobbing against his chest. His hand cups the back of my head as he comforts me with his lips in my hair.

"It's not your fault, baby."

"I know." I look up at him. "But it doesn't change the guilt I feel."

He pushes out a breath before holding me against his chest once more. "I know, baby. I know."

He holds me like that for a few minutes while I give my emotions the release I never have before. All my feelings and regrets come rushing out of my heart, looking like a flood, until finally it's replaced by a sense of relief. Until there is finally room for other things in my heart than just grief.

"I'm not going to New York, Rae," he suddenly huffs, a hint of desperation clear in his voice, "I don't want to."

I hold still, gasping. Shocked.

"I'm not going to let you go."

"You're not?" I murmur, placing my hands over his. The warmth of his hands underneath mine is encouraging, and hope starts to swell in my chest.

He softly shakes his head. "Not a fucking chance. You can tell me to leave. But I won't. I want you. I want to be with you, and I'll be damned if someone snatches you away in front of my eyes. You're mine, baby. I decided," he announces, that arrogant smirk sliding in place, "and you know I don't accept *no*."

I snort, amused by that statement.

"What about your parents? What about the elections? What about Emily?" I do my best to keep my voice calm, but my mind is running overtime.

"Fuck 'em. Fuck it."

"Really?" It's hard to believe him when he's been doing what he's told for twenty-nine years, but I really want to. I want him to choose me. I want him to stay. I want to see where we will end up together.

"I'm done letting my life be dictated for me. I'm gonna do what I want." He pauses, biting his lip. "And I want you. I want to see where this goes. I want you to be mine."

The persistence is clear, and undeniable. And the only reason he's still waiting for my response, my confirmation, is as a courtesy. Because we all know I've been fucked from the beginning.

JENSEN

I wait in anticipation for her to say something. Anything. My heart pounds against my ribcage, the blood running through my veins with a throbbing pulse. I'm not easily scared, but pouring my heart out to this girl has me frightened as fuck. I felt really confident when the words left my body, confessing I'm not ready to give up whatever the fuck is going on between us, but now that she's staring back at me with her brown Bambi eyes flashed with confusion, I'm not so sure.

"Say something, babe," I plead.

"Yes." It's soft, and my eyes widen, not sure if I heard her correctly.

"Yes?" I parrot.

Her face moves up and down with a breaking chuckle coming from her luscious lips.

"I want you too, Jensen. I want to see if this can work. If *we* can work."

Not willing to wait any longer, I suppress the twitching of my mouth, keeping a straight face as I slowly lean in.

"Good, because it might be a bit tacky doing this with some random hook up."

Smoothly, I jump off the hood of the car with a mischievous smile on my face.

"What are you doing?" Her brows plow together as I grab her hips with a rough tug, and she lets out a shriek.

"Making my fantasy come true." I push her back onto the hood while she keeps her head up, her eyes locked with mine. My fingers move to the button of her jeans, loosening them, before I reach for the hem of the fabric and eagerly pull her jeans from her perky ass.

"Oh, shit," she mutters as recognition flares her sparkling eyes. Biting my lip, I throw the blue denim on the ground, then slowly drag her grey lace panties from her hips until they are completely off.

With our gazes still locked, she swallows. "Don't you mean, *my* fantasy?" she quips, her voice hoarse.

I shake my head. "Not anymore, baby."

Then I tilt my neck to look at the sight in front of me. Her legs are open and wide, her pussy shining from arousal, all spread out on the hood of her SUV. It might not be my Camaro, but it's still the prettiest thing I've ever seen. She stares back at me with hooded eyes, her lashes fluttering as she pants when I grab her ankle. The sun shines bright on her vibrant face, the soft breeze blowing a strand of her hair over her cheeks. With my thumb, I rub the skin on the inside of her leg, taking in this image that I want to hold on to forever.

"You look amazing." I place a kiss on her calf, before starting a trail as I move my way up.

"Fuck, Jensen," she huffs when I reach the inside of her thighs. Softly, gliding both hands over the outside of her hips, I move them under her body, cupping her ass to bring her closer to my mouth, and she freezes when she feels my breath on her folds.

"I've been dying to do this since Atlanta. Since your dirty little mind planted that seed in my head."

Before she can say anything, I press my lips against her clit, taking the little nub in my mouth as I tease it with my tongue. She whimpers in my hands, and fueled by her small moans, I start to taunt the flesh directly around it. Gracing her clit with every kiss and every lick. The sweet and salty taste of her juices on the tip of my tongue has me groaning in pleasure as I watch her closely. Her beautiful face is looking up at the sky, her lips parted with her chin held up high, showing off her slender neck. She squirms under my touch, the movement growing my own desire. My dick presses uncomfortably against the zipper of my jeans, but my mind is completely dazed from the sweetness coming from her core.

That same rush of adrenaline surges through me with every game. The scratching of the ice echoing through the rink, while I glide over it, only focused on one thing; getting that puck in the goal.

I'm the puck.

She's the goal.

I delve into her center, making her cry out, before I push a finger between her walls while my thumb presses against her clit. She winces at the intrusion, her head snapping up.

"Oh, my God!" she cries.

I shut her up by sucking her inner folds in my mouth, twirling her around my tongue like fucking gummy bears. A whine rings in my ear, like a sweet melody, going straight to my already throbbing dick. Pushing her even farther, I press a second finger inside of her, then start to finger fuck her in a steady pace. My thumb circles around her clit, and I straighten my back, fully enjoying the view.

She has pushed her white t-shirt up, exposing her grey laced bra while she massages her breast with her eyes closed. Every time I push back in, she lets out a small yelp, arching her back to make me go deeper and deeper. The taste of this girl is addicting, and when I dig in, I want to tear her apart.

I want her to come undone, to be completely surrendered to me, like I am to her just by watching her smile. She pushes me to do better, and think about what I want in life, captivating me with her scornful eyes any time I'm being an ass. Having her below me in complete submission gives me the confidence to do whatever the fuck I want. In any way possible.

"Jesus, Jensen," she puffs, opening her eyes when I replace my thumb with my tongue once more.

"Shut up, baby." Flicking her clit with my tongue, I press her stomach down to the metal of the car, making it unable for her to move.

"Oh, fuck," she calls out, trying to break loose from my touch. "Oh, Jensen. I can't!"

Ignoring her, I keep going, building up her high until I feel her tense beneath me, and a feral screech erupts from her mouth. Her legs shake, and I run my tongue along her clit with a few more strokes until she goes limp, completely spent with her eyes closed. Her pussy drips from wetness, looking sexy as fuck, and I can't resist placing another kiss on her core, coating my tongue with her juices.

Bringing my head back up, I take a step back, looking at her lush body, plastered against the shiny black metal. Her legs are spread, her arms above her head as she pants into the sky.

"Do you know how hot you look right now?"

"My ass is burning on this metal, and my pussy is burning from your touch, so yeah, I have a good idea," she says, like a fucking smartass, smirking up at me.

I quickly grab her ankle, yanking her off the car before I catch her with her ass in my palms. Wrapping her legs around my waist, I bury my face in her neck, sucking on the skin below her ear.

"Cheeky little witch."

"Hmm." She tilts her head, giving me better access while her hands pull my hair. The sensation of the burn on my scalp goes all the way to my legs, and I close my eyes, breathing her in. My body completely overwhelmed by lust.

She pushes me back, her hands moving to my front, grinding her palm against the bulge in my jeans while she gives me a lazy look. A look that tells me *I'm tired, but I want more anyway.*

My hands are locked around her spine as she slowly starts to undo my jeans until they fall down, pooling around my ankles. I pull her hips against me, rubbing my hard dick against her soaking wet pussy. The friction of my boxers against her core makes her huff against my neck, her nails digging into my back as she holds on tightly. I fist her hair, roughly tilting her head to capture her mouth with mine again. A searing shiver graces my spine, sending new spirals of ecstasy through my body when our tongues smash together again.

There is more urgency every time I kiss this girl, as if my mark still isn't complete, and I'm doing my best to burn it into her body. To claim her with every collision of our lips, until one day, there is nothing left but a permanent mark.

"I'm all for feminism, equal rights…" I groan against her lips between kisses, "equal pay, and all that shit."

She pulls back, holding my chin in her hand with a frown. "What is your point, hockey boy?"

A lopsided grin slowly builds. "I mean this in the best way possible," I start, pushing a strand of her blonde hair behind her ear, my mouth hovering above hers, "but you are *mine*. I *own* you. You are spoken for, taken, booked for the foreseeable future. *Claimed.*"

She purses her lips with an amused glint dancing in her gold eyes. "Is that so?"

"Property of Jared James Jensen from this day forward."

A smile travels her face, closing her eyes for a second. "Those arrogant jocks."

"Just one, babe," I mutter, recapturing her lips in a demanding way.

Without wasting any more time, I push my boxers down. My dick eagerly springs free, and I push against the warmth of her pussy, relishing in her wetness as I run my shaft through her folds.

"Are you on the pill?"

She nods, eagerly biting her lip.

"You clean?"

Another nod.

"Me too. You cool with this?" Fucking hell, I hope she is, because I'm pretty sure I don't have a condom and she's too sexy to leave her all willing and wanting.

"Yes, Jensen. Come here. I want to feel you."

She jerks at my repeating touch, showing the whites of her eyes with parted lips. The sun is burning on my neck, but it's nothing compared to the burn that I feel rubbing my tip up and down through her heat. Being on fire has never felt this good.

Listening to her pleading moans, I finally push inside, then tease her by pulling out to go back to her clit, before repeating the process. Her grunts are getting more demanding, sounding like music to my ears, and when her eyes flash with a glow of carnal desire, I thrust myself inside of her, slowly settling in her walls.

"Fuck, you feel so good, babe." I throw my head back, looking up at the sky.

Pulling her closer to my body, I hold on to her hips, pushing in and out of her center. The softness of her walls on my dick feels like bliss; a hot shower after a day in the snow. Thrusting inside of her, she holds onto my shoulders, tilting her neck up. Leaning in, I place blistering, open kisses down her neck, teasing the area below her ear. "You're divine, baby." I take her earlobe in my mouth, scratching the soft flesh with my teeth as I slowly pull back. "You're the sweetest thing I've ever tasted."

"Deeper, baby. I want to feel you everywhere," she huffs against my lips.

Her hands move to my ass, pushing me to go deeper.

"Like this?" I roughly slam my dick inside her, and her body jerks, her eyes popping out of her head with a rumbling bellow fanning my face.

Her eyes close when I do it again, and she presses her forehead against my chest. "Yes, keep going. Like that."

Fueled by her directions, I pick up the pace, wanting to devour her. Wanting her to fall apart in my hands, completely shattered until I'm ready to pick up the pieces. I want to break her and make her for the rest of my life.

While I'm thrusting inside of her, she brings her head up,

looking up at me through her thick lashes. I lick the seam of her mouth, taunting, before nibbling her lip, then press a kiss to the pink flesh when I've let go. Her hand moves up to my cheek, staring into my eyes with an intense gaze. I want to take a snapshot of her face in this exact position, wishing I could frame it and hang it above my bed.

"It has never felt better, Jensen," she speaks softly, but with determination, keeping our eyes locked as if she wants to make sure I hear her loud and clear. "Your body colliding with mine," she continues. "No one has ever made me feel like you do."

A jolt of electricity goes through my entire body when I understand the meaning of her words, knowing she feels how I feel, but also wondering if I will ever be able to come back from this. From her. But I already know the answer to that question.

"I think you're made for me, Rae." I don't think, I *know*.

Driving my hips into her wet pussy, I feel my release building, and I put my thumb in her mouth, wetting it with her own saliva before I press it against her clit. She winces in my arms, and I hold her up as I keep thrusting inside of her, working her clit to bring her to the top of the hill. Each push harder, each pull faster. Her pants are becoming more frantic with every move, and when my muscles tense in my core, she lets out a long cry, like she's a damn banshee in heat. Whatever they may sound like. My face grows stern, closing my eyes as I feel my climax hit me like thunder, a feral groan coming with it before I fall into Rae. Placing my palms on the hot metal of the car, I do my best to hold myself up with my trembling legs.

Our gazes collide, and I watch how she bites her tongue

with a smirk curling in the corner of her mouth while I pant against her face, trying to catch my breath.

"Did you just fuck me on the hood of my car?" She sniffles.

"No, baby," I say, my voice sounding gravelly. "I ate you out on the hood of your car, *then* fucked you underneath the sun. *On the hood of your car.*"

"Show off." She gives me a playful push.

"Next time, it will be my Camaro."

Her face falls a bit, a worry written on her face, and I know exactly what's going through her mind.

"Hey." I cup her cheek and search her eyes. "I meant what I said. I'm staying. I wanna be with you. I don't know what will happen or where I'm gonna be playing next season, but I know I wanna be with you. We will work it out, okay?"

She closes her eyes, leaning into my touch.

Then her kissable mouth opens with a soft voice.

"Okay."

Rae

L ying in bed later that night, my body still glows from his searing touch and the burning sun. My cheek is pressed against the pillow while I'm wrapped under the sheet, staring out of the window beside my bed.

This afternoon was hot.

In multiple ways.

I know it has always been my fantasy, but that was more than I could've ever imagined. His hands on my body, looking up at the sky, the exposure of being naked on top of the hood, the thrill of being outside. If I wasn't already addicted to him, this one definitely tipped over the scale.

"I want you," he said.

Those last pieces of my crumbled heart hope he's serious, but I want to protect myself and be rational about it. There is a big chance that he will start playing for a team at least a plane ride away from here, or that his parents will force him to come home, force him to be with Emily. But right now, he's all mine, so I'm pushing the thought to the back of my mind. Deciding to enjoy him while it lasts in any way possible.

Tomorrow, it's Sunday, and we're going to the riverbank with Kayla and Bodi. Not sure what's going on between those two, but Kayla was clapping like a seal when I asked her if she wanted to come with us. I feel like a little schoolgirl thinking about bringing Jensen and Bodi to the spot where we spent most of our summers when we were in high school, excited about having a relaxed day with just the four of us.

In my head, I'm starting to make a list of stuff to bring, until my eyes feel heavy, and I slowly drift off to sleep. I've barely lost consciousness when I feel the covers rise and a warm hand snakes around my stomach. Before I can completely open my eyes and turn around, heat envelopes my body, a chest being pressed against my back. My body melts when a warm, open-mouthed kiss is placed on my shoulder, and I let out a deep moan.

"What are you doing?" I whisper, closing my eyes to enjoy his touch. He leaves a trail of scorching kisses around my neck that can be felt in my legs.

His hand moves under my silk tank top, massaging my breast. "I can't stop thinking about you."

"You can't be in here," I breathe, having a hard time voicing anything when my brain decides to shut off and enjoy the ride.

He softly bites my shoulder with a grunt. "I know."

"Nana will not be happy."

"I know." His blistering kisses continue.

"She will kick you out."

"Only if you're making too much noise, baby." His hand moves to my hips, brushing his fingers along the hem of my shorts.

"Fuck," he hisses. "You're wearing these silk pajama shorts again?"

"You like them."

"I'll like them better when they are on the floor."

Unapologetic, he pushes the fabric down my legs, and I hungrily push the rest down with my feet, giving him free access to my body. His fingers slowly move to the inside of my thighs, and I push my butt against his hard shaft, desperate to feel him inside of me.

"Now that I've found out how good you feel bare, my dick doesn't want anything else."

"This is a bad idea." He brings his finger up, wetting it with his tongue, then softly moves it through my folds. Pushing the flesh away as he moves up and down, a whimper coming from my mouth.

"Shhh, you have to be quiet, baby." Biting my lip, I close my eyes. The darkness of the night heightens everything I feel, each move more sensual than the other because of my lack of vision. Every time he moves his rough finger through my pussy, I wince in pleasure. When his lips find my skin, I moan in satisfaction. He knows his way around a woman's body as well as he finds his way around the rink. Knowing exactly what he's doing to me with every single move.

"Do you know how sexy you are when you're all flustered and submissive?" he breathes against the hollow of my neck, then dips a finger into my core.

"Ah!" I screech, overwhelmed by the intrusion.

His other hand claps around my mouth, then he gives me a reprimanding bite on my neck. "Be quiet, baby."

Keeping his hand over my lips, he keeps going on working my body like an instrument, and I feel completely surrendered to his touch. My ass is pressed against the bulge between his legs, and every time I move, I deliberately push my ass against it.

"You feel that?" he growls. "You feel how badly I want you?"

I nod, still enjoying how he plays with my clit. He circles, he flicks, he strokes, all thought out actions bringing me closer to my orgasm within seconds. The sensation builds in my stomach, my quads starting to clench until he stops.

"Nah-ah, don't come just yet."

Letting go of me, he pushes his boxers down, and I immediately feel his warm tip pressing between my cheeks. His hand moves over my pussy, lubricating the entire area with my wetness before he starts to run his hard cock up and down my perineum. The tip of his cock feels soft and warm, turning me on even more, feeling him so close to my other opening.

"One day, I'll leave my mark on every single opening in your body, erasing every single man who was there before me." His words sound like a promise that brings a smile to my face, wanting to be owned by him.

I let out a confirming grunt before he pushes the tip of his cock against my entrance, holding my stomach to tuck me farther into his body. I push out a breath, loving the feeling of him stretching me wide, my clit throbbing in anticipation. When he starts to move inside of me, his finger moves back to my front, touching my clit in tentative circles, and I gasp, loudly.

"Shhh, we can't wake up Nana." He chuckles, low and deep against my skin.

"It feels so good, Jensen," I cry, as quiet as possible. "You feel so good."

"I got you, baby." He keeps moving his shaft in and out of my body, with his fingers never leaving my sensitive nub and soon I feel the feeling of utter bliss forming inside of me once more.

"Good girl," he coos hoarsely. "Let it go. Come for me."

A tingling feeling alights in my stomach, spreading like wildfire until I feel my muscles tense, and I go rigid in his hands while he keeps up a steady pace as I ride out my wave in paradise. When my body goes limp, he grabs my hips, slamming his shaft inside of me at a frantic rate, chasing his own peak. With my head still lingering on cloud nine, I let him use me to his own advantage, accommodating him by keeping my body as still as possible. Finally, I feel how he presses his forehead against mine, holding in his breath, his fingers painfully digging into my hips. I feel how he comes inside of me when he exhales roughly against my skin and tucks me even closer against him. With his dick still inside of me, he softly kisses the skin underneath my ear, wrapping his arms tightly around my waist.

"Goodnight," he says, quietly.

"Goodnight?"

"I came here to say goodnight."

My brows shoot up, amused. "That's one hell of a goodnight."

"I know." He pushes a kiss against my shoulder, then pulls out of me before tugging my body to face him. He finds my lips in a heart-stopping kiss, then looks at me with his deep blue eyes. The room is dark, but I can still see the glistering look they are holding, staring at me with lust.

"I think I can go to sleep happily every single night," he pauses, and I feel a finger going through my folds again as he rubs his cum all over my swollen clit, "knowing it's my cum dripping from your sweet pussy."

A mischievous smile forms on my lips. "I won't say no to that."

"Good." He searches my face, the look in his eyes becoming a bit more serious.

"Tomorrow, I'm going to call my parents." My heart stops. "And I'm going to tell them I'm done. I'm going to stay in North Carolina until I know what team I'll be playing for. I'm going to stay with you."

I swallow hard, blinking as I try to process his words while he keeps staring at me. He's sincere. He wants to stay. Whatever happens, I have to take this. Take this moment.

"Yes." I nod. "Yes, Jensen."

He scoffs arrogantly, before a smile slips on his face.

"I wasn't going to take no for an answer anyway," he says before dropping another kiss on my lips.

I'm playing with the gemstones that have taken residence on the entire dining room table while I drink my morning tea. They are all kinds of bright colors, in different shapes with different meanings. My mother used to tell me how every stone had its own purpose. Aventurine, for confidence. Fluorite, for clarity. Rose Quartz, for love. When I was eight, she gave me a sterling silver necklace with a heart-shaped amethyst in the lock.

"This will protect you, wherever you go," she said.

I have never taken it off since that moment. After the crash, I was convinced that necklace saved me, and even though it could all be in my head, it works for me. It's part of me, and I don't feel complete without it. Sitting here, with all these stones in front of me, brings me back to those moments with my mother when we would search for the best stone for her jewelry line. Without thinking about it, I pair stones that I feel would look good together, then put them aside to do it again.

But only half of my attention goes into that. The other half is focused on the handsome man playing a game of catch with my little sister. The smile on his face when he talks to her has me melting inside, surprised by his hidden talents as a babysitter.

"Do you love him?" My aunt walks back into the kitchen, following my gaze before she takes the chair next to me. I freeze, wide-eyed, not sure how to respond, then put my focus back on the stones. We got rid of the elephant in the room, discussing how we want to see where this goes. If we can work. But talking about love is a whole other level.

"That's a pretty big question."

"It's also a pretty big feeling," she agrees.

I stay quiet, bringing my gaze back up. Jensen throws the ball to Lily, bringing out his toned arms and his ripped physique and, instantly, my heart rate speeds up. He does that to me. Just looking at him makes my mouth turn dry and my palms sweaty.

Is that love? I don't know.

"I don't know what love is," I finally say, softly.

"Huh," she snorts. "That's exactly what he told Nana when she asked him the same thing."

I snap my head toward my aunt giving me a knowing look. Her elegant face is framed by her wavy brown hair softly swinging beside her head with every move she makes.

"She asked him if he was in love with me?" I huff, embarrassed as fuck. Leave it to my grandmother to bring out the big guns before she even catches your name.

"Come on, sweety," she drawls as she keeps picking up stones one by one to check the quality, "you know your Nan. Did you expect anything else?"

Good point.

"Well, no, maybe not," I mumble. Jensen is chasing Lily, who keeps running away with a salvo of happy squeals.

"Why is it you think you don't know what love is?"

I shrug, taking a moment to think about it. When I think of love, my parents pop into my head. How they used to steal kisses, share glances from across the room. How they argued, but also made up with that same committed look in their eyes. But I know it doesn't always work like that. I'm not sure if you can fall in love if your heart isn't whole in the first place.

I survived that crash, and I made a decent life for myself.

But I didn't come out unscathed. My heart took a blow, being forced to walk through life as an orphan, and I never really recovered. My heart forever misses the biggest piece, and I'm not sure I'm brave enough to give it to anyone else. I don't think I have the courage to place it in anyone's hands but mine. Not like Charlotte and Hunter, even though I'd love to have what they have. But I don't think that's for me.

I can take risks in life, and I will never decline a challenge, but I can't live without my heart. That's mine. That's all I have, and I need to protect that with everything, even if it means that love for me is nothing more than a memory of my parents.

I've seen love; that's enough for me if it means I get to keep the rest of my heart unharmed.

"They wouldn't want you to be alone for the rest of your life," she tells me, as if she can read my mind.

"I'm not alone." Tears prick under the surface, and I swallow to push them away. "I've got you, Johnny, Chris, Nana, Kayla. I have a bunch of people."

"That's not the kind of love I'm talking about, and you know it." The tone in her voice is free from judgment as she places a warm hand over mine. I sigh deeply, closing my eyes, giving free access to the tears that now run down my cheeks.

"I'm scared, June."

"I know you are, baby. But that's what love is. It's scary."

I shake my head. "My heart isn't whole. I can't lose what's left of it. I can't lose anything else. I can't lose anyone else."

"You think that's gonna work? Look at that man and tell me you don't love him. Tell me you don't look into the future and see *him*."

I look at Jensen, biting my lip.

He's everything I never wanted, but I'd be lying if I'd say she isn't right. We've only been together for a week, but already, he has wormed his way under my skin, making it impossible for me to think about my life without him. Everything before him feels like a distant memory, a faraway past.

"You tell me you can't live without your heart," my aunt continues. "Do you think you can live without him?"

I want to say *yes* so badly. I want to be able to say goodbye and tell him *see you later* whenever our time is up, but the answer is no. Last night, I couldn't sleep because I wanted to remember every second that he was still in my arms, knowing he was about to leave me at some point. I know he said he wanted to be with me, but even if he's staying for now, defying his parents, it won't last. At some point, he's going to leave again, bound to whatever team he's gonna play for. I kept convincing myself that I was going to be fine without him, that he and I were going to have fun while it lasted. Until real life forces us apart. I know he thinks differently; I'm just trying to look at it realistically.

But every time I thought about next week, next month, and even next year, I imagined him being there. Standing next to me. Getting on my nerves about the little things. Kissing my neck when I'm not looking. Annoying me with his cocky behavior. Every birthday, holiday, Sunday. I imagined him there.

Even though that's what I want, my thoughts always end with the same sentence.

"We don't belong together."

"Says who?"

"Says everyone! Says his mother, who's basically trying to marry him off. Says the fact that we've been arguing about bullshit for the last five years! His dad is Asher Jensen. He's running for governor. They want him to fit the perfect picture, and he might be fine wandering off with me now, but I'm never going to be the perfect girlfriend, and I don't want to be."

"Yeah, because he seems like he's the perfect governor's son, right?" she mocks. "Stop finding excuses to ask him to stay. Just ask him."

"He already said he's staying."

June snaps her head my way, her brown eyes scolding, with little specks of gold dancing in around her pupils. Just like mine. They remind me of my mothers, the one thing I will never forget. When I was younger, it was frightening how hard it was to look into June's eyes. I love her with all my heart, and even though she isn't my mother, she's the closest thing there is. But after the crash, having her eyes aimed at me hurt like hell. Like my mother was watching me from a different body. Both comforting and terrifying at the same time.

"Then what the hell is holding you back, girl?"

She holds my gaze, her gaze filled with disbelief. "I've known the boy for thirty-six hours and I'm falling in love just looking at him."

"Yeah, he is easy on the eyes." I swoon.

"Rae, baby. Look at me." I turn my head, doing as she asked. "That's not what I meant. I'm falling in love with him because I see the way he looks at *you*. I see the way he looks at my girl, my niece, my *daughter*." Her words make my eyes flood, and I try to sniff away the tears. "It's the same way your father looked at your mother. It's the same way Christopher looks at me. He's *in love* with you."

"He really isn't. We like each other, sure. Have great sex, yeah. But he doesn't love me."

"Thanks for sharing." She pulls a face. "But you're wrong. You think he'd be playing outside with Lily if you were just a good fuck?"

I frown, letting her words settle, then I gasp for air, my head snapping toward Jensen, who's throwing Lily in the air. His laughter echoes through the yard, warming me on the inside. As if he can feel my gaze, he twists his head, and our eyes lock. For a second, it's like time stands still, and I can feel it. It's like lightning strikes me in an open field; there is no escape, there is no denial. My chest expands and goosebumps trail down my body.

His cocky behavior, his handsome smile, the asshole comments, all combined with the big heart that's hidden in his chest. He's designed for me.

He shoots me a wink, with Lily hanging over his shoulder, and I return it with a half sobbing smile before he gets back to their game. My heart is pounding like it's trying to escape while the clouds in my head are replaced by sunshine.

"Fuck." I place my hands in front of my mouth, shocked at the feelings suddenly flying in.

"Are you finally awake?" June smiles.

"I don't know," I confess, trying to let my emotions sink in. Suddenly, I feel light as a feather, my blood running through my veins with a throbbing pulse.

"What are you two girls doing?" Nana walks into the

kitchen. "Ah, sorting stones, I see. You used to love doing that with your mother, Rae." She pours herself a cup of coffee, then takes the seat in front of me.

"What's wrong, sweetheart?" Her eyes widen when she notices the tears on my cheeks, then she looks at her daughter. "Did that jock hurt her? I will hunt him down with his own hockey stick."

"No, mama. She *knows*."

"She knows?" A confused look washes Nana's face while June nudges her chin to the window. Nana looks around before quickly twisting it back, the confusion now renewed with a knowing look. "You're twenty-four hours late to the party, but glad you finally arrived, kid."

"Thanks, Nana," I deadpan, before rolling my eyes, then glancing back and forth between both women. "Now, what?"

"Now, you go and tell him," Nana says matter-of-factly. Like it's easy.

"What?" I screech. "No! I'm not just going to head out and tell him I'm in love with him. What if he doesn't feel the same?"

"You are blinder than a dead man if you honestly don't see how madly in love he is with you. He's out there playing with your little sister. If he didn't feel the same, he would've left yesterday. He's taking every minute he can to stay close to you."

"Hmm, and he asked you to show him around town yesterday too," my aunt muses.

"Right! He wouldn't do that if you were just a booty call," Nana adds.

"You sound like June now."

"It's true," she replies, bringing her coffee to her lips. "He feels the same, honey. I'm sure. Just go talk to him."

My mind is running on overtime, and the fear keeps me glued to my chair. Thinking about telling him how I feel freaks me out, while thinking about him leaving leaves me breathless in the worst way.

"Just do it. We'll be right here."

I look at the two women closest to me. When my parents died, they both took on their roles, giving me the next best thing. I trust these women more than anything, and seeing them both encouraging me to put myself out there, to offer Jensen my heart, it gives me the confidence I need. Even though I'm shaking on my legs. But it isn't until Nana stares at me with those same brown Bambi eyes, boring into my soul without even trying. "Your mother would've wanted you to have what she had with your father. You deserve to be happy, Rae."

Her words cut me deep, but I believe every one of them. I get up, sucking in a deep breath, holding my body up as my palm stays pressed against the table. I inhale softly, then exhale, doing my best to control my nerves.

"Okay. Wish me luck."

They both give me a supportive nod as they mumble a *good luck*, and I take my wobbly legs into the yard. Opening the back door, I notice Lily on the grass with her favorite doll, without Jensen.

"Hey, bubba. Where is Jensen?"

Her blonde head pops up, looking at me with her bright eyes. "He's on the phone." She points to the gate that leads to the front yard, and I walk around the house to find him. He's standing next to my car, his phone pressed to his ear, his back toward me. His hard back makes me want to wrap my arms around him and press my cheek against him, but instead, I wait until he's done with his phone call.

"Fine. Yes. I understand." He hangs up the phone, then turns around. My lips are pressed together in a tight smile, my eyes beaming as I swallow hard to not lose my nerve.

The features on his face are stern with a hint of fatigue as he lets out a troubled sigh.

"You okay?" I ask.

His eyes move up, a smile haunting his lips. His face is showered with hope as he sees my face, before it's quickly replaced by a dark look that has my smile falling and my heart dropping to the ground. As quickly as my confidence was raised, is as quickly as it's seeping out of my grasp. That feeling of love that was filling my chest in the last sixty seconds is completely replaced with defeat. The hairs on the back of my neck stand up, running a chill over my spine, because I know. I can feel it in my gut. I can feel it in the sharp pain in my heart that kills me inside, just looking at his ominous gaze.

It's over.

We're over.

39

JENSEN

The look on Lily's face reminds me of Della when she was younger. Her light blonde hair shines bright in the morning sun like Rae's, and her blue eyes are blazing at the world with an eagerness to explore. I still wish I'd remember how it felt to be wearing that childish, carefree gaze the entire day.

"You can't catch me! I'm the gingerbread man!" she yelps, avoiding my grasp as she runs over the grass of the yard.

"Don't be so sure, gingerbread man!" I leap forward, my arm circling her tiny body to throw her over my shoulder as a shriek sounds loud in my ear. Girly giggles come from her chest while I tickle her side, and she tries to squirm out of my hands.

The sound of my phone ringing in my pocket makes me hold still, while I still have her on my shoulder. Holding her up with one hand, I pull my phone out. "Hold on, sweetie."

Mom.

Great, just the person I was looking for.

Carefully, I put Lily back on the ground. "I'm sorry, sweetheart. I gotta take this. I'll be right back, okay?"

She gives me a slight nod with a cheerful smile, and I walk toward the right gate of the yard while I answer my phone.

"Morning, mother," I say, my tone bored. I've been preparing myself for this conversation the entire morning, knowing she was going to be calling at what time I was supposed to be arriving. After I acted out this conversation in my head about a dozen times, I just went with *fuck it* like I have been. So, here I am, thinking exactly that. She will probably throw a fit, but she's a grown woman. She will survive.

"I'm assuming you're arriving soon?" I chuckle at the bluntness of her question.

"*How are you, Jensen?* I'm good, mom. Thanks. How are you?"

"Cut the crap, Jensen."

"Mom!" I scold, amused. "Such vile language. What will everyone think of you?"

"I hear you think this is all very amusing, but I've been comforting your girlfriend for the last three days. She tells me you've been ignoring her calls."

My jaw ticks. "She's not my girlfriend."

I walk past the sheltered part of the driveway to the front yard.

"She is until your father is elected." It's unbelievable how you can basically sell your son's happiness for politics and still sound so sure of yourself. As if it all makes complete sense. Most parents would put their kids' happiness in front of their own, but not Kathleen Jensen. To Kathleen Jensen, I'm nothing more than an addition to her perfect picture, an asset gone rogue.

"No." I raise my chin, even though she can't see me while I press my back against the grill of Rae's car, looking at the house. I've only been fortunate enough to have stayed in Rae's family home for less than forty-eight hours, but it showed me exactly what was missing in mine. Rae had given the Lockheart's a hard time, being the heartbroken little girl that she was, but they continued to stay by her side no matter what she did. And even now, after all these years, they treat her like her own. My parents failed to give me even a fraction of the love she still gets every day. The affection, the encouragement. I've come to terms with the fact that it will never be my life. I can settle with that. But I will not settle with my mother telling me what to do any longer.

"No?" My mother sounds surprised.

"I'm not getting back together with Emily."

"Jared James," she huffs, a little indignant this time. "You're not serious, are you?"

I hate it when she calls me by my first name.

"Dead. I'm done, mother. I'm sure dad will become governor without my fake relationship."

I wait for her to throw a fit and start screaming in my ear, but she stays quiet.

"I see," she finally says, her voice soft and warm, making my brows knit together. My heart rate speeds up, realizing something is off. My mother isn't soft and warm.

A sigh sounds in my ear. "Okay, Jensen."

My eyes widen. "Okay?"

You know when someone says one thing and you hear something completely different? She might not be standing in front of me, showing me the expression that comes with it, but my gut tells me this is not an actual *okay*. It's not an *okay, let's do that*. Or an *okay, I understand*. No, it's an *okay* that makes goosebumps trickle over my skin, my brows plowing together.

An ominous feeling building slowly in my stomach, as I purse my lips in anticipation.

"I guess we can figure something out."

"We can?" I sound like a fucking dumb fuck, but I'm honestly flustered.

"Yes. I suppose we can."

"What's the catch?" I ask, suspicious.

"Nothing. I know you never really liked Emily. I'll let her know. Are you still coming to New York?"

A little confused, I clear my throat. I blink a few times while my hand goes through my scruff, and a weird sensation seems to surround me like a cocoon. I'm waiting for the relief, the happy feeling that I'd expect to settle in as soon as I told my mom how I really felt, but I'm just standing here… and nothing. Nothing happens.

"Actually, no. I'm going to stay in North Carolina for a while."

"With that girl?" Disdain is clear in her voice, igniting my annoyance.

"Her name is Rae, *mother*. And yes. I want to see where this goes."

"Probably to shit," she mutters.

I roll my eyes, a tightness forming in my chest. I do my best to keep my mouth shut, taking this win without making things worse. I'd expect her to go ballistic, so I should be happy with the outcome of my rebellion. Part of me is even wondering why I didn't do it earlier, but I still can't lose the nagging feeling.

"Anyway," she continues, "I'd appreciate it if you're home next weekend. We will announce your sister's engagement."

My heart stops. The blood from my face rushes down,

draining me instantly. I push off the car, pacing up and down the driveway.

"Excuse me?" There it is. That ominous feeling, entering the room in its full glory.

"Your sister's engagement," she tells me in a tone that shows exactly how cunning she is. "It's next Saturday. I get that you want to *explore* whatever that is with this trashy blonde, but I'm sure your sister would appreciate it if you could let that be for a day or two and be here."

"Della doesn't even have a boyfriend!" My anger has flared up within a split second, wanting to punch something. The grip on my phone grows tighter, as if crushing the device will crush my mother's devious plan, but I know better. She raised me.

"Well, she does now," she says matter-of-factly.

"She is seventeen!" I roar.

"He's governor McMahon's son. They will make a great couple. Besides, someone has to pick up your slack." I imagine her looking at her nails, a bored look on her flawless face. My jaw clenches so hard it hurts, and I let out a deep grunt while my heart falls out of my chest. I went through every scenario in my head, from accepting the ending of my career until moving to some small town in the Midwest like a forgotten child. Not once did it cross my mind that she'd be evil enough to use my little sister against me. She outsmarted me again, pushing me back against the walls with her freshly manicured nails. She is malicious, and even though that's old news, it never occurred to me how far she'd go to get her way.

"Does Della know?" I hardly believe my sister would agree with this, and as much as I don't want to keep my fake relationship, I can't let my sister take the fall for me. I can't let her ruin her life because I'm a selfish prick.

"I'll tell her tonight."

"You're a shit, mother. Do you know that?" I feel the words from head to toe, meaning every word. "You're a sick bitch, manipulating your children any way you can, as long as you get what you want."

She huffs, shocked, though I doubt the words will affect her. "I'm only doing what's best for all of us, Jared. Your father becoming governor will open more doors than you might imagine."

"I don't need doors to be opened!" I blast. "I just want to be fucking happy!"

"Well, so do I. We all have to sacrifice for our family."

"Pretty convenient. You never have to sacrifice shit, ain't that right?"

"I've sacrificed enough, Jared."

She doesn't get it. She will never get it, and I hate her for it. I hate her for being a shitty mother, and I'm dying to be fucking selfish and tell her to go fuck herself. But Della's happy face pops into my head, and I can't. I can't destroy my little sister's life like that. I'm selfish, but I'm not that selfish.

I shake my head, gripping my hair while I stare out into the street.

"I'll come home." I push out the words like they are venom on my tongue, a lump forming in the back of my throat.

"You will?" she questions, as if she's surprised.

Kathleen Jensen, people, the Wicked Witch of the East, the evil queen, and your worst nightmare all wrapped into one impeccable looking package.

"Don't you dare go through with that engagement! I'll be there before dinner."

"Now, Jared, let's make one thing clear," she chastises. "There will be an engagement announced. If it will not be Della's, it's going to be yours."

"Fine."

"With Emily?"

"Yes," I seethe, wanting to wrap my hands around my mother's neck.

"Well, glad we got that sorted," she replies with a contented tone, as if this was all a big misunderstanding. It isn't. It's fucking hell, and I can't seem to find a ticket out of here. "No more surprises, Jared. Or we will continue with the back-up plan."

"I understand."

"Great. I'll see you tonight."

40

JENSEN

When I turn around, Rae is standing behind me, and a hopeful feeling jams back into my chest until it's smacked out of me all over again.

"You okay?" she asks, her eyes beaming. The sun makes her blonde hair shine bright, her brown eyes peering at me with affection.

I shake my head, barely finding the words. "I have to go home."

Her head cocks, the affection immediately replaced with disappointment, and it kills me inside. I know I'm about to hurt her, to crush whatever is left of her heart, and I can't do anything about it. A trainwreck waiting to happen.

"What?" I can hear the confusion in her voice.

"That was my mother," I explain with a heavy heart. "I have to go home."

She snickers, her beautiful eyes shooting daggers, and she looks like she's pulling them straight from her heart. "I see."

She nods, as if she's trying to grasp her head around the situation, and I reach out to her.

"Baby," I plead, grabbing her wrist to pull her into me. To physically feel her against me, knowing I don't want to end it like this. But she takes a step back, bringing her hands out of my grasp with a look on her face that hits me right in the heart.

A look that's filled with regret and defeat.

Like she gave up on me.

"I'm not your *baby*, Jensen. Emily is," she snarls.

It's a low blow, but I get it.

I blow out a breath, running a hand through my messy hair.

"You know that's not true."

"Do I? Because you just told me you're leaving. You're going to New York. You're going to *her*."

"They are forcing my sister to get married if I don't. I don't have a choice."

"Bull. Shit," she sneers. Her gold eyes are now sparkling with anger. It's the same look she's given me for the last five years, before this, before our road trip, but ten times worse. She's livid.

"You have a choice. But your choice is to be a damn coward. To hide behind your parents' wishes and demands."

"You think this is easy for me?" I shout, my fury rapidly matching hers. "You think I wanna go back to this political bullshit?! I don't! I'd rather disappear and become some John Doe in Bumfuck, Idaho. But my sister is seventeen! I can't let her get married to some pretentious Harvard dick because I'm too selfish!"

"So, that's it? You're just going to get back together with this girl because your parents want you to? God, this sounds like a cheap movie." She turns to walk back into the house, but I quickly reach out, trying to grasp anything to keep her from walking through that door. Pulling her hair, I slam her back against my chest, then grab her waist with both arms before I start to carry her back to her car.

"Put me down, you spineless asshole!" She squirms in my arms, but I keep a tight grip as I open the passenger seat and throw her ass inside.

Her legs are hanging out the open door, and I place my hands beside her thighs, caging her in with my body.

"Scream all you want. I live for that shit. But you do *not* walk away from me until we get this sorted. I'm not leaving like this. *We* are not saying goodbye like this," I tell her.

"And how exactly do you want to say goodbye, Jensen?" she mocks, folding her arms in front of her chest. "As friends? You want a hug and a kiss on the cheek? Or as co-workers, with a pat on the back and a *go get 'em, tiger?*" She throws a fist in the air, then grabs my head between her hands, looking at me through fluttering lashes. "Or do you want us to say goodbye like I'm your secret lover, with passion and lust."

She presses an angry kiss on my lips, and even though I want to hold her tight and keep kissing her until I turn her anger into something else, the venom on her tongue has me breaking our connection.

"Stop. Rae. Please." I close my eyes, dropping my forehead against her shoulder while her hands rest on my neck.

"That's a *no* for option number three. Got it." Her hands fall down to her lap, and I can feel her slipping away. My body feels emptier as the seconds tick by, the time being my worst enemy right now. I just want more time with *her*.

"Rae," I plead once more, even though I don't even know what I want from her right now. I want her to not be mad at me, but I know she has every right to be. I want to tell her I'll come back for her, but I can't make her that promise. I want her to understand, even though I don't understand shit. But mostly, I just want her. I want her in my arms. In my bed. I want to wake up next to her every morning and hold her when it's time to go to sleep.

I want her to know that I *know*. That when Hunter told me, *"When you know, you know…"* I knew. I know she is. She is my endgame. But I can't tell her that now, not while I can't give her any guarantees of when I'll be back.

"It's funny," she snickers, cynical.

"What is?" I bring my head up, locking my eyes with hers.

"You keep acting like you're this tough guy, this NHL bad boy, doing whatever he wants, whenever he wants. But really, you're just a troublesome looking puppet." Her words cut through my soul like a knife goes through butter. With ease, making a clean slice from top to bottom. The worst part? She's right.

My jaw clenches, letting her words sink in while I never leave her eyes.

"When are you fucking gonna grow up and do whatever you want, Jensen? You're twenty-nine, for crying out loud. Act like it!" She pushes me off her, trying to wiggle her way out of the car.

"Stop! Stop, Rae!" I grunt forcefully, holding her back with my arm. "I want to choose you. I do. But right now, I can't. I have to figure some shit out first. You know I don't love her. I love *you*, goddammit!" My hand grabs her chin. "I'm *in* love with you, Rae Stafford."

I can see her eyes starting to sting with tears, her grief hitting me in torturous waves, but quickly, they are replaced by a sinister glare. "I guess you don't love me *enough*."

I physically take a lot of blows on a daily basis, being a hockey player. I always have a bruise somewhere on my body, but it comes with the territory, and I'm not a petty guy. It takes a lot to catch me off guard. But right now, I'm feeling sucker punched by someone from my own team. It is as if I'm being beaten down in the last round, taking a right hook to my face before the light turns out. This beautiful blonde successfully knocked me out, and she didn't even have to touch me to do it.

She roughly slams me to the side, and this time, I let her while my heart squeezes together.

She's wrong. She couldn't even be more wrong than she is right now. But I don't have anything to back my motivation up. I don't have anything to show for it right now, so I let her. I turn my head, watching her as she storms off through the front door. Hoping she will give me one more glance of her pretty face, I keep my eyes trained on her. Her moves are energetic, showing that feisty personality I've fallen in love with so quickly, and when she doesn't turn around, my heart cracks one last time.

41

I storm up the stairs at the same time June walks into the hallway. She quickly notices the distress on my face. "Rae, honey, what's wrong?"

I stop, looking at my aunt giving me a look of pity. I know it is because it's the same look everybody gave me when my parents died. A look I hate with every bone in my body. I don't want people's pity or for them to think I'm some damaged girl. But the truth is, I am. I've known this from the moment I became an orphan, but in the last week something happened. Jensen gave me a feeling I could be more than that. That I could heal with the right people around me. With him around me. I guess I was wrong. Hearts can never be glued, or mended. Once they are broken, there is no fixing them.

"He's gone," I answer, the words leaving my tongue with disdain. "Going back to his family."

June shakes her head. "I don't understand. It's so clear he's in love with you."

"He clearly isn't." I feel the tears pricking in my eyes as a lump forms in the back of my throat.

"No, that can't be, Rae. I'm sure. We all are," she huffs, incredulous.

I stare at her, feeling numb.

"You are wrong," I announce with a glare, then take the last steps to disappear into my room.

42

JENSEN

People pass by me with happy faces. People going on vacation or off to see the ones they love. Their happiness annoys me, souring my mood even more. For everyone around me, the world moves at a steady pace, but ever since Rae left me standing in her front yard, my world stopped spinning. On auto pilot, I called a cab, and in the same numb state, I'm now booking my ticket at the airport. The flight attendant behind the counter tries to flirt with me, but she gets nothing more than a tight smile before I thank her and continue my journey with shoes filled with lead.

The buzzing of my phone interrupts my sulking mood, and I answer it with a deep sigh.

"What?" I bark.

"Wanna tell me why Rae is crying her eyes out right now?" Bodi's voice rumbles in my ear. I can hear the disappointment.

"Not really," I reply honestly. Whatever I tell anyone, I know I'm to blame. I should've known my mother had something up her sleeve to make sure I wouldn't mess up their political plans. But I was stupid enough to think she'd never use my sister against me.

"Yeah, you can share that anyway, mate. This morning, you were all lovey dovey with the girl, saying you were set on staying with her. What happened?"

I grunt, raking my hand through my hair.

"My mother came in like a wrecking ball."

"Ew, J. I'm going to have nightmares now."

"Not the fucking Miley Cyrus one, dickhead."

"Yeah, I *get* that!" he screeches, indignant. "It just happened, okay?"

"You're a fucking idiot."

"Says the man who just left his girl with a broken heart."

I draw in a deep breath, checking the screen in front of me to find my gate.

"She threatened Della."

He clears his throat. "How?"

"She's going to marry her off if I don't come home and get back together with Emily. At least until my dad is elected."

"That fucking bitch," Bodi mutters with clear frustration.

"Yeah."

I listen to the silence as I imagine how Bodi is trying to wrap his head around what I just told him while I make my way to the gate. I could've asked for my mom to get me the jet, but there is not a fiber in my body that wants to talk to the woman unless I absolutely have to.

"Okay," Bodi drawls, "but you're not seriously going to get back together with Emily for another three months, right? Before you know it, your mother will find a way to get you on your knees to put a ring on it."

"You really need to stop with the song references."

"I'm serious, Jensen!" he growls in my ear.

"I know!" If anyone has always been against my parents' wishes, it's Bodi. He's always been trying to get me to do whatever I want, even though he always supported me through everything. He's stood by me, pissing off my mom, because if I wasn't going to tell her to go fuck herself, that was the least that he could do.

"But I can't let Della get married either. She's seventeen, for crying out loud, Bodi!" I add.

"You're really underestimating your sister."

"I'm not. She will probably be brave enough to tell them no, but it's only a matter of time until they find a way to get her to agree."

"Like they are doing to you?" he counters.

"Yeah," I reluctantly agree.

"So, that's it?" Bodi argues. "You're just going to let her walk? Because I can tell you, she won't be waiting for you until you feel confident enough to pull your head out of your ass in a few months."

"Thanks for the encouraging words."

"Just telling it how it is, mate."

I grind my teeth.

"Does Emily know you're not going to be playing for the Knights next season? Does she know you're not going to be living in LA anymore?" Bodi questions. I listen to him, and I frown. Cocking my head as something crosses my mind, like lightning in a thunderstorm, lighting up the dark sky, I pause.

"No, she doesn't," I answer. Thoughts are racing through my head, wondering if I can find a solution with that.

"You'd think she'd be cool with moving to Canada? Or worse, Russia?"

I snort. "Hell no."

"Maybe that's your solution. Where are you?" Bodi asks when the calling out of my gate rings in his ear.

"The airport."

He lets out a reluctant groan. "Jensen, you're not seriously going to do this, are you?" He doesn't wait for my reply. "Don't throw your life away, man. I'm sure Kay will be able to get you a team that doesn't give a shit about what Asher Jensen wants. We just have to find a way to get your sister off the hook."

"I know. You're right."

"I'm right?" Disbelief is etching through his voice, then he quickly recovers. "Okay, so what's the plan? Do you have a plan?"

Shaking my head, a smile tugs in the corner of my mouth. "No, but I have an idea."

"Okay, ideas are good. What is it?"

"I need to make a call. I'll call you back."

Before he can say anything, I hang up the phone, dialing the one person who might be able to help in more than one way.

Anxiously, I ball my hands into fists, walking toward the gate.

"Come on. Pick up," I mumble. I need to have something to hold on to before I get on this plane, and I know just the guy to give me that kind of hope.

"Hey, man! How are you?" His cheerful voice sounds through the line, and I let out a relieved breath. Maybe this isn't all going to shit after all.

"Like shit. I need your help."

JENSEN

A rriving in New York two hours later, I walk through the gate when a surprising face greets me with a beaming smile.

"Finn? What are you doing here?" I throw my arms around my big brother, and he does the same, clapping my back in a friendly manner.

"Came to pick up my little brother."

Confused, we break loose, and I blink in question at the look on his face.

"Bodi called me," he explains.

I nod. I figured.

"He also told me what mother is hanging above your head."

I nod again, despair written on my face.

"Don't worry about it."

I chuckle, cynically. "Unless you're telling me that you'll sacrifice yourself for the wellbeing of your brother by marrying Emily, there's not much you can say that will stop me from worrying."

He pulls a face. "Sorry, man, I don't have high standards, but she's a little too dense for my appetite."

"Right." I grimace.

"I'm serious, though. She's not getting away with this." Finn gives me a serious look, his blue eyes holding no room for doubt. His hair sits styled on his head, and with a rolled-up navy dress shirt, he looks completely believable. "I didn't study law to sit by and do nothing when our mother is being a fucking psychopath."

"Then what the hell have you been doing for the last two years?" I joke, halfheartedly.

"I waited for you to wake the fuck up, but clearly, sleeping beauty needed a pretty blonde to pull him out of his endless slumber." He cocks his head, a mocking grin on his face.

"Does Della know?" I ask when we start walking to the exit.

"I haven't told her yet. I figured it would be best to wait until you were here." He glances at me. "But you know she's not gonna comply anyway."

"That's what I'm worried about. She'll tell mother to fuck off, and I'm not sure what mom will be holding against her. I can't let her fuck up her life to fix mine."

"Neither of you is getting your life fucked up. Whatever mother wants to pull, we will fix it."

We make it outside, and it all feels different. As if the world rushes by in a fast past, and I can't catch up. Don't want to catch up.

"It's gonna mess with elections," I say, still feeling this completely misplaced sense of loyalty. "If dad gets elected, that will help your position too. Help your career."

"You think I give a shit about that?" Finn asks as we make it to his car. There is an offended frown on his face that makes me feel like shit. The last thing I need is turning my brother against me. Right now, the number of people in my corner is nothing to get excited about, and I can use anyone I can get.

"I don't know?" I watch how his usually confident stance breaks a little, a misunderstood grimace visible.

"I don't, Jensen." He grinds his teeth, standing beside his black town car while I make it over to the passenger side. He's peering at me over the roof, his elbows resting on the black metal.

"I don't give a shit if dad gets elected either. I know it seems like I agree with everything they do, but I don't. Our mother is a cunning bitch, and I know she's always treated you like shit, and it's not fair. She let me do my own thing because I happened to have chosen a career they agree with, but I'm not going to sit by and watch her destroy your life. Or Della's."

A little stunned, I blink, realizing I don't know my brother as well as I thought.

"Really?"

"Yes, really, you fucking moron!" He lets out a frustrated breath. "If I have to choose between mom and dad or you and Della, it will always be the two of you. You always just assumed I'd go with mom and dad."

I rub my hand over my face, grunting. I really am a fucking moron. I've been trying to keep everyone happy, but not once did I ask what they wanted or how they felt about shit. Finn is right. I always assumed they didn't feel left out like me. That they belonged.

"You're not the odd man out, Jensen," Finn continues, as if he can read my mind. "We all are. Della. Me. You. You're just really shit at hiding it." He chuckles.

I hold his gaze, our blue eyes showing me exactly how alike we are for the first time. Like he took off his mask, and a face of recognition locks with mine. My shoulders relax a bit as I open the door to throw my bag in the car, then I mirror his stance with my elbows on the metal.

"I envy you, you know?" Finn says, before I can say anything.

"Me?" I blurt incredulously. "Why the hell would you envy me?"

"Because you always had the balls to do whatever you wanted." Pride flashes in his eyes.

"Pfft, don't feel like that," I scoff.

"Maybe. But you wouldn't be the best defender in the NHL if you weren't brave enough to face mom and dad when you did."

"I'm a coward, Finn."

"No!" He slams his palm on the metal. "You're a good brother, and a good son." He pauses. "I know your loyalty. You're a better guy than you like to think. I know that. Della knows that. Bodi knows that." Another pause as he directly looks at me. "Rae Stafford knows."

I stay quiet, my nostrils flaring as I slowly breathe out.

"She hates me, Finn."

I get into the car before Finn does the same and gives me an encouraging look. "She'll come around, J."

"Let's hope so. Gotta fix this mess first."

He starts the car, and we both buckle up.

"We will." He drives his car out of the parking lot and back toward the city. "We just gotta figure out what they are planning to blackmail Della with."

BEING in New York gives me more anxiety than normal when I watch the city pass by me. The crowded streets increase my level of stress, making me realize how good I felt in North Carolina and how much I don't belong in this big city anymore. When we arrive at our parents' townhouse, Della storms out of the house with her suitcase trailing behind her as she comes down the concrete steps.

Startled, Finn and I share a look.

"What the hell," Finn mutters at the same time our mother stalks after our sister. Finn and I both jump out of the car, and Della jumps into my arms the second I'm within an arm's length.

"She is crazy!" she cries.

Protectively, I wrap my arms around her, cupping her head. "What's wrong? What did she do?" I ask, resting my chin on her dyed black hair.

"You get back here, young lady!" My mother stalks down the steps, reaching for my sister.

"Hold up!" Finn jumps in front of her, towering above her. "What's going on, mother?" He straightens his back, making every inch of his length count.

My mother takes a step back, a little startled by the defensive stance of her oldest. She pulls her dress straight, lifting her chin in the air. "Nothing! We're just having a discussion."

"A discussion about what, *mother?*" My anger is reaching a boiling point, and I want to erupt like a damn volcano just looking at my mother's sour face. She looks flawless on the outside, with her hair up in a perfect knot and wearing a black designer dress that's probably highly overpriced. The disdain is dripping from her face, and for the first time in my life, I see her for what she really is to me.

Nothing.

She bore me, but other than that, I have no clue who this person is.

"Jensen," Finn warns, keeping his focus on our mother's blue eyes, which are now shooting daggers at all her children instead of just me. "Speak, mother."

She pulls her head back, a frown creasing her Botox-filled face. "Excuse me?" she snorts. "You do not get to talk to me like that, Finn Jensen."

"I'm thirty-one years old, *Kathleen*. I can speak to you however I want."

Her eyes widen simultaneously with her mouth. "Watch your mouth, Finn, or I will–"

"You will what?" he barks. He takes a step forward, and she automatically takes another step back, swallowing her confusion away. "Force me into an arranged marriage like you've been doing with Jensen? Or how you're threatening to do with Della?"

She looks past Finn, locking her eyes with mine. They narrow, and her lips curl into a smile that doesn't match her eyes. "You." She points at me. "This is all your fault."

She stalks toward me, and quickly, I push Della behind my back, protecting her from my mother's grasp.

"If you would've just done what you're told, your sister wouldn't have to pick up where you left off! You're a selfish little bastard!"

"*I'm* a selfish bastard?" I shout, finally giving my rage free rein. "Everything I've fucking done is for this fucked up family! Because you and dad won't stop until he's the fucking president! You two don't give a shit about us. We're nothing more than your damn pawns! Did you ever care for us once?!"

I already know the answer, but it still hurts when she has

the guts to speak the words out loud. When she finally completely shows the true darkness of her soul.

"I didn't carry and push out three children for them to fuck up everything your father and I planned for! You were supposed to complete the picture! Not break it!"

Her icy eyes grow dark while the heat flushes the fair skin of her cheeks. She snaps her mouth shut, realizing what she just confessed, and we all just stare at her, completely fazed.

"We are just a means to your end? All three of us?" Della asks, softly. She takes a step forward, placing herself next to me, and I look down at her pretty face. Her cheeks are stained with tears and the disappointment is visible in her features. Comforting her the best I can, I throw my arm around her shoulder, so she knows I'm here. But really, I want to drag her away from this and protect her from the defeat she must be feeling. I know, because it's an emotion I've been carrying with me for the last twenty-nine years. The only way to please Kathleen Jensen is to jump through her hoops, but make no mistake—she is not capable of love.

When my mother sees Della's horrified face, she changes her stance, quickly shifting back to the loving and caring mother she pretends to be when we're in public. "Of course not, honey. I love you very much."

I can't call her out on her lie, but I know it is one.

Della shakes her head. "I don't believe you."

"Look, I'm sorry your brother and I don't get along, but it's not true. Of course, I love you. Come on, let's get inside, and we'll discuss this."

"No," I say, firmly.

My mother's brows rise to the sky. I ignore her, dipping my chin to look at my sister. "You can come live with me if you want to. It's your choice."

"If you leave with him, we will *not* be paying for Yale, young lady!" mother says, snapping back to her devilish self in a split second.

I chuckle, not believing my ears, and I hear Della gasp next to me before she purses her lips. Her eyes grow shut, and she shakes her head while Finn and I look at each other. He swallows hard, his shoulders tense, with his fingers balled into fists. Finn doesn't get angry easily, but if he does, he grows quiet. Finding the way to keep his calm and bury you alive with his words.

"Della," he starts, ignoring our mother. "I will pay for your tuition if you want to leave."

"What?" my mother screeches. "You can't afford that."

"But I can," I pitch in, finding Finn's gaze. He nods, silently agreeing to do this together. "You can come live with me, and Finn and I will make sure you can go to school."

"You can't do this!" my mother yelps, trying to grab Della's wrist. But Finn clearly has enough because he roughly pushes her back with a glare on his face I've never seen before.

"Don't touch her! If she wants to leave, she can leave."

"She's not eighteen yet!"

"She will be in two months. But if you want to fight this, I will take you to court, mother," I tell her. "I will take custody over Della, but I doubt you want the media coverage this close to elections." My face is furious, but my voice is calm and composed. It shows the number of fucks I'm giving right now. I'm so sick of this. Sick of her. I don't care if it will cost me all my money, but I'm not going to let my mom control us any longer. I'll spend every dime I have on Della's tuition and live in some one-horse town, if that's what it's going to take.

"I will represent him, mom," Finn adds, and I shoot him

a grateful look. There is a sadness in his voice, but it's laced with determination.

Mother glances back and forth between the three of us while we hold her gaze in union. For what feels like minutes, she keeps her rigid stance as if her brain has a hard time processing. Finally, she grinds her teeth, shaking her head.

Seemingly feeling trapped, she puts her focus on Della, pointing her finger at her with an evil smirk on her face. "You will regret this, young lady.

"Doubtful," I mumble.

She spins on her high heels, strutting up the stairs before disappearing into the house. Della stares at the front door with a vacant look in her eyes, and I run my hand through her hair.

"Are you okay?"

"Did that really happen?" She blinks, and we stay quiet, knowing it's a rhetorical question. "She tried to marry me off," she repeats the question a few times, staring into nothing. Each time her words get more frantic, until finally, she collapses against me. Holding her up, she buries herself into my chest as she starts to sob.

"I got you. I'm here," I chant. "We are here. We got you."

Finn wraps his arms around both of us, pressing a kiss on her head.

"We do, Della. We got you. It's us three from now on," he says with a calmness that soothes my heart, before relief falls over me like a warm blanket when I realize what this means.

I'm finally free.

When I found Sean in that locker room with his dick in some other girl, I was livid. I threw all their clothes on the ice, and I laughed when both of them were shuffling onto the rink with their bare-naked asses. Then I got home, and I felt humiliated, and I comforted myself with a bottle of champagne that I kept in the fridge for special occasions. Thinking getting cheated on was a pretty damn special occasion. Then, at three in the morning, my rage turned into sadness, and I cried my eyes out for two hours, singing sappy love songs. When I woke up the next morning, I called Johnny, told him what happened and how I was going to take the day off. I went to Venice Beach by myself, and while sitting on the hot sand, I stared into the ocean, waiting for the pain to come out. But nothing came. No, if anything, I felt relieved. So before dinnertime, I went back home, ordered a pizza and watched a rerun of Friends, all while feeling pretty good about myself.

If that was a heartbreak, I could handle that. Easy peasy. I've gone through worse.

So, when Jensen went to New York on Sunday, I figured that was what was going to happen. I was angry, then I cried my eyes out, felt like a fool for believing him, but by Monday morning, I thought I'd be all good to go. Ready for my new start. The whole reason I moved back home.

But by the time Saturday arrives, it becomes clear I underestimated my feelings for Jensen. I've been sitting at the riverbank, crying, for most of my days, before I go back home and go to bed. Nana forced me to eat something yesterday, because apparently, I'm losing weight. Which is probably true since the permanent lump in my throat makes it hard to eat anything. Not to mention my lack of appetite. I wasn't even excited when Nana made me fried chicken.

My mind is too occupied with missing him. My car is tainted. I can't drive anywhere without imagining him behind the wheel, reminding myself of the safe feeling I felt while I'd stare out of the window with him next to me. My bed feels empty without him too, even though he was only there for one night. It's hard to admit, but he buried himself in my heart, and he's too deep to get out.

He hasn't contacted me. Part of me hoped he'd text me, call me, demanding me to talk to him. Anything. But after six days of complete radio silence, I've come to the conclusion he didn't mean what he said. Or maybe he did, but it's clearly not important enough.

I'm not important enough.

I'm waiting ~~patiently~~ impatiently, before his engagement is announced on the eight o'clock news, but so far, it's been quiet.

When a knock sounds on my door, I let out a feral grunt. I don't want to talk to anyone. They left me alone for most of the week, just giving me sad glances whenever I passed by, and I'm glad for it, because I could barely handle that. Let alone talk about it or listen to comforting words. There is nothing they can say to make me feel better.

Another knock sounds.

"Rae, open the damn door." I hear Kayla's muffled voice through the wood.

"Go away!" I yell back, moving my body up while glaring at the door. "Unless you have fried chicken. You can put that in front of the door and then go the fuck away!"

I'm not hungry, but I'm willing to try some fried chicken again.

Unapologetically, Kayla bursts through the door, rolling her eyes.

"Heartbreak or not, you clearly still have your humor." She flops her body onto my bed, a beaming smile splitting her face.

"And you are *clearly* deaf."

"Nah." She runs a hand through her brown hair. "I just ignore you when you talk bullshit."

"I hate you." I throw my body back, landing on the soft pillow with a thud, my eyes wide shut.

"Yeah, well, you can hate me some more after tonight. Come on." She taps my leg. "We're going out."

"What? No." My eyes shoot back open.

"We're going to a game."

"What game?"

"Hurricanes vs. All Stars."

"All Stars?" A frown creases my forehead.

"Yeah, it's a charity game. Major League playing the Hurricanes' veterans or something. I don't know. Johnny gave me tickets. He said a game will cheer you up."

I growl, narrowing my eyes. "Johnny is wrong."

She gives me a smug grin, then moves her gaze to her hands, innocently playing with her manicured nails.

"I made a deal with Nana."

My brow quirks up.

"She's going to harass you the entire night if you don't come with me."

"You're a bitch," I say with passion. The only thing worse than a heartbreak is a heartbreak with my grandmother nagging me the entire night. She's been leaving me alone so far, respecting my wish to be alone, but if what Kayla is saying is true… she is probably sick of my sulking behavior. As much as I don't feel like leaving my room, I don't feel like staying in with Nana in my ear either.

"She's going to make fried chicken and said she was going to whip up some cocktails." Kayla smiles.

"Drunk Nana. Yay." I glare.

"Right! I'm way more fun drunk."

I purse my lips, staring at my annoying cousin with a scowl on my face. I know what she's trying to do. I'd probably be doing the same if I were her. My mind isn't jumping for joy thinking about being in a crowded rink, but watching a game of hockey does sound like the perfect way to get some fresh air.

"Are you buying me drinks?" I ask, still scowling.

"Are you gonna let me have a beer?"

"Sure." I shrug.

"Then, yes."

"Popcorn?"

She gives me a dull look. "Sure."

"Hotdog?"

"Geez, Rae. I'm a poor student," Kayla huffs.

"You're buying me a fucking hotdog, Kayla. Or I'll go

and take my chances with Nana. I'm craving for some fried chicken, anyway." I casually tap my chin.

"Fine!" she growls. "I'll buy you a damn hotdog. Can we go now?"

"Give me ten minutes."

WHEN WE LEFT THE HOUSE, I didn't feel as bad as I had for the last week, and I welcomed the distraction of Kayla chatting about some guy on campus trying to get her to go on a date. But as soon as we arrive at the PNC Arena, I regret not taking my chances with Nana.

Anxiously, I look at the big building, my eyes scanning the crowd. I didn't expect to feel as overwhelmed as I am, looking at all those people wearing hockey shirts. The red jersey of the Hurricanes doesn't look like the black Knights shirt at all, but it still reminds me of Jensen. I slowly exit Kayla's car, anxiety probably written on my face.

"It's just a game, Rae. I bet the cold vibe of the rink will help get your mind off things," Kayla offers when she notices my pained expression.

"Right," I reluctantly admit, with a lump in my throat.

"Come on, we'll have fun. I promise." She links her arm through mine and drags me toward the entrance. We shuffle through the crowd, showing our tickets at the register before we find our way to our section. The cold air of the rink graces my cheeks when we walk down the stairs, and immediately, I suck in a breath that calms down my slightly racing heart. Even before I got a job with the Knights, I used to love watching hockey with my family. But since I've had the privilege of watching every home game of the Knights in the rink, it's been one of the things I always looked forward to. The scratching of the skates on the ice, the cold air, the smell of hotdogs.

I love it with every fiber in my being, and for just a second, I can detach myself from the man that is inextricably linked to this sport and just enjoy the atmosphere in the rink.

"Lower Level Center, huh?" I suspiciously eye Kayla when I find out exactly where our seats are.

She keeps a straight face, ignoring my question as she descends to our row.

"Johnny gave you these tickets?" I follow her down with a skeptical frown. Though I know Johnny can get some awesome tickets being a GM in the NHL, I'd figured he gave Kayla some tickets that were giveaways, not the best seats in the house.

Kayla stops at our row, opening her arm to tell me to get in. "Seat eight."

I blow out a breath at her annoying behavior, deciding to ignore it. That is until I spot a head of dark blonde wavy hair and a baby bump sitting next to my seat.

"Charlotte?"

Rubbing her stomach, she looks up at me with that same kind smile she showed last weekend.

"Hey, Rae."

I snap my head back to Kayla, grinding my teeth.

"Johnny gave you these tickets?"

She looks up at the ceiling with a half-smile on her face. "Did I say Johnny? I can't remember."

My head moves back and forth between the two girls as I keep on my feet. I fold my arms together, my back to the ice, giving them both a scowl filled with mistrust.

"What's going on?"

"Nothing!" Kayla screeches with a look on her face that screams deceit. I'm sure that if we wait five minutes, her nose will be as big as Pinocchio's, and she can become his girlfriend.

"We are just here to watch a game. *For charity*. So, sit your ass down and watch the game."

"You're full of shit."

"Maybe. But you won't know until you find out and watch the game."

"Rae." Charlotte's soft voice breaks the tension rising between Kayla and me. I look at her friendly face, her cheeks rosy from the cold air around us. "Hunter is making a guest appearance. I thought you could use a distraction. It will be okay. I promise. Come sit." She softly tugs my wrist, and I hesitantly sit down. A chill shivers down my spine, and I'm pretty sure it's not because of the cold. Though I love how thoughtful Charlotte seems to be, even though we've met once.

"Right!" Kayla chirps. "I'm going to get some beers." She eyes Charlotte's baby bump. "No beer for you, I'm assuming?"

"Kayla!" I seethe.

"What?" She raises her hands in the air.

Blunt as fuck, she is. A little rude too.

"Water is fine." Charlotte chuckles.

Kayla gets up, and I roll my eyes, watching her walk away. I feel a warm hand on my wrist, and I twist my head, looking into Charlotte's mossy green eyes.

"Relax." There is something comforting in her voice that makes me settle a little, but I can't shake the feeling of suspiciousness in my gut. I pull the sleeves of my sweater down my arms, hiding my hands in the fabric while I lean back in the seat. I watch the ice like a hawk, expecting someone to catch me off guard like a jack-in-the-box.

The smell of hotdogs has my stomach roaring, and suddenly, I realize how little I've eaten in the last week. I've been living on tea and biscuits, with the occasional piece of fried chicken, much to the dismay of Nana and June, but I just couldn't get anything down my throat. Breathing the fresh air is comforting for my soul for some reason, because all of a sudden, I feel like my senses are coming back to life.

When the lights go out, Kayla comes back holding three beers and a cup of tea, with a sweet smile.

Confused, I eye the three beers.

"Look who I found!" she booms, excited.

Without waiting for my response, a tall figure pops his head out from behind her back. I cock my head to look at him closely, and it takes me a second before I make out a red flannel shirt and brown styled hair.

"What are you doing here?" I give Bodi a shocked look while my heart rate speeds up once more. My head snaps back and forth between Kayla and Bodi. If I wasn't one-hundred percent convinced something was up, I am now. Wondering if Jensen is here too, I glance past Bodi, a bit dazed.

"Don't worry." His calming voice soothes. "He's not here. I brought you a hotdog." He holds up the bun as a peace offering of some sort, as if he's scared I'm going to bite his head off.

Narrowing my eyes, I grab the hotdog out of his hands. "I thought you went back to Atlanta."

"I did," he explains while both he and Kayla sit down. "But Kayl asked me to come, and I never say no to a good game." He winks.

"Right." I don't believe a fucking word he's saying, so I turn around to Charlotte staring at the ice. When she notices my eyes on her, she smiles.

"Look, I've been hurt many times. Conveniently, by the man I now happen to be married to. I understand your fear, but I'd never do anything to upset you."

"I'm not scared *you* will upset me," I mumble, when I notice Hunter walk onto the ice.

"It's just a game, Rae. Eat your hotdog."

I take a bite of the thing, doing my best to push away the nerves that move through my stomach like wildfire. When I feel the hotdog attacking my taste buds in the most delicious way, I devour the entire thing within a minute, until I let out a satisfied moan while Hunter starts to welcome the crowd. He's wearing his signature snapback with a Hurricane jersey with some washed out jeans, and glancing at Charlotte, I can see the pride dripping from her face.

"He's not playing, is he?"

"No, they just asked him to make a guest appearance to promote the charity. Introducing the new team and new roster."

"Better?" Kayla asks, while I slouch down in the chair, not really registering what Charlotte is sharing.

"So much better." Satisfied, I place my hands on my stomach, listening to Hunter's opening. After a small introduction of the charity chosen for tonight, the teams skate onto the ice, and the crowd gives them a loud applause.

"You know they asked me to play for the all-stars team?" he asks the crowd, and cheering erupts in the arena. "But I declined," he continues, followed by a salvo of boos that makes him chuckle. "I know, I know. But I promised my wife I wouldn't fight anymore, and I'm pretty sure these guys won't hold back once I get on the ice. I don't need my ass kicked on the ice, or my wife will do the same at home." His eyes search for Charlotte in the crowd, and when he finds her, he gives her a short wave and a wink. "I love you, babe."

She rolls her eyes, her cheeks getting a bit flushed, and a grin forms in the corner of my mouth.

"Quite the charmer, that husband of yours," I joke.

"Don't I know it."

"Any players we know of the veterans?" I ask not to anyone in particular, when Hunter introduces the all-stars team.

"Haven't checked. But I'm sure you'll know one or two," Kayla replies before Bodi gives her a small kick.

"What?" she screeches as I watch them carefully. She scowls at Bodi, then gives me her finest smile. "I mean, you've worked in the NHL. I'm sure you'll recognize some of them, right?"

Before I can reply, Hunter's booming voice catches my attention when he starts to introduce the all-stars. A few old names seem familiar, and I start to get a bit excited about the game. But when I think the game is about to start, he chuckles through the mic.

"So, to give the first team a handicap, our center, Korho-hen, and left-wing, Jordan Pence, will be playing for the all-stars team!" Cheers go through the rink, and the Finnish guy skates over to the team, waving toward the crowd. "But to keep it fair, our newest player will be filling the void. This man just won the Stanley Cup."

My heart stops.

"Making him officially the best defender in the league."

Then my heart picks back up, frantically beating against my ribcage.

"And we are very excited to welcome him into the Hurricane family."

My lips part, even though I can't seem to breathe.

"Give it up for Jared James Jensen!" Hunter's words echo through the rink, and the crowd goes ballistic while the world seems to go quiet around me. Time seems to freeze as I watch Jensen skate onto the ice with that knee weakening smile on his face. He skates around the ice, waving to the crowd, and I swallow hard when he gets closer to our section. I blink, trying to keep my emotions in check, but really, I feel like a damn bouncing ball. I want to disappear into the ground, hoping he won't see me, and I want to run downstairs to wrap myself around his body all at the same time.

When his eyes find mine, I gasp, the world around me completely forgotten. He quickly comes to a stop, giving me that smile filled with lust and longing.

The entire rink grows silent, all attention going to Jensen before they all follow his gaze, and eighteen thousand people stare at me all at once. Goosebumps trickle my skin, and I feel paralyzed. His blue eyes pin me down in my seat.

"But before we play, Jensen has to get his girl back." I barely register Hunter's words coming through the speakers until the people around me start to whistle and clap in encouragement.

I glance around me, feeling freaking unsettled with everyone's attention.

"What is this, Kayla?" I clench my jaw, plastering a fake smile on my face.

"I don't know." She shrugs. "Maybe you should go and find out."

I move my attention back to Jensen, who's crooking his finger at me.

I shake my head, nervous as fuck.

"I will get you down here, Rae. Don't make me." It's a clear statement, one that's accompanied by a lopsided grin, but I cross my arms in front of my body, giving him a defiant glare, not sure how I feel right now.

Excited to see him.

Terrified to see him.

Hopeful, watching his smile.

Scared I'm wrong again.

"Just take the grand gesture, Rae," Charlotte whispers in my ear. "You know he's not going to take no for an answer anyway." I twist my head toward her.

"I married an asshole, remember." She winks.

I know she's right. Jensen doesn't half-ass anything. He goes straight for the win, without any apologies. Collateral be damned. I already knew that about him, but I guess I never fully understood how far he'll go if he's really set his eyes on something. He didn't just join my road trip, he hijacked it. He didn't take my heart when I offered, he stole it when I wasn't looking.

"Not a chance, asshole," I bellow at the ice, pursing my lips. Chuckles escape from the crowd, and Jensen breaks out in laughter as he gets off the ice through the bench.

"Don't say I didn't warn you!" He points his finger at me, then his eyes find Bodi's.

"Get her down here, McKay."

"You got it!" Bodi jumps up, his focus on the people in the rows below us. "You heard the man. We need the girl down."

Before I realize what's happening, Bodi scoops me into his arms, and I let out a screech.

"Bodi McKay! Put me down!"

"Sorry, Goldilocks." I'm still scowling when I'm placed into the arms of the first man in the row below us, and I give Bodi a panicked glance.

"Bodi!" I hiss, but my attempts are useless. Within five seconds, I'm being carried from man to man like I'm the object in some relay race until the last man drops me right in front of the man who gave out the command.

Instantly, I'm mesmerized by his deep blue eyes, unable to say a word or even breathe.

"Hey, baby." He smirks.

I frown, folding my arms in front of my body like a moody toddler.

"I'm not your *baby*."

He pulls the front of my sweater, tugging me against his chest. Sucking in his fresh scent feels like coming home, and I have a hard time not burying my face against his body.

"*Fuck it.*" It's just two words, but hope swells in my chest when they reach my ears. For us, they hold a deeper meaning. They hold an answer for the questions we don't want to address, but I know I have to. I know I could assume, and I can't ignore it if I want to take the fear away.

"You broke up with Emily?" I ask, cautiously.

He nods. "Fuck it."

"Your parents?"

He smiles. "Fuck it."

"You don't want to live on the East Coast?"

"I want to be where you are." He brings his lips closer, brushing his nose against mine as he holds onto my sweater, pressing me against his body with his other hand.

"You do?" I can see the affection dripping from his eyes, and slowly, it feels like my heart heals just looking at him.

"Fuck it," he says again.

My eyes dart to his lips, and I lick mine, desperate to kiss him.

"What about Della?" My hands move up his arms, a comforting feeling settling inside of me when I feel his body under my palms.

"She's gonna move in with me. I'm going to be paying for her tuition."

"Really?" I huff, swooning that he wants to take care of his sister like that.

"Fuck it," he repeats.

"Fuck it," I whisper against his lips.

"Can I kiss you now without you biting my head off?" His hand cups my cheek, and I close my eyes, leaning into his touch.

I nod, smiling, and he gently places his lips over mine, exploring with a bucketload of affection. Around us, the crowd breaks out in cheers, and sooner than I want, he breaks our connection.

"I guess they approve, huh?" He presses his forehead against mine.

"I guess so." A giggle comes from my lips.

"I'm sorry I hurt you, baby. I had to fix it first. I didn't want to give you promises before I knew what was going to happen. When I'd come back to you."

I bite my lip, butterflies flying through my stomach. "Are you here *now*, Jensen?"

"Until you kick me to the curb, Rae Stafford."

"Then, fuck it."

45.

JENSEN

That was my best game ever. It's a weird statement since I just won the Stanley Cup, but playing this charity game, knowing Rae would be there waiting for me... well, it's upped my game. I felt like I was flying on the ice, and I haven't left that rush now that I'm freshening up in the locker room. Walking out of the shower with a towel wrapped around my hips, Hunter enters with a big grin on his face.

"Well, she didn't hit you. That's good, right?"

I open my locker to get dressed. "She still might. She's too smart to with eighteen thousand witnesses around."

"No, I saw the look on her face. She's hooked, man. You're good."

"I hope so." I put on my boxers, then grab my jeans.

"You looked good out there. And not just in a red jersey." Hunter takes a seat on the bench, a leg on both sides. "You were on fire."

"It's the blonde." I snicker, putting my shirt over my head. "I'm telling you."

"Can't blame you. I was always better with Charls around

too. I want that Holy Grail in North Carolina next year, so keep her around, man!"

"I'm planning on it."

When Hunter told me Karl Mitchels wanted me to join the Hurricanes next season, I was hesitant, because I always said I didn't want to play on an East Coast team. But Rae changed it all. She forced me to look beyond my comfort zone and pushed me to make choices I had been ignoring for as long as possible. I expected to feel empty when I'd tell my family to fuck off, but after realizing Finn and Della were on my side, I've never felt better. Telling my mother how I was going to do what I wanted from now on didn't gut me inside. It gave me a sense of relief. Like the world was lifted from my shoulders. She still keeps calling me every single day, sending hateful text messages to all three of us, but I don't care anymore. I just laugh about it.

"Alright," he says, tapping the wood of the bench, "I gotta get my wife home. Let's grab a beer when you're all settled into your new place."

"Yeah, let's do that." He offers me his fist, and I bump mine against it before he leaves the locker room, leaving me alone with my new teammates. I get dressed while the other players praise my actions on the ice tonight, brightening my mood even more. And five minutes later, I walk into the hallway to find my girl. I don't have to look far, because when I turn around the corner holding my sports bag, there she is.

Her back is pressed against the wall, her blonde hair covering most of her face while she glances at her phone. Letting out a content sigh, I close the distance between us with a smirk on my face. When I'm almost there, she looks up, our gazes colliding, making my heart race with a passion I have only ever experienced when she's in front of me. I drop my bag, and she launches herself at my chest, wrapping her legs around my waist like a damn koala. Her lips find mine in a breathtaking kiss before she presses her forehead against mine.

"Hey," she speaks.

"Hey."

"Is this real?"

I hold her tight against my body, almost crushing her into my chest. "As real as it's about to get, baby. I'm not going anywhere."

She pulls back, staring at me with her sparkling eyes.

"Your siblings are okay with all this?"

"Never been better. I wasn't the only one ready to tell my parents to fuck off." I snicker.

"What about the elections?"

I shake my head. "Not my problem."

I hope my father wins. I'll vote for him. I'll even go to the election events with Rae on my arm if my parents ask me to, but I'm no longer going to be part of their campaign.

"And you're really moving to North Carolina?" There is still a skeptical look in her eyes that amuses me, and I bite her lip in reprimand.

"The last five days were excruciating without you. I want to wake up next to you and kiss you goodnight. Hopefully, every night, but if you're not ready to move in with me yet, I'll settle for six nights a week."

"Let's take this one step at a time, hockey boy," she tells me, though I can see the excitement washing her face.

"I told you," I continued. "I'm not going anywhere, baby."

I lower her to the ground, then dip my chin and cup her

cheek. She's looking up at me with those gorgeous eyes holding a glint of hope.

"What made you change your mind?" Her voice is soft, like a calming song in my ears.

I push out a breath, a smile tugging on the corner of my mouth. "This blonde decided to leave me in LA, and I couldn't have that. So I forced myself on her road trip."

"Hmm, then what happened?" she purrs.

"I fell for her," I confess. In the last week without her, I've been thinking about when everything changed for me, and I keep going back to the same moment. I've always found her attractive. I've always imagined how she'd feel underneath me, but waking up that first morning with her in my arms, it changed me. I've had plenty of women in my bed, waking up exactly like that, but never has it felt like it has with Rae.

Like she belonged there. Like she is made for me.

"I'm still falling for her," I add.

She keeps her face straight, and I can feel my pulse begin to throb nervously in my neck. I know love is hard for her to grasp, after everything she's lost, but right now, I'll take anything.

"Hmm, can I tell you a secret?" she muses, bringing her lips flush with my ears. A flutter goes through my stomach when her breath fans the shell.

I let out a grunt in agreement, unable to voice anything.

She brings her head back, locking our eyes. "I'm pretty sure she's falling for you too."

"Yeah?" I chirp, relieved. "How sure?"

She nods. "Pretty sure."

"How sure?" I repeat, tickling her side. A shriek erupts from her chest, and she gives me a taunting look before it softens, and her eyes become laced with the love I'm looking for. The love I'm craving from her.

"Positive."

"Are you in love with me?" I ask with a smirk, wanting to hear it. Her hands take a hold of my face, and she presses a crushing kiss on my lips.

"Madly, Jared James Jensen," she clarifies. "I'm madly in love with you."

The front door slams open with a loud thud, and I look into the hallway from the kitchen to see who it is.

"Damn, it's cold outside!" Bodi grumbles, with a scowl on his face. He rubs his hands together, blowing some warmth into his palms.

"It's forty degrees. It's not *that* cold." I frown at his pussy ass behavior.

"I've lived in LA for the last eight years, Goldilocks. It's fucking freezin'." He hangs his coat on the rack before he joins me in the kitchen.

"You do realize you're not the only one, right?" I cock an eyebrow at him, while I start whisking the milk through the mashed potatoes, raking my eyes over his outfit. He's wearing grey pants, with a black dress shirt, and a grey waistcoat tops it off. His dark hair sits casually on his head, and he is clearly freshly shaved, even though he's been rocking a casual beard for the last few months.

"You know it's just dinner, right?"

He dips his chin, glancing at his clothes. "Oh, this? Yeah, I just had a meeting."

385

I narrow my eyes at him, having a feeling he is bullshitting me, but it's fucking impossible to read his face. The man has a poker face that could win you millions.

"Am I the first one?" He glances around the kitchen.

"Yeah, I'm expecting Charlotte and Hunter any second, and Jensen just called. He's leaving the rink right now."

Bodi awkwardly shuffles on his feet, and I look at him. "What is it?"

"Nothing," he says, with that same straight face as he moves to the fridge to grab himself a beer. When he closes the door again, he plucks an opener from the drawer, then leans his back against the counter.

"So, Kayla isn't coming?" he asks, casually taking a pull from the bottle.

I purse my lips, dropping what I'm doing to press my hands against the cold surface of the kitchen island. "I thought you two broke it off?"

"We did."

"That," I pause to point my finger at his face, "is not a face that says *we're over*."

"Then what is it, Goldilocks?" An amused grin forms on his face before he takes another pull, his eyes holding my gaze over the rim of his beer.

"A face that says *I want to fuck her again, because I can't get enough*."

He snorts.

"*A face that says I might actually like this girl*," I add.

"I do like her."

I push out a troubled breath.

"Someone is about to get hurt, Bodi. She can pretend all she wants, but she's not the kind of girl that does casually well. She's not the tough girl she likes to think she is."

"I know." He throws his hand in the air. "I'm not using her or anything."

"I know you're not," I concede. "But you want to keep it casual. She just *tells* you she wants it casual."

"Look, Goldilocks." He gives me a sweet smile. "I don't want to hurt her, okay? We're just having fun. She knows that."

I shake my head. "When shit hits the fan, and it will..." I scowl. "I'm gonna have to pick a side. She's my cousin, and you're my friend. I'm guessing you know what that means."

A skeptical chuckle escapes his lips at the same time I hear the front door open again.

"Baby?" Jensen bellows through the house.

"It won't hit the fan, Rae," Bodi whispers with a ghost of a smile haunting his handsome face. "I promise."

"You can't promise that," I hiss as I walk past him to find Jensen in the hall.

A seductive smile creases his face, as he bites his lip while hanging his jacket on the rack. "You look really sexy with that apron on. Really housewife-y."

He closes the distance while I glance at my pink apron before bringing up my face with a glare.

"Pretty sure that's not a word."

"We should make it one." His cold hands land on the small of my back, then his lips find mine in a scorching kiss. One hand goes through my hair, fisting it before he tilts my head, forcing me to look up at him. "How long do we have?" His lips brush against mine as he hovers above my face.

"Zero minutes, since your best friend is having a beer in the kitchen."

"Fucking cockblocker," Jensen mutters.

He gives me another kiss, then lets go of me when the doorbell rings.

"Can you get that? I'm gonna change."

"Sure." I walk to the front door while Jensen heads up the stairs, giving me a wink when our gazes lock once more. My heart jumps at his smirk, and I shake my head. The tips of my fingers reach behind my back to take off the apron, then I open the door.

"You okay?" I ask when I look at Charlotte's exhausted face. She holds her big belly with a slight roll of her eyes, pushing out a deep breath when she sees me. Her pregnancy glow is basically gone and all that's left on her pretty face is fatigue. I quickly glance at Hunter standing beside her with a pained expression on his face.

"I really want this baby out."

"Err, yeah, can't help you with that," I offer, motioning them to come in.

"I know. It's fine. Just give me a chair and food, and I'll be settled for the rest of the night."

"Well, okay." I take her coat and she waggles off before I turn toward Hunter giving me a sheepish grin. "And how are you doing, *daddy*?"

He takes his snapback of his head to run a hand through his hair. "I feel a little helpless."

"I can imagine. Come on." I slap his shoulder. "I'll grab you a beer."

"Yeah, great," he mumbles, following his wife into the kitchen. When I want to trail behind him, the doorbell rings once more, and I turn back around to open the door.

"What's up, cous'?" Kayla wraps her arms around my neck, pressing her cold cheek against mine. "Is he here?" she whispers in my ear.

"Hmm, maybe," I muse, suppressing a chuckle.

"I want to say *yay*, but I'll pretend to be unaffected." She makes a dramatic straight face that looks more like she's dead rather than unaffected. "How is this?"

"Yeah, don't do that." I frown. "Just be yourself, Keeks."

"Great idea, Rae. Let's put that in the idea box for later." She rolls her eyes, then waves at Jensen walking down the stairs while she makes her *casual* entrance into the kitchen.

A smirk forms on his lips, watching my cousin walk away, then he reaches out to tug me against his chest.

"How are you, baby?" He holds my face between his hands, then pushes his lips against mine.

"I'm good."

"Yeah? All set?"

"Just need to make some gravy, and then we're ready to go."

He twists me in his arms, pressing my back against his chest with his arms around my waist.

"Is this what you wanted for Friendsgiving?" He buries his nose in my neck, placing a scorching kiss on my sensitive skin there.

"Hmm, yes. But I'm starting to have second thoughts if you keep doing that," I purr, leaning into his touch.

"What? This?" He starts a trail of open-mouthed kisses that have me melting in his arms, and I let out a tortured moan.

"Jensen," I growl. "Not fair."

"I know," he whispers in my ear, "but don't worry. I'm saving you for dessert."

He lets go of me, grabbing my hand to drag me behind him toward the kitchen.

"Jensen, you can't say shit to me like that when the night

just started!" I screech, feeling an ache forming between my legs.

"What?" he counters with a playful smirk that makes the flutter grow at a fast pace. "Sounds like the perfect Friends-giving ending, if you ask me."

I shake my head with a half glare. When I told him I wanted a Thanksgiving dinner with our friends to celebrate our new house, he stepped up as the perfect boyfriend, inviting them all for the night before Thanksgiving. He helped with the groceries, and he even helped me with the turkey this morning before he had to go to practice, making it our first cooked meal together. I don't know why that feels so special to me, but it does.

I held off for a few months, telling him moving in that early was too quick, but it's times like this when I'm glad I agreed after his persistence.

The knowledge of waking up next to him tomorrow morning and the promise of his touch before we go to sleep has me happier than ever.

Glancing around the kitchen, a smile slides in place, giving me that feeling I haven't felt in a long time. Peace. Safety.

"What time is Della coming home tomorrow?" I ask, tugging Jensen toward me.

He wraps his arm around my neck, kissing my hair. "Around nine. I'll go and pick her up. You can sleep in."

When Jensen's parents threatened to not pay for her tuition to go to Yale, Jensen and Finn both agreed to pay all her school fees so she could go to college without a worry. But when those three siblings agreed to that, Della dropped the bomb confessing that she'd rather go to Berkely anyway. Mr. and Mrs. Jensen weren't pleased, as you can imagine. So, after endless fights, Della moved in with Jensen for the summer until she went to Berkely in the fall. We kept her room as it is, because we both agreed she shouldn't have to go to New York if she doesn't want to. I've been trying to push Jensen to talk to his parents, to try to work things out, but so far none of the Jensen kids seem keen on working things out with their parents. I'm letting it go for now, but I hope one day we can all have Thanksgiving together.

"It's okay, I'll come with you. I've missed her."

He dips his chin, and I can feel his eyes burning through my body. When I look up, affection is clear in his gaze, and heat flares up my cheeks.

"Are you happy, babe?" he asks, pushing a strand of my blonde hair behind my ear.

"It's perfect."

He grins, licking his lips as if he's going to devour me.

"*You* are perfect."

JENSEN

Sitting on the bench, my eyes follow Logan wobbling around the ice as giggles come from his tiny chest. The two-year-old is holding his father's hand while he's trying to skate, even though his legs don't even have the coordination yet to make the movement. It's freaking adorable, and I can't help witnessing it with a grin splitting my face.

In the past five minutes, I've felt my chest expand, filling with love when I realized that's something I want. To create my own family.

I feel the palm of a hand connect with my back, and I look up into Johnny's smug face.

"Congratulations, *hockey boy*," he beams, using Rae's nickname for me to taunt me. "I have to admit, when you left the Knights, there was no chance in Hell I'd believe you'd be able to get another Stanley Cup playing for someone else."

He sits down next to me, rubbing his hands to warm them from the cold air in the rink. "But you fucking did it."

"I guess the joke is on you, huh?" I chuckle, putting my gaze back on the ice.

"So it seems." He follows my eyes. "Who's the kid?"

"Hunter's boy," I reply at the same time Hunter sees Johnny on the bench and puts his hand up in greeting.

"Cute kid."

"He is."

We stay quiet for a moment, looking at father and son playing around the ice. Hunter throws Logan in the air, and Logan's laughter echoes through the rink.

"I want this," I confess, keeping a straight face.

"What? Your own rink?"

I roll my eyes at his stupid reply. "No, fucker. This. *That.*" I point at Hunter and Logan. When Rae and I first started dating, I treated Johnny as her father figure, making sure he approved of me, of us, because I knew it was important to her. But after being part of this family for two years, Johnny and I developed a friendship. We hang out whenever he's back in North Carolina, we throw barbecues for the family, watch football games together, and I can even say he's my biggest confidant and sounding board when it comes to my career. But nonetheless, I feel like I'll be stepping on his toes if I decide to cross the line I want to cross without informing him first.

"A kid?" His eyes move to his dark blonde hairline as he pulls a disgusted face.

"Yeah." I snicker, softly shaking my head. "Don't you?"

He twists his head back to the ice, then shrugs. "I don't know. I guess I never had anyone that stirred that shit up inside of me." He pauses. "But you do."

I nod, a smile curling the corner of my mouth when Rae's face flashes before my eyes. "Yeah, I do. And I want that." I point my finger at them. "With Rae."

His eyes find mine when I turn my head back toward him. "Why are you telling me, Jensen?"

"Are you cool with that?"

"You having a kid with my niece?" There is amusement etched in his voice.

"Nah, not just a kid. I want it all. I want to put a ring on her finger. I want her last name to become Jensen, and then I want to plant a few babies inside of her until she doesn't want any more of them."

He grunts, though I can see the smile pulling on his cheek. "For fuck's sake, Jensen. Too much information."

We both let out a comfortable laugh. I'm lucky, you know. I might have lost my parents two years ago, but I've gained an entire family. Every single one of Rae's family members welcomed not just me, but my siblings too, with open arms, giving us a family home that we didn't even know we needed. Della is best buddies with Nana, and Finn seems to have found a soft spot for Lily, because the man can't say no to the little girl. Our holidays are completely filled with the traditions of the Stafford-Lockheart family, and I've never felt more at home. If I have ever felt at home before that, that is.

We tried to stay in touch with our parents, but after dad got elected governor, there hasn't been a lot of contact other than a *happy birthday* every year. I guess we served their purpose. But I guess it's true. When we slammed the door in their face, we cracked the window open and jumped out. Or something like that.

"Are you asking for my permission?" Johnny asks with a serious tone.

"No," I huff, giving him an incredulous glare. "I'm gonna do it anyway. But I'd like your blessing. I know Rae would appreciate it," I pause, "and to be honest, so would I."

He holds my gaze with a straight face while I wait patiently. He calls a good bluff. I know that, because we've been playing poker together whenever he's around, but still, a nervous lump forms in the back of my throat when he keeps his mouth shut. Then finally, a lopsided grin appears. "I think my mother will kill me if I tell you no at this point. She loves you."

"I know," I say, pleased.

"But, yeah." The features on his face soften. "I couldn't wish for a better man by her side, *asshole*."

He offers me his hand, and I eagerly grab it as we smile at each other in agreement and, even though I wasn't going to let him stop me, I'm glad I got this out of the way.

"So when are you going to pop the question?" Johnny gives me a curious glance, then folds his hands together, putting his attention back to the ice.

"I'm not sure yet," I respond. My head turns when I hear the sound of the door opening on the right side of the rink. Rae's blonde hair appears, and instantly, a flutter goes through my stomach that seems to only be present when she's in my eyesight. She smiles when she sees me, then starts walking our way with Charlotte following behind her. Her golden eyes shine bright, like they are my light in the darkness, and my heart jumps when I imagine those eyes on one of our future children.

"Soon," I add with a content smile. "Real soon."

ACKNOWLEDGMENTS

This was not a breeze. The book before this made me feel so many things that it made me doubt every single sentence in Jensen and Rae's story. It's a story I started years ago, but couldn't seem to finish at the time. I guess they weren't ready yet, and neither was I.

Biggest thank you to Els, your enthusiasm convinced me this wasn't complete shit and if it wasn't for you, I'm not sure if this one would see the light of day. In fact, if you loved Jensen and Rae, you should thank Els too, because there would be no 9 without her 🖤.

Katie, I feel like the past few months have flown by and in a way, they have. This year has been intense and I literally couldn't have done this without you by my side. Thank you 🖤.

Thank you Rion, Lea and Jordan. Ri, you always know what to say, and always know how to motivate me. Lea, I feel like I keep throwing books your way when you don't have the time and then you surprise me and appear on my docs, it means the world to me. Jor, I know you're out there. I know you read my books. I also know you're busy AF, but know I see you. I appreciate each and everyone of you 🖤.

Thank you, Sheryn, it's so nice to have someone to talk to, share our experiences and keep each other motivated.

Even if you are on the other side of the damn world, LOL 🖤.

And last; Thank you, Mac, you were a try-out, but it's safe to say I'm hoping for many encores. You did great and it's a breeze to work with you! I can't wait to send you my next book. Also I'm gonna keep calling you Mac, otherwise it gets confusing for me, LOL.

ABOUT THE AUTHOR

B. Lustig is a dutch girl who has always had a thing with words: either she couldn't shut up or she was writing an adventure stuck in her head. She's pretty straight forward, can be a pain in the ass & is allergic to bullshit, but most of all, she's a sucker for love.

She is happily married to her own alpha male that taught her the truest thing about love: *when it's real, you can't walk away.*

facebook.com/authorbillielustig

instagram.com/billielustig

goodreads.com/authorbillielustig

bookbub.com/authors/billie-lustig

ALSO BY B. LUSTIG

Numbers:

8

9

BY BILLIE LUSTIG

Normally I stick to the darker side of romance, writing books that come with a trigger warning.

If you're ready for some alpha's ruling the underworld and want to flirt with the dark side, check out my other books:

The Fire Duet:

Chasing Fire

Catching Fire

The Boston Wolfes:

Franklin

Connor

Reign

Killian

Printed in Great Britain
by Amazon

78086933R00237